BETWEEN DESIRE AND DENIAL

BETWEEN DESIRE AND DENIAL

USA TODAY BESTSELLING AUTHOR

SHAIN ROSE

PAGE
&
VINE

Page & Vine
An Imprint of Meredith Wild LLC

Copyright © 2024 Shain Rose
Cover Design by Bitter Sage Designs
Editing: KD Proofreading, Salma's Library

Paperback ISBN: 979-8-9895288-5-1

Note on Content Warnings

As a reader who loves surprises, I enjoy going in blind
with each book. Yet, I also want to give my readers the
opportunity to know what sensitive content may be in my
books. You will find the list of them here:
www.shainrose.com/content-warnings

OLIVE: PROLOGUE

"Olive Bee, you have to stop trying to take care of everyone," my mother whispered as she looked over at me, rubbing lotion on her hands. I'd made a specific salve of oat oil and shea butter mixed with tons of other oils just for her because most lotions didn't work anymore.

Her skin was so dry and cracked it was almost lifeless. My mother, full of life months ago, now seemed extremely tired when she stared at me with her glassy eyes. It's how I knew it wouldn't be much longer.

"I'm going to be fine, Mom. Don't worry, okay?"

She coughed again, then winced as the vibration rattled through her whole body.

"Do you need a nurse? More medication?" I was wound so tight I almost jumped up to yell for someone, but she steadied me with a squeeze of her hand, ever the calming force.

She turned her head and smiled softly, her chapped lips splitting under the strain. I dabbed at them and applied salve for her before going back to holding her thin fingers.

"No nurses. It won't help anymore."

"Of course it will. They have pain medication to tide you over until the next chemo round and then you get a break."

She took a breath, then another as she turned away from me and looked out her window at the rain. It was supposed to be a sunny day, but the clouds had rolled in unexpectedly, unleashing buckets of water. I'd requested we switch rooms so she could at least see the sun some days, but she smiled at the raindrops before she said, "I'm not having more chemo, Olive Bee."

Her words fell over me one by one. The shock of each of them was too intense to believe. "What?" I drew my hand away from hers, recoiling from the instant break in our solidarity against this disease.

"It's too much." Her brows crinkled as she looked at me and then played with the gold necklace she always wore around her neck. It was a calligraphy fountain pen, gold and beautiful. I knew it provided her comfort over the years. She used the pen always to practice her calligraphy before she couldn't anymore, the pain in her joints getting to be too much. "I'm so tired, Olive. And your father shouldn't—"

"Dad should be here," I finished for her, anger bubbling in my veins as I said it.

She smiled softly, but I saw her pain as she said, "Oh, let him be, Olive Bee. You're so mad at him, but you have to let it go."

I wanted to rage on her behalf, to tell her she didn't deserve a man like him. She deserved so much better. But I let it go for her. "You're right. This isn't about him."

"Of course it is. He's your dad. It's about all three of you. I don't care about myself anymore. I had you babies so that we would be a family, and this isn't what a family is."

"Mom, how can you say that? We're a family, we take care of each other." I took her hand back in mine, trying not to squeeze too hard, trying to reason with her when normally it would have been the other way around.

"Olive, you're sixteen. So young. So much life ahead of you. You don't need to be caring for your mother." And that's when a tear rolled down her face. "I was supposed to be taking care of you."

My throat closed up, burned as I tried to hold back my unshed tears. We both knew that was the way it was supposed to be. But life's unpredictable, just like the dark thunderstorm that rolled in on the perfect sunny day we'd planned for. We could plan for everything, but when the lightning flashes, the thunder erupts, and the winds whip around to disrupt our life, we can either wait it out or fight it.

I wasn't ready to fold or give in. I blinked back the tears and tried my best to center myself before I said anything else.

"Oh, don't do that," she said, shaking her head at me. "Don't hold back. It's okay to cry, Bee. I've always loved how you wear your heart on your sleeve. You always let us know what you're feeling. I'd like to see that from you, if only just once more."

"You're not leaving us, Mom," I said, my voice clear and strong so she knew I was determined. My gaze didn't waver either as I stared her down. "You can't. Dad can't even cook a meal, and Knox can barely get himself up in the morning for school."

"I'm going to make sure to teach him to set an alarm, okay?" She chuckled.

"I can do it. I'll wake him up," I reassured her because she wasn't understanding.

"No. Olive, you are a teenager." She enunciated my age again like I was missing something. "Live life like you're sixteen. Make mistakes. Live for you. And when you turn eighteen, you do whatever you want. Go where that big heart of yours leads you. Buzz around like a bee and touch every flower you can. Buzz like a bee and then come back to me." She winked as she said the signature phrase she always used when I left the house.

"How can I do that if you're not doing treatment, Mom? How can I do that if you're not here to come back to?"

"I'm always going to be here in some way, Olive. And don't you know? Bees are strong, baby." She reached out and touched the little plumeria I always wore in my hair. "They go back to the flowers they know, and they find their way. You're stronger than you think. You'll see." She said it with such conviction I was sure she had more faith in me than I did myself. I set my hand over hers and held it close as I bent my head to her chest and cried. Not because she told me I could but because I couldn't hold it back anymore.

I was losing my mom.

I was losing my best friend.

My only friend.

She left us that night after fighting for every extra second she could.

My father wasn't even there to say goodbye.

CHAPTER 1: OLIVE

"I don't love that girl, not when I've felt real love with you." My boyfriend's voice sounded beautiful and poetic in the crisp night air as he talked on the phone. "I'll tell her soon, sweet pea. And of course the project is yours. Olive will understand." The wind carried the words of the man I loved straight to me even though I was around the brick corner. They cracked like a whip on my heart and split it in two.

It was my best friend, Kee's, wedding night. She'd married the man she loved, and I'd invited the man I loved to witness it. We'd watched her say vows in her childhood backyard and then we all went to stay at a luxurious HEAT resort about thirty minutes away. It's there they held the reception where I thought I'd be dancing and snuggling my long-distance boyfriend.

Yet, he'd taken two calls already and then his phone rang again. I told him we didn't have much time together, but he pulled me close and unclipped his one-of-a-kind Rolex from his wrist, "Time is nothing when you're in love. Here, wear this. I promise I'll be back in five minutes. Time me."

And, like always, I'd melted under his spell. I'd missed him so much after months away from one another. My boyfriend and I weren't seen together much. He was my professor after all, plus I traveled for work. But when we were together, Rufford was normally attentive, doting, and loving.

That's why I was shocked he'd been outside for nearly twenty minutes and now I was hearing him on the phone with another woman.

"If she doesn't understand, she still has to pass my class. So, she'll have to comply. It's why I'm here tonight. I told you. She and I need to talk things over."

The conversation felt wrong, made my skin itch and my heart beat fast. I should have announced my presence right then and given him some sort of heads-up that his conversation wasn't private anymore, but one of my biggest problems had always been that I was too curious.

Or paranoid.

"Of course that won't happen. That's over. I've told you that. I love you, adore you, and only you." His deep voice rolled through the air. I knew that phrase—*I adore you and only you*—and it made me feel naive to have believed him.

Those words were ones anyone could interpret. I heard them. I knew the meaning of them. I didn't question my hearing at all.

Yet, I couldn't *understand* them. No way was the man I loved having a relationship with someone else.

I took a step back, not sure how I wanted to react. Then another and another toward the resort's doors. They swung open to make way for the rambunctious, boisterous laughter of a man with a beautiful woman on each of his arms.

Dimitri Hardy was this phenomenal specimen of a godlike man that would have just the right amount of audacity and confidence to entertain two women at a wedding rather than one. He was the brother of the groom and a very close friend of Kee's. We knew each other through her. We weren't close, but when he saw me, his laughter died and those green eyes of his pierced through me, "Olive, what are you doing outside?"

"Oh. Olive, sweet pea, I was just finishing up my call."

Rufford draped an arm around me, but my gut reaction was to jerk away from him now.

Dimitri's gaze narrowed but I hurried to explain, "my boyfriend and I just needed some air." Then I turned to Rufford, "I'd like to talk to you over there."

I pointed around the corner and Rufford frowned but he steered me that way rather than toward the reception. At least I contained myself until we rounded the corner, but then my anger had me blurting out, "Who the hell were you just on the phone with?"

Rufford's beautiful blue eyes widened. "Darling, so sorry I had to take a work call. How is Kee's reception going?" He glanced behind me and smiled at Dimitri, who'd decided to walk without a care over to the side of the building and lean on it, like he had nothing else to do.

Well, I did and I didn't care about the audience. "A work call, Rufford? Do you tell all your coworkers that you adore them?"

"Olive." He reached out and touched one of my shoulder-length curls. "I'm sorry you had to hear that. You know how some of these calls can go. I've got students—"

"Don't play me for a fool." Rage swam rapidly through my veins as I looked at him in his tweed suit and expensive shoes. He had a full head of gray hair that I'd always thought looked so distinguished, but now I felt like the age that color represented mocked me. "I'm not stupid. Don't treat me like I am."

He straightened then, wiggling his tie as he seemed to assess me. "No. You're not stupid, Olive. So, you must know I've been lonely while you've been gallivanting around the nation with Keelani Hale and Dimitri Hardy."

He hurled Dimitri's name as if I should be ashamed of my

actions. I knew Rufford always felt intimidated by Dimitri. He was an overly confident billionaire investor who traveled the globe with us as I worked for Kee handling PR and her hair.

"You knew I traveled for work, Rufford. I told you how my mom said I should ..." I choked back a sob and threw my hand over my mouth, willing back my crying fit. Rufford didn't even try to comfort me. Straightening my spine, I took a breath before continuing. "I've been extremely blessed to have found someone I could work for who became a friend. She gave me the opportunity to heal and feel like I belonged while I traveled with her. It's why I took your online courses instead of in person. But I told you that job was coming to an end."

"Not soon enough," he grumbled. "We should be working together now." I'd had my next plan with Rufford. I'd been ready to take on his research and finish out my thesis. We'd studied the effects of social media on communities and people. It'd been interesting and enlightening. I thought it would be my stepping stone into the field.

"I was supporting myself through college, Rufford. You told me how proud you were of that."

"I am proud you can be so independent, but I, unfortunately, am not as strong."

"What are you saying?" I shook my head at him.

"We've been working hard. I've been up all hours of the night. I needed an assistant. And Veronica was there."

"Veronica?" I choked out the name. He couldn't be serious. "She just started in the master's program, Rufford. And she's ..."

What could I say? *She's so young?* I'd been twenty-two once as well. Three years ago, I'd fallen for Rufford like he was God's gift to man. Maybe even before then. He'd been a professor while I was an undergrad and always praised my knowledge. I was quiet, but he made sure to give me attention. And then after I jumped from major to major, he did a great job of recruiting me into an online master's program for journalism.

I'd been so gullible. I flew out wherever he was just to see him, to sleep with him, to give him my everything. He'd been my first and my only.

"She's what, Olive? She's brilliant, honestly." He said the words almost condescendingly, like he was throwing me in the garbage and replacing me with her.

"You told me that once." Now my voice did shake, and my hands did, too, as I balled them into fists and tried my best to contain my emotions.

"Ah, well. She just has more passion and desire for the project right now. You understand?" He smiled softly and walked up to slide a hand onto my cheek. I didn't pull away. I couldn't. I missed his touch so much even when it was to wipe away a lone tear. Then he tapped the flower I still wore in my hair most days. I had a fake plumeria in every color for every outfit. They reminded me of my mother. Of how she'd been proud of me in her last moments, and now I didn't want him tainting any of that.

I took a step back so I was out of his reach.

"You've been so busy. Let's not fight about it." Rufford's voice was comforting, cajoling, and smooth as he broke my heart further. "You weren't that interested in this topic, and Veronica was."

"I can't believe this." I pushed the glasses on my face up and looked at the dark clouds in the sky, trying my best not to break down fully and start bawling in his arms.

He reached over to straighten those glasses in a soothing gesture. My heart squeezed in pain. I wore the glasses not because I couldn't see but specifically because he told me they made me look more studious. "I love these on you. Can we just focus on that, baby? How good you look and how I missed you?"

I ripped the glasses off instead and put them in my purse. I leaned against the brick wall of the building to look up at him. "I want that. I really do. But I have to know, Rufford. I need you to say it. Tell me you aren't doing anything with her."

My mind still desperately grappled with the idea even though I knew the truth. I'd rooted so much in our future and now it felt like I was free falling. He'd told me so many times he loved me. But now I simply felt like another notch on his bedpost.

"Does it matter, sweet girl? You always want me. I'll take care of you first, okay? You know you need it. Let's talk about this later. Come on." He kneaded my hips with his thumbs and kissed my neck. "I adore you and only—" He stopped himself, probably realizing I'd heard him say exactly the same phrase to her. Suddenly, my body revolted at his touch as I heard those words. Rather than love, I felt disgust.

I shoved him back hard, and he stumbled and swore. "How many *students* have you said that to?"

I emphasized the word, and he curled his lip. "You're all women, Ms. Monroe. You all have come to me. They all have been consensual relationships."

"Or we were all just barely adults and you coerced us into loving you," I threw back without even thinking about it. I gasped as the words left my mouth, and then a sob rattled out of my body.

I'd been duped.

I felt his fear suddenly as he stood there staring at me, and I knew I was onto something. Any other time, I would have concentrated harder, dug deeper, pushed further. I was studying to be a journalist, after all.

Right now, though, my heart was breaking.

I quietly watched as his face contorted with different emotions and then I saw how his brow dipped and his lips pursed. I knew this look. He was going to slather on the guilt now. "You'd accuse me of such a thing?"

"Rufford, you'd never let another person work on your life's research if it weren't someone you're close to. So, she's either brilliant or you're fucking her."

"Yes, well ... begs the question of what you are then, hm, love? You think you're brilliant? Or am I just fucking you?" His tone had changed. There was no love anymore, just the vitriol he was spewing. "I mean, come on. You wanted attention, didn't have many friends because you were spiraling in so many directions after mommy died and daddy wasn't around. Why wouldn't I take my chances on you even if you weren't the brightest?"

I glanced at the watch he'd let me wear. I knew how much he loved it, so I unclipped it then.

He nodded. "Yes, it's best we part ways, I guess. You'll still have to work on a new thesis, or you can drop my class and reapply for another research topic in the fall."

Reapply? That research had taken us over a year. I felt the panic rising in me; the resentment at him still trying to control me. He must have thought it would work, that I belonged to him in some way. "I'm so sorry, Rufford."

"It's okay, Olive. We'll get through this." He reached out like the delusional man he was. He truly believed I was going to simply give him back that expensive one-of-a-kind Rolex like he hadn't just shattered my heart.

Instead, I dropped it on the ground in front of him and stomped my stiletto heel into it.

"Are you crazy?" I heard him gasp. "You bitch!" Maybe I'd taken it too far. I saw his face contort in fury, but it was then and there that a large figure stepped around the corner.

Dimitri Hardy stood taller than all of us, his hair ruffled, but otherwise looking completely put together. The two women he had with him stood off to the side, lingering. His attention wasn't on them though. His gaze, instead, burned a hole into Rufford's face.

"You're not calling my friend that, are you, Rufford?" Dimitri Hardy's voice came out like a smooth drawl, not at all concerned about the domestic dispute he was stepping in the middle of.

"Get out of my way," Rufford growled, and his face reddened.

But Dimitri didn't move a muscle. "You know that's not going to happen, Rufford. Go on now. Leave unless you want to address the woman you supposedly love in a nicer tone than—"

"I don't love her. I loved fucking—"

"God damn it." Dimitri's hand shot out fast to grip Rufford's throat and shove him up against the wall. My eyes widened at how quickly the situation escalated. Even the women Dimitri was with gasped.

He glanced over at them and said, "I'll call you both later. Get out of here."

They listened immediately and then his gaze went back to my boyfriend, struggling like a rat caught in a trap.

Dimitri's grip didn't waver, and he stood tall, so tall and powerful that he probably never ever had to exert power and authority. Seeing him do it for me, for a person he couldn't possibly care much about was shocking. "Tell me, Rufford, why is it that you think I'll let you even mumble a sentence like that without pummeling you, man? Come on now. You that dumb for a professor?"

Rufford thrashed and kicked to no avail, trying his best to loosen Dimitri's hold in his struggle for oxygen. Even if I wanted him to suffer, I didn't want him to have a heart attack.

"Dimitri." I put my hand on his shoulder gently. "You need to let him go."

He pinched the bridge of his nose with his other hand, and it was a perfect representation of how feeble my date was in comparison to him. Dimitri looked completely unbothered by the other man's wriggling, but his eyes held fire as he looked down at me. "Fine." He yanked his hand back and let Rufford crumple to the ground. "Your boyfriend is a prick, Olive. I'm on a date and a work deadline. I hope you're aware I don't particularly enjoy breaking up spats between my best friend's girl and her old fuckboy. So, let's end the night easily rather than with Rufford's bloody nose, huh? You leaving now?"

He didn't glance at Rufford getting up and pulling himself together, but my date was keen on having the last word as he straightened his tweed jacket. "Olive, I'll be in touch about your thesis." He stomped off and left me standing in embarrassment in front of Dimitri who looked me up and then down to stare at my feet.

"You barely cracked his watch."

I glanced at my heels and winced. Great, so he'd seen that. I lifted my chin and crossed my arms. Now was not the time for me to be embarrassed. Instead, I stomped on it five more times before it cracked slightly. "There."

"You done?"

"I don't know." I gulped back the ache in my throat that threatened to cause more tears in my eyes.

"I hope so, because he's old enough to be your grandfather. He's not worth the tantrum." Dimitri was always more honest than I wanted him to be.

"He's not that old." I rolled my eyes at him. "And love can transcend all age brackets. It doesn't discriminate, Dimitri."

He lifted a brow like he didn't agree at all.

I waved him off. "You wouldn't understand."

And that was the problem. Most people didn't. Yet, Rufford had given me life, helped me through my master's program, taken an interest in me like no one else had. He'd given me confidence in myself and direction. Except now I knew he'd actually exploited my lack thereof, and suddenly I felt completely naked without him.

"Oh, Jesus. Are you going to cry?" Dimitri looked disgusted. "Please don't. Everyone will think I did something wrong, Olive. I don't have time for that."

"You know what really sucks?" I sniffled, not at all worried whether Dimitri wanted to listen to me rant or not. He'd been around long enough. He had to call me a friend, even if it was begrudgingly. Sure, more so he was now my best friend's brother-in-law, but before that, we'd all been sort of friends. Dimitri was there to support her, of course, and he mostly endured my presence more than anything as I navigated Kee's business. "This was my fallback after Kee. I was supposed to finish my thesis and continue researching with Rufford. I mean, we never said it out loud, but that was the plan."

"You'll come up with a new plan," he told me, completely uninterested. He was already glancing back toward the reception. The man was a well-known part-owner of a hospitality empire and a ruthless real estate investor. He didn't have time for me.

I didn't have time for this either. I might not have found my way to the right man, but over the past year, I'd thought I'd finally found my way in what I wanted to do. I'd enjoyed researching with Rufford. I thought it was the start of my career. I'd formed that path, dedicated myself to it, and now it was like he was snatching it away. "What if I don't?" I whispered, a sudden ball of fear building in my gut. "I loved him, and he took advantage of that. I wasn't even a smart enough journalist to see—"

Dimitri's green stare hardened as he looked down at me. "Olive, he's most likely been doing this to women since he became a professor a million years ago."

"Well, thanks for making me feel better," I said sarcastically as I glared at him.

He tapped his expensive loafer on the pavement of the alley like he didn't have time for this. "What I'm saying is he's a damn expert at being a dick. The playing field was uneven."

"But—"

"A man that's supposed to love you made you cry. That alone gives you enough reason to walk away from him. Even worse, he did it in the alley of your friend's wedding reception."

"She's my best friend." I nodded, starting to believe what he was saying.

"Well"—he tilted his head and his eyes sparkled—"technically, I think I'm her best friend."

My jaw dropped before a giggle slipped out. "You're kicking me when I'm down?"

"I'm being honest."

"It doesn't suit you." I threw back as I crossed my arms.

He hummed like it was a challenge then suddenly stepped

close to me. The night air shifted as the cool wind whipped between us. "Is that so, Ms. Monroe?"

It was definitely not so.

Our height difference, him being close to six six and me being only five four, along with the tension between us was suddenly amplified. And his arrogant ass knew that everything suited him while he stood there so close to me in the moonlight. Most women—including myself, even though I avoided the pull—were irresistibly drawn to him. His dark wavy hair framed a face that was somehow rugged and refined, every strand falling perfectly into place without effort. Even though he stood there in an expensive tailored suit, he didn't have to try to own the space. He just did with his broad shoulders, his confidence, and a smile that held familiarity but also mystery.

My heart and libido lurched at the same time. For a second, I forgot my heartbreak and that I should be dwelling on that. Closing my eyes, I took a step back to break our connection. "It is. I'm just as much Kee's friend as you are. And probably more so now since I'll be working with her forever after Rufford gets through with me."

"Yes, well, it is probably just best to let it go and do your thesis over," Dimitri said as if it didn't matter much either way to him. "Should we go back to the reception?"

Yet his words rattled me. "Let it go?" I murmured and then, I said it again, "Let it go?" And that's when the ball of fear turned to fury, warped from pain and heartbreak to wrath. I'd let it go with my father, let the rage over him not being the man he should have with my mother go. And I'd regretted it ever since.

I took a deep breath and balled up my fists. "No. You know what? I'm *not* going to just let it go."

I stomped past Dimitri back toward the reception doors and whipped them open without looking back to see if he was following. I didn't have time to wallow. I needed a new plan, and I felt it deep in my bones. I could cry later, but tonight I was making sure I had a place in the master's program that I'd put so much effort into. And I was going to put Rufford in his place at the same time.

I just needed to get some liquid courage to do the deed.

"I'm not letting it go with anyone ever again," I grumbled as I made my way through people dancing and went immediately to the bar. I plopped down on one of the velvet upholstered barstools and leaned over the dark mahogany bar with intricate carvings. "Sir, I need a drink."

I said it loudly enough that the bartender glanced over but then his eyes flicked behind me to Dimitri waving him away. "Hold on a second. Slow down, Olive. Jesus, what do you mean you're not letting it go?"

I glanced at the bartender who had immediately listened to him, and I narrowed my eyes back at Dimitri. "Are you telling him I can't have a drink?"

"I just waved him off for a second." He looked at me with concern. "Let's take a minute—"

"Just because you own this place doesn't mean you get to regulate what I'm doing," I spit out, irritated he was trying to control me.

He smirked. "I regulate everything I own, Olive. If you're standing foot in my investment, I control what you do."

I glanced around the resort. Everything about the HEAT property wreaked of opulence and elegance. Suited men moved around the reception, flowing with the crowd, all very aware of the man I stood with. The bartender listened to him without hesitation, no matter that I was a wedding guest who wanted a drink. Dimitri controlled it all. And it made me want to wreck it.

Rufford had controlled me. He'd manipulated and molded me just the way he wanted me. I'd sent that man hundreds of pictures in the lingerie he'd bought, risked my education to be with him, and now he had the audacity to leave me like I hadn't done a thing for him. "You all think you have control of everything, don't you?" I ground out before I waved at the bartender again and leaned over the bar. He came this time, and I purred, "Give me a shot of Fireball, please."

The man didn't make eye contact with Dimitri and poured the shot fast before he slid it my way. I downed it as I stared at him.

Then, I pulled my phone from my purse and scrolled through my texts to make a point. I clicked the one I wanted to show Dimitri and turned my screen. "Can you believe I sent him this last night because he begged for it?"

It was a picture I'd taken of myself bent at the waist in my torn nylons, looking over my shoulder.

I wasn't at all embarrassed to show Dimitri. He'd seen me and Kee get ready before, and I had to show someone how screwed up it was that Rufford had been able to control me so easily, that I'd been so naïve to believe he loved me. Yet, Dimitri's eyes widened in shock.

"What the fuck, Olive?" He swiped my phone from my grasp, and I thought he'd turn it off right away, but he stared as if he couldn't believe it. I saw how his knuckles turned whiter and whiter from his tight grip.

"Erm ... Can I have my phone back?"

"Fuck," he growled before shoving it back toward me. "I'd

tell you to delete it—"

"But what for?" I shrugged. "Won't do me any good considering I sent it to him. He has it."

"Jesus Christ." He was shaking his head in disgust. "Don't you understand that you risked your whole degree by doing that?"

"It was fun at the time!" I defended myself. "I ... well, I thought I was in love. Plus, he called to tell me this whole cute role-playing thing about how I was a bad student and if I sent him something to show how hard I was trying—"

"Is that request in messages?"

I blew a raspberry. "No." I sounded so dumb now. "He called."

And I'd felt like we were having so much fun too. Now, I stared at my text to him and wondered how many other students he'd gotten to do stupid shit by saying those things to.

"Of course his ass did."

"He said he was teaching me a lesson, Dimitri. But maybe he needs to be taught one."

CHAPTER 2: DIMITRI

"What are you doing?" I stood close to Olive, trying to see what she was doing on her phone, as she sat at the bar. The tiny girl went from crying to looking angry to defeated to now on an evil mission all of a sudden, and that was saying a lot.

Olive never looked evil. She never looked anything but sweet and a little cute, if I was being honest. She dressed in baggy sweaters, wore glasses most of the time, and had holes in her fishnets or leggings most days. I think it was a fashion statement but wasn't totally sure. I remember staring at them for about an hour the first day she'd worn them. I couldn't take my eyes off her skin there, so smooth and exposed. I chalked it up to me being concerned about her appearance, but now I wondered if it was something else.

"I'm being a journalist," she proclaimed before she waved the bartender over again. When the man fucking listened, I was astounded. Didn't he know I was part owner of this resort? She smiled at him sweetly, "I need just one more shot of liquid courage."

"She doesn't need any more liquid courage," I told the man with a mohawk and lip piercing. He was definitely trying to showcase his fucking "bad boy" shit to Olive. He licked his lip and made a show of his tongue piercing too.

That slow smile I knew she normally only got when she was on the phone with Rufford had come out to play, and I knew she'd noticed exactly what he wanted her to. But she patted my hand and said, "Ignore him. He's the bride's friend. He's trying to keep all us bridesmaids in line tonight."

"Ah. I'm very aware of who Mr. Hardy is. It's an honor to be working for you and your brothers." The bartender chuckled a little nervously. "I was told by the groom, though, to give the bridesmaids what they want for the rest of the night. He and his bride just left."

Olive clapped then. "Oh, good. Then I'm in the clear. Hand over that shot." She winked at him, and he winked back before he slid another shot across the bar.

Olive was quick to swipe it up and knock it back.

"Don't you want to card her?" I lifted a brow at him. Olive appeared to be underage. I knew she wasn't, but I wanted a reason to give the man a hard time.

"Already did earlier. Couldn't believe she's twenty-five. That face of yours could deceive the masses, sugar."

That's what I thought too ... until I'd seen the picture on her phone. And when I looked over, I was surprised to see her zooming in and cropping it.

"What the fuck are you doing?" My eyes followed each thumb swipe, and my mouth watered at seeing her ass again.

"I'm writing an article, and I need this picture to show enough of me to get my point across without disclosing my identity."

Against my better judgment, I finally sat down next to her. I'd brought a beautiful woman and her sister to this wedding, and I knew they were down to fuck tonight. Still, I found myself texting them that I wouldn't be meeting back up with them and they could enjoy the rest of the reception on their own.

Olive was taking up my time. I couldn't leave her to her own devices. "Don't do something you'll regret."

"Without great risk, there's no reward," she threw back.

"Normally, I live by a phrase just like that, but—"

"What's the phrase?" she asked as her thumbs moved lightning fast, typing away on that phone like she was reporting an emergency.

"It's 'take a chance and enjoy the damn dance', but—"

"Oh, that's perfect." She nodded without looking up.

"But," I emphasized my hesitation now, "what could possibly need to be written so quickly tonight?"

"Give me a second." She glanced up and narrowed her eyes at me. "By the way, don't you have something better to be doing than hovering over me?"

"As a matter of fact, I did invite a few guests to the reception." I smirked at her golden eyes rolling. She saw the women I was with earlier. "They're willing to wait while I finish making sure my friend doesn't do something she regrets tonight."

She blew a raspberry and I could feel her emotions skittering around in her head, like she couldn't trust her relationships at all anymore. Rufford had already changed her perception and it was a fucking shame. "I'll be fine. You don't have to worry about me, Dimitri. We're not *that* close."

That was a bold statement for her to make. She normally was cordial with me, even if we mostly made small talk. Her cheeks reddened, and it was clear she thought so too as I stared at her, waiting to see if she'd apologize.

"It's just ... we hang out because of Kee."

"Kee is a mutual friend of ours," I confirmed. Keelani Hale, now Hardy and now my sister-in-law, was the glue to our group. Olive was her PA, and I was her childhood best friend. It'd been that way for years. "We've hung out enough for me to care about you, Olive. Don't say otherwise."

She shrugged her bare shoulders and looked away. "Okay."

"Would you disagree?" Now I was curious. Did she think she didn't matter at all to me? Had it come off that way?

"I think you see me as a nuisance. Young. Naive. I think you indulge Kee's wishes of me being around, but you wouldn't entertain my presence otherwise. You see no value in me, and..." She took a deep breath. "You try to find value in everything and every person you surround yourself with. So, I'm irrelevant to you."

"Interesting." It was the only response I could make. I wasn't a liar, and she'd pretty much hit the nail on the head with our relationship up to that point. Except now, tonight, with her in front of me, it felt like something more. "That's what you believe I think of you. What do you think of me?"

"I think you're egotistical. You get to be because you're smart—you didn't get lucky with your investment choices. You're a workaholic. You don't commit to anything except that ... and your friends and family. You're a great friend to Kee. An amazing brother to Dex. But I'm not your friend or a part of your family, so I'm confused as to why you're still sitting here."

"Call it curiosity."

And her laugh rang out through the bar. Her eyes twinkled and her hair almost bounced as she shook with giggles at my statement. "I'm curious. You're not. You couldn't care less about the people who don't add value to your life. Time is money to you, and you love money, Dimitri. So, again, I'm confused," she threw out. It made me respect her even more.

"Honestly, let's blame it on Kee." It was the only rational answer I had right then. "She'll be worried tomorrow if you do something tonight, and she'll call me because of it."

"You act like I can't make an informed decision." Her

bottom lip pouted out, and I found myself wondering how soft it would be against my mouth. My thoughts were still on that photo obviously. It was the only excuse I had.

"I'm not sure you can right now." I pointed to her phone again.

That's when her big, doe eyes narrowed, and she bit her lip. "Okay, since you're the mature one, tell me how it sounds."

She handed me her phone to read the email.

Professor Rufford Butson has been a tenured faculty member at Alcove University for ten years. His research on social media and its impact on teen girls has provided companies with substantial data.

He first liked my social media page four years ago and sent me a private message about how I would be a great addition to the journalism department. I was young, moldable, and gullible. My social media platform showed my life story. I documented my ups and downs in a way that someone could easily assess my weaknesses and strengths. It's apparent now that Rufford Butson took advantage of that.

Our last string of correspondence includes the attached messages and photos.

Yes, I'm a woman scorned. But I'm also a woman seeking justice. I spent most of my time in graduate school in the journalism program working on research with him. Again, please see attached documents. I would like my name to remain on the works I helped to research and publish. I also would like the record to show I requested this and would like to finish my thesis under the supervision of another professor and without Professor Butson being a part of its presentation, submission, review, or defense.

Signed,

Olive Monroe

"You're putting your name?" I asked in surprise as I scrolled up to see the picture she attached. "You cropped your face from the picture to—"

"Yeah, I could hide my identity but, let's be honest, they would figure it out anyway. I just want my degree now. I can't go through a whole new program."

"The university is going to tear you apart," I told her because someone had to.

She sighed and then pulled at the little fake flower behind her ear that she always wore like she was thinking about it. "So be it. Better enjoy the rest of my night before the staff and chancellor read their email tomorrow."

"Alcove University, huh?" I knew the name, knew who funded it, knew I would have ties outside of hers. Yet, I didn't say a thing. This was her battle. For now. "I underestimated you I think."

She chewed the side of her cheek before her chin wobbled. "Most people do. Including my ex, I guess."

"What's your plan for the rest of the night?" I asked her.

"Gearing up to take that bartender back to my hotel room." She wiggled her eyebrows at me and without her glasses obstructing the view of her eyes, I saw how they sparkled with mischief. "Can you believe Rufford didn't even sleep with me when he got to town yesterday?" She slapped her hand over her mouth. "Okay I've come to the point of the night where I'm sharing too much with you."

I hummed. "Or maybe I'm more of a friend than you first thought."

She chuckled. "In that case, friend, I was really looking forward to screwing my boyfriend, but since he's now my ex, I'll be taking home the bartender if he'll have me."

"You're not taking some random guy home." My voice was low as I said it, and I couldn't help how my muscles tightened in anger at the thought.

"It'll be fun." She shrugged and smiled a lazy smile at me. "I've never had a one-night stand before."

Fuck me, she was cute tipsy. I stood up and looked down at her. "And you're not going to have one with him tonight."

Her stare was determined, and I saw the fire light in her eyes. "I'm living my life and getting over Rufford tonight, Dimitri. I'm fucking someone who will make me forget."

"Not him."

"Oh." She licked her full lips slowly. "You offering instead?"

"No." I shook my head, taking a step back immediately, because my dick jumped with her idea even though it was a bad one. "You've had way too much to drink."

"Three shots. And a glass of champagne from earlier tonight is hardly too much."

"Don't make me take you to your hotel room and watch you all night. I have two women and work I could be doing instead."

"Go on then." She waved me away and leaned on the bar. Her damn cleavage was on display, and Mr. Mohawk's eyes were laser focused there.

"That's it. We're going." I put my arm around her shoulders, but she didn't budge.

"I'm not, Dimitri." She looked up at me, and her face was so close now, those lips pouting out lushly like she wanted me to taste them. "I can't leave without someone."

She said the words softly and painfully.

"Olive—"

"I really, truly can't. If I'm alone tonight, I'll just think of him. I'll want only him, and I don't want to want him ever again. I know that sounds crazy but ... I just can't." I saw her vulnerability then, not the determination or the strength. Or maybe that was where her strength came from. She admitted her truth even if it hurt her to do so.

I hated being around women who cried or anyone who was too emotional, honestly, but even the tears in her eyes didn't make me want to back away. Instead, I was mesmerized by them, by the depth in them that I hadn't seen before.

"I'll stay with you, Olive," I said against her ear. "Come on. You don't know that guy," I coaxed her.

"You'll stay with me?" Her eyebrows knitted together. "In my bed?"

Goddamn, she was serious. "You don't want me in your bed, pretty girl. I don't do relationships or sweet nothings or any of that."

"I'm not asking for that. I'm just asking for someone to help me forget the best sex of my life. Rufford was it for me." She said it so seriously and held nothing back at all. Had she always been this honest with me and Kee? "He was all I needed. I hate saying that knowing he used me, but it's true. I can admit that."

"All you needed? There are billions of other men in this world and that's all you needed? You're selling yourself short. And there's no way he was the best you've ever had." Why was I arguing this? I shouldn't care if her best was that asshole.

"Why? Because he's older than you?" She chuckled. "Maybe my bartender will top him."

"He won't because you're not leaving with him." My jaw clenched. "You're leaving with me."

"I'm not leaving unless you're giving me what I'm asking for." She tilted her head and lifted one of her dark little brows at me. "Are you?" She wanted clarification, which was smart considering I didn't intend to offer her any of what she was asking for.

"I'm aware," I said through clenched teeth just thinking about running my hands up her dress over that delicious ass I'd seen in the picture. It wasn't going to happen, but I was still thinking about it as I threw money on the bar and grabbed her purse. "Let's go to my hotel room."

"What?" She glanced around suddenly, like she was nervous. "Well, are you sure? What about your dates?"

"Having second thoughts?" I smirked at her. She might have had a bit of liquid courage in dealing with her university email, but not when it came to me, live and in person. So, I leaned in to cement her hesitations. "Don't worry about my dates, Olive. If they want, I'll have them join in on delivering the best sex of your life for real."

It was a blatant fucking lie. I'd never do that with Kee's friends. I kept my family and business completely separate from my vices and pleasures. Olive was practically both by proxy.

We were here for Kee not to fool around with each other. But then she lifted her chin and stood, straightening that A-line bridesmaid dress before she hooked her arm in mine.

"Sounds like a great time, Casanova," she said condescendingly before pulling me toward the elevators. "Show me the way. I'm ready."

Once I got Olive out of the reception, I'd explain to her that she was going to sleep. Alone.

As soon as the elevator door shut, Olive looked up at me, licked her lips, and wrapped her arms around me. When her mouth met mine, she tasted like liquor and sweet apples. Her tongue slid between my lips because I let it, her hands roved over my chest because I let them, and her hips pressed against me as she moaned because I didn't push her away.

My body was experiencing something foreign, something completely shocking, and something astronomically *wrong*. I wasn't attracted to Olive. How could I have been? I barely noticed her half the time, but in that elevator, I reacted. My cock instantly hardened against her, so quickly that I held her hips for actual support. I couldn't stop tasting her sweet lips even if I tried. And I fucking didn't. I indulged instead. This desire was fierce and wrong. She was young and barely on my radar. Yet, I wanted to explore why the hell I was suddenly craving her.

Finally, she pulled back and opened her eyes. They sparkled with mirth. "Yeah"—she patted my chest—"I think you might do, Dimitri."

"I might do?"

"Sure, the kiss was okay enough." She shrugged and leaned against the railing of the elevator. "So, you'll do just fine at making me forget my ex for a night."

"If I sleep with you—and that's a big *if*, Olive—you'll forget him forever," I told her.

She shook her head and stared at me for a second before a smile so big whipped across her face. "Oh, gosh, I thought that was a joke. You're serious?"

"Of course I'm serious." I frowned at her.

"I don't think so. The kiss wasn't that great. Rufford could do better than that."

Now she was goading me. That was fine. I stepped close to her and put a hand on either side of her hips to grip the railing and cage her in. "I have five more floors to prove to you that what we did right there wasn't kissing," I growled, like I cared. I hated her mentioning me in comparison to her damn sorry excuse of a boyfriend. "It was just a sample. A taste. When I kiss you, you won't compare me to anyone else."

CHAPTER 3: OLIVE

He consumed me on that elevator as his hand slid up my thigh and his tongue dragged around my mouth.

He was right.

I wasn't thinking of anyone else while he did it. His hands were masterful, his tongue skillful, and his body perfection. He brushed his thumb along the seam of my thong, and I pulled my mouth from his to whimper on his shoulder as he dragged his tongue along the column of my neck. I'd never really had a doubt the man would be good in bed.

I'd tried not to imagine it since I'd been with Rufford, but Rufford had accused me of hanging out with Dimitri too much, and well, I couldn't control where my mind wandered in my dreams.

Dreams weren't reality here, though. Reality was much better. His hand massaged my thigh before hiking it up over his hip so he could get closer, but our height difference didn't grant me the leverage I craved. I wanted to rub against him, feel how hard he was for me against how wet I was for him.

He growled and leaned down a bit to grab the backs of my thighs, lifting me up to encircle my legs around his waist, setting my ass on the railing. I wrapped my arms around his shoulders, and that's when my world turned upside down.

Dimitri's cock against my pussy, even with fabric between us, felt life-changingly huge. Tears actually pricked my eyes from desire. My hips rocked hard into him. "I want you here.

Right now, Dimitri."

"We're on a public elevator."

I dropped a hand down between us and tried to unbuckle his slacks. "So what?"

He grabbed my wrist. "So you've got to wait."

"I don't want to," I whined. Alcohol made me bold, and I wasn't about to hide my feelings. This night was for me, not anyone else. I started hiking up my dress, but it was then that the elevator came to a halt with a ding and the door slid open.

"Fuck," he swore as he moved fast to block the view of me from the couple who boarded. He rearranged my dress and wiped at the red lipstick that must have been all around my face. "I should have swiped my HEAT watch," he said quietly, like an apology. I knew those watches were a part of the patented technology he and his brothers had built that was a signature of their empire—exclusive hotels and restaurants for the rich and famous around the world with impeccable security.

Then, he grabbed my hand, threaded his fingers through mine, and moved to my side. When the man who'd boarded the elevator glanced over his shoulder and saw Dimitri, his eyes brightened. "Oh my God, Dimitri Hardy?"

Dimitri nodded but didn't respond.

The man kept blabbering on. "My wife and I absolutely love these resorts. I just have to tell you, what you and your brothers are doing is phenomenal. Businesses are flourishing because of your investments and expertise. I've been a member of the HEAT organization since Carl Milton owned it, and there's been such a shift. Don't you agree, Ms. ...?" He waited for me to answer.

That's when Dimitri's jaw clenched, and he positioned all of his body in front of me immediately. "Discretion within the

HEAT empire is always advised, Mr. Kudrow." The elevator dinged and the doors opened on the floor that held a restaurant. "Looks like this is your floor. Have a good night."

The couple didn't say anything else as they hurried off the elevator, and this time, as the doors closed, Dimitri swiped his watch.

It reminded me how influential Dimitri Hardy and the whole empire was.

When the elevator finally delivered us to Dimitri's floor, I found myself stewing about it.

"Why are you glaring at the door, Olive?" Dimitri asked as he swiped that watch again and held the door open for me. "Change your mind?"

It was a good question. Did I want to spend one night with a billionaire that was probably an entitled asshole? He'd kissed me like he was devouring my soul on the elevator, but I knew he wouldn't provide much more than good sex. "It's not you." I shook my head and walked in. "Just what your company reminds me of."

"Which is?"

"That I was privileged, and my parents—especially my father—always wanted to stay in resorts like this."

"Ah. Yes, you've talked to me before about that community you grew up in too." He nodded and undid his cuff links. Then he unbuttoned his suit jacket, slipped it off, and hung it on the table's chair. "The exclusivity and luxury that community was built on is—"

"Ridiculous." I cut him off. The community was almost as well-known as living in the zip code 90210 in Beverly Hills. "Paradise Grove is as exclusive as any HEAT property." I rolled my eyes. "Big houses, big celebrities, and big egos. Little, itty, bitty hearts. And that's why I left."

Normally Dimitri didn't ask personal questions, but he seemed a bit more interested in this part of my life. "Your father a member of HEAT?"

"I wouldn't know." I shrugged. "I don't talk to him much since ..." I took a breath. "After my mom passed away, he remarried quickly. I'm sure you've heard the story of the big actor turned movie director, Bill Monroe, and Georgette Fenti marrying only—"

"Only two months after Mariah Monroe passed? Yeah." He nodded solemnly but kept watching me intently, like he was trying to see every expression I had. "You have a brother too?"

"Yep. Knox is younger. He's close with them since he's still living at home and all." I bit my bottom lip and glanced around the penthouse. The luxurious leather sofa and the floor-to-ceiling windows with a big chandelier hanging over the coffee table was a classic HEAT statement. "I don't go home to Paradise Grove much now."

I heard the hum of sympathy vibrate through him. I turned around to see him slide his hands into his pockets. He frowned at me before he asked, "Were you close with your mother?"

I turned to stare out at the city below. The night lights twinkled in the distance, and I found myself sighing at the beauty of it all. The world could look like such a peaceful place in the blanket of the night sky and stars. Yet, there was pain and darkness swirling all around down there. "She was my best friend."

"I'm sorry, Olive." His voice was closer and softer now, and I could almost trick myself into believing he cared about me, like we were really good friends.

My heart twisted, and I shook off the pain, my curls

dancing back and forth before I looked over my shoulder to face him. "Don't be. I'm not here for your sympathy anyway. So ... are you going to offer me a drink?"

"You need one?" He stood there, all impeccably styled, not one of his dark locks out of place in that penthouse suite he likely owned. He was tall and always commanded attention when he walked into a room, but he never asked for it or sought it out. That quiet confidence ignited the attraction and chemistry I'd had with him in the elevator again.

"No." I licked my lips as I appreciated how his suit hugged his muscular frame and broad shoulders. His tie had been loosened but the deep forest green of it brought out how striking his eyes were as they raked over my body. "I think I just might need you, Dimitri Hardy."

"Should I tell you again that you don't really want to sleep with me?"

If he backed out of this now, I'd die of embarrassment tomorrow. I probably already would, but I followed through as best I could now. "You could, but that's only if you want me to sleep with someone else tonight."

His eyes darkened then, and his brow dropped as he commanded, "Take your dress off, but the heels stay on."

I glanced behind me at the window. Could people see into this suite?

"Don't want anyone to see?" His voice sounded as if it was taunting me almost. "If you're nervous, we can turn all the lights out."

I whipped back around to unzip the dress and then I let it fall to pool at my feet. I would manage to exude as much confidence as he did even if I had to fake it. "Do I seem nervous?"

"Undo your bra and get rid of your panties. Show me all of

you. I'll judge how nervous you are then."

I undid my bra and let that fall too, holding his stare the whole time. When his gaze finally drifted to the rest of my body, I pushed down my panties and let out a breath. My knees were practically shaking, along with my whole body, but I wasn't going to admit to it. I'd never had sex in front of a window before or done anything remotely like this. Rufford had been vanilla, but I knew as Dimitri's eyes glowed with hunger, he was anything but.

"Fuck me. You're as pretty as an angel, Olive, and I normally fuck like I'm in hell. Maybe I'm the one who needs a drink," he murmured before turning to the minibar and grabbing a bottle of champagne. "Want a little champagne?"

I shrugged. "It's your bottle to open." I saw the brand name and tried not to wince. I knew luxury, and I knew there was a $100,000 price tag on something like that. "And pay for. We probably won't finish it. It would be a waste."

"I own the hotel, Olive." He popped the cork and walked forward. "It's mine to waste, right?"

I was so mesmerized with how close he was to me, how exposed I felt standing there completely naked in just my heels, that I didn't answer.

He chuckled and then murmured in my ear, "Open your mouth. Let me give you a taste."

This I could do. I could listen even if I couldn't talk. I closed my eyes, my heart beating fast, and opened my mouth slightly.

I felt Dimitri's hand go to my neck before his thumb moved over my pulse point. "Open wider, and eyes on me, Olive." I snapped them open and frowned at him in question. Why did he care if I was looking at him? Like he could read my mind, he said, "I want to see that pretty color in your eyes all night when I'm bringing you to the brink."

Staring into his emerald eyes, completely naked, as he tipped the bottle felt much too intimate for the one-night stand I wanted. And then he took it to the next level when he squeezed my neck hard enough that the liquid couldn't flow down nor could I breathe. It was just a few seconds of him filling my mouth with champagne, of the bubbles fizzling on my tongue, of him holding my gaze but my whole body shivered, my nipples tightened, and I was instantly wet.

He eased off his grip and watched as I drank it. "You swallow like you want my cock in your throat, pretty girl. Do you?" he asked before he used his thumb to tip my chin up and expose my neck. Then, he did the most ridiculous thing. He poured that hundred thousand dollars' worth of champagne on my throat, my breasts, and down my stomach. The fizzy liquid ran over my clit and my thighs. He set the bottle on the counter and wasted no time sucking the alcohol from my neck. His hands skirted down my body to squeeze my breasts and then moved the cool liquid back and forth over my nipples.

"Dimitri, this feels so good." I squirmed against his touch.

He dropped his head as his arm wrapped around my waist and then he pushed me back to gain access to my chest. He took his time sucking one of my breasts into his mouth, his tongue swirling over me. Round and round. It was like he was lapping the champagne from me, taking me in, enjoying my taste.

My nails dug into his shoulders, but he didn't stop. Instead, he hummed so loud that the vibration had me jerking my hips against him. He nudged his thigh between my legs and dropped his hand to my ass to rock me into him, over and over.

And I whimpered, "I want you, please."

Dragging his teeth slowly against my nipple, he took his time, licking it after biting. Then he looked down at me grinding against his thigh. "That's it," he murmured. Yet, he kept a firm hold on my ass, controlling my rhythm. The friction of the fabric over his thigh had me climbing closer to the orgasm I so desperately wanted. "Look at you, getting what you want. So greedy like you can't wait. It makes me hard, Olive, seeing you want it so much." I bit my lip as I rode his thigh harder, the shame falling away because he wanted me too. He felt this pull also. And then he let go of my ass and smacked it, telling me, "Go faster. The way you want it. Take what you want. All of that orgasm is yours."

And I did. I rode his thigh hard and fast and uninhibited. I cried out as an explosion shot through me just as fast, but much more powerful than I ever experienced. I couldn't think about anything other than how good it felt and how my body needed more as I clutched him close.

It was an awakening or a revelation of sorts. This was better than I'd ever had, and it was something I could have more of now. My heart raced and my breath came fast as I crumbled against him, the high subsiding.

"You look flawless when you come. Like a damn goddess," he murmured against my curls. "I don't know if I want to keep seeing that or ravage you until I've broken you enough to see a flaw."

I nodded at the idea. I wanted all of him then. I wanted more of this, needed more of this, and wouldn't stop until I got more. I dropped to my knees, ready to unbuckle his trousers and see how I could make him feel as good. Yet, he scooped me up like a baby and laid me on the bed instead, shaking his head.

"I'm not done, Olive. I still want more of that champagne."

I nodded glancing over at the bottle. "I can pour some down your—"

"No." He slowly grabbed my thigh, pulled me to the edge of the bed, and spread my legs apart. "I want to taste my champagne on your pussy."

He took the bottle from the counter, and I could only watch as he poured more on my bundle of nerves, so swollen and sensitive now from the last orgasm that I arched and hissed when it hit.

He kneeled on the floor to suck my clit.

I was writhing now, my legs spread as he licked my pussy with champagne on it over and over. The bubbles popped on my clit, and the cool liquid rolled over my sex before his warm tongue sucked it away.

I couldn't stop from crying out again and arching. "Please, Dimitri. This is too much."

"Not enough," he said against me and kept going, faster and faster. But he was right, it wasn't enough.

"Please. I want more," I cried because my pussy was convulsing around nothing. I wanted his cock, but instead, he sat back and brushed his fingers over my arousal.

"Look how wet you get for me even when I lick it away. I love how greedy this pretty pussy is for me."

I couldn't believe how filthy his mouth was behind closed doors, but my nipples puckered, and I moaned as I heard him saying it.

"Maybe we shouldn't waste a single part of this champagne, Olive. Maybe you should show me how you like to ride a cock, huh?" That's when I realized he still held that bottle and now he was tracing the cool rim of it round and round the edge of my entrance.

I whimpered and clawed at his wrists, trying to get more of something, anything to bring myself over the edge I was teetering on again. "Yes," I whispered, not even knowing right then what I was agreeing to.

Dimitri slid the cool glass in slow as he moved over my body and planted one arm above me as he moved his whole body to the rhythm of the champagne bottle fucking me. He tipped it up and it immediately hit my G-spot. His thumb rolled over my clit to pinch it into the hard glass, moving it back and forth on top of it.

It was a feeling I'd never experienced, a vulnerability I would crave for the rest of my life. I surrendered again to the pull of him, to how he took control of me. I cried out as blood roared through my veins, ablaze with desire and ecstasy.

He watched me the whole time, mesmerized. Then, he pulled the bottle from me slowly. "The bottle's glistening with your come and my champagne," he said. He brought it to his lips and held my gaze as he put it in his mouth and sucked on it before licking the rim. I gasped at seeing him do it. "Champagne and honey might be my two favorite flavors mixed together now," he murmured as he sat back and stared at me naked on his bed.

I sat up to crawl to him, ready now to have all of him. My hand went into his trousers just as his phone started to ring. He glanced at his watch. I saw a woman's name and immediately wondered if he'd want me to continue.

"Answer it," I told him, my hand moving over him now. He frowned at me. "Is it your date, Dimitri? Want to go meet up with her instead of having me?" It was a bold thing to say while my hand was wrapped around his cock.

He stopped my hand, pulling me from his trousers and

crawled over me to say, "I've got you here all night. Why would I meet up with anyone else?"

"Get real." I shoved at his broad shoulder and then chuckled when he yanked my hips closer against him. "I probably can't do much more anyway. I'm freaking spent."

"Do you truly believe that?" He searched my face to see if I was serious. Then, he rearranged me so that I was in the middle of the bed under him. "Is that all your professor would give you? He didn't teach you that the best way for your pussy to feel good is to keep going?"

"You tasted me about a billion times just minutes ago," I reminded him.

He hummed. "I tasted you with champagne. What about without it?"

His hand touched my hips and then between my legs, his middle finger pushing against my already swollen clit. His finger was able to move over it smoothly because of how wet I still was, of how wet I was getting again.

His words had me tightening my thighs though. I swallowed, and the gulp was audible. "That's not ... We've done enough."

"You not into me eating you out?" he whispered against my ear.

How would I know? What we'd just done was the only time someone had gone down on me. It was fantastic, but I couldn't be sure that without champagne ... "I ... Rufford and I didn't normally get to that part."

"What do you mean?"

"I mean it's obvious I enjoy sex. Probably to my detriment. Rufford always told me I was too impatient. I wanted it too much. So, we never ..." I shrugged not sure what to say.

"What about with others?" Dimitri kept his finger moving over me the whole time.

It was probably a tactic to get me to tell the truth or something. I fell for it though. I was rolling my hips and writhing against his hand as I moaned out, "It's only been Rufford, Dimitri. I ... He's the only one."

"Fuck." Dimitri dragged out the swear. "Fuck. I'm going to be up all night, aren't I? Proving to you what a disservice that dumbass did."

"I said you could— Actually, you should leave," I whimpered out as I rolled my naked ass against his hard cock. It was growing by the second against me, and I loved the feeling. "You had a date tonight. I know you did."

"Yep. Two actually. But I'm not leaving you for anyone. I sent them home. This ass is mine for the night." He squeezed the side of my hip and then commanded, "On your back, baby, and spread your legs. I'm going to show you what it's like to have the best sex of your life tonight."

"I think you've already accomplished that," I mumbled as I laid onto my back and spread my legs a bit.

"Wider," he murmured as he undid his shirt and pulled it from his shoulders. I didn't move as I watched him strip completely down. His body was pure muscle, toned to perfection. "Olive, are you listening? Spread your legs wider. Show me my pretty pussy."

I did as I was told. I'd already gone this far. I'd already lost what I thought was the love of my life, and now I was going to be without sex for a good amount of time after this.

"Now, thinking and knowing are two very different things. You need to know I'm the best you ever had, Olive." He hovered over me, completely naked, with his gaze locked on mine.

Normally, his green eyes were a light misty color, so light, so laid-back and relaxed.

I wasn't sure who Dimitri was as a person. I knew he was exceptionally smart by how far he'd come professionally, but he didn't really associate with those he didn't need to. He avoided confrontation, and he enjoyed himself to the extremes. He didn't seem to worry about much, but here, his gaze was darker, determined, and full of a desire to prove his point.

He moved down my body slowly and lapped at my chest, taking his time to swirl his tongue around each of my nipples.

"Please hurry," I whined. I'd told him I didn't have a handle on my sex drive.

"Patience, Olive."

"I don't have patience. I just told you that." I clawed at his shoulders now.

"Should I teach you what it feels like?"

"Let's just have sex, please."

He chuckled and let me ride his fingers faster. He kept with the pace of my hips as I gyrated on him, but I wanted more. "If you need to get off, go ahead, Olive. We have all night."

"All night for what?" I was panting as his thumb pressed against the bundle of nerves that probably didn't need any more attention but still loved to get it all the same. "I just want to come. You said you wanted me to come again, so let's just do it."

"No." He shook his head against my stomach, and I gasped at the sensation of his five-o'clock shadow there. He kissed down further, and I felt my legs trying to close, unsure of how close I wanted him to get to my pussy. "I didn't say that. I said I wanted to taste your pussy."

Having him fuck me was one thing, eating me out was another. Rufford wanted nothing to do with that. "I just think it's easier if—"

"Do I look like a man who wants an easy fuck, Olive?" he said, now right above my clit. I practically felt his breath there and stopped rolling against his fingers to look down at him. Vivid green eyes held mine, and I wanted to believe there was hunger in them.

"You look like someone who could have one," I whispered out. "I think any woman would sleep with you, seeing you like this."

"And yet I'm about to eat out my best friend's bridesmaid, knowing the repercussions are going to be pretty damn bad."

"We're not telling her." I hurried to make that clear. "We're not telling a single soul."

"Oh really?" He worked my sex, and I whimpered at his large, calloused fingers gliding over me, the motion was slow, excruciatingly so. Then he brought those two fingers to his mouth and slid his tongue between them, not looking away from me for a single second. "You taste like you have goddamn honey inside you, Olive. I get you all night. Why would I hide it when I'm enjoying it? When it's nothing to be ashamed of?"

"Because ... this is just one night. And it would only complicate our friendships with Kee."

He growled against me. "But it's the best night, right?"

"I think so," I whimpered because his mouth feathered over my clit as I said it.

I couldn't breathe, couldn't think, could barely even form a sentence. He nipped me then, and I convulsed against him, my thighs clamping down on his ears.

"You know so. Tell me." And then he sucked on my clit hard before his tongue slid down to my pussy. He pulled back to swear and say, "You drip this sweet honey all for me, Olive.

So fucking sweet that I'm going to lick up every last drop of it. Make sure when you come, you say what I want to hear."

"What do you want to hear?" I didn't care. I'd tell him anything. I'd lost my mind. I was clawing at his dark hair now, trying to get him to finish what he'd started.

"Say I'm the best sex you've ever had. That you know it. Me and no one else."

"Jesus, you're egotistical."

"You think so?" He chuckled, then his tongue slid into the most sensitive part of me. He moved it fast, like he knew it's what I needed, and his fingers worked my clit, my ass, my body in a way I wasn't used to.

Dimitri had perfected whatever this was. If there was a class for pleasuring women, he could have had a doctorate in it. I should have been embarrassed with the mewling I did, the arching, the clawing, but he egged me on.

Every time he'd pull away from my pussy to work his fingers in me some other way, he'd tell me, "That's it. Take what you want. This orgasm is yours. Look at the work you're putting in fucking my hand. You deserve to feel good. Feel fucking perfect. Take what you want."

I screamed out right as he curled his fingers in me, and the blinding euphoria shot through me.

He didn't hesitate or let up. He pushed me further, sucking on my clit and pumping his fingers up and down so fast and hard that suddenly my body felt like it was going to implode.

"Dimitri, I can't ... You have to stop. I'm ... I think ... I've never felt this good, and I can't control—"

He sucked harder, and something unraveled inside me. My orgasm gushed onto his face, and he hummed as it happened, like he wanted every drop still.

I heard how he lapped at it, how he practically drank my come into his mouth. And he didn't shy away from licking every single part around my folds to get all of it. He slid that expert tongue over my inner thighs, and I felt his five-o'clock shadow scrape against the sensitive skin. My legs tightened around him, and I could've held him there all night because suddenly I wanted to.

When I rocked against him one last time, he moaned out, "Look at you. Fucking incredible. Your body wants even more, I can feel it." He crawled up me and turned my face to his. I knew I was blushing, but he grabbed my jaw and chin so that I had to look him in the eyes. "Ashamed of how much you like it, Olive?" I bit my lip because I didn't want to answer, but he used his thumb to pull it from my teeth immediately. "Answer me."

"I just broke up with my boyfriend. I really shouldn't like it this much ..."

"He was cheating on you. You should do whatever the fuck you want," he corrected me before he leaned closer—so close that our lips touched—and murmured, "Now, tell me how good you taste when you're doing exactly what you want."

And then he kissed me hard, stuck his tongue so far in my mouth I had no choice but to suck my juices from it. I tasted sweet and salty and mixed with him. I tasted of desire and sex, and it was addictive.

As I arched into him, I moved my hand down to grab his cock and centered his hard tip right against me. "I won't be able to stand it if you don't fuck me, Dimitri."

"I probably shouldn't. You're right about complications."

Now he was trying to deny me? "You should. Just one time. I'm on birth control, you can have me bare if you've been..." I drifted off, not knowing how to ask.

"I get tested regularly, Olive. But don't trust any guy who says that. *Fuck*." He swore under his breath and I watched how the cords in his neck tightened. "Do you know what saying that to a guy does?"

"Yeah, it gets him to screw me, which is what I want. It's only going to be tonight anyway. Might as well make the most of it."

"God damn it, Olive. We're going to regret this." But I felt the tip of him at my entrance. There was no way I'd regret feeling all of him in me. There's no way he'd regret it either. He was throbbing in my grip, thick and solid and bigger than I'd ever experienced.

"Fuck me like you mean it, Dimitri. Don't let me down."

CHAPTER 4: DIMITRI

How could I deny a woman panting with desire underneath me and begging me for the best sex of her life?

Better still, how could I deny Olive Monroe? The second she dropped that dress in front of my window, I knew no other woman would compare to her. So strong even in her vulnerability, she met my challenge head-on.

And now, she was already a fiend for what I could to do with her sexually, and I was a fiend for her addiction to it. Her body was perfection, so small and yet so full of curves that I could get lost in her forever. Every sound she made when I touched her was almost as intoxicating as the way she tasted against my lips too.

I couldn't deny her if I tried. It's how I'd defend myself later, but now, there was no defense.

I thrust into her hard and didn't hold back, all our boundaries and reservations gone. I didn't care right then that she was my best friend's assistant or that she was younger than us or even that she'd just broken up with her boyfriend.

All the worries, all the hesitations were gone. We got back to the animalistic need within us to be a part of one another, and that's what I needed most now.

"Harder," she begged.

I pulled out slowly as I stared into her hooded eyes. I took my time really observing her in that moment. Her curls were sprawled out on the pillow, dark and shiny against the white pillowcase, her breathing heavy. Her breasts rose and fell fast, and I saw how they were peaked, full and ready for me to give them more attention.

"You hide these tits from the world, I swear," I growled as I brushed a thumb over her nipple and leaned on my other arm, hovering over her.

"Yeah, they're too big." She rolled her eyes, and when I pinched the nipple, she whimpered. "And too sensitive."

I rolled it now, giving it extra attention as I watched how her eyes glazed over, so responsive to my every touch. "Hmm. I disagree."

"Seriously. They just"—she waved one hand at them— "harden easily and people see, and then if you touch them ..."

I dipped my head down to run my tongue over the other one, and she screamed then gripped my hair and pushed me against them. She liked to be touched so much I wasn't sure I'd be able to remember anyone before or after her.

"God, that feels so good. You have to stop or I'll—"

"Come again, Olive. But I want to feel it this time." I threaded my hands through her hair and looked at her seriously now. "Come on my cock. Show me how you like this."

I twisted her nipple and pulled her hair back so I got exposure to her neck. I was being rougher than I normally would be the first time with a woman, but I saw how she liked it. Her breathing was erratic, her legs spread further as I thrust into her and rolled my hips, and she cried out loudly as I pinched and twisted her nipple hard.

I felt her pussy, so tight already, convulse around me, and then something came over her. She rolled us and climbed on me like she wanted the control.

"Not enough," she moaned in my ear. Then she spread her

legs wide, gripping my shoulders and lifted herself from me to then bear down hard with everything she had.

My cock was ready to explode as I hit deep into her walls and felt her pussy stretching to accommodate my size. "Damn, you're tight. You feel good riding my cock like you need it. Fuck. That's it. Give me that pussy just how you want to."

Her legs quivered as she increased her speed. Holding onto the headboard, she leaned forward. "It's so good, Dimitri."

With her tits bouncing as she rocked over me, I couldn't look away as I held her hips. "You're the unexpected sort of stunning that people never get to see." I don't think she cared at all what I was saying. Her eyes were glazed over as she moaned and rode me harder. "You're beautiful under me, Olive, but above me, you're flawless. You're—"

She covered my mouth and murmured, "Please don't talk." And she lifted herself up and ground down onto me again. "I want to get off, not get taken for an emotional ride that means nothing."

I gripped her hips harder but let her control the rhythm. She needed it. She wanted it.

And all I wanted to do then was give her that moment. We reached a high together but she controlled the pace. She controlled me. I watched how her body tightened, how she moaned for me, and then how she rolled off of me after like it was all she wanted.

She didn't snuggle up to me or say a thing as she fell asleep. Yet, once her eyes were closed and her breathing slowed, I murmured, "You really are flawless, Olive Monroe. He never deserved someone as perfect as you." I pulled her close in the night then and, in her sleep, she cuddled close.

I held her through the night, never letting go.

CHAPTER 5: DIMITRI

The next morning, I stretched in bed, thinking I could coax Olive into morning sex, have some breakfast with her, and do all the things you do after a good night of screwing around. I wasn't even opposed to cuddling her this morning. I'd enjoyed doing it last night.

Except, I woke up to my phone ringing and when I grabbed for it, I saw her side of the bed empty and completely made up. I couldn't help the pang in my chest at that. "What do you need, Dex?" I answered the call as I walked through my place, smelling sweet honey-covered apples all around me but finding no Olive anywhere. I checked the bathroom, the other room connected to the en suite, and even looked out at the balcony.

She'd left me like I was a shitty, dirty one-night stand she was ashamed of. And if that's all she wanted from me, that was fine. I didn't do more than one-nights with women anyway.

Dex blabbered about work on the other line. "So, you going to that ridiculous HOA community meeting? It sounds like they're pulling strings with New Haven City to make sure you can't renovate your condo complex and get companies in your new office building there." New Haven City was a large, vibrant metropolis hub. It was a powerhouse of business startups and innovation. But for some reason, the city was continually blocking my office building and I'd finally found out it had to do with Paradise Grove.

"Paradise Grove is going to be the bane of my fucking

existence," I growled and winced as I thought about how I'd pried into Olive's upbringing just a tad. She'd grown up in the community I was now invested in. I'd actually researched the place after I'd become intrigued, hearing her talking to Kee about it.

I liked risky investments, and with land available near the exclusive community situated right outside a big city, putting in for a bid to build there was a great opportunity to turn risks into rewards.

"It should be the bane of your existence," my older brother reminded me. "You wanted to invest in this shit. Not me. Now you took your chance and what do you always say? Enjoy the dumbass dance?"

"It'll work out." I walked over to her half-made side of the bed and threw the blankets off just to mess it up. I was still more than a little irritated she'd left me this morning.

"Or just admit it was a bad one, bro." Dex chuckled like he was excited about me losing my ass on this.

"You bet on this being a bad investment, didn't you?" My older brothers always acted like I made bad decisions.

"Dom said it was going to be and Declan said he wanted nothing to do with it. I merely said I thought you'd stop investing time and money in a few months, and—"

"And so there's a fucking bet between you fuckers," I concluded, my competitive blood spiking.

Then I heard Kee in the background, and Dex grumbled, "Why do you need to talk to my brother the night after our wedding?"

"Because he's my best friend, you idiot," she said before her voice became clearer. "Did you see Olive leave last night? I can't get ahold of her."

"Was I supposed to be watching over her?" I growled in irritation.

"No, you big baby." She tsked. "It was just a question. She didn't answer her phone this morning."

"Pretty sure her and Rufford had a spat. She's probably nursing her wounds."

I heard Kee sigh. "Right. I saw that coming from the way he was so distant with her. I should swing by her hotel room and—"

"Enjoy your first morning of marriage, Kee. Olive's just fine. I'll check on her." I winced immediately and then pinched the bridge of my nose. In the past, it would have been so easy to handle a small problem like this for Kee, but now I'd slept with her friend. "I'll call you later."

I hung up and punched Olive's number. It rang once, then twice, then went directly to voicemail.

She was ignoring me? I hated that she thought she could and that it was the best option she landed on. So, I did what I shouldn't have. I pulled up the hotel registry and figured out her room number. These were the benefits of being part owner.

I called her room's phone from mine. That way, she wouldn't know who was calling.

"Hello?" Her voice sounded laced with sleep and confusion. I glanced at the time. It was a bit early after what we'd been doing all night, but I didn't care.

"You're ignoring me when I gave you orgasm after orgasm last night?"

"Dimitri?" she murmured, like she couldn't believe it.

"Who else would it be, Olive? You have some other guy last night too?"

"Oh, shut up," she grumbled as I heard rustling. "Why are

you calling me?"

"Why weren't you in my damn bed?" I said back even though I wasn't supposed to be calling about that.

I was met with silence, a long tense silence I didn't at all feel comfortable with. Normally, there was no vulnerability when I was with a woman, no questions about how she felt, no worries that I might be bothering her. With Olive, I thought of all those things at once.

"I needed to sleep. So, I came back to my room."

"You couldn't sleep next to me?" I sounded like a butthurt reject.

"I don't really sleep well next to other people," she confessed. "Anyway, it's not you, it's—"

"Are you feeding me a line right now?"

"Well, you sound like you kind of might need a line," she said quietly before I heard a giggle.

"Are you laughing at me?" Why was I completely offended?

"Dimitri, I think my intentions last night were clear."

"Crystal. I know what we did was just a hookup," I corrected her pointedly, my voice almost a growl.

"Oh, okay." She cleared her throat. "Good. Then, if there's nothing else—"

"Kee wants to know if you're all right. I told her about Rufford and—"

"You did not tell her that we slept together, right?" She cut me off with a screechy voice. Then I heard more rustling. "I'm up. Do you want to talk about this? We should definitely talk about this. She cannot know. I can come back to your suite if you want to discuss how to handle it and—"

"You want to see me now all of a sudden?" I grumbled.

"I don't give a crap about seeing you, Dimitri. I just need

you to promise you will not tell her anything."

"Why?" I didn't want to tell her either but, damn, she was adamant.

"Why?" she repeated and her voice got higher. "Why? Because she's employed me for the better part of my adulthood when I needed her, and I cannot have her thinking I'm sleeping around with her best friend."

"Is that all I am? Your friend's best friend?"

"Yep," she said loudly, like it was obvious. "You're her very rich, very annoying, very entitled, does-whatever-he-wants-and-shows-up-whenever-he-feels-like-it best friend. We barely even talk because you're working in the corner all the time. Barely friends, Dimitri. Barely. And if she thinks I just had a total lapse in judgment because of a breakup, which I did, I will look completely vulnerable and she'll worry. I'm her assistant. I'm supposed to worry about *her*."

"Kee's taking a break from the limelight."

"Not only is she taking a break from the limelight, but she doesn't need to worry about us on top of everything. She wouldn't want to know that her friends ..."

"Hooked up and had great sex?" I finished for her.

"Please don't ever say that again. But yes. She'll just worry that it's going to cause a rift."

"I don't hide the women I sleep with, Olive. I don't really hide anything I do at all."

"I'm well aware of that. But we aren't sleeping together. We *slept* together. Once. It will never happen again."

Damn, that was a shot to my ego. "Olive honey, you sound so sure."

"Do not ever use that name again either."

"Don't like me bringing up how you taste?" Now I was

goading her just to piss her off after she'd irritated me.

"You're literally the worst person ever to talk to in the morning."

"Had you stayed with me, we wouldn't be talking."

"You know what, Dimitri?" She spoke fast now, didn't even let me reply. "You really think I just wanted to wake up with my one-night stand that I don't care about? I just broke up with Rufford, and now I have to deal with my heartbreak." I heard how her voice wobbled and I hated that I heard the sadness there.

"Olive, if you want—"

"No. I don't want anything. I have to deal with that and the shitstorm of my email I sent last night. I really don't have time to deal with you too." Her tone hardened.

I frowned about that email and about her university situation in general. "You said that would be fine. If it's not, let me know, and I can—"

"It is fine," she shrieked. "I know it's fine because I was sad until you called and made me so mad that I don't have any more capacity for emotion."

"Well, I guess my charm works." I sat on the bed and smiled as I listened to her throw anger at me. "Want to come over and see if other parts of me work too?"

"I really can't with you right now. It's too early and quite frankly, when we slept together, I wasn't expecting this the next day."

"What?"

"You talking freely about how we fucked. I do not want to deal with you or your mouth right now."

"What's wrong with my mouth?" I wasn't sure why I kept egging her on, but I genuinely was enjoying myself more than

I had in a long time. "You seemed pretty happy with it on your pussy last night and on your—"

"I am so mad at you I can't even see straight. Do not call me back when I hang up, and do not ever bring last night up again. We are done, and I am done with you. When you see me around Kee, act like you did before. Got it?"

"Maybe."

"You'd better get it, you dick." And then she hung up.

Well, she didn't exactly sound sad anymore. So, that was a win in my book.

I tried to forget how she spit the fire from hell at me but tasted as sweet as heaven as I looked over my schedule for the day. Thoughts of her lingered in my head, bouncing around and causing havoc a lot longer than I would have liked.

It's when I concluded that this had to be one of the best and worst one-night stands of my life.

Maybe I never had noticed her until last night. But I wasn't going to forget her being in the room after the night we'd had. Not for a long fucking time.

CHAPTER 6: DIMITRI

Three Weeks Later

Three weeks of not contacting Olive hadn't exactly been a slice of heaven. If I was being honest, three weeks of her avoiding me had been absolute hell.

I was supposed to be a workaholic, but instead of focusing on my investments, I was wondering about what she was so damn busy with that she never contacted me once.

She appeared around Kee when she was needed, which was most of the time, but suddenly I felt out of place. She was hanging out with my best friend, we'd always gotten on just fine, but now I wondered who she was talking to, what she was thinking, what her plans were after getting Kee's marriage out to the press.

When I walked into Kee's record label office, I found them all looking perfectly content. Platinum records hung on the walls and my brother sat with his laptop, making calls. Olive's curls bounced about as she buzzed around fluffing Kee's dark hair while discussing wedding pictures.

No one even looked up at me when I appeared in the doorway. My gaze, though, tracked Olive's whereabouts like a damn obsessed puppy. She wore one of those big sweaters again with holes in her leggings as she pointed to a photo and mumbled that it could work for the magazine. Olive had become a jack-of-all-trades where Kee was concerned, working as her PA and helping with PR, but Kee had shifted her focus out of the spotlight when she'd married my brother. Instead of continuing to be a pop star, Kee was running the record label my brother had bought for her.

She'd already informed us she wasn't going to release another album for a year or two. Normally, my focus would have been the business, but instead, I found myself asking about her team and wondering about Olive.

After she'd avoided me so diligently, now I had a reason to approach her. Quite frankly, this was me focusing on business.

I watched them fuss over a picture before Olive pushed at the pink flower in her own hair and stood up to stretch. She froze when she saw me but then turned to Kee. "You're not doing any appearances for the next month. So, I'm guessing you'll have some time off?"

It wasn't just a month that Kee wouldn't be doing appearances, but she nodded softly, not willing to tell Olive that her position as an employee wasn't needed.

"Means you're free for a whole month, I guess." I walked into the office and blurted it out, looking to finally get a rise out of her. I wanted her to acknowledge me, pay attention to me, stop ignoring me. Her honey-colored gaze cut across the room to scowl at me but she didn't say anything at first.

So, I goaded her more and brought up our night from three weeks ago. Her eyes widened and she got up fast, grabbing my arm. "Let's go."

She hustled me out of the office and down the hall to another empty room before she slammed the door and glared at me like she could appear mean even though I was a whole head taller than her. "What the heck was that?"

"You're avoiding me. So, figured I'd incentivize you to stop by offering to talk about the night we had three weeks ago."

"In front of Kee?" She threw up her hands. "We agreed to not talk about that night."

"I'll definitely keep that agreement if you can help me out with something. I have a favor I need to ask of you," I told her, not at all intimidated by her anger. Instead, I found myself eyeing her up, wondering if her cheeks would redden further, if her breath would catch as I pushed her more.

She crossed her arms, and her curves drew my attention too. I knew exactly how well they fit in my hands, and I tried my best not to rearrange my damn trousers while she glowered at me. "You're threatening to tell Kee about our night for a favor? Not really a favor, Dimitri. More like blackmail."

"It was a way to get you to stop avoiding me. It worked, didn't it?"

"I'm not avoiding you," she said, but her gaze skittered around the room.

"You've been avoiding me for the better part of a month, haven't talked to me since Kee's wedding night unless she's in the room."

"Did I ever talk to you before when she wasn't in the room?" She had me there, and because of that, the silence stretched between us. "We're not really that good of friends, Dimitri. Let's not pretend like we are." She sighed. "I'm trying to deal with my own stuff, get my ducks in a row for the university hearing, preparing to restart a whole year of master's program work. So, I'd rather not—"

"I thought you said that was all under control"

"Yeah, well, I was lying." She winced.

"But a year? You were almost done with your thesis," I said, confused.

She wiggled the glasses she had on and looked away. "Yeah, and Rufford reassigned me."

That motherfucker really had some balls if he'd done that. "What happened with your email?"

"The university buried it. They asked if I wanted to come in to discuss the allegations because the email screenshots looked cropped and Photoshopped. He's claiming I forged all of it because he didn't think I was fit to continue the thesis. I'm over it. I'm just going to restart."

"So, you're letting him get away with it?"

"No. I'm not letting him do anything. Don't say that. I hate when people say I'm letting a situation happen." She stomped her foot, and I saw the fire back in her eyes that I'd seen a month ago when she sent that email. "I'm picking my battles. I'm mad as hell about this, but I want to graduate, not get thrown out of the master's program. I already have no plans for ..." She threw up her hands. "Anything honestly. And so I'm just stressed." She rubbed at her temples and took a deep breath before she continued. "I also don't want to sit through a meeting while he degrades me and the relationship we had."

"The relationship you had?" I frowned at her feelings. Why would she try to hold that in a high regard still? "He groomed you, took advantage of you, and manipulated you. He screwed you over, Olive."

She propped her hands on her hips as she stood taller to scold me. "We still had some good times, Dimitri. I cared about him," she said quietly.

"We had good times too. I don't see you wanting to preserve shit about the tumble we had in the sheets."

"Is there something to preserve? Because from what I

remember, you and I both got off and that was about it. There weren't any 'sweet nothings' exchanged." Yeah, well, she'd made sure of that by leaving fast the next morning.

"Your pussy was sweet enough for me. I've dreamt about it ever since."

Her little mouth formed an O of shock before she poked my shoulder. "Don't you dare say stuff like that around me."

"Why not? You don't like a compliment?" I couldn't help but smirk at the heat rising to her cheeks.

"I'm going to go if that's all you needed to say to me."

"No." I grabbed her elbow gently as she started to turn and spun her back. "Fine. I didn't bring you out here to discuss that actually, although I don't think avoiding me over the last couple weeks was necessary."

"Then what did you bring me out here to discuss?" She folded her arms across her chest and tapped her shoe on the floor like she didn't have time for me.

She was about to make a lot more time. "You mentioned that community you grew up in ..."

"Paradise Grove?"

"Yeah. That's the one." I nodded.

She combed her curls back away from her face and asked, "What about it?"

"Your father still lives there." I cleared my throat, not sure how she was going to take this. "He's also on the HOA board there."

"I mean, maybe?" She narrowed her eyes. "Why would you care? And how would you know?"

She took a step back then, but I took one forward. "Now wait. Hear me out."

She put up her hands to stop me from coming toward her.

"You asked me information about Paradise Grove the night we hooked up."

I nodded. "That's true, but it had nothing to do with our night together."

She shook her head at me and laughed, but it sounded hollow. "Were you pumping me for information?"

"I was curious." I bit the bullet. "I'd invested in Paradise Grove and the land surrounding it awhile back and—"

"You're joking. Why?" she blurted out. "Why would you invest in a small community like that?"

I combed a hand through my hair. It'd been about a year ago I'd listened to her and Kee talk about how she grew up in some gated community that held more pain than joy for her. "I listen to people when they talk. You talked about a luxurious enclave with Kee and I—"

"That was me talking about my childhood! I hate that place. It wasn't an invitation to go research it and invest in it."

I slid my hands in my pockets. "It's what I do."

"You realize you should be ashamed, right?" She wrinkled her nose in disgust. "I thought I was talking to friends."

"You said the other night we weren't even that—"

"Oh, shut up. Don't feed me a line about us not being friends so you can profit off what you overheard. You sound like an unhinged investor too obsessed with money to realize that he's using people's personal stories to make deals."

"I like taking risks, Olive. You've moved on from the community, right? So this one felt like a fun one, innovative and on brand for HEAT."

"Oh, it's on brand." She scoffed. "Good luck."

"Well, now." I rubbed my jaw, trying to approach this differently. "Do you think you'd maybe like to explore why you hate that place so much and maybe visit with me? Go to a meeting and—"

"Are you kidding?" she whispered.

Fuck. This wasn't going well. "Look, Kee is a part of the HEAT empire too now. We won a bid on developing a border area and some of the land within Paradise Grove. It's a vibrant community that I want to make better."

She lifted a brow. "I highly doubt you're doing this out of the goodness of your heart."

"Fine. I purchased a house there so I can understand why their little community meetings that they mask as HOA meetings are somehow pulling strings within all of New Haven City."

"Sounds about right. Paradise Grove always has been able to influence all of New Haven. So, they invited you to a meeting?"

"Not really. But I'm technically living there so I'll just show up. I bought the place merely to go to these ridiculous meetings that seem to hold so much weight. I haven't put much effort into the house at all."

"And I'm sure all of Paradise Grove is seeing that you're not putting in any effort." She rolled her eyes. "Great. They probably think you're just going to flip the thing. And they don't allow flips. And they don't really allow anything to change in New Haven unless they're completely on board. So good luck."

"Ah, so just everyone knows about Paradise Grove influencing the city ordinances?"

"Sure." She shrugged. "My father and stepmom talked about the meetings and the happenings in town enough."

And that's how I knew right then and there that Olive had to help me. She had a knack for retaining irrelevant information most of the time, but in this case, I needed it. "Right, well, it's an exclusive community, as you know, but we need to revamp some of the buildings, and I need the board to agree."

"They won't." She actually chuckled, shaking her head at me. "I mean, seriously, Dimitri, I wish you good luck. Not that you deserve it after selfishly asking me for information."

"I was making conversation that night, Olive."

"You don't make idle conversation." She bit her lip and then whispered in a voice that held pain, "Were you disappointed I didn't stay over the next morning because you missed out on asking me more questions?"

My gut twisted with her query. I wouldn't have her think that, I couldn't. I stepped close to her before I could stop myself to remind her of the chemistry we had. "I wanted you to stay until the next morning so I could fuck you again. My business is separate from me touching you, Olive Honey." I pulled at the collar of her sweatshirt, yanking her close so that we were chest to chest.

She gasped out my name. "Dimitri."

"I'm trying to be professional because we're in our friend's office, but I'm happy to remind you of how my cock feels in your pussy if you want. I don't think about much else when you're around as of late."

She licked her lips, and I saw her amber eyes glance down before she shook her head. "That was a one-time thing."

"I know. Want to make it a two-time thing right now?"

Her breathing had accelerated, and I was suddenly ready to forget about the fact that we were in an office if she said yes, except she closed her eyes tight and admitted, "I have a date tonight."

Immediately, my hand dropped from her collar as if it'd

been electrocuted. "A date? What the hell for?"

"Yes, a date. Some guy I matched up with on an app."

"Just a guy on an *app*? That doesn't sound safe."

"It's fine, Dimitri."

"How the fuck do you know? You haven't met him," I scoffed.

"I'm a big girl, I can take care of myself." She chuckled like this was all fun and games. "Anyway, I'm trying to get back out there. I want to see who else can make me feel like, well, you know." She waved a hand in the air like I was supposed to get it.

"Feel like I made you feel?" I finished for her. "You're not going to find that on any damn date," I practically snarled.

She dragged her teeth over her bottom lip as she looked me up and down. "Well, I want that, Dimitri. So I'm going to find it. Even if I have to go on a million dates."

I leaned forward until my mouth was close to hers as I placed my hand on the wall behind her. "If you're saying you want someone to fuck you like I do, just ask me to fuck you, Olive."

She shook her head, but I swear her pretty eyes dilated. She wanted this as much as I did, and when I reached down to trace the rip in her leggings so I could feel her bare skin, she sucked in air like the chemistry that ricocheted around the room was making it hard for her to breathe. "Dimitri, we're in Kee's office space."

"So? You think I care who sees me touching you?"

"You should. Your brothers are out there somewhere too. What if someone walks in?"

"Then they'll see that you don't need to go on any dates. They'll see you have a man willing to take care of your every need right here." My thumb slid across her smooth, soft skin and inched higher up her thigh. She whimpered at my touch and her hands fell to my shoulders. "This isn't right, and you know it. We can't sneak around in the middle of a workday and—"

I tore her leggings just enough so I could push her panties to the side and graze my hand over her pussy. "You must like sneaking around because you're soaked. Or do you just get like that when I'm around, Olive Honey?"

"It's not for you," she said, like she was trying to keep her dignity, but her thigh wrapped around my hip, and she rocked against my hand.

"Bullshit." Olive was as hungry for sex with me as I was for her. Her eyes glazed over as I worked her clit back and forth and then slid a finger inside her. She was climbing closer and closer to the edge.

"What if it's not you? Maybe I just like the rush of doing something here, Dimitri. Don't you?" She gripped the lapels of my suit. "I want it here. Right here, right now. And I want you to show me you want it too, like you can't wait another second for it."

I hummed, "So you want to see *me* lose control? Want me to fuck you where everyone might find us?"

Her gaze was hooded, and her skin shimmered with the faintest glow of sweat. "Yes. Please. Show me, please."

Her words held weight, held emotion I wanted to dig into, but now wasn't the time. Now was the time to show her she'd get everything from me. I wanted to fuck the confidence into Olive that she needed. I wanted to show her that no man should ever deny her or make her feel like she was less than flawless. "I'm never going to resist anything when it comes to you, Olive."

"Good," she whispered before her hands went to my belt

buckle. I let her undo my pants while I kissed her neck. She gripped my cock and moaned, "You're so big, Dimitri."

I ripped her leggings further. "You like how big it feels? You want me to bend you over that desk and remind you?"

"Yes." She nodded fast. "Fuck me over it. Please."

She chanted the words as I pulled her over to the large mahogany desk and turned her to face the door. We both were looking at the entrance to the room, knowing it wasn't locked, that anyone could come in at any time. Yet my cock was out and throbbing, my body wound tight from her ignoring me, from wanting her, from seeing her but not being able to have her everywhere over the last three weeks.

She placed her hands on the dark wood, and I leaned over her, pulling her panties and leggings down, and nudging the tip of my cock to her entrance. "Olive, I hope someone comes in."

She whipped her head around and glared at me. "You should have locked the door. No one better see us."

I laughed before I grabbed her curls and pulled so her back would arch that ass out just for me. "I'm not stopping even if someone does see, Olive." I slammed into her, wanting her to feel every inch of me at once.

She gasped loudly and dug her nails into the wood. I hoped they left indents. "I'll fuck you anywhere. In a dark hotel room or in the light of day in front of this whole office. You know why?" I thrust in and out again, and she moaned, rolling her hips. "Because I want everyone to know I'm sleeping with you. I'm going to continue to sleep with you. And I'm going to fuck you till you understand I'm the only one who can do it this good."

"Oh, God. It's too good. I can't wait, Dimitri. I'm going to lose it."

"Come on me, Olive." I smacked her ass once, then twice. "Give me all of it."

That's when her walls constricted around me so tightly it was like she'd never let me go. Her body was on board with us fucking, and mine was too. I roared as I thrust into her one last time and buried myself deep, so deep I hoped she wouldn't be able to remove me.

It was a revelation that flew through me fast as I breathed in the sweet scent of honey all around. I wanted to imprint on Olive's life, make her mine, and make her see she was irresistible to me. She didn't have to be that for every guy, just me. And I was ready to do anything right then to do that.

CHAPTER 7: OLIVE

"Oh my God." I wiggled out from under Dimitri, regretting indulging in sex immediately. The desire to have him again had grown every time he'd walked into a room over the last few weeks. Seeing him want me, seeing how he moved with enough confidence to take me, well, it was hard to resist.

Now, though, reality set back in. "Get up. Hurry up. I think I hear someone coming."

"You just came." He chuckled. "I did too. That's probably what you're hearing."

"Please don't start with that." I was wiggling my sweater around now and trying to rearrange my leggings. Could anyone see that the hole on my thigh was bigger now? "We need to look presentable when we walk out of here."

"I'm not concerned," he said literally sounding like he didn't have a care in the world.

"Dimitri." My tone was exasperated. "Kee cannot find out about this. I can't believe I lost control and did this again when I have a freaking date tonight and—"

"Don't even think about going on that date," he growled.

"Oh, don't be ridiculous." I waved him off, but he stepped up to me and grabbed my chin.

"Are you seriously contemplating being with another man when I just fucked you into oblivion?"

"Of course I am. I'm trying to get out there and date. I don't want to be lonely or feel like I'm not good enough anymore."

Why had I told him that?

"You won't be because you're coming to Paradise Grove with me where I need you," he said as he straightened and rearranged his pants. He zipped them up and buckled his belt, appearing one hundred percent professional again.

"Um ..." I tried to smooth down my curls without a mirror and rearranged the flower that was falling out of my hair. "No thank you."

His jaw flexed, and I immediately wanted to smooth my hand over his cheek and soothe his frustration. Getting feelings involved along with our physical attraction would be disastrous, so I took a step back.

"Look, it's a weird place. Just sell your investment and contract. Chalk it up to a loss."

"Why would I do that?"

"Because Paradise Grove doesn't accept outsiders. And I get it. The community looks amazing, right? It offers what most people dream of. The iron gates open to beautiful homes with lush landscaping and the nice hall and the pretty golf course and the exclusive services and amenities offered to everyone there." I was talking fast now, rattling off all the things I knew people wanted. "It seems great that you'll be rubbing elbows with all those amazing elites at private social gatherings but it's *not*." I remembered how they'd shunned me before I left, how I was made to feel so small.

"It actually sounds like the perfect place to expand our hospitality empire into real estate and master-planned communities."

"So that's what you did?" I shook his head at him. "And how did it turn out?"

"Well, I've been blocked for a whole year on getting offices into the building we constructed just north of the community boundary. I'm finding that Paradise Grove is to blame because they have more pull than I anticipated. So, you're coming with me to change that."

Crossing my arms, I lifted a brow at him. "Why would I do that?"

"I'll pay you what Kee is. I just need you to fly in for a week and give me the rundown." He looked me up and down, and I swear he contemplated how he could make this work. "I'll call your university."

"What?" The word slipped out in disbelief.

"I'll take care of it."

"Oh, just like that?" He didn't have that much power.

"If I have it taken care of by the end of today, will you agree to go later this week with me? That Paradise Grove meeting is on Friday."

"Well, Kee probably needs me to—"

"To what, Olive? She's got a whole team here and you know it. I'll cover your salary in exchange for your commitment to getting information regarding moving my plans along. I'll be happy to hire you rather than have you sitting here fluffing Kee's more-than-adequate PR team."

"Wow. Don't pull any punches." That hit a nerve. It was a reminder of what I already felt—that suddenly I wasn't needed here either.

Still, he didn't stop. "Be a part of something you might be interested in. Give it a chance. It's your hometown after all. If you have some sort of problem there, don't just let it go. Go back, take a chance, and enjoy the dance."

"That the saying you love so much?" I remembered him telling me he lived by some motto. But now he was throwing it in while he stressed me out. I rubbed at my temples. "You're going to give me a freaking migraine."

He frowned and nudged my hands away to rub my temples for me. "You get them a lot?"

It was such a small gesture but one that had me biting my lip far longer than I should have as I stared into his eyes. "I guess so. My doctor thinks it's potentially hormonal, but it's probably just stress, considering ..." I shook my head and stepped away from him. "It doesn't matter."

He slid his hands into his pockets. "You'd be less stressed if you took me up on this offer."

I thought about it. I'd just screwed him while bent over a desk. Going to my hometown together was a recipe for disaster, and yet I didn't feel like I had anything else. I didn't feel like I wanted anything else. If he could smooth over my university issue, I blurted out, "I'll go for one week."

"Fine." He clapped his hands together. "That's perfect. Act like you like me during that week and give some key pointers at this HOA meeting coming up. I'll give you the details. They need to believe I'm trustworthy. And—"

I held up a finger. "Let's see what you're capable of doing with the university first. I'd like to know before I text Rufford back."

"Your ex is texting you? What the hell for?"

"To apologize. He wants to talk and maybe help figure out what we can do for my thesis. He's sorry, I'm sure—"

"Fuck that guy. He's about to be out of a job soon, and—"

"The university believes him, Dimitri," I reminded him.

"We'll see." He chuckled before he pulled out his phone and dialed a number. I was shocked that within a second or two, he had the chancellor on the phone.

"You know the chancellor?" I whispered. He had a direct line to the freaking head of my university?

"I own most of that university. Rufford is getting fired already. I made sure of it." He glanced at me and smirked. "What do you want? To graduate now?"

"I haven't even done my thesis! What do you mean?" I started to panic. "I didn't think ... Well, I don't want to be there another year. Maybe ... could I do it over the summer?"

"You can do whatever you want, Olive." He winked at me and reiterated what I wanted into the phone. "And you'll make sure this issue is taken care of? I don't want Ms. Monroe doing more work than her fellow graduate candidates or getting treated unfairly. I want Mr. Butson out of there by the end of the day, got it? It would be bad for the Hardy name and Alcove University if he wasn't."

Then he hung up and said, "The university agreed that you can pick a new topic and do the research through the summer to graduate in August. No meeting to discuss the email. You good with that?"

I stuttered over my words. "But normally we must have a year of research going into—"

"But that's not what you wanted. And I'm getting you what you want. I told you I'd pull some strings. You're all set." He slid his phone back in his pocket and leaned forward. "Want to say thank you?"

He was shameless. "No. My thank you is going back to Paradise Grove with you."

"Great. You can fly in at the end of the week then? There's a meeting that day that I'd like you to come to. No decisions will be made, but it'll be a great segue into you showing them I'm a valuable part of the community."

Maybe I should have been excited to go home, but home was supposed to be a place you felt comfortable, where you belonged, where you had memories that you cherished.

Yet, Paradise Grove definitely didn't encompass any of that for me.

CHAPTER 8: OLIVE

"I don't know if this is such a good idea without me," Kee whined over the phone.

"Why wouldn't it be, Kee?" I dotted on a little lip gloss and fluffed my brown curls in my compact mirror before straightening the pink flower in my hair. Honestly, I'd been thinking the same thing when Dimitri's driver picked me up from the airport later that week. It seemed Dimitri had my whole itinerary planned considering he'd booked me a private flight so I could read the entire way there, and then Mr. Preston hurried me into the SUV and said he had to get me to the meeting within the next hour.

I barely skimmed the email he'd sent me. There was enough building ordinance jargon to bore anyone to sleep. Instead, I contemplated how my life was spiraling faster and faster out of control. I was headed back to my hometown to meet the guy I was sneaking around on my best friend with. I hadn't told my father or my brother I was coming back, and I had no idea what I should research for my thesis that was due in four months.

"I mean, you're home, Olive. And you don't love that place. And you're with Dimitri." She emphasized his name like that was reason enough. "He can be pretty rude sometimes or too charming and ..."

"And what?" I wiggled my glasses in the compact mirror, the ones Rufford said framed my face so well. I growled and pulled them off. I wasn't sure that's what I wanted anymore.

"And I want you to stay friends," Kee concluded. "I like my best friends being friends."

"Nothing bad will happen. It's only a week." My statement was met with silence. "I promise, Kee. I'll keep you updated."

She mumbled a resigned yes and then asked, "Has Rufford called? I'm happy to hear Dimitri was able to work out your thesis timeline."

"It was nice of him," I muttered. Too nice. And I hated that I couldn't stop thinking about all he'd done for me already. Yet, it did keep me from being too depressed about my loss of a relationship with Rufford. "Rufford called once or twice. I didn't answer."

Technically, he'd left me five messages and texted me in anger about his firing. I'd even gotten a message from him that day.

> **Rufford: You can't ignore me forever. I apologized for calling you names about me being fired Olive. But we need to work this out. Call me back.**

I blocked that number.

> **Unknown: You're being immature. Your age is showing. Can you just answer?**

I sighed as I glanced through them again.

"Don't give in, Olive. He's a dick who doesn't deserve anything from you ever again."

"You need to stop worrying about me and enjoy your husband, okay?" I reminded her. She was married and had everything to look forward to, and I would be A-okay.

When I got off the phone with her, I sighed, hoping my reminder to her was true. One week in my hometown was manageable ... even if my life was spiraling down a drain faster than water.

I stared out the window as Mr. Preston drove, nearing closer and closer to Paradise Grove. I knew I'd been afforded opportunities that most didn't get because my parents raised my brother and me there. And it was a beautiful place, straight out of a fairy tale even. The weaving brick roads, the tall trees that had been growing for hundreds of years, the perfect landscaping of each yard, and the historic homes that had been updated and expanded over the years.

But every fairy tale had shadows and dark spots, right? Paradise Grove had those too.

The driver hadn't said a word to me but scanned a HEAT watch that made the iron gates open slowly. We used to always have to key in a code to be buzzed in, but it seemed Dimitri had been able to implement small changes. Yet, as I stared up at the shiny gold lettering that read Paradise Grove, I knew not much could have changed.

The large houses stood tall and iconic against the backdrop of a sunny day. We passed the large park that boasted lush grassy fields and tennis courts, and I saw in the distance the country club with the golf course beyond. The further you went into the community, the larger the houses got. The largest ones were on the lakefront, and I eyed the trees that draped over the street as we got closer and closer to the Seymour Hall, where all Paradise Grove meetings were held.

"I'll drop your suitcase after I drop you off for the meeting, Ms. Monroe," Mr. Preston informed me.

"I appreciate that."

He chuckled. "I appreciate you packing lightly. One suitcase is no problem at all."

Well, I rented a completely furnished apartment on a month-to-month basis, so I didn't have a lot of stuff. My whole life was easily packed up in a suitcase or two because I traveled a lot with Kee. Or at least I used to. It's the way I liked it. No roots and no home, because wandering the world seemed better than planting roots in a place you didn't love.

"Makes it easier," I agreed with Mr. Preston as we rounded a corner.

My heart sank as I stared at the corner home where I'd lived my childhood. There sat the Monroe estate. My maternal grandparents had acquired a corner lot with extra yard space, and the house itself had been a small place until my grandmother, in her old age, updated and built on for the family. She wanted my mother to inherit a home that had changed with the community, and every year people renovated and upgraded. Now, there on the corner, stood a six thousand-square-foot home in all gray brick. It was a statement, they'd felt, that they were there to stay.

To my parents' credit, they never moved after inheriting the property. I'd like to think it was because my mother knew how much it meant to my grandparents and wanted to keep it in the family.

We passed it on the way to Seymour Hall, where the meetings had always been held. It stood like a castle with its large pillars out front and stone architecture on top of a small hill. We rounded a fountain and Mr. Preston said, "I do hope the meeting goes well, Ms. Monroe. Mr. Hardy is doing so much for the community."

"Do you think so?" I asked him, genuinely wanting to know the answer.

He nodded and his gray brows knitted together. "The HEAT empire makes good money, but they invest in the best places too."

The car slowed. "Maybe," I grumbled more to myself than him because I was still skeptical.

"He puts in a lot of work too. He wants to show he's doing good everywhere, you know? Not all investors take the time to figure out how to integrate the buildings they're constructing into the community. He made sure to have that condo for the office spaces. It was smart. And he's doing research on what are good wages for those working under him in these boutiques he's getting set up. Also, I think he's running a study to see if expanding the community would be to the detriment of the residents—"

"A study?"

"Well, there are 300 homes now, but he could add HEAT Lane along with the condos for 400 as long as he can prove it's worth it."

I didn't know what to say. Dimitri had to know how clinical it all sounded, didn't he? I kept the thought to myself and waited to arrive in front of Seymour Hall. Dimitri Hardy stood out there on his phone, taller and larger than I remembered somehow. Out in the daylight, he appeared more on top of the world in his expensive navy suit tailored to perfection and his Italian loafers. I took one last breath from the safety behind the closed door of the vehicle and then got out.

"Olive, you made it." He pulled me in for a hug, and I swear he breathed in my hair before murmuring, "Apples and honey. My favorite."

I rolled my eyes and pulled away from him. "Don't be weird."

He chuckled. "I'm just setting the tone. We're supposed to be friendly, you trust me, and you think all my ideas are good ones. Got it?" he said to me before we walked into the conference room.

"Yeah, yeah. I read over the email you sent on the plane." I'd mostly skimmed it, but he didn't have to know that. "I'll try my best, but—"

"Where are your glasses?" Dimitri asked, assessing me instead of worrying about the dumb meeting he'd flown me in for.

"They're ... well, I don't need them. I just wore them because Rufford thought they made me look studious and more educated, I guess—"

"What a dumbass," Dimitri grumbled. His piercing green gaze held mine and somehow our stare felt intimate as a small smile slipped from his lips. "Your eyes are even more striking without glasses."

The butterflies in my stomach couldn't be fought back when he said that. I looked away. "Don't be charming for no reason, Dimitri. Let's get this meeting over with so I can get out of here, okay?"

"Fine. Fine." He draped an arm around my shoulder, and we walked in together.

"This is a private meeting, Mr. Hardy. You can't bring—" I recognized Lucille's voice just as I stepped around Dimitri so she could see me. "Olive Bee?"

Her frown immediately burst into a smile. Lucille extended

her arms to me in her white wool suit jacket that matched her wool skirt. She'd always been a vision of timeless elegance, I recognized that while growing up. It hadn't looked like she'd aged at all in the last few years, either, as she'd always been a woman who regularly went to the spa and took care of herself.

I walked toward her with a genuine smile. Lucille was a staple of the community but also had been a friend of my mother's and grandmother's. She'd never had children, but she'd also been a sort of mother hen in Paradise Grove. "Oh, Olive Bee, it's so good to see you home. Did your father send you to fill in since he's not going to be here again, or ..." She trailed off and frowned at the fact that Dimitri was still standing beside me.

"I'm actually here because Dimitri invited me."

Lucille huffed and patted her perfectly dyed blonde bun. Her blue eyes were focused solely on me as I said the words. She straightened her jacket, trying to piece together how I would be here with him.

"She's my guest, Lucille." He smiled at her. "She's in town to stay with me."

"Why I ..." She trailed off as her eyes ping-ponged between us. Finally she came to her own conclusion. "Where?" Lucille's eyes narrowed. "You must be moving back home, right, Olive Bee? Technically, Mr. Hardy has already agreed that no more employees would be moving into the condo building until next year or until we approve a revision of city ordinances. If you're working for him—" She cleared her throat and patted her hair, glancing around at the other board members before murmuring, "Well, we could make an exception, but you know how everyone is."

"She's not working for me. She'll be moving into my place

for—"

"Oh." Lucille's eyes widened and then got bright. "Oh!"

"No. Not like—"

"Well, that shouldn't be a problem at all then. Oh, Olive, your mom would have been so happy. And this will actually be quite a great addition to the community with all that Mr. Hardy is doing. We haven't completely understood it, and you know how it is, we just want someone we can trust to sort of buffer these things. No offense, Dimitri."

He smiled, and I saw how his beautiful, stupid emerald eyes twinkled like he'd just struck gold. He even nodded along with her, and then he put his hand on the small of my back. "Yes, yes. Olive and I have been together awhile now, but we've been keeping things quiet until ... Well, I really missed her, and we've decided it's time she be around more often. Right?" He wide eyed me. "Olive?"

This wasn't the place to make a scene even if I wanted to. Plus, Lucille didn't need to feel as though she'd been lied to at the moment. So, I pasted on a fake smile and nodded before she clapped her hands together to wave us in. "Reggie, would you get Olive a seat?"

She pointed at me and Reggie, the sheriff of New Haven, who nodded at me. "So good to see you here. You here for your dad or—"

"She's here with Dimitri, Reggie!"

Dimitri maneuvered us over to the conference table while Lucille informed most everyone. I whispered to him, "This is not going to stick. Especially if I'm not here."

"We'll work it out." He chuckled like he enjoyed a challenge. "Just go with it for now."

"So ridiculous."

And that's how the meeting went. Ridiculous in every way. The board members discussed lawn care, then they discussed the dry cleaning that was picked up weekly because Renata, a woman who'd moved in five years ago, still didn't like how they dropped off her clothing.

Finally, Lucille looked over at me, and I saw the genuine happiness on her face when she said, "I think it would be a great idea for Olive to give us some information on Dimitri's updates. She's now back home, where she's been missed."

Reggie, who'd been a part of pushing me out years ago, huffed in his chair.

Lucille's eyes cut to him, and her tone hardened. "I also think it's a good idea for Olive to work with me on writing up our quarterly *Paradise Grove News*. She can contribute a couple articles going over the changes we're so worried about. You're about to graduate with that degree in journalism, right?"

"I am but—" How could I tell them that I wouldn't be here that long?

"She'd love to do that, wouldn't you?" Dimitri squeezed my thigh as I glared at him. But he didn't give me a chance to answer. He rolled right on. "Also, I can answer any questions you have today, as I know there have been some concerns you all have shared with the city."

He continued on, answering questions and going over his plan for implementation of the office spaces in the new building he'd already constructed. They'd moved in some HEAT employees, but renting out more office space was prohibited after a new city ordinance was passed. "It's clear that you all worked to block that with the city."

"Don't point fingers, Mr. Hardy. Everyone is just trying to understand what this will mean for the community," Lucille said quietly, like maybe she could be the peacemaker. "With Olive here now, well, I think we'll see."

A few others agreed, but it was begrudgingly and under their breath, and I felt the tension in the room. I knew Lucille's husband, Earl, used to stare down any car that even looked like it remotely didn't belong in the neighborhood. And Reggie had stopped people walking into the community if they weren't recognizable.

"You say that, Lucille, but, Olive, you know how nice it is to keep things small here. Why would we want that large building to be corporate office space next to our homes?" Walter, an older gentleman that was the father of my younger brother's friend, Esme, rubbed his bald head and then his large belly in frustration. "I don't know who's going to be in there."

I glanced at Dimitri as I tried to recall parts of the packet I'd skimmed on the plane. Dimitri tried to help me, "Well, as you know, it's an opportunity for new businesses to—"

"I've heard what you think." The man's gruff voice cut Dimitri off as he stared at me. "I'd like to hear from Olive."

"Well." I cleared my throat. Walter always cared mostly about his property value even if it didn't benefit those around him. "Don't you think New Haven City is filling up with corporate spaces? Why not have Dimitri control what we have in ours? He's here, a part of Paradise Grove now. He'll make sure it's up to our standards."

Melly, a woman about the same age as me who'd gone to high school with me, too, bounced in her chair, her chest jumping with her and putting her ample cleavage on display. "I already like what he's doing with the boutiques by the golf course."

I thought I heard Reggie mutter something about the

retail space looking like a strip mall, but I didn't comment on that. Instead, I said, "Right. Dimitri is working hard on the boutiques. And I grew up here. I'll have the best interests at heart with him."

"Oh please. He drag you here just to help him with this? You get bored fluttering around the country with pop stars and wanted to try something new? Your father's gonna love this." Walter grumbled.

"Now, Walt—" Lucille started.

"Earl would say the same damn thing." Walter pointed his meaty finger at her, and it shook with anger. "And you know he's not going to be on board with any of this."

Lucille glared at him like she was about to say something, but Dimitri beat her to it. "Walter, look." His voice had shifted. It was lower, meaner, colder. "My girlfriend and I have been together long enough that your insinuation is disrespectful."

"Dimitri, it's okay. I can be a bit noncommittal."

"No." He frowned at me and then touched my cheek. "I'll be clear now while we're all in a room together. I've invested a significant amount of money into this community, not just for me, but for my girlfriend. It's of value to her and of value to me. I intend to keep investing because she's committed to you all, and I'm committed to her."

I wasn't sure if he was winning over the men in the meeting, but Lucille had stars in her eyes, and Melly looked completely in love with him.

"Olive wanted to be here to focus on her thesis in a place where she felt comfortable. It's time to settle down and maybe look at expanding our family." Family? I almost choked on my own tongue. Yet, he put his arm around me like he was a doting boyfriend, like we'd done this a million times. Then he squeezed my shoulder. "Didn't I tell you this was the perfect place to settle, Honeybee? That's what you all call her, right?"

Lucille had pulled a handkerchief from her wool pocket and dabbed the corner of one eye. "Yep. We love her middle name. Her mother was such a treasure, as I'm sure Olive Bee has told you, that's how we all referred to her growing up because her mom loved it so much." I gulped down the ball in my throat at the memory of my mom yelling for me to come home from down the street. "Oh gosh. You two are just perfect together. I'm excited to hear how you met. This is so wonderful."

Dimitri just continued on, "Yes, Honeybee has told me so much about her."

What a fucking nickname. I tried to stomp on his foot under the table, but he moved quickly.

"Sure. My Darling D is such a good listener ... when he's home." I fluttered my eyelashes at him as he wrinkled his nose at my nickname. "But he travels a lot. I'm sure he's been neglectful with keeping this place up to the standards of Paradise Grove."

"Actually, I try my best to help Dimitri out with that." Melly added in.

Lucille tsked as if disgusted and rolled her eyes. "Good thing Dimitri has it covered now, Melly. You can stop waltzing over there to water his plants even though you know I do that in the morning."

"I don't know why any of you women are over there watering his plants when he's trying to ruin the very community we've built," Walter said with venom in his voice. "How's Earl feel about that, Lucille? Where is he, anyway?"

She cleared her throat and her eyes narrowed. "That's not your concern. My Earl will be here when it comes time to vote, or I'll vote for him."

The man huffed while Melly smiled sweetly at Dimitri. "Dimitri, if you still need help watering the plants, I'm happy to do it—"

"I appreciate the offer"—Dimitri nodded at her and then winked at me as if it was a joke how much these women were doting on him—"but Olive and I will have all of that under control now, won't we?"

"I guess," I mumbled. I wasn't going to do any gardening at all, and I'd be gone next week, but I just had to get through this meeting.

"And she and I will be providing you all with enough information in the mailing along with at the next meeting to make sure you're all comfortable with the condos and offices, I promise."

"I'm really looking forward to it." Lucille sounded genuinely happy for us.

I wasn't. I wasn't at all.

CHAPTER 9: OLIVE

"A freaking family, Dimitri?" I screeched once we were alone in the car with Mr. Preston driving us back. I was almost hyperventilating—and it was just a pretend idea.

He looked me up and down, then squeezed my shoulder. "Breathe, Honeybee. You look terrified of even pretending to want a family."

"I am," I blurted out. I shut my eyes as if I could hide from him, because he didn't need to know my fears.

He chuckled at me, though, so relaxed while I was wound tight. "What's so bad about a family with me, huh? I'd be a good-ass father. And—"

"Families inevitably fell apart. So please stop talking about it," I blurted out. My heart twisted at the idea of having children and losing them like I'd lost my mother or being like my father that neglected them. I didn't go into details with him about it though.

Still, the smile dropped from Dimitri's face and a frown replaced it. He waited a moment before he asked softly, "Olive, do you really think that?"

"Mine did." I winced as the words tumbled out.

He stared at me for so long, like he was studying everything about me before he said, "I hope you know that's not always true."

"Maybe not for yours." He waited for me to continue on with my thoughts.

Dimitri was someone I was finding I'd confide in without even thinking about. I didn't know if it was because he'd been around here and there for years or if it was because he'd already seen me break down with Rufford. It's like he'd seen me at my worst and now I wasn't scared to show him any part of me. "I just ... when my mom passed, things sort of crumbled."

He took my hand in his, like he wanted to provide comfort if just for a moment. "I'm sorry."

"And I hate saying that because I had great memories before, you know?"

He nodded. "Even when there's the bad memories, there can be the good ones too. Both can be true."

"Yeah." I sighed and squeezed his hand before letting it go, trying to distance myself a bit. "It's just most of the time, now, with my father, it's bad."

"I hope you know, even if your family now isn't good to you, you can find someone who will be. You can find a family, Olive. You know that right? Hell, now I'm inclined to show you that and make you believe it."

What could I say to a man that had beliefs like that? I sighed and patted his shoulder, trying to dispel the tension in the car. "Maybe. But I doubt you'll change my mind. So, you better start coming up with a plan to tell them the freaking truth. They aren't going to trust you if you're flat out lying to them once I'm gone after this week."

"Or maybe we try and see how this plays out? Act like we're thinking of having a little one together." He wiggled his eyebrows at me, like he was trying to lighten the mood too.

"You're ridiculous."

"Oh, come on. I think about having kids now all the time, if I'm being serious. My brothers and sisters are bringing the next generation to life. My nieces and nephews are a damn riot. It'd be fun as hell to have some. Fun as hell to act like it too. So, say you'll do it with me?"

I swear the man enjoyed taking chances and dancing on the edge. "You know, some girls would kill for the chance to have you saying this to them? Like you could make me obsessed with you by just offering up this idea."

"You're not some girls, though. I'm realizing that very quickly. Play house with me, Honeybee."

He gave me his green puppy dog eyes and I had to quickly swing open the door of the SUV as Mr. Preston pulled up to the massive home to get away from him and his outlandish ideas.

Instead, I focused on the home I'd be staying in. It looked straight out of a *Coastal Living* magazine with its beautiful wraparound porch and white siding. Yet, I could see it wasn't at all quaint with the high roof and massive pillars supporting the overhang. I waited for him to open the door with his HEAT watch, a mere scan of a small pad instead of using a key.

"I'll get you one of these soon so you can get in and out whenever," he murmured as he held his hand out of me to walk in first.

Immediately, when I stepped in, I could smell the fresh paint, but it didn't take away from the old charm the place had with the architecture of the doorways having arches, the exposed wood beams on the cathedral ceilings, and the dark flooring that matched those beams.

Dimitri slipped his shoes off as he watched me take in the space. There wasn't much furniture, just a large white couch and a table and chairs in the dining room. The open concept was beautiful though with the granite countertop overlooking the living room and connecting to the dining room.

"The place is beautiful, Dimitri." I turned to him. "But I won't need a watch. As I said, I won't be here long."

"Why exactly can't you stay a bit longer?" He narrowed his eyes on me as I ran a hand over the white couch and felt the plush fabric that I could tell was expensive immediately. "It seems Lucille loves you, and an opportunity to write in her paper—"

"She *seems* to love everyone, but she's also the most nosy person you'll ever meet."

"Still, if you have a foot in the door with her, that will be good for getting an ordinance passed for my condos and office space."

I shrugged. "Paradise Grove is her first priority. And then probably her husband, Earl."

"He wasn't at the meeting." Dimitri frowned.

"He's probably busy." I shrugged and looked over at the staircase. "I'm guessing there are guestrooms up there, if it's okay with you, I'll stay there for the week."

He ignored my questions and kept trying to convince me. "Come on, it's clear Lucille wants you here for longer than that. According to the board, the next meeting is in a month and a half."

"It's also clear I can't be here that long."

"Explain to me why you can't again." He stepped close as he waited for a response, and I sucked in a breath at his proximity.

"I have obligations back in—" I didn't even know where at this point, but surely there was somewhere I belonged.

Dimitri didn't give me time to dwell on it. "Kee isn't an obligation anymore. Only your thesis. Take a job with HEAT."

I threw up my hands. "That's hardly what this would be."

"I'll pay you double your old salary with Kee."

"I don't need a salary. So your bribe is shit." It was a snotty thing to say, so I normally kept it to myself, but my bank account had always held more than enough in it. My mother made sure of it before she passed, and Kee also paid me well.

"It still provides you with purpose. You need something other than 'assistant to a celebrity' on your résumé if you want a job apart from that. Unless you plan to follow her around for the rest of your life?"

"So what? I'm going to add 'fake long-term girlfriend' to it instead?" I held up a hand so I could finish. "Also, I was never following her around. I resent that. And you know what? I'm not going to entertain this conversation any longer. You can do whatever the hell you want the next few days. I'll talk to my parents and Lucille for you, but then I'm gone."

He stood there in his perfect suit with a look of determination not resignation. "You so afraid to spend a little time with me?"

"Afraid of *what* when it comes to spending time with you?"

"You know what." He looked me up and down, and suddenly my body heated like a match thrown on hay.

I blamed it on the fact that without Dimitri, I was practically experiencing the definition of a dry spell now that there was no Rufford. *And* after sleeping with Dimitri twice, I'd been having dream after dream about him. "You've lost it, I swear."

I stormed past him, but he grabbed my elbow. "Have I though? Because I don't recall you blushing like this when you're simply frustrated. I must have missed it all these years."

"I'm not blushing. And I'm also not frustrated. So, you're missing a lot." I stepped back and away from him quickly. His touch was electrifying; it sparked a yearning in me I didn't know existed before. "I'm done with this conversation. I need to go"—I hesitated, trying to think of an excuse to get away from him—"visit my family. I'll be home later."

"Want a ride?"

I stumbled toward the door like it was a damn fire escape. "No. I'll walk." The fresh air would be nice, anyway, after feeling the heat of our tension.

When I got to my parents' house, I didn't even attempt to walk in. Instead, I sat down on the porch and dialed the number I knew by heart.

"Olive, it's three o'clock. I'm still at work. Can I call you back?" My stepmother answered without even a hello.

"I know, Georgette. I'm in Paradise Grove though. I thought I'd maybe stop by ..."

"Oh. You're here?" she screeched into the phone. I heard rustling and then, "Well, I wish you would have given us more notice. Your father is on a work trip, and your brother has been having a lot of anxiety lately. I have a million calls to still make today and—"

"I don't have to stop by."

"The front door camera alerted me that you're on our porch." The annoyance in her voice was palpable. "I'm in the home office. I'll be busy for another fifteen minutes, but you know where the spare key is. Why don't you see if your brother is up for a visitor?"

She hung up before I could respond, and even though I knew it was a silly situation to have affect me in any way, my gut still twisted.

I took my time lifting the flowerpot to grab the spare key

underneath it and then unlocked the door to walk in.

The entryway with its large staircase and extravagant Greek god statue was a statement to those entering that we kept up appearances, or maybe that we cared a bit too much about appearances. It wrapped around the chandelier hanging from the cathedral ceiling, and I took the oak stairs two at a time to go knock on my brother's door.

I heard his grumble first and then, "Come in."

Maybe I expected at least a smile. Or a hug. What I got was a painful reality shot at me like a bullet ready to kill.

"You're here?" His voice was just above a whisper and dragged out so slow and so garbled I almost didn't recognize it.

Knox was full of life and potential. Almost too much I used to think, because my parents loved to show him around. He was big and tall and got good grades, did all the sports, did all the things my parents told him to.

He fit in in Paradise Grove. He'd been the shining star, and I was the one they tried to hide away.

Yet, now, he sat there thin, so thin I was concerned he'd gotten sick. "Hey, yeah, I'm back for a bit. Thought I would come by." It was all I could say as I took in his room, the blacked-out curtains and the mess. We were Monroes. We didn't have a mess in our house. I spun around and around, trying to find evidence of his illness, trying to find the reason behind his change.

"Well, thanks for coming by." He didn't even lift his head. He'd learned how to dismiss me after my mom passed. We'd both dismissed one another day after day until we weren't much of siblings at all anymore.

Now, though, the dismissal atmosphere felt catastrophic. My brother didn't seem as strong as he used to, and without that strength, I saw the weakness there and didn't want him to give in to it.

"What's going on, Knox?" I asked the question quietly, hoping I could prompt some sort of real response.

"Olive, you've been gone for years." He shook his head slow, smiled lazily, but his eyes weren't steady. "You know what? Forget it. I'm just tired."

I stepped closer, trying to get a read on him. "Do you need me to get Georgette?"

He rolled his eyes but his whole head moved with him, and he fell back into his bed. There was no attempt to get up. Instead, he reached for his nightstand, patting his hand around without looking. "I'll be fine. Give me a few."

He pulled the drawer open, and that's when I saw them.

Pills. So many pills I gasped before striding forward and grabbing one.

It was prescribed to him.

Then another.

And another.

Every single one had his name on it. "What do you need all this for? Do you— Are you sick, Knox?"

"I just have anxiety, Olive Bee. Don't worry about me."

And I witnessed how easily he popped a lid and threw back two.

I was his older sister. I probably should have stopped him. Or said something rather than standing there with my mouth hanging open. But all I could do was stare.

We'd been distant for so long, and now I wasn't sure how to come back from that. I scanned his room and saw the trophies from football, the medals from track, a couple of gaming systems, and a dresser with a few pictures on it. One was of me and another of him and my parents. We were all smiling, and I remember that day, we'd gone down the street to Fitches for custard.

"You remember this?" I pointed to the picture, and it took him a second to register but he nodded once before glancing away. "That was a good day."

"Not many of those here," he grumbled before sighing and sitting up again to swing his legs off the bed. "Why are you back?"

How could I even explain that to him now? "I sort of have a job here for a few days and—"

"Oh, work. Of course." His tone was hard, his shoulders stiff. And then he turned a glare so cold on me, I wasn't sure I was looking at my brother. "Go work then, Olive. No need to check in on me."

"Knox." His name came out a plea with all the emotions I couldn't express behind it. "Maybe we should talk or—"

"Nothing to talk about. You left. I got Georgette and Dad, right?"

"I thought that's what you wanted." But the hammer of guilt at being the oldest sibling and leaving behind my brother to endure them alone slammed down pretty hard at that moment. Knox had been a kid when I'd left for college six years ago, but every time I came back, his disdain for me grew.

My father had made clear how I didn't belong next to them at a dinner party one night two years ago. I remembered how I stood there as Georgette called me a failure and how their friends, people I'd grown up with, stood by and agreed.

Paradise Grove either accepted you or it didn't. Somehow, without my mother, I'd been pushed out. And that night, Knox hadn't said a thing. He watched me run upstairs to my room and pack my things. He told me it was for the best anyway. So, two years ago, I stopped coming. Two years ago, I decided to only call.

"You told me it was for the best, Knox."

"Well, hell, anything is better than here, right?"

Maybe two years had been too long. "Look, can we talk about Dad and—"

"Oh, good." My stepmother walked in, her wavy hair pinned up and her suit jacket still perfectly in place. "You found your brother. Knox, do you want any lunch?"

"I ate," he grumbled and then turned his back to us. She gave me a look as if she was annoyed and waved me out.

I touched his bed before I left, hoping he would be able to feel me trying to connect. "I'll be back, Knox. Maybe we can go to Fitches?"

He didn't respond, but he didn't have to. Something was very wrong with my brother, and I needed to find out what.

I walked silently down the steps and followed Georgette's heels clicking on the dark wood floors into the living room. "Would you like a drink, Olive? I have tea or—"

"What the hell is going on with Knox?"

CHAPTER 10: OLIVE

The silence in the room was so loud I might have asked for headphones had I not wanted to witness my stepmother's obvious discomfort.

She floundered for a whole second before she straightened and smoothed her black work pants. "Oh, so no niceties, I guess? You want to just jump right into your theatrics? Because I don't. I'm not in the mood today. I'm not going to tolerate you being emotional for no reason while you're visiting me."

"I'm not visiting *you*. You were too busy, remember? I'm visiting Knox. And obviously there's something wrong."

"Honestly," she huffed and turned toward the fridge like my questions were all too much for her. "Why is your first reaction to think something's even wrong?"

"Is that a joke? Have you looked at him? Two years ago, he was twice the size he is now and—"

"So he lost some weight." She shrugged. "I wish I could lose a few pounds." Her canned laugh skittered around the kitchen, and I stood there in shock as I took in the clean counters, the expensive art on the walls, and the fancy table settings even though no one would be coming to dinner.

"This isn't a joke about weight, Georgette. I'm asking you about my brother. What's wrong?" I whispered, trying my best not to scream at her.

She rolled her eyes again and turned to the cabinet I knew was full of liquor. "I guess you're going to make me deal with this instead of your father. In that case, I'll opt for liquor."

She took a swig of pure vodka before she got a glass out to pour more than two fingers. My stepmother didn't drink hard liquor except at home where she could hide how she downed it. She poured me a glass, too, and slid it my way.

I crossed my arms, not willing to drink with her. "Tell me what's going on."

She scoffed like I was being ridiculous. "How about nothing? Don't make a mountain out of a mole hill. Jesus, why are you always so dramatic?"

"This is concern, not dramatics," I clarified without raising my voice, though it shook with rage.

"You were *always* too concerned." She waved me off. "Was it those theatre classes and programs we allowed you to stay in after your mother passed? And then you would write those books with so much drama in them, I wondered what was wrong with you."

"No need to wonder anymore. I've been gone, living on my own for years."

"Exactly. You've been gone, and we've been living here as a family without you while you flounce around with that Keelani girl doing God knows what and wearing those stupid flowers in your hair." She waved at the small plumeria I had behind my ear.

I'd confided in her once that it felt like a connection to my mother, that I enjoyed having a bright color in my life even on a gloomy day. I offered her one once, but she'd wrinkled her nose and told me they would look immature on her as a lawyer. And since that day, she'd reminded me of her disdain for them.

Still, I took the high road because it wasn't about us today. "Kee has provided me with a lot of opportunities, Georgette. It was a college job that allowed me to travel. I wanted to see the world. You know that. So if we could focus on Knox—"

"What real opportunities? You come back here after two years to tell us what? Did you even get that ridiculous degree you were so obsessed with because one professor thought you showed promise?"

Her words were pointed and cruel. They hit fast and precise too. I remembered how she'd laughed at me that night when I'd told them all I was changing my major. It was the night I knew I wouldn't be back to visit. "I'm working on it." My confidence shrank as I answered her.

"Great. You're working on becoming a journalist. God. Don't you realize you have a status to uphold as a Monroe? Your father is a major player in Hollywood. That makes you part of it too," she grumbled into her tumbler before rounding the island to go sit on the barstool. "We raised you to be so much more than this. Then, you come to a party and announce you're changing majors."

"I was doing what I wanted for once. What my mother had always told me to do."

"Your mother," she scoffed. "As if I didn't have a hand in raising you up to what you should become."

"Raising me? My *mother* raised me, Georgette." I wouldn't take away that credit ever.

Georgette's eyes narrowed, and they burned with that evil fire I knew she had in her. "Your father should have smacked you harder across your face the night you left. You were always ungrateful, and here you are, bringing her up in my house. Being ungrateful again."

And that's where the problem has always lied with us. I wouldn't erase the memory of my mother. Ever. "This is *her* mother's house, actually." I raised my chin, ready to go to war with her, but then I held up my hands. "You know what? It doesn't matter right now. Nothing matters but my brother. I'm not here to get into it with you."

She flexed her thin fingers on the tumbler before she downed all that was in her glass. Then, she reached for mine. "Fine. Then, leave. Call your father about Knox. He's the one running around with him half the time. I only took Knox to the doctor for his anxiety because your father was busy."

"Dad was busy?" I deadpanned. Of course he was. Busy like he was when Mom got sick too.

"He's taken much more of an interest in Knox as of late. They have actually been working on business outside of Paradise Grove."

"What type of business?" My father had always been very involved in the film industry, but he made time for nothing else.

"Well, that's not your concern. They're providing for this household." She said it so fast and in a high-pitched voice. I narrowed my eyes to try and find the lie. Something wasn't right as I watched her smoothing her hair like she was irritated that I'd even ask. "Plus, it's good for your brother to make connections in high places. Networking helps with success."

"But with who? And if it's the wrong sort of people, and he's acting like this—"

"You think your father wouldn't have your brother's best interests at heart? Also the doctors prescribed this dosage." She justified it again, as if his temperament was fine as long as doctors were involved. "We have worked on it, and we have balanced everything."

"That's not balanced." I pointed upstairs, fury in my voice as I said it.

"How would you know?" She rolled her eyes and poured herself more vodka. "You haven't been around."

"I've ... been working." It wasn't a good enough excuse. I knew that. I took a deep breath as I settled on what I knew had to be done. "But he needs someone." He needed support. He needed a family. He needed our mom.

But she wasn't there. And I couldn't bring her back. All I could offer was myself.

"Well, he's got his friends and us." Georgette checked her watch, making it obvious she wanted me gone. "Anyway, if you're waiting to see your father, you won't."

"Knox's also got me. I'll be here." I was going to make sure I'd be here whether he wanted me to be or not. I chewed my cheek as I stared at the stairs.

Georgette didn't seem to care about the proclamations I was making. "Whatever. I need to get back to work. So you need to leave. And don't go bother Knox with a goodbye. He's quiet, which means he's asleep. Next time, call before you come over too. Unannounced visits aren't best for our family." She waved me toward the front door, making it clear she didn't feel I belonged in that family of hers.

I didn't. And my brother didn't either.

I wiped away the tears forming in my eyes and told myself I needed a new plan. Suddenly I'd discovered the roots I'd had in Paradise Grove were all tangled up and buried deeper than I realized as I thought of my brother being a shell of a human here in this place. I wouldn't leave him here.

Not again.

I tried not to talk to a single person on the way back to Dimitri's. I stalked down the sidewalk, passing a couple of homes with my head down, but I was just one house away when

I heard, "Olive Bee? That really you? You're back?"

I winced before looking up and seeing Jameson standing on the porch of the house next to Dimitri's.

"I go just by Olive now, Jameson."

He chuckled that familiar laugh that used to give me butterflies. "Aw, well." He shook his head like he wasn't going to listen. He was a few years older than me, but we'd always found a way to hang out when we were young, and then we sniffed around one another as we got older. He'd come back from college for my mother's funeral and walked with me for hours that day, telling me leaving home would be the best thing I could do if that's what my mom had wanted for me.

"You finally home to stay?" He lifted a dark eyebrow that matched his almost jet-black hair.

"For a while." I crossed my arms and rocked back on my heels before I saw a little girl come running full speed out of the house. She didn't even hesitate when she got to the porch stairs, and I gasped just as Jameson caught her in his arms without even turning his head.

The smile that spread across Jameson's face showed me that he was attached to her. "She's practicing being a flying squirrel."

"Oh." I didn't really know what to say. Jameson with a kid was surprising enough, and him being responsible was even more so. "You have a daughter."

He smiled big. "I do have a daughter, Olive Bee." He looked down at the girl with his same jet-black hair and said, "This here is Olive, Franny. We call her Olive Bee sometimes because her middle name is Bee after bumblebees."

"She's no bee, Daddy." She glanced at me. "I'm Franny. I'm four."

"That's very nice." I nodded, wanting to back away. I wasn't good with children, wasn't even good with my younger brother.

"Olive Bee, you okay?"

"I'm ..." The question brought tears to my eyes, but I couldn't fall apart on the street. "I'm fine. Just catching up with everything that's been happening here."

"A lot has changed." He said it with a heaviness as he stared over at my family's house.

"Yeah. None of it feels right." I crossed my arms over my chest.

"Just watch where you're digging. You know how Paradise Grove is." He said it lightly, but there was a hint of truth in his tone that I caught.

My gut feeling of something being wrong grew, but I held the idea close to my chest. "A lot has changed. Too much." I sighed. "But I'm back. So, maybe we'll see how I end up fitting in here now, huh?"

"You won't fit in with that Hardy here with you. He's got no idea what it takes to build up a community like ours." He chuckled. "How did you get tangled up with him?"

"Same circles, I guess." I shrugged. We'd have to get our story straight if I was staying.

"No one likes that condo building, the idea of that office structure, or the strip mall he's trying to get passed."

I smiled softly, trying to appear positive, like a nice girlfriend would. "It'll all work out. I wouldn't let him put anything here that would be bad for us."

"Why not?" He smirked at me. "We used to hate this place."

"Yeah, well, we're both back, right?"

"I never really left," he admitted and looked at his daughter like he was contemplating if this was the right place to raise her.

"You got any plans to leave that Hardy in the dust so I can really stall his building plans?"

I sighed and shrugged. "You all love to give a newcomer a hard time."

"Truthfully, I'm going give anyone who's dating you a hard time. I thought you'd come back for me one day."

I hummed. "Maybe you'll give him a chance for me then?"

"We'll see." He winked, and I waved at him as I walked toward what I'd decided was going to be my new home for the summer.

I contemplated my stepmother's words as I made my way up our driveway, and when I swung open the door, Dimitri was sitting in the living room, working like he wasn't at all concerned that I'd left for an hour. "Getting your luggage packed now?"

"I'm staying," I announced to him. "All summer. What do you need me to do?"

CHAPTER 11: DIMITRI

Olive Monroe stood there in her gray sweater with a new look in her eyes, determined and full of fire. And tears. It was the second time I'd seen her vulnerable and broken. And the urge to help her pick up the pieces and comfort her was there again.

That was an obvious issue. I wanted to fix all her problems when we weren't even dating. Instead, I'd bribed her into coming here and had goaded her into faking a relationship with me all summer just so I could be around her to see all her emotions unfold.

"What just happened?" I slowly closed the laptop I was working on and set it aside.

She combed her hands through her curls, and when they flew over the little Hawaiian flower she always wore, she threw it off and let it land on the ground. "I can still stay, right?"

I'd really believed that people who wore their hearts on their sleeves never appealed to me. I prided myself on avoiding them actually. I thought it was best to spend less time on relationships and more time on business. Yet, with Olive, I studied every emotion on her face. They were like fireflies that I wanted to lock in a mason jar and watch light up the night.

She was open with me about her family in that car and suddenly, I knew I was considering doing everything I could to be a part of her life that made good memories with her.

"Yes, of course," I responded and then waited for her to explain her abrupt change in plans.

"You won't be here much, right?" She looked up toward the ceiling, then brushed away some of the moisture on her face.

"Why?" I said slowly. If she was here, I might just opt to stay. I wanted to see

"Does it matter why? Don't you only care about getting what you want? It's a good investment." She tapped her foot on the ground like she was impatient for an answer even though she wasn't giving me any information.

I liked to take a risk here and there. Shit, I'd spent millions on investments that tanked because, even with all the facts, jumping into an uncertain situation sometimes paid off. It's why I also went skydiving or swam in shark-infested waters or pushed myself always. We couldn't grow without it.

Here, though, I hesitated. Olive was more dangerous than shark-infested waters. She was a woman I was quickly getting attached to. I obsessed about my investments, not women. Yet, I found myself constantly wondering about her. I'd scheduled her itinerary for Paradise Grove and watched her damn flight, tracking it to make sure she arrived on time. Then I'd jumped on an opportunity to act like we were planning a family in front of all the important players in Paradise Grove—and not because it'd be good for my investment.

Watching her respond to that brought me joy I hadn't felt in a long time. And the idea of a family with her grew in my head like it might be a damn fun adventure.

This line of thinking wasn't good for me. Not at all. Not if she wasn't going to reciprocate the feelings. I needed to pull back and maybe even abort that plan now. "Well, I don't only care about the investment. And, yes, I do care about getting what I want." What I wanted was yet to be determined. "I just recently was trying to come to terms with you not being here."

"How do you expect to win over the community?" She put her hands on her hips. "Walter and Reggie hate you. Jameson—who, might I add, has a lot of pull around here—thinks you have no idea what you're doing. And I'm pretty sure everyone wants you out. I'm your only hope."

She was bold in her anger. "You're a shot in the dark."

"Without me, you don't even have a gun to shoot." She lifted her chin, still fighting me with tears in her eyes.

"I want to know what happened to make you want to stay." I wanted to know every single thing about her, but this was a start.

"I just need to do some stuff. I won't be in your way. You'll barely notice I'm here." She smoothed a nonexistent wrinkle on her legging, and I recalled how I'd torn a large hole in another pair the last time I'd seen her.

"That's impossible, Olive."

She frowned, her full lips pouting out. "Why would it be impossible?"

"Because if you're here, my attention is on you and your sweaters and your haggard-looking leggings and the bright flowers in your hair—"

"They aren't haggard!"

"If you're here, I'm thinking about fucking you. Twenty-four seven. I notice you in every room. And I notice when you're not in the room." I told her the truth, laid it out for her to understand.

"Dimitri." She breathed out my name before she started nibbling on her bottom lip. "You probably shouldn't say stuff like that to me when I'm here."

"I will." I wasn't going to lie about it.

"Well, you won't even be here much." She turned to look

out the window of the living room. "I just need to stay."

The quiver in her voice had me getting up and moving over to stand beside her. "Tell me what happened."

She shook her head, pursing her lips. "I'll stay upstairs, out of your way. You stay out of mine, okay? Completely out of the way," she said louder, like that was going to help me stop asking the question.

"Well, I can be here all day every damn day, in your way, if you don't explain to me why you look like you're about to burst into tears."

"There's no looking like it, Dimitri. I *am* about to burst into tears!" she blurted out.

Then there was one sob. And another. And then I pulled her into my arms. She basically wore her heart on her sleeve, and I was finding I wanted to bubble wrap it up, not because I was uncomfortable when women cried but because her cry made my own heart hurt.

It all should have felt too intimate, but instead it felt right. Especially when she curled into me and her tears hit my chest. I let her cry, and my arm wrapped more tightly around her while my other hand threaded through the curls in her hair. She didn't hold back for probably a whole minute, and I didn't ask for any more explanation. Support didn't look like prying, and I knew she needed unconditional compassion more than ever now.

Finally, she stepped back and looked at my shirt. "Sorry." She glanced around and stepped away, hurrying over to the kitchen where there was a white towel hanging from the oven handle. She pulled it from the bar and brought it over to blot out the tears on my shirt. "I can wash this for you, if you want. I don't think it's ruined. I don't have makeup on or anything."

"No makeup?" I murmured and stepped back to really study her. Olive's skin was flawless without it; a tint of rose touched her tan skin as she rubbed at her nose.

"Don't look so closely, Dimitri," she said softly, waving the towel in front of her face but I was taking in how her long dark lashes were a deeper hue from being wet, how her curls were a bit of a mess now that I'd run my hands through them while she cried.

"Why wouldn't I look at you closely without your makeup on? It's when I get to see the real you, without hiding a single thing. I want to see the perfection you hide from everyone."

"Kee's right. You can be too charming sometimes." She sighed before jumping to the other topic on her mind. "So, want to show me the upstairs?"

"Right. About that ..." I smirked because I knew she wasn't going to like the revelation once she was up there. "I don't have much furnished or anything."

"Oh, well." She narrowed her eyes and took a big breath, like she was resigning herself to something. "I can make do."

I hummed. "I haven't decorated. We'll need to get more furniture, and I'd like your ideas on renovation and decorating so that when I sell the house, it'll look good for potential buyers. What do you think about the arches—"

"Most of the homes here are historic, Dimitri. You might want to get over the idea that you can renovate any of it. And as for redecorating, I'm sure you can get someone to come in and do it for you. Keep it to yourself, though, because no one will love the idea of you leaving quick and moving." She brushed a hand over the wooden staircase railing and pointed to the crown molding along the trim of the living room. "*If* it were a possibility, the architectural structure of this place with its open concept is ideal for selling anyway. This is a highly sought-after location."

I smiled at how quickly she could file through her knowledge and provide me with information. "You'll be perfect at helping redecorate, it seems. You already know a little."

"I don't. I did a bit of research a few years ago for a paper, but real estate is fickle. Design trends come and go quickly."

"You know about real estate too?"

"I don't know a lot about anything, Dimitri. Just a little of everything. Mingling in my dad's and stepmom's circles in this town, and at Kee's events, made it necessary." She sighed like maybe she wasn't so excited about how she'd lived her life so far. "I pivoted a lot in life for people I cared about, probably too much. We strive to make our families and friends and partners happy even when we should be focusing on making ourselves happy first." I wasn't sure she was talking to me anymore. She was staring through me, the house, and the world at that moment. Her eyes looked haunted, but then she blinked away the darkness. "Anyway, my past doesn't really matter."

"It does," I corrected her. "It makes you who you are. Plus, I need to know about you, and you need to know about me if we're going to pull off being a couple."

"I think we probably need to pull back on that idea." She wrinkled her nose.

"We can figure it out over dinner. And you can tell me what happened at your family's house."

She sighed and combed some of her curls back into place. "It's just family stuff."

"'Just family stuff' is probably the most important stuff. So, I'm here when you're ready to share." I leaned over to the island counter to grab my phone. "What do you want for dinner?

We can go over how we met while we eat. Tell me what's good around here."

"Haven't you been staying here on and off?"

"Not really." I flew in and out for meetings.

"All the more reason Paradise Grove won't trust you," she grumbled as she grabbed her phone too. "I'll put in an order for some pizza. What do you normally like for toppings? There's great Italian down the street."

"Pepperoni is fine. And do you think it's necessary I'm here that much?"

She scoffed as she typed in her phone and mumbled to herself while she presumably ordered before she looked up at me like I was dumb. For some damn reason, I wanted to prove her wrong. "I'll be here, I guess. So, I'll schmooze Paradise Grove for you. You of all people know it takes that to win a deal."

"You're right," I said softly, thinking I was trying to win her in the deal, not the damn town.

"They won't trust you if you don't attend certain things over the next few months and aren't around. I can fill in most of the time, but you will have to at least come back when needed."

"What does 'when needed' mean to you?"

"Do you have that full of a schedule?" She read my question the wrong way. My ass was sitting there thinking I might just be able to weasel my way into being here all the damn time. She turned to make her way into the kitchen like suddenly she owned the place. "I mean, you were around quite a lot for Kee and seemed to be able to get most things done on your computer."

"Kee's my best friend. And we were dealing with the opening of a resort. Plus, she was engaged to my brother. So, I was with family and doing business."

"Okay, in that case, you can put on your calendar the annual Paradise Grove Carnival at the end of summer."

"The board meeting is in a month and a half. I won't need to go to anything after that."

She hummed like she disagreed. "That's if they pass what you want them to."

"They will because I have you."

Her amber eyes hardened as she glared at me. "You have to be around too."

"I will." I smiled, liking that the woman was putting her foot down about me being around when I intended to be anyway. "There's a grill out at some point, right?"

"We used to have weekly cookouts on Fridays in the park, but I'll have to check on that."

"Every single Friday?"

"Yep. It was a lot. But, I'll be honest. People expect you to show up. Mom and Dad started to miss them as I got older and she got sicker, and one time they almost weren't let into a board meeting because of it. Granted, they claimed the board meeting was to discuss the weekly cookouts, but that's a lie." She scoffed. "Lucille had a few choice words for board members at that point. She was always very good friends with my mom's parents before they died in a car accident."

"I'm sorr—"

"Don't be." She waved it off. "I was young. But Lucille has always had a soft spot for my mother and maybe me and my brother, Knox, too."

"I see that. Your brother still live down the street?"

She took a shaky breath and nodded. "I'm staying for him. And to figure out what's going on. I just think ... something's not right. And the dynamics of this community truly sway so much that happens." She chewed on her lip.

"What are you thinking?"

"If you need information about the community and I don't have a thing to research, maybe the sociology of a small community would be a good start? I could ask around and make nice with everyone."

This is how I knew Olive was resourceful. "That's perfect. Any information we can gather as to why they wouldn't want condos and offices will help. And if you go to most of the upcoming events, along with helping Lucille with that mailer, I'm sure we can gain a meaningful outlook on everything—"

"You should go to this one coming up, though." She glanced at me as she dug through the white cabinetry and found a glass that she then filled with water. "If you're not busy."

"If I'm not here, I'll fly back in." I needed to keep priorities in place somewhat, I reminded myself. But as I turned away from her, I spotted the flower she'd pushed out of her hair on the floor. I picked it up, unable to leave it there for some reason.

She always wore them. I didn't know if they meant anything but I held the flower in my hand as we walked through the dining room. "Let me show you the place."

CHAPTER 12: OLIVE

I followed him with my glass of water in hand. We went through the kitchen to the back porch where he showed me an elevated hot tub surrounded by pavers and stones. It all was atop a hill with a view of his acreage that couldn't be beat. We passed a study and two rooms on the first floor before arriving at the primary suite. "I've been staying here," he said, gesturing.

"Makes sense." I shrugged and then padded across the room to peek into the bathroom.

I gasped at what I saw then. "Wow. This is heaven in a bathroom, Dimitri. Did you help design this?"

"Probably a bit too much. But I enjoy the luxury of it."

"I love it. Look at this bathtub." I giggled and skipped over to swing first one leg and then another into it. "This is what dreams are made of. I love a good bath"

A claw-foot tub sat in the middle of the tiled wet room where a rain spray ceiling mount was installed above it. "The layout was bigger than initially intended, and the marble mosaic tile along the walls is much too expensive to profit from on a flip, but I wanted it for when I was here. If you like it, you can stay in this room."

I bit my lip at his offering, and somehow, us in that bathroom seemed much more intimate than it should have. Then, I cleared my throat and got out fast. "No. I ... that's not a good idea. Like I said, the upstairs works just fine for me."

"Let me show you," he said, casually, but as he passed me,

he slowed to put the flower back in my hair.

"What are you doing?" I whispered.

"Putting things where they belong," he murmured back to me before dragging his finger across my cheek and down to my chin where he lifted it. "Better, Honeybee. Much better."

Dimitri Hardy was more observant than I gave him credit for. It was like he knew that damn flower was symbolic in some way. He didn't say more about it, but he positioned it in just the right place on my left ear, like he'd known where it went all these years.

I stepped back because I didn't want to indulge in the desire that was starting to brew much too quickly for a man I was going to be living with. Not that we'd be together a whole lot. He's bound to be gone most of the time, I told myself. I'd have friends around. I'd meet new people. His building of the office near Paradise Grove was going to bring in herds of newcomers, much to the dislike of Paradise Groveians. As we made our way up the oak stairs, I noticed that the hallway on this floor wasn't decorated at all.

It smelled of fresh paint, but it was all white. Two rooms and a bathroom with no furniture.

"So, you really haven't been living here at all," I observed.

"Nope."

"So, who did your bathroom?"

"Just an interior designer, but—"

"Well they should help with decorating the rest then, right?" I told him. "I can't decorate. Honestly." Nor did I want to. The idea of making a house a home had me itching to leave it.

"They'll need direction."

"Direct them then." I wasn't going to.

"You're here. We're gonna play house aren't we? Why can't you?" The man smirked, and I knew he was trying to irk me. He truly must have enjoyed getting a rise out of me.

"The goal of me being here, for you, is to make people think you're a part of this town so you can get them to approve your ridiculous plans. Not decorate this home." Then, I looked in the next room and saw no bed either. "Is there only one freaking bed in this place? How do you have no furniture?"

"Well, as previously stated, I'm not here often." He shrugged.

I turned slowly to face him. "Where am I supposed to sleep?"

He smiled big now, like he wanted to make a joke. "In my bed, next to me."

"Absolutely not."

"Why? You afraid I'll make you feel good again?"

"Nope." Instantly, my body tightened. I'd probably indulge with him again if he weren't friends with Kee. Or if I knew I didn't need to stay with him and had a separate place to retreat. Things would get messy too fast living under the same roof. He was a bad idea. Yet my heart and body didn't want to listen to my head. "We can't sleep next to each other. We need boundaries. I'm here to help you and ... there are issues with my brother, so I need to be here. Without complications." I tried to be honest.

He leaned on the doorframe and stared at me in the white room. "Okay." His voice was resigned. "I'll sleep on the couch for a day or two. I'm going to head out of town anyway, won't be here long."

"Work?"

"Duty's always calling, Honeybee."

"Probably not the best nickname, considering ..." I wasn't

going to finish that sentence.

"I have the Bee to make it nice and sentimental, and I coined the honey after I tasted you. I'm not dropping that nickname for anything."

"Please stop," I whined. "There has to be some sense of restraint while we're both staying here. I'll stay upstairs once we have it furnished, and you can stay downstairs. It'll afford us some privacy."

"I don't really know why we need privacy."

"Because, Darling D, I like my personal space."

His eyes narrowed, "Why does that nickname feel like a slight?"

"Because it is one after you started calling me Honeybee in front of everyone."

"Is the D for my name or for—"

"I don't know, Dimitri. Do you think it's darling?" I asked him sweetly.

I knew he wanted to say more, but the doorbell rang.

"Pizza's here." I turned and went to the door. I swung it open and smiled when I saw Esme, a blonde sapphire-eyed teenager who was one of Knox's close friends. I gave her a hug as she welcomed me back and then saw that Jameson and Franny were standing beside her.

"Jameson and Franny came to deliver pizza too?"

"Esme drove with the pizza light on her car, and I wanted to say hi because she never delivers!" Franny announced.

"Guilty," Esme admitted, laughing. And then she flipped her long, straight hair like she'd done years ago when she was going to share some gossip. "Dad came home from the board meeting in a tizzy, saying you two weren't really living together or dating. Guess I'll have to report back that you are."

That was when Dimitri came to stand beside me, his big arm wrapping around me to pull me close. "Really dating. Really living together. And really enjoying it too." He took his time looking down at me and then rearranged the flower in my hair before he kissed my temple softly. The gesture was so intimate that I felt myself melting into his touch so much that I purposefully steeled my emotions and stiffened in his hold.

"Daddy, I thought Olive Bee was *your* girl who ran away?" Franny bounced in front of us, her hands clasped.

Jameson looked at me, his icy blue eyes serious all of a sudden. "The girl who *got* away, Franny. Not ran away."

I bit my lip at his admission. At one point, I would have wanted to hear that, but now I was standing there with Dimitri by my side, trying to ignore the pull between us.

"She's back now. Next door. So, why does he get her?" She pointed at Dimitri. "Don't you get her back?"

Jameson scooped her up and bounced Franny on his hip. "Maybe I'll be given the chance to steal Olive away for a lunch or two, huh Dimitri?"

"It's Mr. Hardy, Jameson." Dimitri corrected him and I felt his body tightened next to mine. The tension in the room suddenly shifted, crackling between the two men. When I looked up at Dimitri, his stare was cold and hard as he held Jameson's gaze. "And I'll be clear now so there's no misunderstanding, I don't let anyone steal my girl away from me for anything."

"Not even for a favorable vote from the board?" Jameson pushed him, raising an eyebrow.

"You could offer me this whole place on a platter and I wouldn't want it without my Honeybee."

The silence stretched after his response. He'd said it so definitely. Like I meant something to him all of a sudden.

And I think he would have kept up the act all night had Jameson not chuckled and stepped back toward the door. "We'll see, huh? Either way, me and my girl Olive need to catch up."

"She's no one's girl but mine now. It's best you remember that."

Jameson didn't say anything else as Franny yelled bye. Esme wide-eyed me, pulling me in for a hug and to whisper, "Awkward. They both want you."

After she left, Dimitri turned to me and said, "We're going to have to work on your public displays of affection."

"Why's that?" I leaned against the countertop, looking at the pizza box instead of him.

He stepped close suddenly, and I felt him everywhere. It was like I couldn't escape how my body responded to his, how his touch ignited a fire in me that I couldn't put out. "Because you're stiff even when I kiss your head in front of your friends, Olive. Or is that because Jameson isn't just a friend?"

He caged me against the counter, and I licked my lips while I looked up at what seemed to be burning jealousy in his bright-green eyes. "Dimitri, Jameson is just a friend." Why did I have to defend myself?

"Really? How long ago was that crush you had on him? Because I'm convinced his crush for you is still going strong."

"He likes any single girl within a two-mile radius," I chuckled and patted Dimitri's chest.

Jameson had always been a womanizer, but we'd gotten along fine through the years. He had his own issues to deal with, but having a family who put their burdens on their children gave us something in common and made him an ally. It's what we bonded over.

"You're *not* single. You're mine. Do I need to remind you

of that?" Dimitri growled. "Maybe I need to go to lunch with you two."

"Well, considering you're not going to be here much, you'll probably miss out. Right?" Why did I throw that out like I wanted him to be around?

"All the more reason for me to establish that boundary right away."

"What boundary?"

"That he can like every other woman in a two-mile radius, but he can't like my woman."

I laughed at that. "Get real. Even if Jameson and I quietly see each other, it'll be no skin off your back. He'd be discreet. Believe me, he's probably hooked up with half the women in this community and none of them know it."

"You'd hook up with him?"

I scoffed because this conversation didn't matter. "Dimitri, my sex life is close to nil right now. I left Rufford, slept with you only to learn what I've been missing out on, and now I have to spend a stressful who knows how long in my hometown while working on finding a career. If I want to destress with someone, I will."

"Or you can destress with me." His forehead fell to mine as he cut me off with that soft statement, and my stomach dipped at the thought. He continued on. "We're supposed to be together."

I couldn't contemplate this idea. It'd mess everything up. "Couples swing and cheat all the time."

He jerked back to stare into my eyes. "We're *not* being a couple that does that."

"We're *not* a real couple. Our relationship is a fake one," I reminded him. "Plus, like I said, if Jameson were interested, he would be discreet, I can guarantee it. Just like when you are traveling and want to be discreet, that would be great too."

I hated saying that. It felt like a knife to the gut thinking about him sleeping with someone else, but honestly, it made things much easier. We were establishing realistic expectations.

"You think I'm going to go fuck someone else, Honeybee? When I still think about the taste of your pussy?"

"Jesus, Dimitri." I shook my head at him.

"You're mine, Olive. As long as we're here. Don't forget."

Right. As long as we're here. And that meant he was concerned about his investment, not me. I reminded myself that as I squeezed his arm and slid under it to step aside before my body reacted to him being this close. "Well, Jameson is harmless to our efforts, and me having lunch with him will ultimately help your cause."

"I don't really give a—" He took a deep breath and pinched the bridge of his nose. "I don't think it's necessary."

"I think it doesn't matter one way or the other. He's a friend I need to catch up with. I should talk to him about my brother too." Jameson always knew what was happening in Paradise Grove. He'd know if my brother was talking to people he shouldn't be.

He hummed as if assessing something. "You want to talk with Jameson about your brother but not me? That's interesting."

"I just ..." I chewed on my cheek and stared at Dimitri. I was going to have to put some trust in him if I wanted this to work. "You're close with your siblings, Dimitri. In a way, I wish I was close with mine."

He nodded but waited for me to continue, and somehow his silent acceptance made me feel like I could share what I was ashamed of.

"You'll think less of me when you hear that I left Knox when

I went to college and stopped visiting after having a falling out with my father and stepmom. I was selfish in protecting my own sanity rather than—"

"Selfish? I've seen you taking care of Kee, not traveling the world, Olive." He frowned at me. "You put her first a lot."

"Right, well, of course. She's a good friend, but I could have been caring for my brother, too, and I should have weighed the priorities more."

He scoffed at that. "Olive, did you put yourself first much as a kid?"

"I mean my mom was sick ..." My mouth snapped shut and I frowned before I chose my words carefully. "I am happy for every day I got with her, but you don't put yourself first when someone is sick. I tried my best to care for her when my father wasn't around which was most of the time."

"Right. So, I think you're selling yourself short. You then came and took care of Kee right?"

"Hardly taking care of her. I did her hair and was a friend to her."

"Kee needed you always, Olive. You know that. She dealt with a lot being in the public eye and you were there for her."

"Maybe," I begrudgingly agreed.

"And now you're back, figuring out things with your brother. I'll say it again, don't sell yourself short."

Dimitri Hardy was making me feel better while we stood there in the living room, and I was completely falling for it. Him giving me grace now had me appreciating having him with me while I navigated being back home. It made me wonder if I'd been selling *him* short. "I appreciate you saying that even if you don't technically know everything I've been doing in the last few years."

He chuckled. "Well, we need to work on changing that, considering the circumstances." He stepped up to me, closing the distance between us so that our chests were touching, and I took a sharp breath. My resolve at denying myself his touch was waning now and any touch from him felt like lightning through my veins. It reminded me of the times I was with him. My body hadn't forgotten even though I desperately wanted it to.

"How do we go about that?" I shouldn't have asked.

"You share with me certain things, and I share with you certain things. We learn." I licked my lips and his eyes snapped to them immediately. "Don't you want to share so I know how to make it look like you're my girlfriend?"

"I ..." I squeezed my eyes shut, trying to figure what he meant by that. I stepped back and turned to grab a slice of pizza. I took a bite and mumbled, "I'm going to unpack and rinse off quick."

He went to grab my suitcase. "I'll take your luggage to the primary suite. You can unpack and use the dresser and closet. There's a ton of space."

I hurried to finish my slice as I shook my head. "No. I can do it. Or we can just put it upstairs for when we order another bed and I stay up there."

"I'm taking your things to our damn room," he grumbled and walked off. I followed him as he combed his hand through his hair like he was trying to shake off the tension between us.

"You're right. I'm not even thinking. I need to look like I'm living with you anyway," I agreed as we walked down the hall.

I swore I heard him grumble that it wasn't the point, but I couldn't be sure. "Just put your stuff wherever you want, okay? Our bedroom should have enough space for both our things."

"It's your bedroom," I corrected him.

"Well, ours tonight since you're sleeping in *my* bed. I'll let you unpack, but call me if you need anything, Honeybee. Anything at all." His voice rumbled under my skin and caused me to shiver.

"Thanks," I murmured, but he was already gone, leaving me to unpack and then unwind in that oasis of a bathroom on my own. I searched the cabinets and found his designer must have taken great thought into what should be stored here. There were plush towels, soaps with gold specks in them, and bath bombs that I was sure Dimitri didn't use.

Someone had stocked and decorated this bathroom for a king. Or for Dimitri, hoping he would be thankful. It was a reminder that I might have Jameson after me, but Dimitri probably had hordes of women after him.

I sighed and grabbed a bath bomb. I wanted to relax for just a short minute, to decompress alone, to relieve the tension of being in the house with him.

Dimitri didn't know me or my past. He didn't understand that this town could turn a person inside out and eat them alive. I was bringing him into that, shaking things up, and he was shaking me up in the process.

I let the bath bomb spread across the water and turned on the rain spout from above. The pink foam fizzed, smelling like sweet fruit. I breathed out as I got in the hot water and let it work on loosening my muscles. I was surprised to find the bathtub had small jets too.

Everything melted away—every worry, every concern—and all that was left was the thought of being in his home, in his space, completely naked, like I belonged there.

He may have had another woman create this oasis, but I sat there with the smells of him all around me and the echo of his voice still in my ears. I felt how he'd breathed my name in that kitchen, how his eyes raked over my lips as I bit them, and my hand immediately slid between my legs. Desire is always strong when a release is needed. I wanted him even though I knew I would have to deny myself. Here in the bathroom alone, I could envision him though.

I slid my hand into the water, down my body, and then between my legs. I imagined him with me, how his hands felt, how he was rough but so gentle when he wanted to be. The moans I let escape were small as I worked myself higher and higher.

"Honeybee." My name rumbled from deep in his chest as my eyes flew open to see him leaning against the doorframe.

"Oh my God!" I jumped and a bunch of the water and bubbles sloshed over the tub onto the tile floor. It'd been designed to take water into a drain three feet away, so I wasn't concerned about that. I was concerned that he was standing at the doorway, leaning against the frame, looking like absolute perfection with just sweatpants on.

"Don't whisper my name when you come. When you're in my house, scream it nice and loud so I know you're thinking of me."

"What are you doing in here?"

"I came to put on my sweats after I showered upstairs and heard you saying my name."

"So, you just walked in?"

"It's my bathroom. You said that. Plus, I thought you might be calling me because you needed something. Maybe to destress?" He brought up our conversation from before and that smirk on his face was almost irresistible.

"You were supposed to be giving me time to relax," I

reminded him.

"I still am." He looked into the bubbly water, and I didn't shift to cover anything of mine now. "I just want to witness my girlfriend relaxing. Maybe learn a bit more about what she likes."

I looked down and saw how his sweatpants were pitching a large tent. I couldn't look away either. I licked my lips and tried my best to will myself to close my eyes, but they wouldn't listen to me at all. "You should leave."

"I should. But you know I'm not going to."

CHAPTER 13: DIMITRI

The bubbles in her bath were sparse enough that I could see how her nipples tightened, how the blush on her chest and neck rose to her soft face. I saw how she wanted this as much as I did. "There's not a chance in hell I'm leaving now, Olive."

I wasn't good at denying myself anything. Most risks I thought were worth taking, but I had hesitated first with her which meant she was one of the biggest risks of all. She was the one I was going to have to go all in on. I had to. Yet, I had to be careful with her, ease her into the idea, and make sure we navigated it all perfectly for it to work out. I wasn't about to share her with Jameson or any other fucking man, that was for sure. The thought alone had me wanting to rage.

"This ends badly for all of us." She seemed to be reminding us both. "We don't want to be in a screwed-up situation while I'm here. When things go sideways with us, we need to remember we still each have a friendship with Kee."

Did she think our friends couldn't overcome us being together? I wasn't going to be able to explain it to her now. My brain wasn't currently functioning. It was short-circuiting as I stared at her. It wouldn't be something I would admit later. I'd chalk it up to my dick taking control, but right then, it didn't feel that way. This was more than lust. I wanted to own this woman in the bathtub in a way I'd never owned anything. I would have given all my prime investments for it.

"Friends with benefits then," I countered because I was

used to negotiating. I could start there and work my way in.

"Have we reached the official friend level?" She smirked.

She wanted proof; I'd give it to her. "Sure. I've known you for years now, Olive. I know you like doing my best friend's hair. That you talk incessantly about absolutely nothing with her, but it still brings you joy. I know you like flowers in your hair but are subtle with everything else you wear. You're quiet but observant and somewhat nosy. You care about your family even if they've given you hell in the past. I also know the warm amber color of your eyes mists over every time you're upset and darkens when you're turned on like right now. I know how greedy you can be too when you want to fu—"

"Okay. That's enough." She held up a small soapy hand. "Tell me something about you now. I want to know you just as well."

I stepped forward and tried not to scoff at her question. "We don't need to talk about me."

"I want to." Her bottom lip pouted out, and she dragged a hand slowly over the bubbles across her knee. "We're living together, Dimitri, so I should know things too. I know you like to invest, take risks. I know you have brothers and are Kee's friend. I know what the magazines tell me. But you're mostly working when you hang out and, well, I ..." She sighed. "Never mind. This should just be us getting off, right?"

Her words jolted me and felt like a punch to the gut. I immediately wanted to tell her to take that back.

Still, she kept going. "I mean, I know that. Friends with benefits. After Rufford, we had fun, and this can be fun now too. Probably will be better than the other dates since—"

"Other dates?" My gut twisted, and I felt my neck tighten.

"Well, I told you I was dating that day in Kee's office. Not that I'm looking for anything serious ... just new, you know, stuff." She waved down at my cock like I got the idea, but then her eyes locked on the bulge there. I'd been hard for her all day. I wasn't about to hide that now. "So, we can do that, right? I mean with Rufford—"

"Olive, Jesus Christ." She was rambling about other men fucking her while she stared at my dick. "Stop talking about other men or I'm going to shove my cock down your throat to shut you up." I wanted to squeeze her neck while I did it so she couldn't get a word out about another guy.

"Right. Of course. Oh my God. This is all stupid." She licked her lips because she still couldn't rip her eyes away from me, and I saw how her hand slipped down her leg into the water. I knew she put it between her legs as she whimpered, shifting in the bathtub. She hadn't learned to control her desire yet. I hoped she never did, because I loved watching her struggle with it. "Dimitri," she breathed out my name. "You should probably just go."

"Go? Go where? To the next room to fuck my hand to the image of you? Why not give yourself some relief too? You know you don't want me to leave you here unsatisfied. You want to come on your hand when I leave or have me give that pussy what it really wants?" I lifted a brow and put my hand in my sweatpants.

Her eyes were glued there as her lips parted, dazed. "What does it really want, Dimitri?"

Fuck. She was showing me by asking that— she'd for sure pick fucking me over sanity. "It wants to ride my hand, have my cock fuck it into submission. You want to be owned by me, Olive. I'm your boyfriend now. I can show you a damn good time. Better than those dates you've been on. You and I both know it."

She shook her head. "If we do this, it's just fulfilling our desire right now. Not again." Her breath was coming faster now.

I hummed as I smiled. She'd give in again. I think we both knew that now. "You know, my parents let me get away with everything when I was in high school. They had my younger twin sisters to focus on, and my older brothers had already set the tone, so I ran wild. Did anything I pleased. Dabbled in whatever. Took the initiative to get what I wanted."

"Why are you telling me this?" She frowned and started to sit up. Yet, I shook my head and took her chin between my fingers so I could drag a thumb over that bottom lip.

"Because. You wanted to know something about me."

"We don't have to be friends, Dimitri," she whispered.

I knew that. But I wanted to give her what she asked for, needed to. She'd compared me to other men she'd been with, and I wanted her to understand this experience would be something different.

"I think we can be friendly though, right?" I leaned in and tasted her lips, relished in how soft they were, how they pillowed out to taste mine back. "I'll give you a little of me and then take a lot of you."

"Tell me something else?" Her breath came faster still, like this was a fucking turn-on for her to know more about me.

I shrugged as I stood back up and stared down at her. "I've taken a lot in my life. I like to take. I like to own. I like to show everyone what's mine. It's why I invest ruthlessly and get what I want."

"What is it you've wanted most?" The woman was so inquisitive even while moving under the water, and I indulged her as I stared at how the bubbles floated around.

No one had ever really asked me that before. "To experience life, maybe. And not crave any desire I couldn't have."

"Do you think you want for anything now? Or you get it all?"

"I'm staring at a breathtaking girl in my bathtub in a neighborhood I practically own. What do you think?"

"I think you don't own Paradise Grove yet or this girl."

"I will own both, Olive. I won't stop until I do."

She chuckled. "You don't want to own me for long, Dimitri. Just for now. This once. I think you'll probably only want this tonight ..." I opened my mouth to stop her, but she kept going. "Just like I only want this one more time too."

Damn, that hit my ego where it hurt.

"You were so good last time," she praised. I could see how her body was almost arching toward me, and I believed she meant what she was saying. "But I still want to see other men. You will too. You can't possibly be satiated with just this when you've been out there conquering the world. And I want to see what else I can feel when ..." Her words drifted off and a blush touched her cheeks.

"When what?" I asked as I pumped my cock. She had fantasies, and I wanted to hear them.

"I don't know." She shook her pretty curls in front of her face before murmuring, "When I do different things like we did in the office. When I thought someone might walk in, I liked it. So, I'm going to pursue it more with other people. And you can too."

"Are you setting boundaries with me, Olive?" I asked and immediately felt myself wanting to push at them. "Are you saying I should see other women? Because I won't."

"I think it's best."

"I won't argue with you about it now." Instead, I'd nudge her in the right direction over time, make her see that I could give her all she wanted. I'd fuck her in an office or on a damn rooftop for all I cared as long as I got to keep her as mine. "Right now, you get what you want. So, what do you want from me? Tell me."

"Well, I ..." She shifted in the bathtub and her hand finally came up to twist the little flower in her hair. She did it when she was nervous and embarrassed. And I loved seeing how she blushed along with it.

"Don't get shy on me now. Tell me."

"I want to see how you want me. I ..." Her eyes dragged over my cock as she hesitated. "I'm not used to seeing a man show me that."

She hadn't been spoiled with attention, hadn't been given the reinforcement she deserved from her prior lover. I had an urge to change that. "You know every man would want that?" I motioned over her body. "But are you going to show me how you want me too?"

I wasn't sure she'd rise to the challenge, but her little body rolled in my bathtub as her tits emerged from the water while she moaned my name softly. Then, she held my gaze with no shame and only desire in her eyes as she sat up and went to the edge. Lifting herself, she perched on the side and spread her legs. Water droplets and bubbles slid down her tan skin as she dragged her hands up her thighs. "I already came, Dimitri. Maybe I'm done."

"You already know how many times I can get you there in one night. You're not done. Roll your fingers over your clit."

She did as she was told but pleaded with me too. "Show me."

"You want to see what you do to me?"

She bit her lip but didn't look me directly in the eyes as she nodded fast. I shouldn't have cared, but it wasn't enough. Even though this was only supposed to be relief for both of us, I wanted her begging only for me. "Look at me, honey." Her eyes caught mine. "Say it out loud. And say my name, Olive. I'm the man you're begging tonight."

"Please. I want to see your cock, Dimitri. I want to see how I make you feel."

"That's right. I like that mouth saying every filthy thing to me." I pulled my cock out and walked toward her. I pumped it slowly, biding my time. I wanted to have her all night again, to show her that she wanted it too. She'd talked about being discreet with another man just before this bath of hers, and it'd made me see a color I wasn't used to.

Red.

Maybe even darker than red. Black.

I'd wanted to fuck her on that table right then and tell her there was going to be nothing discreet about our relationship.

When I stood on the other side of the bathtub, directly in front of her, I commanded, "Get on your knees in the water."

She didn't even hesitate. I caught the smile on her face and how she rushed to do as I told her. The way she wanted to experience everything sexually so quickly had me thinking of all the things I could do to her. "Want to taste me?"

"Yes," she said, her eyes locked on me and her lips so close that I felt my dick swell in my hand.

"Open your mouth, then. You get me fucking those pink lips for one second."

I threaded my hands through her hair, and she put one on my hip to anchor herself but one was still between her legs.

Then she took me back in her throat, farther than I expected.

"Greedy fucking girl." And that was the problem. Olive Monroe was greedy and desired almost everything I shouldn't be giving her.

Her eyes drifted shut as her head bobbed over my rock-hard dick. I gripped her hair hard, pushing her further onto me than I should. I wanted her lips only around my dick, her moan only humming over my skin. I had to make her see that she wanted the same.

"Do I taste good?"

She hummed out a yes.

"I'm the cock you want. I'm the one you need fucking this little mouth of yours. Remember that," I said before yanking her hair back and exiting her mouth with a pop. She'd have sucked me dry if I'd let her. "Remember you're mine." I didn't say for the time being. She was mine now. Always.

Her lips were shining with my pre-cum and her saliva as she breathed fast, her breasts going up and down as I held her hair so her gaze met mine. "Dimitri, I want you to come."

"Of course you do. You want everything when we screw around."

She glared at me like she wasn't sure if that was an insult. "You're the one who came in here to listen to me."

"I did. I like you greedy, Honeybee, don't get me wrong. I wanted to see why you were saying my name."

"Well, you saw," she said, her eyes narrowing.

"Yeah, I did. And I want to see again," I told her as I pulled my shirt off and shucked my pants to the ground. Then, I stepped into the bath with her. She was getting cold now, her skin had goose bumps, so I pulled her up to stand in front of me and turned the rain spout on above us. I let the water cascade over her body before I kissed her, tasting the lips that had just been wrapped around me and nearly made me come way too early.

I sucked on her bottom lip, then thrust my tongue into her mouth. She met me with the same eagerness as she draped her arms around my shoulders. My other hand squeezed the curve of her ass, and she whimpered. When I slid my hand to her pussy as I kissed her, I felt how wet she was, how slick her opening was, and I knew she needed more.

I needed more. "You going to come for me again?"

"I will," she said almost in irritation as she tried to pull me back to her mouth. "I'm going to orgasm on your cock, and you know it."

I shook my head. "Step apart for me," I commanded, and she listened because she liked to obey. I made note of that for later.

I lowered myself to sitting before stretching out between her legs as I reclined back in the tub. I placed her right calf over the side as I admired the shape of her smooth legs. She balanced on one foot but then leaned forward to place a hand on my shoulder as I stared at her before me with the water running over her body, her calf hanging over the edge.

"Now the other," I murmured and watched as the recognition of what I wanted hit her. She knew if her other leg was draped over the opposite side, she'd be essentially suspended right above me, her pussy spread wide for me to see. "Dimitri, I'll be completely open in front of you—"

"Just how I want you." I nodded and slowly grabbed her other wrist, then brought it down to my chest so she could use me for leverage. We both stared at one another. "Even if it's just for tonight, I expect you to trust me."

"This isn't about trust," she countered, "it's about giving into our desire for a night."

"If you think hitting a high with someone doesn't require trust, you've missed the best part."

Biting her lip, she looked away for only a second before she allowed me to help her drape her left calf over the other side.

"Will you touch me?" she whispered, but I couldn't answer her.

She'd captured my damn soul hovering over me, her legs spread as the water hit both of us in that tub. Her curly hair looked like ringlets falling over her chest now and her pussy dripped water and her come down into the water right above my cock. "You have to touch yourself, Honeybee."

She whimpered. "Why? I want your hand between my legs, Dimitri. It's better."

I shook my head. "If I touch you now, I'll explode. Let me watch you. Fuck your hand like you want to fuck me."

She bit her lip but leaned back to slide one of her hands up her thigh to her pussy. She was eager with her movements, fast with her fingers, and she dipped them into her core and groaned. Immediately, she balanced herself on the tub so she could arch backward and thrust her hips across her fingers.

"Slow down," I growled, because I wanted her to remember this. "And look at me."

I gripped my cock in my hand right below her and squeezed as she caught my gaze. "Look at what you do to me."

"You do the same to me," she whimpered. "I'm so close. I want to go fast."

"Roll your thumb slowly over your clit, honey. Slowly," I warned.

She shuddered over the feeling, and I pumped my cock

once. "It's too slow."

"It's just right. Your pussy is dripping, greedy girl. Slide a finger in now."

"Dimitri," she whispered as she did, and her nipples puckered with just one finger in her.

"You want my whole cock in you, don't you?"

"Yes. God yes." The way she was riding her one finger told me she was almost there. I wanted to see her unravel, see how she got there just from me commanding her.

"Move that finger inside you, Olive." I pumped myself as I watched and brought my other hand up to one of her breasts to give her even more satisfaction. Her skin was so smooth and supple as my fingers played over her nipple. Her eyes widened when I pinched and pulled before she swore under her breath on a moan. "That's right. Feel how I play with you while you play with yourself. Curl that finger in you now. Say my name as you do it. Ride your hand hard, baby."

She cried out when she did as she was told, her whole body arching in the water splashing down on her. She almost fell forward, but I slowly lowered her, my hand still rubbing her breast in soft circles. She was fully vulnerable and beautiful. Completely at my disposal. I slid one of her legs from the rim of the tub and then the other so that her pussy was nestled right against my cock all while she took quick breaths coming down from her orgasm. I took the finger she'd had in her pussy and sucked the come from it.

She watched with wide eyes, her head on my chest. "That shouldn't be hot."

"And you shouldn't taste like honey."

"And I shouldn't be on top of you in the bathtub." She giggled.

"And I shouldn't be contemplating how much more you can take."

"A lot more," she whispered. "All of you in me."

"I'm a little concerned that once we're done here, I won't be able to picture any other face but yours when I want to fuck."

"Then maybe I should turn around? I'm still on birth control," she said. "You know what that means. You can fuck me just like this."

I think right there I should have stopped us. There wasn't a way I could get over a woman like this—one I'd overlooked for years and now couldn't look away from. She knew she had me by the balls when she spun in the water and then straddled me to bear down on my cock. She did the maneuver perfectly, like she'd practiced all her life.

She was made for me, and in the water on that night, I took her hard, her back facing me like she thought I didn't want to see her.

"Look back, Olive."

She looked over her shoulder and smiled. It might have been the first real smile I got that night, and then she met my thrust with her own, and I came deep in her so hard I might have blacked out for a second.

She screamed at the same time and tightened around my cock, the water sloshing over the edge as she fell back onto my chest.

It had barely been a minute of us breathing heavily when she moved to get up. I pulled her back. "Where the hell are you going?"

She giggled and shoved my arm off her waist. "Our pizza is getting cold, Mr. Hardy."

"Don't call me that."

"You just told Jameson to do so." She rolled her eyes. "Should I keep calling you *Darling D*? A good nickname for my pretend boyfriend."

"No. Unless the *d* stands for *daddy*." It was a joke, but she smirked.

"I'll call you daddy if you like it ..." She stepped out of the shower and turned off the water before looking back at me and purring, "Daddy."

Fuck me. I didn't usually like being called that, but anything she did lately was getting to me. "You need to be careful with that mouth of yours."

She rolled her eyes and toed the small seam in the tile. "Was it your idea to have a drain wrapping around the tub?"

"Sure. I thought it would add some fun." I smiled at her. "I was right, huh?"

She walked over to the cabinet and grabbed a white towel to wrap around herself. "I'm sure a lot of girls like it. I'm going to get dressed and eat."

"I'll be down in a second."

"Oh, don't rush. I'm going to scarf down my food and pass out anyway."

"That tired?"

"Well, we expended a lot of energy." She sighed and looked out at the bedroom. "Should we order beds tomorrow? Till you leave, you can just sleep on one side of the bed. It's a king anyway. And since we already ... well, since ..."

"I already fucked that pretty pussy of yours?"

"Oh my God. Do you always get like this after sex?"

"I'm not sure. I'm not usually around women much after I sleep with them, and you left me fast the last couple times we screwed."

"Great that I know how to leave right?" She shrugged and I wasn't sure if she meant it.

"No. I want you staying and cuddling—"

"I don't want to cuddle," she clarified. "Let's just practice not talking about it and try to avoid the topic in the future. You can sleep in the king with me. No wandering hands though. Got it?"

I looked her up and down and contemplated how long I would have to play this fake dating game. For the time being, I would. "As long as yours don't wander either."

"Please. We got that out of the way. It's not like we'll want to screw again anytime soon."

She knew how to take my ego down a notch or two, but when I glanced at her, I saw how the blush stained her cheeks. She shook her cute curls in front of her face and continued. "Believe me, we've done enough to hold us over for the time being."

She left the room to get dressed as I grumbled to myself, "Speak for yourself, Honeybee. Speak for yourself."

CHAPTER 14: OLIVE

Dimitri was true to his word that he wouldn't have wandering hands in the bed we shared that night. Or the night after that.

He left for a week, and I told myself it was for the best. We'd had our fun. When he didn't text me the first day, I decided I needed to work on establishing even a small relationship with my brother while rekindling other friendships in town.

My brother didn't answer my texts or calls, but Lucille did. She talked my ear off about how my mother would be so proud of me having a hand in Paradise Grove's magazine. Then, she invited herself over but gave me until the end of the week. She was a busy woman, she reminded me.

So, for the next six days, I tried to keep busy without texting Dimitri. What he was doing wasn't my concern. Instead, I made it my mission to walk past my father's house once a day in hopes of talking with Knox.

He was never there.

I worked on my thesis, unpacked all my clothes, and shoved the little box of keepsakes I had under the bed. I watched TV and texted Kee probably too much about the dating app I was on.

That day, I'd even texted her pictures of all the guys I'd thought would be worth a date.

Kee: Yes to all of them if they get you out of your Rufford slump.

Me: I'm not in a slump. It's been a month now without him, and I'm completely fine.

Kee: That's what I like to hear. You need to get back in the saddle with someone else.

Me: You're one to talk.

Kee had pretty much saved herself for her high school sweetheart and it worked out for her. Not so much for me and Rufford.

Kee: You're right. I'm not. But Pink says it'll help. Get over someone by getting under someone.

Me: I've been on dates. Gotten under someone too. Don't worry.

Kee: I hope you're being careful though! I haven't worked much lately and recently gotten into documentaries about dating apps and some of these men are spreading diseases. Birth control and freaking wrap it up, Olive.

I winced at her lecture text because I'd let Dimitri have me without a condom.

Kee: How is your birth control by the way? Still getting migraines on that pill?

Me: Yeah, I think it's mostly stress though.

Kee: Just get off it if they keep happening.

I sighed and threw my phone down on the table. She was making the dating app not fun at this point. Plus, it was right on time and Lucille knocked on the door.

She waved from the side window and pointed toward all the papers she had under her arm. I hurried to let her in, and she smiled big at me in her purple tweed dress. "I'm so happy we're doing this. I have so much to show you!"

She set her armful of papers on the dining room table as I offered her something to drink and she showed me all the different sections of the magazine. "You'll get a 200-word article in the opinion section."

"The condos are already standing and so is the office building, Lucille. Don't you think maybe more facts—actual *real* information—would help rather than just an opinion piece?"

She fluttered around the dining room and peered down the hall. "You need to add some touches to your living space, Olive."

She wasn't at all concerned about the article we were discussing. "I'm more focused on what I can put in here to make Walter and Reggie change their minds about the office space."

"Don't forget Earl too. He wasn't at all on board with

Dimitri's plans from the beginning." She sat down at the table and opened up the laptop she'd brought. As she typed away, she hummed, "If I made a few changes, I could maybe get you on the front of the magazine for a feature. People wouldn't like it. It would stir things up a bit though. Let's see here."

She pulled out some wired glasses and put them on. I stood over her shoulder and made light conversation. "How is Earl, by the way? I haven't seen him since I've been back."

She straightened her dress and fluffed her shoulder-length hair. When Lucille had a meeting, she dressed up even if it just encompassed coming over to my house. "He's been busy. Have you seen your father?"

"No," I grumbled and went back to skimming some of the articles she was adding into the little magazine.

"You should call him, Olive."

"What could I possibly need to call him for?"

"Oh, I don't know. To tell him you're home?" She grabbed my phone that I'd placed on the table and waved it in front of me. "Be good to him even if he's not to you."

"This isn't how I wanted to spend my day," I ground out before I swiped the phone from her and pounded the number in. Lucille always had a way of making everyone feel like she was their grandmother who knew best. You just didn't want to disappoint her.

My father answered on the first ring. "Olive." His deep timbre rumbled through the phone. "I was expecting a call from you."

"Yeah. I'm in Paradise Grove. I thought I'd let you know."

"Your brother already did. I'm out of town for the next few weeks, but there's a grill out soon, right? I'll fly in. And the board meeting, I believe, in about a month or so. I'll be back for that."

"I've heard you agree with the city ordinances. You don't want to fill the new office building with businesses."

"I'll agree to anything to keep that Hardy boy out of here. And if you're really shacking up with him, I suggest you stop."

"What?" I rolled my eyes. "You haven't met him, and he's—"

"I don't care what he is. He's in business with people we won't associate with. Your mother would have wanted—"

I winced at him bringing her up. "Mother is gone."

Lucille's eyes cut to mine then, and her manicured hand immediately fell over mine.

He sighed, "I'm not an idiot. She may be gone but her legacy in this town lives on through us. We have a status to uphold."

"Speaking of that, Knox isn't well."

"He'll get better. He's fine. He's been working with me, doing great." I heard someone in the background and knew my father was focusing on work rather than family.

"Doing what exactly? Because if he's hanging out with the wrong people ..."

"I've got my son under control. Get yourself under control if you know what's good for you." He hung up abruptly.

I was white knuckling the phone, ready to tell him off, and my hand shook as I set it down on the table. Lucille patted my other hand for a minute or two as the silence stretched between us.

Then she murmured, "Maybe you shouldn't write the article. Maybe we should—"

"I'm writing it." I grabbed the paper and clutched it to my chest before smiling at her. "I'm going to write it and it's going to be great, Lucille. My father doesn't get a say in who I'm dating."

"He won't ever vote for your boyfriend to be around. He's trying to push Dimitri Hardy out one way or another."

"Is everyone trying to do that?" I inquired, because I was starting to think there was an underlying reason. It wasn't simply about the condos and office building.

Lucille sighed and looked out the window. "Oh, our little Paradise is a complicated place. You know that. I just hope your brother starts to see that your dad isn't the best influence."

"But a father should always strive to be that for their son."

"Not all people are meant to be parents, Olive. You've learned that the hard way." She pulled me in for a hug right as a text lit up on my phone.

She looked down and saw the notification just like I did.

> **Kee: And if you do get off the birth control, wrap it up. Unless you want littles running around.**

I snatched the phone up, but Lucille was already smiling big. "You're getting off birth control to start a family?" She clapped her hands together, tears in her eyes.

And that's when I heard the garage door opening.

Dimitri must have gotten home. Not that he'd texted or called. I glanced at Lucille, and she tilted her head before she patted my cheek. "Oh, has he been gone all week? I haven't seen him outside lately. You must have missed him."

She wasn't moving to leave at all. The woman was nosy, and she wanted a show.

Shit.

CHAPTER 15: DIMITRI

"Oh, he does know how to answer," Kee mumbled into the phone as I pulled up into our driveway.

I sighed at Kee's immediate whining. "I'm busy, woman. And I'm about to be home so I gotta say hi to Olive and—"

"I was just texting her. Why is she staying there so freaking long?"

"I offered her extra work while she finishes her thesis." That was a good, plausible reason.

"What type of work?" Kee inquired, and that's when I knew I was going to have to drop a little more information than I wanted to.

"She's just acting close to me so these people here trust me a bit more."

"How close?"

I relented and explained our fake dating idea.

"That's .... She didn't even tell me! This is stupid."

"Why?"

"Because ... well ... I don't know. I'm not there! I just hope you're being nice and not messing with my sweet friend, D." She sighed and then continued, "*And* you better not try to hook up with her."

"Olive's a big girl. She can make her own decisions," I told her as I tried to chuckle but winced instead. She was going to be real pissed when she found out. And she would.

I'd spent a whole week away, and instead of fizzling out,

my feelings only grew for Olive. I wasn't used to the intensity of them, to worrying about her, to wanting to be near her. Those feelings had become unavoidable, and I knew I was going to have to admit them to everyone soon enough.

"She's also probably the most complicated woman you've been around for years. She's embedded in our friend group and—"

"And we'll cut your dick off if you hurt her," Pink, Olive's other friend, said in the background.

"That's aggressive." I rolled my eyes.

"I agree. But I really will rip your eyes out for looking at her wrong," Kee threatened, and she never did that shit.

"What the hell? Why aren't you warning Olive off? I'm your best friend."

"I have three best friends. You, Pink, and Olive. Olive's the most vulnerable right now. Especially when it comes to men. Rufford hurt her." Kee sighed, like she knew more. "Her father practically abandoned her when her mother was sick. You know that, right? She thought she found a man in Rufford who would never make her feel that way again, and then he did the freaking same. Such a douche. And he's probably still trying to screw with her. Has he been calling?"

Damn it. Had he? "I don't know." But I was going to figure it out. I made a mental note to ask.

"She needs to forget him, but she needs to be careful who she's hooking up with. I'm worried about her."

"Don't be. I got her. She's fine," I reassured her, though not solely for Kee's benefit. I knew I had Olive and that I'd never let her get hurt in the same way again. "Gotta go. Call me when you need me."

"Never if, always when," she grumbled and hung up.

I hurried to get out of my car, on a mission now to see the woman I'd been thinking about for a week.

When I walked in, she stood in my living room, her hair pulled back with a few curls cascading down around her face and a little O shaping her mouth in surprise. She looked surprised to see me.

Immediately, I regretted my decision to leave at all. Sure, going to check on investments for our HEAT empire in person was always helpful, but mostly, my brothers had a decent handle on the hospitality aspect. Maybe I should have stayed here and made sure Olive got used to me being around.

Then again, I visited Declan, saw the next gen, and found myself watching how my older brother had found joy in his family, and I found joy in that family too.

The little one ran the show with my sister-in-law and my brother, but they smiled at every single thing that kid did. I did too. Would I be the same way with a kid?

Would Olive?

My mind ran away with the idea, and I got lost in how I'd dote on them both, on how she'd be scared but I'd ease her worry and keep her safe from the disappointment she'd experienced with men before. I'd be able to show her how good of a family man I could be.

Olive cleared her throat and snapped her pouty mouth shut before waving me in. "Oh, Darling D, didn't know you'd be home today." She said it sweetly, but I knew what it meant. I hadn't communicated with her in the way she wanted. "Anyway, Lucille is going over the magazine with me." She tilted her head toward Lucille. I hadn't even noticed the older woman standing at the table, smiling with hearts in her eyes at us both. "You need anything to drink, or are you hungry?"

A drink? For her fucking boyfriend who hadn't seen her in a week? "You think I want a drink?" I lifted a brow. She shook her head slightly as if warning me off. She walked to the kitchen, but I was following her and watching how she jumped to take care of me immediately.

I pulled her away from the fridge she'd just opened, wrapped an arm around her waist, and bent to taste those lips. Her teeth slid over her bottom lip before her body melted against me and her gaze dipped. I took that mouth like it was mine, like I'd been starved for it, like I was never going to come up for air. I didn't want to.

I loved how her arms automatically went around my neck, how her mouth opened for me as I slid my tongue against the seam of it. She didn't stop or hesitate. Maybe she couldn't. Maybe she needed me just as badly as I missed her.

I knew I had to pull away to keep it PG, but I let out a low sound of disapproval as I did, and my eyes didn't leave hers as I said, "Missed you, Ms. Monroe. So much that I might drag you with me next time." I touched that pink flower in her hair while I considered how I was going to cull the feelings coursing through me. I wasn't going to scare her off.

"Well, you'll have a little one to text that friend of yours about sooner rather than later with this kind of love," Lucille said, and Olive jumped back from me like she'd forgotten Lucille was still in the house.

"What's this you're talking about?" I tilted my head and glanced at Lucille, who had tears in her eyes like a doting grandma. I swear, she was the happiest woman around Olive. It showed me that Olive had roots here even if she didn't want to.

"Olive's friend Kee told her to wrap it up if she didn't want kids. I saw the text." Lucille laughed and waved off her meddling.

"Guess that friend doesn't know you're already trying."

Olive quickly shook her head, "Oh, Lucille, we're—"

I undid my suit jacket, hung it on one of the dining room chairs, and cut off Olive because I was about to really consider it. "I'm ready for one that looks just like Olive right now."

Lucille chuckled and packed up her things faster than I'd thought she could move. "Well, don't let me keep you. I'm so happy you both found each other. This is so exciting, Olive. This is what you should write about. How Paradise Grove will be perfect for the next generation."

"I don't think—"

"Yeah." I rocked back on my heels, looking her up and down. "How perfect it's going to be walking down the street with me, chasing around our little minion."

Lucille squealed and waved goodbye, leaving us standing in the living room looking at each other.

"Dimitri Hardy," Olive started with her pretty brown eyes narrowed on me. "Stop with the family talk."

"I won't. I saw my nephew this weekend with Declan."

"Oh, well, that's nice."

She went to the dining room table to straighten papers, cleaning up to busy herself, but I wanted her full attention. "It is nice." I put myself between her and the papers, took her wrist, and pulled her close instead of having her fiddle with something else. "Made me want a damn kid more than I ever have before."

"Well, I'm sure there's a lot of women who would—"

"Only one woman I can picture having my kids."

"You're getting a look in your eye. Is this how you get when you want to take some ridiculous risk, Dimitri? Because I'm not the one to do it with."

"You agreed to this."

"Don't unleash your risk-taking, adrenaline-seeking behavior on me right when you get home." She started to comb loose tendrils of her hair back into a bun, like she did when she got nervous.

Her anxiety caused something in my chest to burn. I wanted to dig until I found the root of her worry and find a way to ease it. So, I asked her the question I really wanted to know and that she'd avoided the first time we talked about. "You told me the first day we were here that you don't like the idea of a family. Now I want to know, is that why you don't want kids?"

"Please stop." Her breath came faster. "You need to focus on making Paradise Grove like you. That's all we're doing here. Okay? That is it. I haven't talked to you in a week. You can't just come home with outrageous plans all of a sudden. We're friends helping one another out."

"I made it to the level of friendship now?" I smiled and took a step back. I'd drop the idea for now. Solidifying myself in her life was a win for today. I'd work on the rest.

"You proud of that?" She finally smirked and I saw how she instantly relaxed.

I just kept going so that she'd forget being nervous, forget anything that was in the past that might have hurt her. "Next, I'll be boyfriend, Olive. Then, I'll be baby daddy."

She shook her head. "Friends. That is it. Put me in your friend zone and lock me up in there, okay?"

There was no way I'd do that. "Fine. For now."

"Good. I'll kiss you in public for the benefit of this stupid agreement we have," she clarified with a hand on her hip. "That's it."

"Fuck that. I'm kissing you everywhere, Olive," I growled and yanked her body to mine before I devoured her.

CHAPTER 16: OLIVE

Dimitri might have had a lapse of sanity when he got home. Maybe he'd missed screwing around with me, which had him considering more. Yet, after that, we fell into a perfectly cordial, friendly routine for a whole week. We ate quietly together while we both worked, went to bed at about the same time every night, and made small talk.

But he respected my space. He held my hand during our scheduled daily walks around the neighborhood but did nothing more. He even made sure to sleep with his head at the foot of the bed and mine at the top.

Not that it stopped my body from gravitating toward his every night. I hated myself for it too. I'd specifically told him I didn't like to cuddle, and the statement was true in that I didn't want to get attached.

Rufford had never cuddled me, and so I told myself it was unnecessary. Still, somehow, I would wake up with my ass tucked into Dimitri's crotch every single morning, like I was hungry for his touch even in my sleep.

Today, I moved faster than lightning to get out of bed and put on a sweater and leggings, got ready in the bathroom by throwing on a bit of concealer, mascara, and the pink flower in my hair before I pulled it back into a ponytail, and went to make myself coffee.

I didn't look his way at all, didn't stare at his perfect bare chest, didn't wonder what he was dreaming about. Not even for a second.

"I can handle anything if I keep my legs closed," I mumbled to myself as I went to the kitchen and opened a dating app. "Or I'll find someone else." I'd swipe right as much as I could for now. Maybe I'd start communicating with someone fun and forget all about Dimitri.

I lowered my head on the counter and groaned for a second.

"I feel that way about mornings too." Dimitri's groggy voice sounded from the hall, and when I looked up, I wanted to groan all over again. He'd left his shirt off when he walked out of the bedroom. And I practically had to wipe drool from my face.

I needed to focus on something else. "Actually, I'm feeling that way about helping Lucille with the finishing touches on the article at the moment."

And about my eyes traveling up and down his abs. And about me wanting him when I should have been trying to find a not messy date.

"That hard to throw an article together about how good it will be to have more offices nearby?"

"It should be snappy and cute, Dimitri. The whole magazine is that way. The information you sent me was not. Plus, people won't just be entertained with your data." I hated that Lucille was right that they would probably enjoy a family piece more. I busied myself by going to check for breakfast food in the refrigerator. "Want me to make breakfast? I need to stop at the grocery store—"

"Isn't there a delivery service for residents?" He shrugged. "I'll have coffee for now. And you did read the email I sent, right? It's a green energy building with mostly companies that

HEAT supports which are all reputable. Anyone moving into the condos for work will contribute to local consumerism."

"Most everyone who lives here doesn't care about a few stores in your strip mall."

"Plaza of boutiques." He rolled his eyes and grabbed the coffee pot to pour some into a mug. "Anyway, spin the narrative then. Those working there will mingle, be a part of the damn country club, and offer investment opportunities." Then he smiled and side-eyed me. "Or put you and me on the front and talk about what we want for our new family."

"Stop." I held up a hand. "Not in the morning." He was laughing at, I'm sure, what looked like disgust on my face.

"Kids in the morning are a little difficult, but we'd make it work, Honeybee." Then he sipped his coffee while he looked over the mug with his green eyes staring at me.

"I'm not even going to respond to that. Your *first* idea might just work. This town was always mulling over money."

His eyes twinkled with mischief still. "My second idea would work better."

"You're incorrigible." I stared into the fridge like there was something really interesting in there before announcing, "I'm going to go to the grocery store and maybe for a walk so I can consider options to write about."

"A walk without me? We're supposed to go together." He set down the mug and stood next to me until I had no other choice but to close the fridge and meet his eyes. He pulled at a loose curl that must have escaped my ponytail and came to stand beside me so we were both leaning on the counter, looking out over the island toward the living room window. His bare shoulder touched mine and I almost gasped at how electrifying it felt after being against him in bed this morning.

Then he murmured, "Our walks are supposed to be every day together. We're supposed to be holding hands, kissing in the streets."

My heart picked up speed, but I shook my head fast. "I don't think our PDA needs to be that intense. I'm doing a good job establishing us by just talking to people around town. Reggie even stopped me the other day to tell me he was actually happy with the security measures you've implemented."

"As he should be since he's the sheriff. If you're going to the store, maybe we can go to the furniture one and—"

With him this close, I didn't want to do anything but jump his bones. "*I* am going to the grocery store by myself. And I already ordered a bed frame and mattress for upstairs and a desk. I'll move right up there when they come and be out of your way."

He hummed and walked over to his briefcase near the couch to pull out his laptop and sat down there. Still without a shirt on. "Who said you're in my way?"

"When I moved in here, Dimitri, I told you I would live upstairs." Sliding on my shoes, I rearranged my sweater and made a mental note that we needed a mirror in here too. "Then you'll get the bed back to yourself and—"

"But then I won't get to wake up with you right against me," he said without even looking up from his laptop.

I froze. "What?"

"You told me you don't like cuddling, Honeybee, but I wake up at sunrise to your body plastered against mine. I've always been an early riser. But did you know I go back to sleep with you against me every morning?"

"I ... I don't know what you're talking about," I murmured, backing away from him. I needed to leave right now because if I didn't, I knew I'd do something I'd regret like straddle him on that couch. "I have to go."

"Take my car if you're getting groceries," he yelled after me as I rushed to grab my purse.

"What car?" I glanced outside and didn't see anything in the driveway or on the street. All I saw was Lucille digging a very large hole in her backyard.

"The one I had brought in for when I got back from the airport." He shrugged. "It's in the garage."

I wasn't staying to talk to him for a second longer. I needed to find another man and not try to make Dimitri fill Rufford's shoes. Or I needed to be on my own. I flicked on the lights and gasped when I saw the most expensive-looking car I'd ever laid eyes on. And I'd been in a Rolls-Royce, a Bugatti, a Porsche, you name it. This was something else though.

I grabbed the keys from the hook. I circled the front and then back. It was a sleek matte black, and every angle was a curve of perfection. My parents always had nice cars, but this was one of a kind. I pulled the handle and the door freaking lifted into the air.

When I got in, I let out a sigh of pure ecstasy as I brushed a hand over the white leather. All custom interior with lighting along the dashboard that turned on when I pressed the ignition.

"You like it?" Dimitri said, standing in the doorway.

"Maybe. What is it?" I rubbed my hand over the wheel.

"A Pagani Utopia."

"It's pretentious."

"Yep. Just like the town you grew up in." I wouldn't argue with him there. "You know how to drive stick?"

I snapped my gaze to his. "I learned how to drive using stick shift."

"If you say so." He pressed the button to lift the garage door. "And you don't want company?"

He was leaning against the doorframe in those sweats and combed a hand through his thick dark hair.

"I don't think so. Although, you sure you want me driving this? I might crash it." I gripped the steering wheel and twisted my hands over it a few times.

"I trust you, Honeybee."

"I'll be gentle with her," I reassured him.

"What pretty thing with this much power wants to only be treated gently, Honeybee?" he asked and winked at me. "Pushing her to her limit will be when she's most beautiful. If I were you, I'd take the risk ..."

"'And enjoy the dance?'" I took a shaky breath, listening to his words. "We still talking about the car?"

"Maybe," I heard him murmur. "Maybe not." Then, I eased off the clutch and gave her some gas quick, backing out of our garage and leaving him behind.

It was only a few winding blocks to get to the local grocery store, Santelli's. It was another family-owned business that had carpeted grocery aisles, fruits lined up perfectly, and only sold organic produce. My mother used to say it was ostentatious, then she would feed me grapes right there while my father shook his head at us and said we were going to get him in trouble.

She was the logic and light in the family, the one who kept us grounded. I tried not to well up, but my eyes became blurry thinking about it. I swiped a few different frozen meals, some chicken and beef, and some produce before checking out. When I packed up my car, I saw Esme across the street walking into the library and thought I should say hi and maybe ask if she knew anything about my brother doing business outside of town.

Yet, when I got in there, she was nowhere to be found. I went past the sleek oak shelves and finally reached the quirky front desk employee to ask if she'd seen her. The woman in her early twenties wore red glasses and had her brown hair tied in a high ponytail.

"Oh, she's um ..." She glanced at the back wall. "I'm sure she'll be right back. She went to the bathroom."

So I went to the bathroom to check but didn't see her. When I came back out, though, she was standing right there. "Hey. Zen up front said you were looking for me."

"Hi. Yeah, I saw you come in and just thought I'd, well, say hi and see how things are going."

"Good. I have a part-time job here, so I'm just about to start my shift."

"Oh. Well, maybe you'll be seeing a lot of me in the coming months." I sighed and looked around. "I'm doing research on the sociology of a small community for my thesis."

Esme laughed and nodded. "Oh, because of our families? I'm guessing your father told you that you had to keep it anonymous, am I right?"

"He did," I answered, not knowing why he would say that, but it seemed she was going somewhere with it and I wanted to know where.

"With each of our families having such a rich history here, it's so interesting. I've found that many private, upscale communities have these secret groups embedded in them too. Were you coming to grab a book from the society stacks? Zen was concerned about whether or not you knew about them, but I told her you did, of course."

"Right." I had no idea what she was talking about, but this

was how Esme was. She shared way too much before she realized she shouldn't. I knew now I had to know. I pried further, even though I shouldn't have. "What book do you think has the best information in it?"

"Here." She turned on her heel. "I'll show you."

Esme had never been good at keeping secrets. I knew she was in love with my brother the moment she stepped foot in my house, and this was no different. She was blurting out things, totally assuming I knew them all.

"Honestly, I think your brother is barking up the wrong tree with the people your father is having him meet with. My dad too. This was never in the society's partnerships, you know?"

"I know Knox isn't doing well, that's for sure."

She shrugged as she glanced around, making sure no one was with us, and then she pulled an older-looking book against the wall, and a doorway swung open to a back room. Stacks and stacks of older books lined the walls and there was a table and leather chairs in the center of it all. She walked to another book on the far wall and pulled that to open yet another hallway. She then used her key to unlock the door on the other side.

"So the book I like best is only because my great-great-great grandfather is in it. I haven't read them all. You'll probably like it, too, because I'm guessing your great-great-great grandparents are in it, considering they were a huge part of the Diamond Syndicate coming over to the United States and influencing the spread of the society across the nation."

"The Diamond Syndicate?" I murmured but then I cleared my throat and nodded vigorously. "Yes, of course, the Diamond Syndicate."

Esme had caught me though. I saw how her eyes widened

immediately. "You know about the Diamond Syndicate, right, Olive?"

"Mm-hmm," I said, but it was quite obvious from my tone that I did not.

"Olive," she hissed, stumbling back, "how do you not know but your brother does? Oh my God. My dad is going to kill me."

She tried to snatch the book she'd handed me back, but I wouldn't let it go. "Stop. I won't tell anyone," I reassured her.

"Are you kidding?" Wildly, her eyes ping-ponged around the room while she combed her hands through her hair. "You need to leave."

"Why? I'm supposedly a part of whatever secret society this is."

"We're never supposed to talk about it unless it's with each other. I thought that your mother would have ... This is bad."

"How do you know and I don't? Why was this kept from me? And ... you said Zen knows? She hasn't even lived here her whole life."

"She's from a different community where the Diamond Syndicate is also based." Esme waved me off as she took deep breaths. "You can't tell anyone and—"

"I won't. It's not a big deal." It felt big, like my mother and father had kept a massive secret from me my whole life.

"It's a huge deal. You don't understand. Cousin Ricky started spreading rumors about this, Olive. He ended up gone. My dad keeps saying he's vacationing in Bora Bora, but he's gone gone."

"What?" I whispered.

"Ricky was working with those men your dad and Knox are working with. In the mob. Ricky was selling drugs for them and I told Knox this. He got mad and now he won't even look at me. I'm telling you—"

"You think Knox is selling drugs with these men?" I repeated softly.

"I don't know what he's doing but it's something. And he's doing it to make your father happy. Yes."

"You can't be serious. If that's the case, we should go to the c—"

"Sheriff Reggie Boone lives across the street from us, Olive. He was the one talking to my dad about Ricky."

"I ..." I glanced around and everything felt dizzying. "I might be sick."

"Don't you dare throw up back here," Esme yelled, and she rushed me out. "And don't you dare tell anyone that you know. Not your dad, not your brother, not anyone in this town ... and especially not Dimitri."

Well, that wouldn't be a problem ... or so I thought.

CHAPTER 17: OLIVE

That afternoon, my mind raced through my memories, through my childhood and high school years. When my father went to meetings with the board, I wondered now what those meetings consisted of. And then I mourned the fact that none of us were close enough to discuss something like this.

How had I fallen so far from the family tree? How had I lost such an integral part of me?

I knew how, but I didn't want to accept it.

I thought of stories I'd heard as a child about secret societies, of the tales we told each other until we got to high school and realized they weren't true. And then I thought of Knox, of what he must know, of what he was going through. I called him but was sent to his voicemail. I called him again. And again. And again.

"Olive, I don't want to talk." He finally picked up the phone and I almost dropped it with just hearing his voice.

"Knox! You answered," I stuttered.

"To tell you to stop calling," he ground out. "I'm in the middle of something."

"Where? Are you home?" I heard men in the background. "Are you with Dad because—"

"I'm with Dad out of town. Stop texting and calling."

"But we should talk." I hesitated for a moment. "Without Dad. And without Georgette. We need to talk, and you need to—"

"Stop bothering me, Olive. It's for the best." He hung up and I was left wondering what to do. Did I text him and push him further? How involved was he? And if he wasn't, I didn't want to ask and get him involved.

That left me with the book I'd schmoozed Esme into giving me before I left the library. She'd given me her number and said I should call her with questions—only her, no one else. It was old and leatherbound and held secrets not even I was certain I could keep.

I told Dimitri I was going to work on my thesis and he nodded, waving me off in the living room. He was busy working and I would be busy reading the rest of the night in the primary suite where I closed the door behind me. I started to read about how this society was men and women walking among us with much more pull than I could ever have imagined.

They were entangled with the government, law enforcement, investors, and such influential people that they could sway decisions on every aspect of the community. I read how they went from implementing small changes in a school a hundred years ago to influencing how and where drug cartels land within the state.

I took notes, mapped out relationships, figured out how embedded this society was in about everything I'd ever known. They were connected in the highest social circles of business tycoons around the world. An online search revealed they were also connected to a biker club. It was all hearsay, but it made sense.

No mafia.

The Diamond Syndicate was founded hundreds of years ago in Europe and the mastermind wanted a group of knights to protect the morals of society along with influencing power to do right. When they migrated to the United States, they kept those morals and brought extreme amounts of money over. Yet, they kept the syndicate as a sort of secret society where they could mold laws, increase power, and exercise influence. Supposedly in the last couple hundred years, in this region, they kept the mob from infiltrating communities that were near, kept men and women from paying for protection. They claimed that they would strive for an idyllic community around it.

Except power breeds greed, and some had fallen victim to giving up communities to the mafia. Some were corrupt. And exceptionally powerful.

It made sense that Paradise Grove would push back on Dimitri's offices if the companies he were bringing in didn't align with the Diamond Syndicate.

I knew that Dimitri's sisters had married Armanellis, a powerful Italian mob family. That family wasn't listed anywhere in this book. Could they be a direct threat to the Diamond Syndicate? Dimitri bringing that link to this community could potentially disrupt their harmony.

I took notes on how this society must have influenced our town. I started writing it into my thesis, although I wasn't sure what I would end up using.

The excitement I felt being able to put it down on paper, to expand the history of this community, to tie in how it affected the greater society, it felt like a perfect thesis at first. Yet, when I came to the descendants of the Diamond Syndicate, the excitement was squelched.

I saw my mother's parents pictured, a wedding photograph printed in there.

My mother had never told me she was a part of the syndicate, never once said a thing to me about them.

And I couldn't figure out why. I racked my brain, but I knew I couldn't tell Dimitri about this until I learned more, until I knew why my mother kept it a secret from even me.

I was so deep in my reading that I didn't feel the migraine until I glanced up at the time. I found myself squinting away a visual aura and having to wobble to put away the book in a dresser drawer before I laid down for an hour-long cat nap.

I woke to Dimitri still in the living room on the phone like he was planning to be there all night.

And even though I was thankful my headache subsided, I was now irritated he hadn't come to bed yet. Every night, I'd fall asleep to him lying on his side, his body heat warming mine. It was clear he didn't care to do the same. I sighed as I looked over at myself in the mirror. I'd made sure to wear big, baggy clothes to bed more for my own sanity than anything else. Yet, I spent every night sweating in those long pants.

If he didn't even come to bed early to talk with me before falling asleep, it was obvious he wasn't thinking of me in the same way I'd been thinking of him. So, I stomped over to my dresser again and flung off my sweater. I was going to sleep in the crop top and shorts I normally did.

I'd be just as comfortable as him now, and I wouldn't think about him one bit. Who thought about people that were just friends anyway? We were platonic, and I could keep things that way. I would deny any other feeling I had from now on. I ripped the sheet away from the pillow just as I heard his voice down the hall.

He walked into the bedroom in time for me to act like I

was gently, without any rage, folding down the soft white silk duvet filled with down. I turned to say, "You finally decide to—"

But he held up his hand and then pointed to the phone. "No. The governor of Hawaii declared a climate emergency." He laughed at the person on the other line. "You realize their water levels are less dangerous than Florida's, right? We need to be diligent with this investment even if it comes at a loss." One more pause to listen. "I'm sure it will. You shouldn't have invested if you didn't know the risk. Now, my girlfriend needs to talk with me. So, call my assistant in the morning if you need to discuss something further." He hung up the phone and took a deep breath as he scanned my pajamas. "You're going to bed?"

I glanced at the clock on the nightstand. "Um, yes. It's eleven."

"You've been in here for hours."

"Right. I was working on my thesis and then I napped after getting a migraine."

He stopped walking mid step and looked up with concern. "You're still getting migraines?"

"It's fine." I waved him off. "It's just stress. I took a nap, and it went away."

Still, he walked to my side of the bed and put his hand on my waist to look closely in my eyes. "Come get me if you have a headache next time." Then he had me step back as he moved between me and the bed. "I can turn down the bed, Honeybee."

"So can I, Darling D," I singsonged.

"But you don't," he clarified as he started folding the sheets down. "I do. And if you're ready for bed, you come get me."

"For what?" I said as I let him fiddle with the blankets. He seemed to think fluffing my pillow a certain way was helpful to me. I didn't correct him. The man was attentive if nothing else.

And right then, it occurred to me that every night this week, he had actually stopped working when I told him I would be retiring to our room. I'd say, "You don't have to come to bed with me," but he'd still come anyway.

He frowned at me. "You haven't talked to me at all today. Normally, we lie down and you divulge something."

"Oh, so you're coming to bed for information?"

"How am I supposed to learn about the mother of my future children otherwise?"

"Oh, don't start with that." I waved him off. "And if you wanted to know about your friend, you could ask. I'd have an opportunity to tell you before bedtime if you weren't on the phone all day." The reply flew out of my mouth before I could stop it.

"I'm not getting the sweet honey today. I'm getting Olive with bite, I see." He looked me up and down, and I took another step back.

We'd gotten along fine this week. I shouldn't have any complaints. Yet, he'd been extremely nice, too nice, like he didn't want to jump my bones with the same fervor in which I wanted him. Still, it shouldn't have been his concern. I knew that. I rubbed at my temples because my head was starting to hurt. "I've just had a long day."

"Your head still hurt? How bad do these migraines get? You said you asked your doctor about them."

"I get visual auras sometimes. But I'm good about it. Nothing to worry about, really, according to the doc as long as ..." Here he was getting information out of me.

"As long as what?" He smirked.

"Nothing."

"Come on. Tell me," he said softly.

"It's just stress. The doctors keep saying it may be hormonal and that maybe switching my birth control could help but—"

"They think it's your medication?" He sounded shocked. "Why are you on it then?"

"It's not. It's fine." I waved it off. "I get them when I'm working a lot, and I was doing a ton with my thesis. You get it. You worked most of the day too."

He nodded after rearranging the pillow one last time, then he turned to face me head-on and took a step toward me. "I have." He motioned for me to get in the bed, then he pulled the sheets up close to my chin and tucked the blankets around me like I was a child he was taking care of.

"What are you doing?"

"Tucking you in tight."

"Don't want the bed bugs to bite?"

"With what you're wearing, Olive, *I* just may bite." A smile slipped. At least he had noticed and wasn't as immune to me as I'd thought. "You're blushing." He dragged a finger across my cheek. "Tell me what you're thinking."

"We're technically friends, right? Complete friend zone and all?"

"I'm regretting that idea more and more every day." He sighed and tucked in my left side a little tighter.

"It's the right idea. I'm fresh out of my relationship with Rufford, who made me incapable of trusting anyone. And I'm sure you sleep with women in every state you fly through."

He chuckled. "I'm not just flying around states." See, he didn't deny it. It meant he had women in other freaking countries too.

"Right. So, when you say things like you might just bite me instead ... I'm really not sure—as just a friend—if I should tell you not to or indulge and say I don't mind a bite here and there."

He let out a low growl but didn't really say what he wanted one way or the other. He just kept looking at me with those green eyes, like he was assessing all the things. "You give me the go-ahead and I'll fucking ravage you right now, Honeybee."

"Again, not sure what to say."

"You don't have to say a damn thing. I just want you to know it." He took a step back and sighed. "My day has been particularly frustrating. So, we should get some rest." Right after he said that, he looked down at me and reached behind his head to pull his shirt slowly over his body.

I watched the shirt rise inch by inch and every ab of his appeared below it. The V of muscle showing on the edge of his slacks was much more defined than any other man's I'd ever seen. I had the urge to drag my tongue across it and started imagining how it would taste.

"I'm going to shower," he said through what might have been clenched teeth, then he disappeared into the bathroom.

My desire for him was getting out of hand, and I refused to envision the water running down every ab, the way his arm would flex as he washed his hair, how big his—

I grabbed my phone to look at my dating app instead. I would find someone to talk to. I even swiped right and messaged a few guys, determined to do better.

I wouldn't fall for a friend, especially not when he was a Hardy who could have any woman he wanted. I'd already made a fool of myself by getting cheated on by Rufford. Not again. Plus, I wanted to experience different things. I'd told Dimitri that time and time again. Back to swiping.

His eyes were nowhere near as interesting as Dimitri's.

They didn't pierce my soul. Left.

That jawline couldn't compete with any Hardy brother. Left.

There was no way he was as tall as Dimitri. Left.

I sighed deeply and I heard, "That guy looks like an asshole. Swipe left again." I jumped and turned to see abs with water droplets now on them.

"Jesus, Dimitri. Put some clothes on." I covered my eyes so I wouldn't keep looking at his half-naked body.

"Olive, I have a towel on." He chuckled and went into the walk-in closet only to come back with shorts on but no shirt.

"Are you sleeping without a shirt on again?" I said, frustration laced in my tone.

"Are you sleeping in what you're wearing?"

I took a deep breath. "I can change if it makes you uncomfortable." I was regretting my decision to get his attention now that I had to stare at his response.

"I'm not uncomfortable with your bare legs next to me." He walked to his side of the bed where he grabbed the pillow from next to my head and placed it at my feet. Sleeping with his head at my feet was so juvenile and yet completely necessary at this point. I was too attracted to him to do otherwise. Then he flipped back his side of the comforter, and I felt the cool air on my legs and toes. "But then again, I have less restraint after a long day, and I'm not used to being frustrated all through the night." His voice was strained, low and raw.

"I understand." I licked my lips, not sure exactly what he was frustrated with. Me talking to him, lying next to him? "You took a lot of phone calls. It's got to be a long day dealing with all of what you do. Are you talking to clients all day most days?"

He rubbed at his jaw. "You think I'm frustrated with work?"

"Well, yeah. I get it. I hear you talking to people all day and it sounds tiring," I blurted out.

His eyes narrowed on me as he sat on his side of the bed. "Are you listening to my calls?"

"No. Of course not."

"If you're going to lie, take a breath before answering." He chuckled and laid down. "It will be more believable."

I sighed. "Okay. Sorry. I just hear you talking and can't help but—"

"Be nosy?"

"I like to classify it as being informed about my current surroundings."

"Curiosity killed the cat."

"Knowledge is power," I argued back and even pulled my arms from the blankets that were restraining them so I was able to sit up higher and lean on my elbows to look him in the eye.

He chuckled. "Ignorance is bliss."

He wasn't going to outwit me. I crossed one ankle over the other, and my toe touched the side of his arm. "'Nothing is more dangerous than sincere ignorance.'"

Just as I was about to shift my legs away from him, I felt one strong hand reach over and rub over my foot. "Really? Martin Luther King Jr?" He smiled big at me.

"I only quote the best." I shrugged, not pulling my foot away quite yet.

It was right then that his thumb pushed into the arch of my foot though, and I couldn't control how the shivers shot through my body or how good the sensation felt. A moan escaped as I practically melted back down into the pillow. "Oh, gosh. That feels too good. So nope." I tried to pull my foot away. Of course, he didn't let me. I glared down the bed at him. "I can't handle you doing that to me tonight, Dimitri."

The goose bumps I felt over my skin, the way I was already breathing more rapidly, the way I knew I wouldn't be able to resist if he kept on.

"I can't handle not doing it." Suddenly, his eyes were a darker green and they simmered with a heat I wanted to experience. "I'm not frustrated with my workday, Honeybee."

"What's frustrating you then?"

"You walking around in your skimpy pajamas, you sleeping next to me, you being everywhere in this damn house but not with me at the same time. So choose ... me giving you a massage as a friend or fucking you against that headboard as your boyfriend. Which do you want?" I bit my lip now to stop myself from answering, because we both knew I'd pick the wrong one. "Jesus, Olive. Don't tempt me if you're not sure. Take the massage."

"Fine. But the massage is ..." I gasped when he pushed the right spot again. "Tempting enough."

"Let's focus on something else then. Why the fuck are you on a dating app?"

CHAPTER 18: DIMITRI

A damn *dating* app. Was she trying to kill me? I could handle a long workday, I could handle giving her time, I could handle pretending to be just her damn friend for a few weeks.

I would not endure watching her date other men though.

I fantasized about the woman having my damn children at this point. It was obsessive and not what I planned for, but it didn't matter. I was beyond that now.

"Because that's how people date and hook up, Dimitri," she said like I was an imbecile. "I told you I wanted to see what people had to offer. Haven't you used one?"

"I can honestly say I haven't." And she wasn't going to be using one for long either.

"Really?" She looked shocked. "Not even in college?"

"In college I was studying and—"

"According to some, you were setting fire to buildings and hooking up with every woman you could."

He chuckled. "The fire was an experiment gone wrong."

"How exactly does that happen in the middle of the night?"

"My chem professor unlocked a couple doors for us to get into a restricted part of a lab late one night, and she was showing me how two chemicals can react, but then we weren't paying attention because ..." I drifted off with the story.

See, this was the difference between me and Olive. She'd tell me all about a dating app because I was truly just her friend. I wouldn't tell her about hooking up with a woman because I didn't see her as a friend at all. After the bathtub, I'd thought of her every second of every day. And I'd worked hard to quell the thoughts, but they weren't going away. I knew that now.

"What?" she encouraged me but then narrowed her eyes. "You were fooling around with her?"

Her eyes darkened, I swear, and I could see how she was turned-on by talking about me being with someone else. She was insatiable. "You want me to tell you about it?"

She took a deep breath and closed her eyes as if she needed to break our connection. "Stop it." She yanked her foot out of my grasp and sat up on her side, causing the blanket to fall from her chest. She was wearing something completely different from what she normally did. It was a cute white top that barely covered her midriff. I couldn't look away from how bouncy her tits looked or how her thighs felt so smooth next to mine. "It's bad that I almost said yes. It's—"

"Or maybe it's good. You're finding out what you want to experience. You like me talking through sex out loud, I'm happy to."

"I would probably enjoy listening to that story, but we're staying focused on the PG version. Weren't you scared?"

"Of the explosion or—"

"Of breaking into the building with her and doing that?"

"I'll only live once," I said.

"So, you should probably try a dating app." She giggled to herself and threw herself back onto her pillow to look at her phone again. "I've had some good dates on this app. I'm actually surprised you've never tried one. How old are you, anyway?"

"Old enough to know I can fuck you better than any of the men on that app." I squeezed her leg as my mind wandered to who'd she'd been with since me. "How many dates have you gone on?"

"Oh gosh. Does it matter?" she breathed out, and I felt how her thigh shook under my touch.

"To me it does."

"Why?"

"Because I want to make sure each of those guys is forgotten by the time I'm done with you tonight."

"You've been done with me since we announced our friendship, Dimitri," she said even though her voice was breathless, and she spread her legs as I pushed her panties to the side.

I felt her slit, wanting to see how turned-on she was. "Why are you wet then?"

"Barely," she teased me. "I've been much more turned-on before. I've actually had some great conversations with guys on here that—"

I swore into the night. "Watch yourself, Olive. If I lick that pussy, it's going to be soaking, and you know it."

She singsonged, "I don't think so."

I sat up and started to inch her shorts down. She wanted to be a smart-ass, I was going to see how much of me she could handle.

"Dimitri, what are you doing?" she whispered.

"Lift your hips, honey. I want to see how wet you are."

"Really?" Instead of being embarrassed, she was intrigued, and I could see the hunger in her eyes.

Once I had the shorts off, I hummed as I stared down at her bare pussy with her tan thighs closed. Already, I saw how her clit glistened. "Not wet enough, huh?"

"No," she said in a breathy tone.

"Want me to make you wetter?"

She bit her lip. We were crossing the line again, and saying yes meant she condoned it. She nodded her head and watched as I gathered spit and let it fall from my mouth directly onto her clit. She gasped at the cool liquid running onto her and between her legs. "Already wetter, and I haven't even touched you. How much do you want me to?"

"Depends on if you can lick me there and make my pussy wetter than anyone ever has before." The smile on her face was devilish even as she blushed. I loved seeing how she wanted to push my limits.

"With your filthy mouth, I should bite you for punishment instead."

She still had that phone in her hand as I ran one finger over her slit, and she clutched it to her chest as she shivered. She wasn't paying that app any attention as I rubbed her back and forth. I was trying to keep my other hand to myself, to not completely position myself between her legs and taste her, and to keep this as just a lesson. She needed to know I was the one who'd give her pleasure now, that she didn't have to look anywhere else.

Yet, even as her hips rocked back and forth, she sighed, returning to her phone. "So, I think maybe this guy might be nice."

Fuck. Was this really happening? Was she looking at other men while I got her off?

"Show me."

Her eyes jumped over to me as she held her phone over her shoulder like she was hiding the screen. "No way." I slid a finger into her slow and her eyelids drooped as she whimpered, "None of them are going to be as good as this."

"What?" I asked. She'd murmured the last sentence, but

I wanted her to shout it from the rooftops. Damn right no one was going to be better.

"Nothing." She shook her head back and forth, her eyes closed while her hips pumped up and down on my finger.

And I heard her arousal, so soaked it made sounds with her movements. She couldn't give a shit about those guys when I was making her feel like this, right?

"Olive, come on, I'm a *friend*," I taunted her. "You said that's what we are now. Show me a match. I'll tell you if you should swipe right or left."

"You know the difference?"

"Just because I don't indulge in the app doesn't mean I don't know how to use it."

She sighed and wiggled away from me. "Fine. Be honest, okay?"

"Nope." I gripped her thigh and held her close. "You show me *while* I touch you."

"What?"

"You heard me." My voice was low and in command.

"This is a bad idea," she warned but I wouldn't agree now. She'd been sleeping against me every night for a fucking week, and I couldn't handle it anymore.

"Why? If a man isn't getting you as excited as I am, you shouldn't be indulging him anyway. I'm just giving you an example." I took my time dragging my hand up her leg before I pulled it around my waist so I could sit between her legs.

I touched a drop of arousal that dripped from her and dragged it up against her clit. She hissed and I chuckled. "I wish you could see how pretty your pussy looks right now. So ready for me."

She took a shaky breath. "Dimitri," she moaned, and her

eyes were finally on me, all warm chocolate lit with a hungry fire that I wanted to see.

"Go on." I tilted my head toward her phone. "Show me a guy."

"I don't care about that right now." She rolled her hips to get more friction on her clit, and I gave her what she wanted, pressing my thumb against the swollen bundle now. I saw how her nipples puckered under her shirt, and she bit her lip probably to stop from begging for more.

"I do." I cared that she was looking elsewhere when I only wanted her to look to me for everything. I pulled my hand away and lifted an eyebrow. "If you want to come, you're going to be a good girl and listen. Can you?"

She narrowed those pretty eyes at me before she swore under her breath. "Fine." She pressed a few buttons on her phone and turned it toward me as I slid a finger into her and rolled my thumb over her clit to the left. "Left."

"Jesus," she murmured as her thumb swiped across the screen. I kept my rolling motion on her clit as she showed me more.

"Left, Olive. Left again. Left," I repeated as her hips rode my hand, her arousal now dripping down it. "Please tell me we're going to get something better than this."

"Some of them are nice," she said breathlessly. I hummed and leaned down to suck her clit into my mouth. My tongue pressed into that sensitive spot, and I got to taste how sweet she was.

All for me.

"You don't want nice, Olive. You want this. Me making you come and telling you none of those guys can take care of your pussy like this. You know that."

"I do," she whimpered. "Please. Please."

Her hips moved faster now. I knew what she wanted, but I needed to make her work for it, show her how it felt to have me every time. Not only once or twice. Because we weren't just friends indulging. I was involved. I was obsessed. She'd become the investment I wouldn't walk away from, not this town. "That's it. So sweet that you'll beg me to give you that orgasm. Show me another match."

"Dimitri." She whined my name now, but she held up another.

"No picture with him."

"I don't know." She was past caring.

"Well, maybe he's the one. You matched with him otherwise." I slowed the pace at which I was pumping into her sex, but I slid two fingers in now. "Tell me about him."

"I don't know. I don't know, I don't know." Her legs shook, and her clit glistened with the movement. I wanted her in my mouth again, but I had to make it clear.

"What's so good about him?"

"He's tall. He's got the same interests. He's my age. I don't know why the app likes him."

I hummed. "Swipe right then. Let's see."

She swiped right fast and then threw her phone down and screamed as I pinched her clit hard. "You think he's going to make you feel this?" If she had answered yes, I probably would have brought her to the brink all night.

I slid another finger in, and her hips bore down as her hands went into her curls and she arched her back. Damn. She was beautiful when she came undone.

"It's so good, Dimitri." Her breath caught on my name, and I tried to catalog the sound of it. "So, so, so good."

"I should be doing this to you every single night I feel you against me. When you tuck in so close to me like you're all mine. You want it, don't you?" I wanted her to admit it. Because every morning I felt her jump away from me out of bed and then I had to lay there and will myself not to go after her.

"I want you, yes."

"*Only* me." I curled my fingers in her so I could pump the spot I knew was most sensitive, and her whole body tensed as she gasped and moaned my name. "You see, Olive, it's *only* me who can make you come like this."

"Yes, only you," she chanted it like she believed it. "Jesus—"

"No, baby. Me. Not a man on an app and not Jesus. I'm your almighty now. You praise *me*."

She whimpered as I tapped her G-spot over and over, and she milked out the last of her orgasm. I watched how her tits bounced with her movements, how her plump lips formed an O, how her eyes locked on mine as I held hers. She was at my mercy, and I was officially fully invested.

I was going to do most everything in my power to keep her mine. Yet, if I fucked her senseless while she looked at other guys on dating apps, I had a feeling things would get murky.

It was the first time in my life I was nervous about the risk I was taking, the first time I wasn't sure I wasn't going to enjoy the dance.

She needed to feel as obsessed as I did. She had to want this too. I had to make her understand that being just my damn friend wasn't enough.

The question was whether or not she would think so. Olive had the ability to break my heart and destroy me now. It would be her choice in the end even though I wasn't sure I wanted to let her choose.

CHAPTER 19: OLIVE

He slid his fingers out of me, and I spread my legs because I was more ready than ever for his cock. He was by far the biggest man I'd taken, and I wanted to feel him again, I wanted him to slide into me and fill me the way he had before. I craved him now, my pussy practically convulsed at feeling the emptiness his hand left.

Yet, he simply stared at me with those green eyes and placed his three fingers that had been in me into his mouth. He sucked them dry before saying, "Sweet pretty little pussy you have there, *friend*."

His voice delivered even the filthiest of comments in such a smooth and erotic way, it didn't register at first what he was saying. When it did though, my stomach flipped in revolt. Were we still just friends after that?

He squeezed my leg as if he was trying to be soothing as he continued. "I hope you make sure to hold those guys on that app to this standard. You deserve it."

I felt my whole body flare with embarrassment. Was this a brush-off now? Was I someone he was simply having fun with? If so, then he could finish what he started. I expected him to lower his shorts and position himself over me, but he actually moved back to his side of the bed and laid his head down on his pillow by my feet.

"What are you doing?" I blurted out, shooting up from the blankets.

"Going to bed."

"What? Why?" I frowned at him as he turned onto his side and stared at me. "Aren't we going to ... you know?"

"I know what?" I heard the mirth in his voice.

"Well, I just figured you'd want to do stuff for yourself after ..." I couldn't bring myself to say more, so I let the silence stretch between us until he spoke up.

"No. If we're just friends, let's call it a night. I have meetings in the morning."

I wanted to scream at him. This wasn't how this was supposed to end. He was supposed to bang me against his headboard and tell me I was the best he ever had. Then, we would go to sleep and deal with the consequences later.

I took a deep breath and tried not to care.

Maybe he had someone else in a different place that he did that with. My stomach truly rolled then, and it felt like food curdled inside it too. At least here I wasn't being led to believe there was something more between us. "Right. Of course. I get it."

"Get what?"

"Well, I know that you have women I'm sure you meet when you're traveling." Saying it out loud made total and complete sense, but my stomach twisted in knots. "You'll leave again soon. So, actually, well, thanks for even doing that with me," I grumbled in embarrassment.

"What did you just say?" he murmured low.

"Never mind." I scooted further onto my side and hit the nightstand light. I just wanted this night to be over. "Also, you don't have to sleep with your head down there."

He rumbled out, "I think I might at this point."

"I really and truly don't care if you're up here." I sat up to fluff my pillow angrily before reaching over the side of the bed to grab my shorts. Once I'd slid them back on, I threw my body back down. "It'll only be a few more nights till the mattress for the other room is here anyway."

I turned away from him and tried not to think about it. This was for the best. I should be trying to text no-face Mr. Perfect and hopefully build a connection. But then I felt rustling behind me and the wind of his pillow *whooshing* past as he put it next to my head.

Then his body curled around mine, and his arm tightened on my waist before he yanked me close. "I just tasted your pussy again and you think I'm considering flying around the country to have another woman?"

"Well ... I ..." What was I supposed to say?

His hand smoothed the skin of my stomach as I felt him shift, then he was under my blankets where he could get close enough that I felt his length against my ass. "This is what I feel every morning. Your ass against my dick nestling closer and closer."

"I know," I admitted, wincing. "I drift over to your side when I'm sleeping. Like I said, the other bed will be here soon, and we can put a pillow between us in the meantime. I'm sorry—"

He chuckled as he lowered my shorts from behind. Before I could say anything else, his bare cock was against my ass, and he murmured, "You think all I want is an apology even with my hard cock up against you?"

"I ... I don't know." I hoped he'd want more.

"I try to hide how much I want you daily, Honeybee, and it's pure torture. You're the only person I think about when I'm in bed with you, the only person I've thought about for days, and the only person I'll think about when I'm traveling."

"Oh." I breathed because now his length was moving up and down so close to my pussy, that I was wet all over again.

He gripped my hair and pushed me down to an angle so that my center was more accessible to him, and he pulled my hips up toward him. "Say it'll be the same for you, Olive. Tell me you'll think about me fucking you too."

"I will. I am thinking it right now."

"I want you to think about me sliding in and out of you all the time." He put the tip of himself right at my entrance. "Not some damn guy from an app."

"Dimitri," I breathed. This wasn't fair, and he knew it. "You're *supposed* to want me to find someone on the app."

"You don't need to find anyone but me." He slid into me then, his cock stretching me just like I remembered—almost to the point of pain but somehow with only pleasure. "I fit this pussy perfect. I make it soaking wet so that I can fuck it. I make you come so good I'm the only one you want inside you."

I moaned and cried out his name, but I didn't agree. I wasn't supposed to want him like that. We were in denial if we thought this would ever work.

Yet, I couldn't resist the desire, couldn't resist him. I let him grab my hair roughly as he fucked me from behind and took every inch of him because I wanted it. I wanted him and he knew it.

He knew he had me at his mercy.

He murmured in my ear, "Tell me I fuck you best, Honeybee. Tell me this sweet pussy is mine."

"For tonight, it's yours, Dimitri."

He growled and pounded into me harder, his grip becoming bruising on my hip. I loved the feeling, like he wanted to own what he could. "For just tonight or forever? I'm not going to forget how this feels. And you better not either. You're mine. *Just* mine."

He said it over and over as he fucked me roughly and came deep inside me. I convulsed around him then, too, crying out as bright-white light burst all across my world. The orgasm was so overwhelming that it actually hurt to come back to reality as my body relaxed. It was like I wanted his come to stay within me for much longer than a night.

I was wrong and delusional to think this would last more than just the night. I took deep breaths and closed my eyes tight as his hands drifted through my hair, then to my breast to rub my nipple, and then over my stomach to pull me closer to him.

He couldn't possibly think we were going to cuddle now.

This was over.

It had to be.

I tried my best to break away right after.

"What are you doing?" he grumbled into my neck as he nuzzled closer to me.

"I should go wash up so we can go to sleep."

"Wash up in the morning," he murmured like he was half asleep already.

I was falling asleep too. "Dimitri, cuddling after sex is blurring the lines. And I told you I don't cuddle."

"There are no lines. You're here. With me. You're mine. My cock's so far in you right now, I'd venture to say I'm yours too." He kissed my neck, bit at my ear and sucked it better, then pulled out of me. He got up to go to the bathroom. When he returned, he had a warm washcloth. He tapped my thigh. "Open for me, honey."

"I said I was going to go clean up myself."

"And yet, I'm here, doing it for you."

I tsked, not sure why he needed to, but his eyes were on my legs now, determined. "Why?" I asked as I spread them for him.

He slowly dragged the warm cloth up each thigh, then against every sensitive part of me. "Showing you what boyfriend material is."

I couldn't look away from him as he said it, as he focused on his task, as he cleaned away the evidence we'd made together of our desire for each other. "No way a guy is going to do this every time."

"I will if you want me to," he said softly. "Or I'll leave myself all over you if you want me to."

"Why would any girl want that?"

"Because it means your mine, Olive. Women want to be mine."

I hated that I got butterflies with the way he said it, with how the warm cloth dragged over my clit too. "They must know it's nearly impossible to be yours."

"Is it?" he whispered, and I didn't know what to say so I didn't respond. I let him move another clean cloth all over my body, and he did so slowly and precisely before he discarded it into the dirty laundry and then laid down next to me, bare naked still. I felt his cock again, wanted him again, almost arched into him again, but then he murmured, "Go to sleep, Honeybee. Go to sleep."

CHAPTER 20: OLIVE

He woke up before me the next morning and, when I rolled over, I knew exactly why. My phone said it was nearing noon, but I saw the visual aura as I stared at it. My head was pounding, and the migraine was back with a vengeance. I groaned in pain before I stumbled to the bathroom and got a washcloth to drape over my eyes as I laid back down in bed.

I stayed like that for probably far too long.

"Time to walk—" I heard him from the doorway. "What the fuck is going on? What's wrong, Honeybee?"

"Shhh." I kept my eyes closed and tried to will away the pain. I needed to keep up my end of the bargain, and our walks around the neighborhood together were important. "Migraine again. I'll sleep and then we can walk—"

"Damn it. All morning? I thought you were just sleeping in," he murmured, and his voice was way too close, like he'd rushed over and was kneeling next to me, like he cared.

"It's fine. I'm going to call my doctor soon and get things changed. I just need an hour and we can go—"

"We're not going anywhere." His tone was final. "I'll get you Advil." There was a pause. "Motrin? What do you need? How often do you get these, Olive?"

"It's fine." I winced though. "Just Motrin please."

I heard his footsteps leave and come back. I heard the blinds of the bedroom being closed, the door being shut, and then he lifted the cloth from my eyes. He stood there with a look of concern that I wasn't used to from him. "I got Motrin and water and an ice pack for your head."

When I reached for the pills, he shook his head and held them out of reach. "Open your mouth." He was so gentle as he placed them on my tongue and then lifted my head a tiny bit so I could drink the water from the glass. Then, he set it on the bedside table and disappeared into the bathroom to run cool water on the cloth again for me. "Close your eyes again."

"Dimitri, I'm fine. I can take—"

"I'm taking care of you now. Please just let me." He left no room for argument as he put the cloth back on my eyes and then the ice pack. I felt his side of the bed dip as sat down next to me. Then, he pulled me into his lap so that my head could rest against his chest.

I fell asleep to his fingers massaging my temples.

He was becoming a good friend. One that I would miss, but shouldn't. I dreamt of him and then woke to my headache gone, though he was too. I heard him rustling around in the kitchen.

I knew I had to thank him and tell him that what he'd done was completely unnecessary. It was more than that, it was unwarranted and shouldn't be done in the future.

I padded out to the living area, still in my small shirt and shorts from the night before, ready to tell him how wonderful he'd been. Yet, I found him at the sink, frowning down at my birth control in his normal white collared shirt and slacks. He was reading the back of it with disgust on his face.

Then he was shaking his head and grumbling to himself.

"What are you doing?" I asked, tapping my foot on the ground waiting for his explanation.

"Your head feel better?" He threw the question my way, not

answering mine.

"Much better." I nodded.

"Good. Have you read all this?" He held up my pills, and I groaned before closing my eyes and rubbing them.

"Sure ... at some point I did, or my doctor told me." As I opened my eyes again, though, I saw him popping each of my pills into the sink.

"Dimitri! What are you doing?" I screeched, frozen in place from what I was seeing.

He looked up, his eyes completely determined as he dragged one thumb hard against the packaging. I heard them pop from the foil quickly one by one. A whole damn row of birth control. "Getting rid of these."

"Are you stupid?" I yelled and rounded the island fast, trying to reach for the package but he held it out of reach and waved it in my face. "They're gone already. All down the drain."

He didn't apologize. He didn't look remorseful. Instead, he turned the garbage disposal on.

"You idiot! Those are stopping me from having a literal *baby* that I don't want."

"Interesting." He leaned against the counter, like this was completely normal. "Why don't you want a kid again?"

"You think we're going to have a casual conversation right now?" I said, my eyes wide in shock as I felt my blood starting to boil. "Is this a joke? Of course I don't want children! It's why I'm on freaking birth control!"

"Well"—he tipped his head back and forth—"people get on it for a lot of reasons. My sister-in-law—"

"I do not care." I stomped my foot, ready to shoot fire at him. "I do not want children, Dimitri."

"Why?"

"What's it to you?" I threw up my hands. "You just got rid of my birth control!"

"I did." He nodded and meandered over to the plush white couch, not one ounce of him concerned. "They're probably giving you migraines."

"You ... I ..." I took a deep breath. We had to live together, we had to be nice. I didn't need to lash out or overreact, I told myself. "I'm going to ask you to call my doctor tomorrow and tell them I need new birth control because of you."

"Oh. I do want to talk to your doctor." His misty green eyes were vibrant with an angry glow as they snapped to my direction. "I'm going to ask why the hell they're giving you a drug that can intensify migraines and blood clots."

"What?" That couldn't be right.

"Says on the back of the packaging. You're not taking that shit anymore."

"Obviously. Since you put them down the drain. That was a complete overreaction, Dimitri," I said, still in disbelief.

"Honeybee, I saw how much pain you were in. If someone causes that, you can expect a reaction more catastrophic than that in the future."

I shook my head at him, not really knowing whether to be mad or think he was sweet for watching out for my health. "You realize that's not the way to handle it? You can't just do the first thing that pops into your—"

"I've never been a person who doesn't weigh the risks, Olive. I knew what I was doing when I threw them down the drain."

I placed a hand on my hip and popped it out then. "So, you're willing to have me sleep around with no birth control?"

He got up from the couch, walked right up to me, and

crossed his arms while towering over me. "You're only sleeping with me."

"Oh, please. Even if that's the case, which it will *not* be"—he grumbled it would be, but I kept going—"what if we have a slip up? I'd be a terrible mother, and I don't want children with—"

"Me?" He was waiting to finish that sentence for me. He even smiled then, like he'd truly thought about it, like he was a deranged psychopath. "I wasn't joking when I said I wouldn't mind having a kid with you, Honeybee. You'd stick around, we'd cause havoc in this little Paradise you call home, and I'd get to see you carrying what's mine inside you."

His gaze had grown hungrier and hungrier. "Dimitri, that's ... do you have some sort of freaking breeding kink or something?"

"I didn't before. But I do now. With you. Only you." The flutters in my stomach needed to stop.

"That's absolutely not happening."

"It'd be a damn good adventure, and if you took the chance, a really fun dance, Honeybee."

"A good adventure for any guy?" My tone was rising. I felt myself losing control of my emotions again. "Because, technically, it could be any guy that I'm sleeping with!" I waved at the garbage disposal. "I could go out tomorrow and fuck someone and that could be—"

"You so much as look at another man and he contemplates fucking you, I'm going to kill him."

"That's not ... You don't get to decide who I sleep with." I shoved his shoulder now.

"Yes. Actually, I do. I'm your boyfriend," he said like it was a fact.

"Oh my God. Are you completely out of your mind?" My hands went to my curls to pull at them. "You helped me pick out guys to freaking date last night. You're my fake boyfriend!"

He hummed as if he wasn't exactly agreeing to that anymore. "Don't hum like you're not sure about it. That's what this is." I motioned wildly between us.

"You're very cute when you get worked up, Honeybee." He leaned against the counter now, completely casual.

I walked up to him then and poked him hard in the chest. "I'm not just worked up, I'm pissed the hell off."

He frowned. "You're that mad?"

"Are you fucking kidding me? Of course I'm mad. Say what you did out loud. Think about it."

"I got rid of your birth control." He rubbed his jaw. "Well, okay. Saying it out loud does sound controlling, completely mad, even unhinged. Yet, I'm finding that I am all those things when it comes to you."

"Well, I hope you feel like you made a great choice. Because now, when I go on a date with Mr. Perfect, you can think about how I'm not on birth control. And just so we're clear, I won't be sleeping with *you* at all."

He shook his head and his muscles tensed. "Honeybee, good luck with that."

Then, he walked out of the room and left me to think about our relationship for the rest of the day.

And while I was alone, my phone buzzed with a text from Mr. Perfect.

Mr. Perfect: I like the flower in your hair in that picture.

> **Me:** I'd say I like something in your photo if you had one, Mr. Perfect.

> **Mr. Perfect:** Well, Flower Girl, sooner or later.

> **Me:** Why don't you work on updating that pic while I work on my thesis.

> **Mr. Perfect:** What's the topic? Maybe I can help?

> **Me:** The nuances of a small community, how it can affect those in it. It goes hand in hand with my job this summer.

> **Mr. Perfect:** What's your job this summer?

> **Me:** Essentially getting information for a client about a community.

> **Mr. Perfect:** Interesting. That all?

I didn't get that question. Was he saying I should be doing more? I narrowed my eyes and put the phone down.

It wasn't *all* I was doing. Instead, I was faking a long-term relationship with Dimitri. Well, technically I hadn't faked a damn thing the other night. I sighed and checked my email to see when the mattress and desk would be here.

They'd been delayed. But only a couple more days.

That was for the best. Sleeping next to him proved to

be detrimental to the platonic part of our friendship. His outrageous behavior was blurred by our close proximity, and I was finding myself considering it, which probably made me even more outrageous.

That night, I went to bed early without telling him I was. I didn't have a thing to say to him. Our relationship was murky already.

Still, though, I felt him tuck me in like he always did and murmur, "Good night, Olive." And then he pulled me close and snuggled me. I didn't roll away. I slept soundly because of it instead.

CHAPTER 21: OLIVE

The next couple days, Dimitri tiptoed around me. He was tentative and overly helpful to the point of me feeling like I couldn't even be mad at him for what he'd done.

One morning, when I woke, he was gone.

Not just in the other room but had left the whole house gone. No sign of his expensive loafers or car anywhere.

When I checked my phone, I saw a text from him.

> **Dimitri:** Went to the office for the day. Text me when you're up and let me know how you're feeling. Stop by if you want.

> **Me:** I'm fine. I'll stay here and work.

> **Dimitri:** You could work on your thesis or that article here. When is the article due?

> **Me:** No. I also need to make some calls to my doctor.

> **Dimitri:** Give it a few more days for me, huh? See how you feel?

I wanted to tell him he had no right to ask that of me, but

I knew we still had to live together, and he'd meant well. After researching the side effects of every pill on the market, I knew I was probably going to wait to go back on it anyway.

> **Me: I'll do what I choose to. Are we walking together today or not?**

> **Dimitri: Sure. I'll be home on time.**

It was for the best, anyway, considering I needed to work too. I pulled the Diamond Syndicate book out again, this time along with a box of keepsakes I'd initially packed when I came to live with Dimitri.

The box only had a few things my mother had given me: A gold necklace that held a calligraphy pen she always wore around her neck, a few pictures, and her journals. She'd told me to keep them with me always and to wear the necklace if I wanted.

I never did.

I told myself it was because calligraphy was her hobby, not mine. I told myself it wouldn't look good on me. I had a lot of excuses. Really, it just felt like it was still hers all these years. Now, I rolled it between my fingers, letting myself miss the way she held the pen, wrote with it, sat up at night at her desk with it.

It hurt to feel the memories but felt cathartic too. I placed the pen back in the box but chewed on my cheek. Trying to be closer to her even though she was gone suddenly didn't seem as scary. Suddenly, it seemed right.

I pulled up calligraphy pens on my phone and scanned through them, ordering a few things. I'd try the hobby and maybe just see if I liked it too.

Then, I stared at a framed picture of my mother and me while I dialed Esme's number.

"Please tell me you're not calling about—"

"I am. And you didn't tell me almost everyone knew about this but me," I ground out.

I'd mapped out how Jameson's family was involved and also Lucille's husband Earl.

"It's not everyone. My dad, Jameson and his dad, definitely Lucille and Earl. Your dad ... well, okay, it's a lot of people you know in the neighborhood. But your mom was influential and—"

"Why didn't she tell me?" I sighed as my fingers danced over the gold etchings of the pen.

"Oh, Olive, I'm sure she wanted to tell you in her own way. She might have. Or maybe she didn't want you all mixed up in this mess until you were old enough. Look at Knox ... he's making all the wrong decisions." I heard the pain in Esme's voice then. I knew she'd been close to him, that they'd once considered each other best friends.

"What wrong decisions, Esme?"

"Not my story to tell, Olive." Esme's tone sounded guarded and stilted then, like she didn't want to talk anymore. "I gotta go, okay? Just be careful with that book." And she hung up on me.

I realized nothing would be disclosed to me if I didn't become closer with people around here. So, I got dressed in some black yoga leggings and a sports bra tank to go on our walk, hoping to continue building those relationships.

Dimitri arrived not much later, right as I was finishing stretches. "That outfit should be illegal."

"I wear this every time we walk."

"And every time I wonder if Jameson is going to take his eyes off your chest," he growled. I wasn't going to remind him that these walks were essential to establishing us in the community, that this was how we made friends, and that Jameson had always been a sort of flirty friend of mine.

"You're just imagining things." I brushed off his comment and tipped my head toward our room. "Go, hurry up and change so we can get this over with. I want to stop by the spa today, too, and see if I can take on some part time hours." He eyed me up one last time before he walked down the hall.

"What for? You need more money?"

I ignored that. He and I both knew I didn't need the money for living expenses. I needed the town gossip to include me, that would help to establish better friendships with people, crazy as it sounded. "It'll help me with the article and thesis."

He came back out from the room wearing black gym shorts and a thin light-blue T-shirt. His pecs were outlined and his arms on full display. In his hand was one of my fake plumerias. He smoothed some of my curls before he placed it gently behind my ear.

"Thanks," I whispered.

He nodded at me as if all was right in his world before holding up his pointer finger. "Let me get your water bottle. No ice, right?"

I narrowed my eyes at him going into the kitchen to fill the bottle. "Why are you helping me get ready?"

"Why wouldn't I?" He held out my black water bottle. "I'm your boyfriend, right?" As we walked out onto the porch, he put his hand on the small of my back.

"You're overdoing it behind closed doors," I told him.

"Nope," he replied and his p popped loudly. "This is how it's going to be, Olive. I'm your boyfriend. I take care of you. You accept it. Now, I'll call Madi today at the spa and have her add hours for you. She's the manager."

"Who? Wait ... just like that?" I threw my hands up.

"Yes." As we started our walk, we fell into sync, and he grabbed my hand. It was normal that we held hands on our walk, yet every single time, I got butterflies. "Just like that, Olive. I hired her a few months ago, but she lives twenty minutes away because we can't get the condos approved for renters. Yet."

"So, she'll just give me a job?"

"If I say so, she will."

"Seems a bit like favoritism."

"And don't you all do the same? I bet if you called Esme's dad asking for a job at the pizza parlor, he'd give you one."

"Yes, but ..."

"But what?"

I didn't know what. It felt weird that he'd infiltrated my hometown, that he had that much pull right away. It made me wonder even more if the Diamond Syndicate was intentionally blocking him.

Right as we got to the end of our sidewalk, we saw Lucille and waved to her. "Hey, you two. Your plants are going to need some watering soon."

We both frowned over at the bushes and flowers that had definitely seen better days. "I'll hire someone," Dimitri mumbled to me before he yelled back to her, "Olive keeps me busy inside, Lucille. But we'll definitely get to it. I'll be out of town soon, so if she needs a bit of help, feel free to remind her."

Her eyes scanned the block and then lit up. "Or Jameson can help."

Jameson sat on his porch swing next door, like he always did, reading to Franny. He heard his name and looked up. "Happy to help with whatever." He winked at me.

Lucille started to cross the street while Dimitri grumbled something that sounded a lot like, "I'm sure he would be happy to help." His hand tightened around mine before he let it go. Then, he wrapped his arm around my shoulders, and if I didn't know any better, I would have guessed Dimitri was jealous and trying to stake his claim.

"What are you two up to other than your normal daily walk?" Lucille asked as she got closer, wiping dirt from her garden apron.

It was good to hear she'd become accustomed to us walking. We'd made this our normal route because we'd strategically wanted to pass most of the board members' houses. Now I wondered if everyone on that board was a part of the Diamond Syndicate. It included Lucille and Earl, Jameson, Jameson's parents who lived a block down, my parents, and Esme's dad.

I sighed as I looked over at Dimitri's condo building in the distance. From everything that had been added, I couldn't fault any of it. There was security, a beautiful new building, and a fresh retail space that was lush with flowers, new roofs, and updated interiors.

He'd produced value. But if he brought in companies that were linked to enemies of the Diamond Syndicate, it didn't matter.

"Just talking over me picking up a few hours at the spa," I informed her.

"Oh! That would be wonderful. I'd love to have you do my hair. And how's your article coming?"

"Almost done," I said even though I wasn't. I contemplated

my conversation with Esme instead, wondering how embedded she was in this secret society.

Jameson asked, with what seemed like too much interest, "What article?"

Lucille waved him off. "Don't worry, Jameson. You'll see when it comes out. You know how I like my magazine to have surprise articles."

"We shouldn't have too many surprises, though, Lucille," he said, his voice holding a bit of warning before he continued, "By the way, you guys coming to the grill out on Friday?"

I'd seen it on the weekly community calendar and remembered we'd been invited. Dimitri was going out of town though the very next day. "Oh, probably not. Dimitri—" I started just as Dimitri said, "Yep."

"Won't you be working the next day?" I whispered to him.

"Doesn't mean I can't go out with my future wife the night before."

My heart thumped against my rib cage at his loving stare. I smiled sweetly, trying to cull my reaction as I turned to Jameson. "We'll be there." I nodded. "It's an enchanted forest theme, right?"

"Melly!" He waved at the woman who was coming out of her house. "You putting on some extravagant show at that grill out? Enchanted theme?"

Melly held on to her gardening tool like she was just out to weed the flower bed but pranced over in the tightest white jean shorts and cowboy boots. "Oh, you know it, Jameson. You planning a good costume?"

He shook his head, but her eyes were now laser focused on Dimitri. "Dimitri, please tell me you're coming. I know you've never been, and I'd love to show you how we do it here in Paradise Grove."

She blatantly ignored me.

Lucille was on to her, just like I was, though. "Melly, I'm sure Olive will show him when she attends *with* her future husband."

Melly's free hand went to her hip. "Of course. I know that, Lucille." She glared at the older woman before changing the subject. "By the way, where's Earl? Haven't seen him around lately," Melly threw out, and that's when I saw Lucille shrink a bit, like she didn't want to discuss Earl at all. He had a temper, and growing up, we heard the fights, but we never knew much else about him. He was a good man according to Lucille, and he'd been a fine officer before he retired.

"Melly, don't pry," Jameson scolded her.

Lucille nodded a slight thank you to him before she touched my shoulder. "Let me know your hours when you start working, Olive Bee. And send me your article soon. We're printing the magazine late next month," she grumbled and then stalked off.

"She's losing it, I swear. How she even gets that magazine done is beyond me," Melly whispered to us. Even if I wanted to gossip, Lucille wasn't one I would talk about.

"Lucille's always had her wits about her," I retorted, but Melly had already shifted her focus to Dimitri.

"Dimitri, I'm so, so, so excited for those offices to open and newcomers to start moving in. We need something more around here obviously."

"I think they'll do well," Dimitri informed her. "So well, in fact, I'm doing research on another community we're looking at investing in."

"Getting bored of this town already?" Jameson quipped.

"Never going to get bored with this one, Jameson. This one

has my girl's heart." He kissed the side of my head.

"Yeah. She's got everyone's heart even if she doesn't know it," Jameson said, his eyes on me. "Olive, you have some free time to get lunch this week or next? I'd like to hear more about the article you're writing."

"Oh, sure. We'll plan something soon, okay?"

Dimitri didn't say anything, but I felt his hand steer me forward, like he was done talking with Jameson for the day. "We'll see you guys later."

Jameson said goodbye, and I looked up at Dimitri as we walked, "What other community?"

"I'll show you." He got a gleam in his eye. "We can look at it later tonight and you can tell me what you think?"

A little piece of my heart lurched. "Why?" I whispered.

"You grew up here. You probably know more about them than I do."

"So you want *my* honest opinion on another huge investment you're going to make? You think I'm qualified to give that to you?" I looked down at the sidewalk and tried not to read too much into it.

"Why wouldn't I want your opinion? You might be the most qualified since I'll be wanting you around while I'm working on it."

It was a small moment, so small no one else would have noticed. Yet, the small moments made the biggest impact in a person's life sometimes. "I just ... I used to work on research with Rufford, and he would say what I thought didn't matter and—"

"I don't give a fuck what that guy had to say, Olive. Your opinion matters to me."

"Okay," I whispered because that meant more to me than

I realized. It occurred to me right then that Rufford really had never respected me, nor did my stepmom or father. But Kee had, and I'd followed her around the world. I might just follow through with Dimitri's plan, too, if he made me feel important enough.

Then Dimitri announced, "You know, I have to leave again Saturday. You should just come with me?"

"Oh." His announcement felt like a knife to my gut for some reason. It twisted in like I cared whether or not he would be here. "No. I need to stay and make sure we get the mattress delivery and finish up this article. The board meeting is coming up."

"So?" He didn't seem to care at all about the HOA and the ordinances now.

I reminded him, "So, we need to get people to vote for your condos and offices, Dimitri. I'll stay here and work on that."

"Maybe. Or maybe not," he grumbled, and for just a second, I wondered what it would be like if he wasn't there for the investment. What if he was there for me?

That day, I chose not to be mad at him about the birth control or about hooking up. I chose to consider what it would be like if I really dated him. And what I considered made my heart thump wildly, happily, and fearfully.

Yet, it stuttered to a stop as we neared my childhood home. No one was ever home when I usually passed, but now, I froze on the sidewalk when the front door opened and my brother came outside with a basketball. He'd always played, but I hadn't seen him do so at all since I'd been back.

"That your brother?" Dimitri asked.

I nodded and bit my lip. All this time, I'd been hoping to catch him outside, but now that it was happening, I wasn't sure what to do.

"Yeah, but he's ignoring me and mad at me, Dimitri," I whispered because that's all I could say without letting loose the emotions I was feeling. I hadn't exactly told Dimitri what the problem with Knox was, just that there was one. I couldn't explain to him the drugs. It felt too complicated, too painful.

And maybe he saw how stuck I was there on that sidewalk, because he didn't miss a step. He gripped my hand and pulled me a little forward before looking me in the eyes to ask, "Want to do this? Is it time to introduce me to your family?"

He was standing with me, not leaving. He had my hand in his like he was there to give me the support I needed. It made me want to move forward, to take a chance, and not run away. I took one breath before I said, "It's now or never."

CHAPTER 22: OLIVE

My brother tucked a basketball under his arm and glared at us as soon as he saw us making our way over. I tried to talk fast under my breath to Dimitri. "So, we don't get along, we haven't in years. He's not been himself lately. He won't want to talk to you or me."

"Best time to make amends is the present time," he murmured.

One foot in front of the other, I thought of what I would say when we got to the driveway.

But when we got there, nothing came out.

I stood there with Dimitri, staring at my brother, whose eyes looked much more lucid than the last time I'd seen him. But everything else was still so different. He used to be so much bigger, was still taller as he stood there, but the muscles he'd had before were gone as he dribbled a basketball in front of us. "Guess the rumors Dad told me are true." He looked us up and down, disgust in his eyes. "You moved back here for him."

I folded my arms across my chest and nodded. "I moved back to be closer to home and you *and* to be with him. Yes."

"Dad's not happy about it. Can't stand that you're basically working with the enemy." His choice in words held so many meanings—Enemy of Paradise Grove, of our family, of the Diamond Syndicate or something deeper than that? I wanted to ask but couldn't with Dimitri there. Knox just shook his head at me like I should know better. Turning his attention to Dimitri, he asked, "You enjoying the ripple effect you're having around here?"

"Just trying to make Paradise a little better," Dimitri responded. He wouldn't be deterred so easily. "You play ball?"

My brother nodded before he threw the ball harder than needed right at Dimitri's chest. Instead of getting furious like I instantly did, Dimitri chuckled and grabbed the ball fluidly. He dribbled once, twice, three times, then executed a flawless jump shot.

Although I was impressed, my brother rolled his eyes like a snobby teenager and walked over to grab the ball as it bounced away. He dribbled and jumped in the way Dimitri had to make a shot from the exact same distance. As he retrieved the ball, he asked, "So, you plan on sticking around once your investments are settled, Mr. Hardy? Or this all for show?"

"Probably depends on your sister." Dimitri shrugged, and I glanced at him in question. He had a serious look in his eyes as his gaze bounced between us. "It started out as a show."

"Dimitri!" I gasped his name, not sure what he was doing.

"We're honest with family, Honeybee. I'm being honest with your brother. He needs to understand, I was originally here for an investment but now I'm only here for you." He said it so genuinely, tears sprang to my eyes immediately. His focus now was on Knox though. "She only wanted to be here because of you. So if she stays after we figure it all out, I'll stay. If she doesn't, I'm willing to go where she wants."

"So, this between you is real now?" Knox asked me instead of Dimitri.

"Real for me," Dimitri answered. "Can I talk to you inside? Invite us in for a water?" he asked my brother.

Knox's gaze flicked to mine. "Georgette isn't home. Hasn't

been here for a few days." I wasn't sure if he was giving me a heads-up or trying to coax me into agreeing to come inside.

I chewed on my cheek before I said, "I'd love some water, Knox."

So we followed my little brother inside, and my whole body broke out in a sweat from the anxiety that rolled around in my blood. How could I know where Knox's head was at, what he'd done the last few days, how he'd felt?

We hadn't spoken since last week when he'd explicitly told me to stop calling and texting. He'd done it at our father's request, I was sure ... but still.

And I hadn't really talked with Dimitri about it either. How could I explain the Knox situation to Dimitri, who knew nothing about any of it?

Knox sat at the island and waved me over to the sink. "Help yourself. Sure you still know your way around."

I sighed and grabbed two glasses from the cupboard, one for me and one for Dimitri. I looked at Knox, really looked at him, to see if he was completely aware today before I asked, "Want water or—?"

"I can get my own water if I need it."

"Okay. How's it going, Knox?" I tried again. "You seem better since the last time I saw you—"

"You don't need to act like you give a shit if I feel better or not," he grumbled, his tone laced with venom.

"Careful." Dimitri's voice was low.

"Careful?" My brother didn't seem to weigh anything regarding Dimitri logically. He appeared aware and not as tired as when I'd last seen him, but there was no way he thought he would be able to square up to Dimitri. "What the hell are you going to do about it?"

"Look, we don't know each other real well, Knox, but I don't let anyone talk to my girlfriend that way. Whether it's a stranger, a friend, or a brother. Her father could look sideways at her, and I'm going to have something to say about it. You get me?"

"My sister can handle herself."

"I never said she couldn't. But she doesn't have to when she's with me." Then, Dimitri rubbed his jaw. "I got sisters too. And quite frankly, she shouldn't have to when she's with you either. She's *your* blood. *You're* supposed to take care of her."

My brother scoffed but his dark eyebrows dipped a bit, and I saw something like guilt flash across his face when he glanced at me. I was older, I was supposed to take care of him, and even though Knox sat back down and didn't look like he wanted to argue it, I needed to say something. "Dimitri's right. You're my brother. We haven't been acting much like siblings the past few years though. I should have come home more."

I would be the bigger person. I wiggled the flower in my hair and tried to maintain eye contact with him. Admitting to the heartache I might have caused him by leaving him behind wasn't easy, but I stood tall as I faced his response head-on.

His fists clenched and his frown deepened. Then he breathed out what looked like a load of tension and combed a hand through his short curly hair. "Dad and Georgette are a fucking lot, Olive Bee." He said it so quietly, and his jaw flexed as he whispered my name like he needed me to understand, to connect to him again. "Dad and ..." He hesitated like he wanted to say more as he looked at Dimitri. "This year has been a lot."

I rounded the island and threw my arms around him. He didn't return the hug, and he felt so stiff and small under my hold, but I still squeezed him tight and said, "I'm here now. I'll come over and—"

"Or you can come stay with us," Dimitri offered.

"What?" I gasped and my curls whipped around as I looked up.

"We've got room if you're not feeling it here." So nonchalantly he offered his house to my brother, so easily he made me think he was a different sort of man than I'd ever met. He was ready for a commitment, ready for the responsibility.

And Knox actually thought about it for more than a second, longer than he should have if he was happy at home. "Nah. It's fine. My stepmom and Dad haven't been home much anyway. I got things to do this summer, too, and my friends—"

"Who are your friends, by the way?" I asked, trying not to sound intrusive. "Esme said you two weren't hanging around much anymore."

"You talked to her? When did you see her?" His eyes were like lasers on me now, bright and aware.

"She stopped by with pizza the other night." I didn't mention the library.

He kicked at nothing on the ground as he asked, "What else did she say about me?"

"Not much." I crossed my arms. "Just that you don't hang out anymore."

He let out a small "ha" and shook his head as he looked down at those fisted hands again. "Yeah, I don't know. She got her own friends, I guess."

"Really?" I asked and then threw out, "Because she looked pretty sad about not seeing you."

Dimitri cleared his throat. "So, you play basketball?" he asked, changing the topic, before I laid into my brother. That's where the conversation was headed, because Knox and I both knew Esme was a great girl.

"Used to."

"Your fadeaway still looks decent for a quitter."

Dimitri's words had me snapping my gaze to Knox. And I saw his face reddened. "I'm not a quitter."

"You just said you *used* to play," Dimitri continued.

"Yeah. I did. I can't now." Knox puffed up his chest.

"Oh, you break a bone?" Dimitri lifted an eyebrow, waiting.

"Wow, you're extremely inquisitive today." I wanted to steer him away from this particular conversation, but Dimitri wasn't even looking at me.

"I'm working with my dad now. Plus, I'm just not into it anymore."

"Why'd you go out front to shoot hoops then? Didn't make varsity and quit?" Dimitri was egging him on. We all knew it. But I saw some of the determination in Knox's eyes that I was used to, saw a little of the competitor he used to be.

"Man, I made varsity freshmen year. Could now if I tried."

"So, you're either a quitter or not good enough. Which is it?"

"Dimitri." I glared at him.

My brother didn't let me say anything though. He grabbed the ball and said, "One-on-one. Let's go right now."

A smile more genuine than I'd ever seen whipped across Dimitri's face. "I'm going to beat you, kid."

They both walked outside, leaving me standing in the kitchen wondering what had just happened.

CHAPTER 23: DIMITRI

I knew love between siblings to be almost unbreakable, so seeing Knox and Olive at odds pushed me to invest in something I normally never would.

Life's a series of choices. You choose to put your time into a person or choose to walk away. The risks were great with staying. Your time, your love, your heart. But the rewards could be great too. Not always. But that was the risk. I didn't need to weigh the pros and cons anymore. I wanted everything good for Olive. Everything good for us.

She just needed to warm up to the idea of it. It meant I'd invest in her family too and everything she held dear. I'd take care of her—her health, her relationships, everything—to ensure she'd have the greatest outcome.

I was convinced she was the mother of my future children after all. Even if she was avoiding the pull between us and acting like what we had was all fake, even if she was talking to men on damn apps, and even if she was going to be the biggest risk I'd ever taken.

She was worth it, I thought, as Knox shouldered me hard in the chest and pushed past me to toss in a layup.

"Damn," I swore under my breath when he threw the ball at me with extra force. "Four to nothing. You're playing like you want to prove something, Knox."

"And you're playing like you never had anything to prove at all."

I smiled at his comeback. "I don't have anything to prove, kid."

"I'm not a kid. Don't call me one."

"When you act like an adult, I'll give you that title."

"You really think coming here and being a dick to your girlfriend's little brother is gonna get you somewhere?"

I dribbled the ball back and forth in front of him. "She's not with me because I'm good with kids." Although, I did want to prove to her I was good with them.

He grabbed for the ball, but I moved back and took my time squaring up for a jump shot. It sank right in.

He went to retrieve it, mumbling swears under his breath. "I told you. I'm not a kid. If anything, Olive's more of a kid than me. She's dramatic as all hell and doesn't know when to stop dreaming. She never commits to one thing."

He dribbled back to the grass where we'd both decided to be and eyed up the hoop. I took a step back. He wasn't focused. "Gotta dream big to make it big."

"She made it big to you? She's following some celebrity around and now is back home doing nothing."

Teens could be little shits. He said it so easily, as if it wouldn't hurt his sister's feelings. But she'd come outside and was standing on the porch listening to us. "You're not doing much yourself, Knox." She stood up for herself, and I was proud to hear it, but I saw the pain and anger in her eyes.

He tried to fake one way, but I was ready to block the other way and caught him. He didn't stop though. He tried to plow through me but this time I planted my feet, steadied my stance, and when he rammed into me, he bounced right off and fell back into the grass.

"I told you to watch the way you talked to your sister." I

reached out a hand to help him up, but he swiped it away before scrambling to his feet and throwing the ball away from him. "This is dumb."

I nodded at him, not willing to argue. "Yeah, sports are pretty dumb."

"What?" He frowned at me.

"I played them through high school. Didn't really help me at all."

"Well … they teach discipline and teamwork and determination." He caught himself defending the sport he'd quit.

"I guess." I shrugged. "I was able to build my empire without the sport."

"So you just got your discipline elsewhere?"

"Maybe a little from basketball. Mostly from my family. I wouldn't have gotten anywhere without their support."

Knox's eyes flicked to Olive's. "Yeah, well, maybe one day I'll find a family that does that."

"Maybe you already have one, you ass," Olive whispered. Then she glared at him. "What have you been doing when you go out of town?"

His jaw worked up and down over and over as the birds chirping around us filled the silence between us. "What's it matter to you?" He held her gaze, and it seemed she was willing him to say something further.

"You need to stop whatever you're doing."

"It's not your concern," he said the words definitely.

Their communication was broken, and I saw the pain in both of them. I saw how Olive opened her mouth once but then closed it. She was scared to push him, and I think instead she tried to convey without words how she hoped he'd see she was at least there. She was trying. I was willing to stay and try with her. It's what family needed even when they thought they didn't.

But then a black SUV pulled up, and a thin woman in a pantsuit got out. She looked at the three of us before her blue eyes landed on me.

"Hello." She stood stoically for a moment before walking over and extending her hand. "Mr. Hardy, so nice of you to come by. I told Olive we should all get together sometime soon."

"Well, I'm going to the grill out on Friday. So, maybe I'll see you both there?"

Knox blurted, "You're going to the grill out?"

"Why not?"

"You haven't been to one since you moved in." His observation showed me just how much this community was talking about me.

"Well, Honeybee can't pass up a good time." I went to stand beside her and wrapped my arm around her waist even though I felt her whole body stiffen at first. She consciously relaxed a split second later.

Knox's eyes widened. "She's going too? You realize *everyone* will be there." He said it directly to his sister and now his dark eyes lightened with the information. "All of Melly's friends."

"Yep?" Olive wheezed.

Knox snickered. "You hate them."

"No. I don't hate anyone," Olive barked out way too fast and way too loudly. I would have bet my whole savings on the fact that she did now.

Knox laughed outright then. "And it's going to be a lavish party, Olive Bee. Did you read the whole invite? You know it's in Melly's backyard with her pool and all her friends?"

The color drained from her face and Knox bent over, literally laughing his ass off. Olive chewed her cheek for a few seconds before a small smirk played over her features. Then she started to giggle. It was that sibling bond and some inside joke, the one you shared even if you were pissed at each other. They laughed harder and harder. And Knox's laugh was infectious, loud, and completely unrestrained.

"You're a freaking jerk, Knox, but I don't even care. If a laugh at my expense brings you this much joy, you can have it." She tried to lift her chin and hold her head high. "I'm completely over Melly and her high school antics."

"Sure you are." He wiped at his dark eyes that looked a lot like Olive's.

"Shut up, Knox, I am!"

"Knox, dear, shall we go make some dinner together?"

He looked at his stepmother like she was full of shit before saying, "Yeah, gotta go. But maybe I'll come to the grill out just to see this." He waved between both of us and then glanced at me with some hesitation before saying, "Nice game, and, uh, sorry about what I said before, guys. Good seeing you both."

I think Olive and his stepmother were shocked because they didn't say a damn thing as I wrapped my arm around Olive and steered her away as I waved to them.

The whole way home, I smiled like I'd won a prize.

Olive said, "Why are you smiling like that?"

Instead of holding her hand loosely like we had been, I maneuvered my fingers to intertwine with hers. "Didn't you hear, Olive? He said, 'nice game.'"

"And that means something to you?"

"Sure. I'm showing you how good of a dad I'll be. Even with a moody damn teenager." Her eyes bulged, but I kept a freaking straight face because she had to know how serious I really was. "I'm winning over your little brother, Honeybee. And that is a victory in it of itself."

CHAPTER 24: OLIVE

Dimitri doted on me for the rest of the week even though I reminded him we were keeping it friendly over and over. I had to be the rational one even if he wasn't. We were friends who'd indulged in benefits. But we were stopping that now. The only time we touched was at night when I found myself cuddled against him.

I couldn't resist it. At least not until the bed came.

On Friday, Dimitri went to the office, and I tried my best not to get nervous about the grill out that night. I also tried my best to stop thinking about him and about how he'd interacted with Knox, how he'd smiled at me after, how he hadn't stuttered at all about being a father.

I needed to be rational. So, I went back to the dating app.

> **Me: Sorry I didn't respond before.**

> **Mr. Perfect: I figured you had moved on, that I'd offended you somehow.**

> **Me: No. I've just been busy.**

> **Mr. Perfect: Gotcha. Seeing someone now?**

> **Me: No. I'm not.**

**Mr. Perfect: You sure? Normally
what happens when you stop talking
to someone on a dating app.**

> **Me: No one serious.**

At least, I was trying to make myself feel that way. I got up to shower and then worked on getting ready for the infamous grill out while he messaged me back.

**Mr. Perfect: Tell me about this
not-so-serious person. Why isn't it
serious, and how can I make sure we
get to that point.**

> **Me: Well, with him, it just can't be.
> We're not compatible. Plus it would
> ruin friendships.**

**Mr. Perfect: I highly doubt that,
Flower Girl. Highly. I think you'd be
compatible with everyone. And you
sure it wouldn't make friendships
better?**

It was an odd thing to say, but I wasn't very invested in our conversation at this point anyway. Kee was calling and I answered right away to tell her all about how this grill out was going to be the absolute worst.

"There's just something about seeing everyone you grew up with and not having a job, a real boyfriend, a freaking path, even," I said into the phone.

I walked over to the package I'd set on my dresser earlier that day and I opened it up as I listened to Kee. "You have a job. You're my assistant," Kee corrected me. "And Dimitri is *acting* like your boyfriend in front of everyone, right? I'm still mad I heard about that from him, by the way."

She knew we were pretending for the sake of Dimitri's investment. "I know. I'm sorry. It's been a whirlwind here."

She sighed. "Well don't stress yourself out. Just remember, no one knows you're faking it there. And they don't have to know."

"But I know," I whined because every girl should be able to whine to her best friend about things that shouldn't matter. It's what friends were for. "I know I'm destined to live a life of being single."

"Are we going to mope this whole phone call? You're talking to guys. You sent me pics of them."

"I know." But Mr. Perfect wasn't giving me the butterflies the way Dimitri did, not that I could tell her that.

"So focus on him."

I heard Pink yell out from the background, "And other guys too." Then Kee was scolding her, saying I didn't need to sleep around.

"Well, I am still messaging a guy. So, we'll see." I opened the package and stared at the calligraphy pen I pulled from a thin black box. "And I'm starting a new hobby. Calligraphy."

"Calligraphy?" Kee sounded confused.

"Yeah, I got the ink and the pen. Something my mother used to do."

"She's doing calligraphy?" I heard Pink blurt out. "As a hobby? See. She's bored. She's filling her time with arts and crafts. She needs men."

"I do not." I rolled my eyes and took a moment to hold the pen between my fingers and feel its weight. "My mom used to do it and I figure why not try, right?"

"I didn't say it was a bad idea," Pink clarified softly and then chuckled. "I just think you need dick in your life too."

"Well, maybe Mr. Perfect will provide that."

"Oh, is this the dating app guy?" Kee asked. "See, you got Dimitri and the dating app. You're way better off than most of the women there. Plus, you may be trying to leave me after you finish your thesis, but you're still my assistant."

God, my life was a hot mess. I thought back to how my stepmother told me to be a lawyer and wondered if she'd been right. "Keelani Hale, you're taking a year off. You have a whole damn PR team and marketing team that—"

"I still trust you and Pink more than any of them though."

My friend was forever loyal. And loyal friends were to always be valued over pride and ego. I opened the ink bottle on the dresser and grabbed a notebook from my nightstand to test out the pen. I drew *friend* on it and smiled at the curve of the ink. "I trust you guys more than anyone too. I told you, you can text or call me at any time for advice, and I'll fly out to do your hair whenever you want free of charge. Or you guys can fly here and—"

"I *have* been wondering a bit about this weird-ass community Dimitri is so obsessed with. Wonder if it's as fucked-up as the gated community I grew up in." Pink cackled before she said, "But seriously, Bane is acting weird about it too."

"Why?" I asked, because Bane was her enemy but also maybe her lover, and he was a man of mystery who intrigued every single person who encountered him.

"Probably because he knows how toxic ours was, and now

he wants more toxicity in his life. He'll probably try to buy it out from under the Hardys."

"Good luck," Kee grumbled. "Even if Dimitri isn't answering me half the time, I know how invested he is in Paradise Grove. Which makes me curious. What are you two doing over there other than faking a relationship?"

"Nothing," I blurted out as I dropped the pen and screwed the ink bottle back on tight. I needed to finish getting ready for the grill out anyway. I grabbed my purse and shuffled through it to find my lip gloss so I could put some on as I looked at myself in the full-length mirror next to the dresser. "We're not doing anything at all."

And of course that was the exact moment Dimitri came to stand in the primary bedroom's doorway. I saw him leaning against the frame looking like a tall drink of water in the middle of a desert with condensation dotted across the clear glass and maybe some ice cubes thrown in. I was suddenly hot and thirsty. "A suit?" I whispered to him.

He smirked at my lie and then whispered back, "It makes a lasting impression."

"He didn't answer when I called him yesterday," Kee told me. "And he hasn't called me back. It's unlike him."

"He works a lot," I murmured as Dimitri pushed off the doorframe and came to stand behind me. I was fiddling with tying my green halter crop top. It was a knitted fabric that had tiny gold strands threaded throughout. It was as close to the forest theme as I was getting and I was happy it matched my bikini bottoms along with bringing out the gold flecks of my eyes. Supposedly, we were all supposed to dress for her pool too. With loose wide leg pants over my bikini and sheer cardigan cover-up to match, I felt confident enough.

But then Dimitri's hand slid under the cover-up and around my waist, I gasped, and he took the phone as I heard Kee say, "What's wrong?"

"Nothing's wrong, Kee," Dimitri said as his hand moved over my stomach. I could barely make out what he was saying as my body reacted to his calloused hand, how it felt so rough but so gentle against my skin. We hadn't been touching like this, hadn't been putting our skin right up against one another's. "We're going to a grill out. So, we need to go and get ready."

He paused for a moment, just his thumb moving up and down on my hip now. And I almost whimpered, "Dimitri ..."

"I haven't gotten back to you because I'm working, but we're fine. I'm taking care of your girl." More silence. Then, "Should I be?" He chuckled and I looked up at him with question. "I'm kidding, Kee. She's safe with me."

He frowned at her next question. "Well, I fly out of town tomorrow. So, you can imagine. And she'll call you all next week. Just don't worry so much." Another pause, then he said their best friend phrase, "Not if, always when." Finally, he placed my phone on the dresser next to the mirror.

"I love that phrase," I told him because I saw how good of friends they were, that they'd become family over the years.

He chuckled. "Really? You used to repeat it every time I said it to her like you thought it was ridiculous."

"No." I shook my head. "I thought it was nice that she had a friend like you. You've always provided unwavering support to her."

"I always do for people I care about."

"What did she ask you?" I said softly.

"If I'm taking care of you in more ways than one."

"Oh," I whispered and tried to step forward, but his hand

was still at my waist and held me there suddenly. "Well, like you said, I'm safe with you, right?" I almost squeaked out.

"Safe like I'm going to protect you from getting hurt forever, or safe like I'm not going to touch you all night?"

"Both?" I squeaked, trying my best not to lean into his touch.

"My hands are already wandering all over you, Honeybee, and we're not even in public yet. So you should probably change if you don't want me touching you all night." He took a deep breath, then slid his hand away, like he was employing restraint just for me.

I felt instantly colder, like I was missing something that should have been on my skin always. "Actually, if you don't mind touching me tonight, now's the time," I said, as I pulled my hair up in a bun. "We should really look like we've been together awhile for everyone to witness here."

He stuck his hands in his pockets, his eyes scanning me again, as he sucked on his teeth. "If I don't mind touching you, *just* tonight, Olive?"

"That's what I said." I looked in the mirror at him and his green eyes were ablaze with hunger now.

"I'm dying to touch you every single night. You get that, right? You realize that every day I spend nearly *all* day talking myself out of it."

"Dimitri—" I started.

"Please tell me you're going to put on another shirt."

I grabbed for my small purse and frowned. "What for?"

"Are you serious?"

His jaw worked up and down, up and down before he dragged one of his big hands over his face. "I'm positive that if you don't cover up a bit, I won't be making a good impression on anyone tonight."

"You're a big boy." I patted his chest. "You can control yourself."

"I'm aware. I'm just not sure other men will and I'll end up mauling all of them."

"I can take care of myself."

"And yet, when you have a boyfriend like me, I'm inclined to take care of you instead."

I rolled my eyes. "There will be tons of other women there to look at tonight. Melly normally invites all her friends. You'll see. Your eyes—and every other man's—will be glued to them."

"You're the only woman who holds my attention, Olive Monroe. I don't think it's ever going to stray from you again."

I chuckled at that. He was about to be reminded that there were much prettier women in the world than me. "I think you've been cooped up too long."

He sighed. "I'm starting to think you don't have a high enough opinion of yourself."

"I have a realistic one," I told him as I slipped on my wedge heels and pointed to the door.

"Realistic? Have you looked in the mirror lately, Honeybee?"

"I just was."

"So, then you must not be looking." He stopped me and turned me back toward the mirror. "Really look at yourself, because some god took extra time on you."

"Dimitri, I'm standing at about five four to your what? Six foot four or something insane."

"Little over six six." He smirked.

"And do you work out every day for like five hours?"

"I work out enough."

"Right. I go for a light jog or walk only to spy on the neighbors and my family."

"I'm starting to think you're as nosy as Lucille."

How dare he. "I'm doing it for you."

"Keep telling yourself that."

"Anyway, I appreciate you trying to make me feel confident, I do. But it's not like I'm fighting of the masses."

"You seemed to have a lot of matches the other day."

"To hook up," I told him. Didn't he get the point of the app?

"So you just want to hook up with them?" He narrowed his eyes. "They're not worth it."

"Oh my God. That's beside the point."

"Do you really think Kee would want you going out and taking a chance—"

"You told me I should be taking chances and enjoying dances."

"What fucking dance are you seeking?"

"Well, hooking up normally leads to a great—"

"Don't finish that sentence," he ground out.

I blew a raspberry and waved him toward the door. "Let's get walking before I decide these heels and this party aren't worth it."

His eyes were on my legs. "The heels are fucking worth it all right. The party? I'm not sure."

When we walked into Melly's backyard that night, I expected her to have gone all out because every person who volunteered to host a grill out normally did. But even I stood there with my mouth open for a minute. Her backyard was larger than most as she had the woods behind it, but she made sure to showcase the expansive estate nestled among the lush trees. Lights were threaded in the woods, illuminating a path with a sign pointing into it saying, *Enjoy the enchanted woods.*

Women dressed like fairies held champagne trays and one sauntered up to us immediately, her task obviously to greet guests. "Welcome to Fairy Land," she said and waved at the glasses she held. Smoke flew in front of her wand over our drinks and somehow they sparkled into the night. I took two because I knew I would need them.

Dimitri shook his head and smiled down at me. "She has enough for both of us."

The fairy fluttered away, but my attention was on him. "I don't have enough. You should have taken one. You're going to need it."

He chuckled. "I enjoy a party." He shrugged as I watched him take in everything. The pool's sleek curves were lit up by an ever-changing colorful light, and there were five waterfalls cascading into it. A transparent floor was seamlessly suspended over the water, and people walked across it, oohing and aahing at how it held them.

"Eep! You both made it." Melly's high-pitched voice could be heard from the house as she barreled across her patio to come hug Dimitri. She had to stand on her tiptoes to meet his tall frame, and she folded into him perfectly, her shimmering white pearl fairy dress much more revealing than mine. "Do you like the theme?"

Dimitri nodded and I agreed with him. "Sorry we didn't dress up much." I shrugged. Women were dressed to the nines, but the men hadn't really indulged. I saw Jameson from the corner of my eye as Melly rambled on about how she had a live band for the whole night. Jameson rolled his eyes, and I snickered.

But Melly kept going on and on. She had Dimitri's full attention because why wouldn't she? She was a tall, beautiful brunette who knew how to flaunt what she had. And then she snatched even more of his attention as she said, "We are holding a little impromptu meeting about some of the points that will be addressed at the next board meeting soon. I'll put in a good word for you, okay?" She placed a hand on his arm, and my body instantly wanted to rebel and lash out at her. She was touching what was mine. Didn't she know that?

But I took a deep breath. This is what we were here for, to engage with the community. Even so, Dimitri stepped back and put his arm around me. "I'll be at the board meeting. In three weeks, correct? I'd love an invite to yours, too, if possible."

"Oh, that's just a couple of us girls. We get together every now and then. But I'll speak highly of you, promise. If you'd like, we can catch up on your plans for the condo and office building in a bit. I think that's the biggest concern right now, correct?" The woman had an uncanny knack for ignoring me, and so I knew inserting myself here would do us no good.

I tried to step away quietly, but Dimitri's hold on my waist tightened even as he continued to talk with her. "I hope it's of no concern once I let everyone know how rentals will work. And the office building will be the same, but I don't believe we'll be renting it out much at all. Most everyone working there will be a part of the HEAT empire."

"Oh, I know that," she said like they'd been partners in his business for years. "We just have to convince everyone else, right?" Her laugh was so soft and perfect as she leaned into his side.

"Of course." He shrugged.

"Now, I have to mingle." She waved at another guest. "But catch me for a dance later so we can talk about this more, okay?" She fluttered her eyelashes.

That's when I stiffened, and I knew Dimitri felt it. "I probably won't," he admitted to her with no remorse on his face. "I intend to dance with my girlfriend all night."

Melly quite literally said "Oh" as if she was surprised to find me there. "I'm sure Olive won't mind letting me sneak you away for a dance or two though."

"It's fine." What else could I say?

"She wouldn't mind, but I mind letting her sneak off with another man." Melly looked as if she'd been turned down in front of all her best friends. Maybe she had. Rina and Willa were actually right beside her. They were tall and skinny and stunning in their own ways. Just as Melly was.

Neither of them, like Melly, made any attempt to say hello to me even though we'd all been in high school together. "Well, either way, we'll see. Olive, so glad you could make it too. Watch your step next to the pool tonight." She bustled away, and her friends followed as Dimitri kissed my forehead.

"You're laying it on too thick," I murmured to him.

"No. I think it's just right. You're mine around here. They need to know you deserve the same amount of respect I do."

"They don't give me any respect at all, and they never will. Melly is a lost cause, hence her pool remark."

"What happened with the pool?" He frowned.

"Melly used to live with her parents a few blocks over. They had a pool too. She invited Olive over and then pushed her in during prom pictures her senior year of high school," I heard Knox say from behind me. I turned to see him standing between my stepmother and my father. He stood tall with a small smile on his lips, and he winked at me like he and I had a secret to keep. "They're assholes."

There it was. My brother exactly the way I remembered him. I pulled him in for a hug and he let me. Something was different about him tonight but also completely the same as he used to be. I might have held onto that hug a little longer and squeezed him a little tighter. "It's really freaking good to see you tonight, Knox."

"You just saw me." He laughed softly. "Don't be dramatic." But he patted my back like he understood and let me hug him extra.

It may have been dramatic, but I didn't just mean it was good to see him here at the party, I meant it was good to see him looking aware, looking like he could handle socializing, looking like he wanted to be out in public.

When I pulled away, my father hugged me and said he was happy to see me too in a clipped tone. His tense jawline led me to believe otherwise as he and Dimitri eyed each other up.

My father was a tall, good-looking man. His dark wavy hair and bright brownish eyes the same color as mine had always landed him acting roles when he was younger, especially with his charming smile. Now, as a director, I think he held most people's attention and respect. It was what made his career and what broke his family. Women had always thrown themselves at him, and he never resisted. Not when he was with my mother and not now with my stepmom.

It's why I still couldn't look him in the eye with respect, even when he tried to be consoling and sweet to me. I never forgave him for not being there for us at the end of my mother's illness, and maybe he never forgave me for not forgiving him.

"Good to see you, Dimitri. Olive tells me you two are sharing a house for the time being." He extended his hand to shake Dimitri's.

Dimitri shook it but said, "Well, we're sharing more than that, Mr. Monroe. She's been my girlfriend for quite some time."

"Right. It's not something either of you has mentioned over the last year to anyone in Paradise Grove or it seems I would have heard about it?" There was question in his tone.

I watched Dimitri smirk, and a gleam shimmered in his eyes at the challenge my father threw his way. "She was traveling with my best friend, Kee. We wanted to make sure it was serious before we moved in together and let family know."

"I'd still like a call from you, Olive, with news like this. You should respect your father enough to do that."

Knox sighed and groaned, "Dad."

I tried my best not to explain myself immediately. It's what I would have done had I still lived at home. I would have tried to smooth things over and take care of everyone. Now, it felt futile. Knox was already struggling, and I'd already left.

Dimitri didn't have me contemplating what to say for long. "Respect goes both ways."

Dad narrowed his eyes at Dimitri and turned to my stepmother. "Why don't we go get a drink? We can rehash family business another night. This one is for fun. Right, everyone? Olive, call me this week." He held my gaze before he nodded to Dimitri, then he turned to Knox.

They exchanged a glance, but Knox shook his head. It wasn't the first time I'd seen that look in my father's eyes, and it wasn't the first time he tried to quietly throw his weight around. He grabbed Knox's arm, but my brother, although he'd lost muscle, still yanked it away from my dad.

"Knox," I said softly, because that look I'd missed—the one where he was sort of himself—died right there as he stared at my dad.

My father glanced around and then waved him off before smiling big and turning toward the bar with his wife.

There was silence between the three of us now even though the party's loud music and laughter filled the air. The tension was louder than any of the surrounding revelry. My gut twisted at thinking of what Knox and my father might have been going through. "Knox, can you—"

"Don't. Just ... let's talk a different day." A frown wrinkled his forehead as he stared at our dad.

"Dad's probably just stressed." Why was I making excuses?

"Doesn't matter." He glanced away, and I saw the moment he recognized two men I'd never seen before. He perked up like suddenly he had more energy. Normally I would have been happy to see him excited, but this was too much. He waved to them before he turned to me and hurriedly said, "He'll forget about it tomorrow when he's packing to be on the set of another movie." I took a deep breath and Knox patted my shoulder. "Go enjoy the enchanted woods, Olive Bee."

I cleared my throat as I watched him hurry off. "I'm going to go make sure he's okay," I said to Dimitri, but he caught my arm and pointed.

Esme was beelining toward Knox on a mission. "I think she's about to do that for you." I chewed on my cheek, not sure if I should intervene. "He's got to make his own decisions."

"He's making the wrong ones, and I wasn't there before to steer him in the right direction."

"Sounds like you were a kid growing up too, Honeybee." He nudged my shoulder. "And you're here now. When he inevitably falls further down the shithole he's digging, we'll be there to get him out."

My eyes snapped away from Knox to Dimitri's as he said we. "Oh, you don't need to be a part of this. It's my problem to—"

"Your problems *are* my problems." He smiled down at me, and I wasn't sure if this was just for show or not.

I shook away the thought and sighed as I looked on at the whole town packed in Melly's backyard. "Sorry. Everything here is so much more complicated than you probably thought," I whispered. "My father is ..."

"Don't be sorry for someone else's actions. They aren't your responsibility." Dimitri pulled me close to whisper, "Now, want to dance on that ridiculous dance floor?"

"Nope." I couldn't shake those terrible memories of falling in no matter how long ago it was.

Dimitri stared at me as the melody of the band swelled with a slow song. "Come on. I'll hold you close. Won't let you fall overboard. I promise."

"I'll pass."

He hummed. "But Olive, aren't you the least bit interested in the *experience*?"

"Seriously? I'm not that curious about everything," I grumbled, but now I was thinking about it and wondering a little. "Maybe you could go out there and tell me?"

He shook his head. "I go only if you go."

I glanced around and didn't see Melly or any of her friends. And the people standing on the clear plastic were doing just fine. Yet, I didn't like how the platform only covered about three-quarters of the pool. Sure, there was a bit of a clear ledge so people wouldn't fall in, but years ago, that wouldn't have mattered. My fall back then had been epic.

Still, I couldn't pass on the opportunity and sighed. "Let me put down my purse." I walked over to the lounge chairs and realized half of the guests were now in swimsuits. It was unusually warm for springtime, sure, but Melly had also been squawking about how the pool had been "heated to perfection." My being in a bathing suit was a smart decision in case I did fall in anyway. I shimmied out of my pants and coverup and went to go meet Dimitri at the edge of the shimmering water.

When he saw me, he stalked off the dance floor and started marching me back to the lounge chairs. "No." He shook his head. "Absolutely not."

I halted as I chuckled. This man made me feel like my ego should have been bigger, like I was worth it even if I didn't have a job, didn't have anything to brag about at this virtual high school reunion masquerading as a grill out. "Stop it, Dimitri. Don't worry about what I'm wearing, and let's go dance."

"You're in panties and a bra, Olive." He pulled me over to the side of the backyard. "How the hell am I not supposed to worry about that?"

CHAPTER 25: DIMITRI

"It's a bathing suit—like every other person has on here. And if I happen to fall in the water by some ill-fated turn of events, I don't want my stuff all ruined."

I'd stared at Olive all night like she was mine. She was sleeping in my bed. She was sharing my food. My home. *Our* home now. I'd started to see little things of hers everywhere. Her flowers in a bowl on the bathroom counter, her clothing in the drawers, and her notes about her thesis everywhere.

She had invaded my life, and I couldn't look away, not even for a second. She had started to become mine. Not just my fake girlfriend. My real one.

It's why I unbuttoned my suit jacket and practically growled as I stared at her. I wanted to jump at whoever looked at her longer than they were supposed to. I held it out. "Put this on."

"What for?" She looked incredulous. Or confused. I wasn't sure which. "I don't even know why you're wearing it. It's like seventy degrees and balmy."

My blood began to boil thinking about her not listening to me, my muscles tensed. "Because every man out here has their eyes on you."

She glanced around in disbelief. But I know she caught how Jameson waved at her. Motherfucker. I didn't care how nice he was to his kid and everyone in town. The man barely worked. What type of hours did he have when he was on his porch every damn day, anyway?

"Dimitri, no one is looking. Even if that were the case, who cares?"

Who cares? Did she think it was okay for men to ogle her? "Are you kidding me right now?" I harrumphed. "I do. Me. Your boyfriend. You're mine, and I'm not here to show off every part of you to anyone else."

"But, Dimitri, this between us is—"

"Say fake, Honeybee. I dare you." Something percolated in the air between us, and she knew it. I pulled her close and slid my hand up her body to her collarbone and then to hold her neck. The view of us to anyone around must have been extremely intimate when she shivered at my touch. She couldn't deny this. Couldn't deny us. Couldn't say everything was fake between us when I squeezed just a little and she gasped.

Her eyes darkened and narrowed, and I wondered if she was going to meet my challenge. "Well, it *is* fake." She pushed me with a smirk on her face, and I felt how the blood rushed through my veins. Didn't she know I lived for this sort of thing?

I brushed a thumb over her lips slowly. I was proud she'd defied me. Then I took the jacket I was still holding behind her and stuffed her right into it.

Challenge met. I was going to make it completely clear to everyone that I didn't want them staring at her.

Her mouth dropped open. "Seriously? This is absolutely ridiculous, Dimitri. You shouldn't even care." She stomped a foot.

"And yet here I am ... caring way too fucking much," I whispered to her. "I actually just decided. I'm done tiptoeing around making you feel comfortable with this. So, you better learn what that means."

She crossed her arms. "Oh really? You just deciding we're going to do this for real? *This* between us is for one purpose only." She narrowed her eyes and looked around before pulling me away from the crowd and into a dark corner of the backyard near some shrubs where no one was paying attention. "It's serving me by allowing me to do a new thesis because you have some ridiculous strings you can pull around this country, I guess. And this serves you by allowing you to win over this community. That. Is. It."

"I don't think that was really ever what this was for," I said back, looking her up and down. "I had ulterior motives from the beginning after I heard you scream my name in that hotel room."

"Well, you shouldn't," she clarified, like she had a choice in the matter. She didn't. She was going to have to start understanding that. I was going to protect her now and call her mine every chance I got. "You should just be worried about the board, okay? Having me in a damn corner all night is not going to help with that."

"You half naked isn't going to help it either," I threw back just to rile her.

She shook her head and whispered, "Actually, it totally would if you'd go along with it. It would even be to our benefit. Maybe if I flirt a bit, I'll get people to lighten up at the next board meeting, Dimitri." She wide-eyed me as if trying to refocus me on our original goals. "If I'm being honest, I know we're both jealous people. Just don't think about it." She blew out a breath as her cheeks brightened.

"You don't want me walking around talking with anyone either, and you know it. I can see how even the thought irritates you."

"It doesn't." She did a terrible job of being convincing. "Just stay focused on the true objective, which I guess is to mingle and dance happily around on that flimsy see-through platform. Let's show everyone a good time."

I narrowed my eyes. "Show who a good time, exactly, Olive? Because you're not flirting with anyone here but me."

"What do you mean?" Her hands fisted together now as she whisper-yelled at me. "Couples do it all the time. I'll get in good with the men tonight. You get in good with the ladies. Next board meeting, you might have a leg up."

"Not fucking happening."

"And why is that?"

"Because I might be invested in this community, but I'm more invested in *you* now," I murmured almost to myself as I pulled the lapels closed around her. Looking directly into those mesmerizing eyes, I intoned, "From now on, you're mine for real. I'm going to treat you like it, too, whether you like it or not."

My tone was direct, commanding, and left no room for argument. Every person who knew me well knew I saved it for when I meant business, because normally I was pretty laid-back.

Olive didn't seem to get the memo. She crossed her arms and looked up at me like I was a damn idiot. "I didn't agree to that."

"You're going to now, though." My hand slid under my jacket and smoothed over her skin slowly before I pulled her close to my side and started walking her back to the dance platform. I felt her body stiffen, her hesitation palpable as we approached the pool.

Someone had ruined her confidence long ago, and I was

going to get it back for her now. I rubbed my thumb up and down to the beat as I glanced at her and murmured, "I got you. Take a chance and enjoy the dance with me."

I waited for her to take the first step, then I synced up with her right away. Slowly and with purpose, we walked out onto the clear platform, and my grip on her waist didn't waver at all. She needed to understand that I would either catch her or we'd fall all the way through together, but I'd be there to save her nonetheless. More than anyone else had.

Once we were in the middle of the platform swaying to the song, a smile spread across her face so big that I knew nothing was going to stop me from having her. "I think I like conquering fears with you, Dimitri."

I hummed. "Be prepared to conquer all of them with me," I said softly before kissing her in the middle of that grill out, for every single person—including Jameson—to see.

Then I dipped her fast and pulled her up to kiss her again. She giggled the whole time. "You know, you're not thinking straight tonight." She still tried to be the voice of reason.

My hand dipped even lower on her back and then I pushed her against me. She gasped as she felt how rock solid I was against her belly. One of my hands threaded through beautiful curls so I could tilt her face up to mine as I bent close to her ear to say softly, "I'm thinking as straight as my cock, Honeybee. I've got every single one of your curves pressed against me, and I'm convinced all the men here have been cataloging the slope of your neck and the flare of your hips and the way you can rock that ass back and forth fluidly in those damn heels."

"Dimitri," she moaned my name, "this is to better your investment."

"Right. I'm fully invested in *you*. So, find another way or don't. I don't really care at this point. But let me be clear, you flirt with any man here, I'm going to choke him out for flirting back."

She pulled away to look at me, to try to find the lie.

There wasn't a single one.

She sighed and murmured, "You know what? Right now I don't care. Because we're dancing over a freaking pool." And something about the way she finally relaxed in my arms led me to believe we'd turned a corner. She and I were going to be a force together.

So, I fell into step with her. Maybe we should have talked it through more right then, but we weren't immune to the pull we had on one another. We deserved that moment, and we took it.

We didn't simply dance. We waltzed and then fox-trotted and then let loose when the beat changed. We both genuinely laughed when I finally wiped sweat from my brow and told her I wasn't going to keep up with her dancing all night.

I took her around to mingle, always staying at her side, and she talked to every single person she could about how anything HEAT-related was a great addition to Paradise Grove.

I wasn't trying as hard. Or at all. "Relax," I said as we walked away from Esme and her dad. "You've made an impression on at least fifty families tonight."

She looked around. "You think?"

"I know. And you approach at the right angle every time."

"My article will be perfect too. You'll see."

"I have no doubt. You're quite good at just about anything you put your mind to." She'd been a jack-of-all-trades for Kee, for her mother it seemed, for her family, and for me now.

Laughing, she shrugged. "I told you, my family raised me to know a little bit about everything." She took two flutes of champagne again and smiled at me when I lifted a brow. "Oh, don't comment on my alcohol consumption. I'm at what feels like a high school reunion, okay? Plus, I need to go to the bathroom. Which means I guess I have to go into Melly's house, huh?"

"Want me to go with you?" I'd escort her just about anywhere while she wore that suit. I'd walk into the bathroom with her, help her take it off, and maybe have a few minutes of fun too.

"No. Stay and mingle." She smacked my arm. "Stop avoiding what we came here to do. You haven't been trying all night. Just go be nice to someone. Tell them what they want to hear."

I didn't care to do that at all anymore. "We'll see."

"Dimitri, it's the only way for us to make this work." She popped out a hip, and I stared at her with those curls blowing in the wind and that smile on her face like she might be relaxed enough with me to let loose now. Except she was still working angles on this deal we had while I was purely enjoying her instead.

"Make what work, exactly?" My mind was only thinking about making things work with her.

"To get your condo rentals and office spaces approved," she whispered and wide-eyed me. Then she downed her champagne and set the flute on a standing table. "When this is over later, you'll thank me. Now, let's hope I don't get lost in Melly's ridiculous house."

She spun and set off to make her way inside. The woman was on too much of a mission tonight. I didn't like it. Not when I realized my mission had shifted. I was less and less concerned about this community and more and more concerned about her.

And I didn't like it. I was feeling like my ego was being knocked down about ten fucking notches as the thoughts raced through my head. I knew she'd messaged Mr. Perfect again on her app tonight too.

I shouldn't have known that, but my obsession with her was borderline unhinged.

No, completely unhinged.

I wouldn't apologize for it either. She might have been reminding me that this was only a transaction between us, but I was about to remind her that we were so much more than that.

CHAPTER 26: OLIVE

Why did Melly's house have ten hallways and a hundred rooms before I found the bathroom? And why did the bathroom have to look perfect?

Her house was decorated in soft neutral tones and beautiful arches in the doorways and gemstones that popped with just the right colors on the counter of the bathroom as I peed. Plus, she had a pool. And her life together.

She'd told everyone tonight she'd just landed another great client for her advertising business. And I could only admit in the quiet of this bathroom that I was utterly jealous of all of it. Of every single person I'd mingled with. I'd pasted on a smile and told everyone how amazing they were doing. Yet, I felt the burden of my own future crushing my soul. The thesis and the leatherbound book had me wondering where exactly I belonged.

I took a deep breath and straightened my outfit before flushing the toilet, washing my hands, and splashing some cool water on my cheeks. Stop moping, I told myself. I was here, I was working, and I was forging my own path of life. Just because the road was a bit rocky didn't mean it was lesser than someone else's.

And then I heard whispers outside the door. "Esme! How are you? I saw you by Knox." She responded with something noncommittal and then the woman said, "Right. Right. He'll come to his senses. He always does. Can't say the same about his sister though. My God, right?"

"What about her?" Esme replied, her tone off.

"Well, Knox told me that their father isn't happy about that relationship. So, I'm sure Dimitri and her won't last. I mean, come on. How could it? The girl's a mess."

"Why would you say that?"

"She's still getting her master's. I also heard she slept with her professor. There's no way Dimitri *Hardy* stays with that. I'm just hoping my girl Melly can sway him tonight. They would be the cutest couple."

That's when I chose to swing the door open and try my best to stand tall as I walked out and away from them. Esme called my name, but I didn't want to hear what she had to say right then. I just wanted to get out of there.

I knew I wasn't a ten in anyone's book. I knew this whole grill out was going to feel like a damn high school reunion gone to shit, but I'd come and I'd been a part of it. I'd done it and now I wanted to leave. Yet, just as I turned the corner, I heard my name from Melly's mouth.

"I did push her accidentally on purpose into the pool once. It was so long ago, though, and you know how teens are. I was a brat but turned out okay, right?" Her voice snaked out like a conniving purr, and I knew right then who she was talking to.

"Sure," Dimitri said back to her. His tone was noncommittal, but I hated that he'd even agreed.

"So, please tell me it's not that serious between you two. She just doesn't really seem like your type."

"She *isn't* my normal type," he responded, and my heart cracked a little.

"I didn't think so." Could Melly sound more excited? "She's cute, but I see you with someone a bit more, I don't know, comfortable in their own skin, right?"

"In the past, it's what I went for. She's definitely different."
Different didn't feel like such a good thing when he said it like
that.

"I think at some point in our lives, we would have made a
great match, Dimitri. And to think of all the stuff we could have
done around here." Her laugh was so soft and muffled, like she
was right against him. "Maybe we still could, hmm?"

I hated that I thought the worst as the silence stretched.
I didn't even really give myself more time to think about it as
I cleared my throat and walked into the room. Melly gasped
loudly and jerked away from him with a smile on her face as
she wiped away her red lipstick, and I glanced at his shirt to see
a smudge at his neck.

"I'm leaving," I whispered because it was all I could get out.
And then I stalked off toward the patio doors, beelining for my
purse, pants, and cover-up as fast as I could.

I heard him call after me, but I didn't want to talk to him.
It wasn't that he owed me anything; we weren't really together.
It was that he was doing that with her, a woman who was well
aware that we were supposedly together, yet she was maliciously
trying to hurt me again. And he was allowing it.

I stormed out, ready to go grab my belongings. I didn't
get far at all though. Dimitri sped up to me, his eyes filled with
worry as he raked his hands through his hair. I couldn't tell if
that look was because he was guilty or because he didn't want
me mad or to make a scene.

I couldn't be for sure of anything, not when my heart
cracked with betrayal.

I was going to cry. My life was an absolute disaster. I was
spinning off in so many directions that I couldn't keep any of

them straight. That girl outside the bathroom with Esme was right.

And just as the first tear fell, Dimitri walked right up to me and said, "I'm carrying you to the enchanted woods, Honeybee. Don't fight me."

Then he scooped me up like a child and walked right down the glowing pathway. I don't know if anyone looked or saw us, and I didn't care.

I needed a moment while I crumbled. After that, I would deal with the fact that the man who was saving me from complete embarrassment in this moment was the man I hated because he'd caused it.

I wove through the woods Melly had in her backyard and passed two large bar areas, one that seemed to be offering cigars too. The grill outs were obviously a way for each of the neighbors to show off extravagance.

Not that I cared much about that anymore.

I was more concerned about the shimmer I saw in my girlfriend's eyes as I carried her to a secluded area and plopped her down in front of me.

"You should have let me leave," she murmured and wiped away at her eyes. "I just need a minute to collect myself."

"I'd rather spend a minute with you collecting yourself then another second with the people at this party."

She hiccupped out a laugh that sounded like it was mixed with a sob. "They never got to me before my mother passed, you know? I didn't care if anyone made fun of me because I knew I could go home and tell her about them. I knew I could call her or ditch class to get home to her. I knew she'd tell me it was fine that I had, that I never should have to surround myself with people who aren't worthy of my time."

I nodded and let her pace back and forth in the grass. "She sounded like she was a good mom."

"The best. And you know, now that I'm back, I keep finding out more and more about her."

"Like what?"

She looked away for a moment and then said, "I think

she truly would have built us a bubble and protected us from everyone she felt would wrong us. And I sort of hate that she can't be here to do that, because ... I think Knox needs it." She sighed.

"It's okay for you to need that too, Olive." I stepped in her path now and touched my hand to her cheek. "And it's okay to miss her. But you don't have to run from me or from how someone out there is making you feel. You're entitled to be here just as much as anyone else, you know that?"

She shook her curls back and forth. "You don't get it. Melly's right. You should be with someone like her, and you probably want to be."

I slid my thumb across her smooth skin to wipe away one tear. "I wouldn't touch that woman with a ten-foot pole, Olive. You could drag me across hot coals at this point instead of having me look at another woman, honestly. You have my attention 24-7, and I'm struggling with how to not act on it."

She closed her eyes tight and murmured, "Her lipstick is on your collared shirt, Dimitri."

"Fuck me." I groaned. Melly had tried to lean in and kiss me, but I'd sidestepped her, and she'd fallen into my shirt. "I didn't do a damn thing with her, you know that, right?"

"You know, in my heart, when Rufford cheated, I knew. Right away. With you, I knew right away too, Dimitri. It just ... it hurts to see the idea of it and to see she'd be that cruel still. I know, though, you wouldn't cheat, even if this was only fake."

"But you know it's not fake with me and you, right?" I needed to hear her say it now.

She nodded instead and looked up at the sky. "I don't know if I can add one more complicated thing to my life though. I can't ... What would we even tell Kee?"

"I'm not worrying about that now, Olive. I'm just enjoying the dance." With that, I pulled her close and kissed her softly.

She gripped my shirt and moaned into me. When she stepped away for a second, she murmured, "You know, my brother and dad and Georgette would actually tell you that you're indulging in my dramatics tonight."

"Hardly. I was the one who carried you into the woods."

She giggled. "Like a caveman."

"Because I am one when it comes to you. I'd fuck you in the woods if I could." She bit her lip before she glanced away. "You want me to do it?" I asked as I touched the blush on her cheeks that was suddenly there. "I've been waiting to fuck you all night."

"We aren't supposed to do anything else, Dimitri," she whispered. "Remember, you crossed the line with the birth control. It was completely reckless, and even if you're reckless, I shouldn't be. Melly's friend just said that in there. I'm a perfect example of a mess. Complete chaos. And even still, I'm about to give into you because I'm getting to the point where I can't deny myself."

"Good. Don't deny yourself. Give in. How are you supposed to experience everything you want to after Rufford without giving in to me, huh?" I wrapped my arm around her waist and lowered my face to her neck. She tilted her head, giving me instant access to drag my tongue over her soft spot. "You going to deny me even while standing here in Melly's backyard?"

She licked her lips so slow. "If you try," she glanced around, "I might run."

"But if I catch you, Honeybee, I'm taking what I want." I dragged my hand over her chest and then twisted her nipple through the fabric. She gasped as she watched me do it.

"You want this? Me? All my chaos over Melly?" she said, a vulnerability in her tone, like she needed to hear it. "Tell me, please."

"I only want you. I'd run through the damn woods for you, chasing you like I'm as unhinged as you tell me I am. I want only your pretty pussy. I want to fuck you against a damn tree and make you scream my name for everyone to hear."

She was panting now and clinging to my suit jacket. "You'd do that here?"

"I'd take you anywhere. But *especially* here."

"Melly could find out you did that in her backyard," she warned, but I saw how her nipples puckered as she said it, like she wanted that woman to know how we truly were together.

"I hope she does find out, Olive. I hope she does. You have five seconds to run. When I catch you, I'm not going to stop until you scream."

She didn't even let me finish. She bolted off through the woods, and I only counted to three because I wanted her that bad.

I sprinted through the grass in my expensive loafers, not caring about anything but catching her. I swerved around some hedges before the forest thickened a bit. I heard a branch break under her weight, then a gasp once or twice.

I turned in the night at a snapping branch. When I heard her breathing turn rapid as she ducked behind a large tree, I walked slowly toward it. "Honeybee, you can't hide from me. I'm always going to find you. Don't you know that?" I reached around the tree and grabbed her arm. She yelped as I pulled her to me. "Caught you," I murmured against her neck.

She didn't face me as she said, "So take what you want." She bent at her waist and put her hands on the tree.

I took my time getting rid of her bikini bottoms, sliding them inch by inch down her thighs. "Look at how you get ready for your boyfriend even after you ran from him."

"Well, it's only for a little while," she murmured but I heard the taunt, and I loved her goading me, loved that she wanted me to fight for her.

I also wanted to punish her for that statement, so I smacked her ass in response. She gasped and wiggled her ass like she enjoyed it. "It's for however long I say, Olive. Remember that. And remember, you might run from me, but you like to be caught by me, and ..." I moved close to her, completely lost in the sight of her bent and ready for me. I thrust in fast. "Fucked by me."

"Oh my God," she cried as I filled her to the hilt. I didn't stop as I untied her bikini top and slammed into her harder and harder while holding on to her tits, squeezing them like I wanted to consume every aspect of her.

It wasn't just a want now. It was a damn need to own her. I fucked her in those woods like I would never let her be free and growled in her ear, "Don't run from your boyfriend again, Honeybee, unless you want me to fuck you like this over and over."

She cried out that she was coming, that she couldn't stop, that I shouldn't stop either. She begged for me not to stop over and over until we both were spent and collapsed on the forest floor.

I barely could move as she murmured, "So much for not screwing around in private." Then she groaned. "And being safe with a freaking condom."

She slapped my chest, but I wasn't going to apologize. "I'm clean, and I already told you, I'd have a baby with you. You want to remember condoms, just tell me, Olive, but I'm probably not going to at this point." I chuckled because I wasn't afraid of babies with her. I wasn't afraid of anything with her at this point.

"That is the absolute wrong approach."

I hummed. "I'm going to fuck you anywhere I can, Honeybee. Anytime I can."

Didn't she understand that already? That girl controlled me, not the other way around.

CHAPTER 28: OLIVE

I was standing naked in the woods next to my fake—but maybe now real—boyfriend contemplating if I could handle being pregnant with a baby of his when I heard her.

"Dimitri. Dimitri!" Melly was literally singsonging his name through the enchanted woods, and there was absolutely no way I was going to right my bathing suit in time. "Go out there and talk to her."

"What? No way," he said as he trailed a finger over my breast and took his time enjoying how I shivered under him. He was smiling and truly had no concerns about having a family with me. He looked relaxed, even; like him shooting his come in my not-protected-from-pregnancy body was a good idea.

"Seriously, go." I shoved him fast. "Oh my God, she's going to come back here."

"So what? I'm not going over there. She's a parasite of a woman that infects your head with thoughts that I might be interested in her over you anytime I look her way. I want nothing to do with that. Not when we're talking about having babies together."

"This is not a joke!" I said but I caught myself giggling. "Just go. I'm not concerned about Melly anymore. I believe you want nothing to do with her now. I just screwed you in the woods on her property." He smiled as his eyes glazed over. "Get it together!" I shoved him. "If you don't get your ass out there right now, her and her friends will see me naked in her freaking woods." I scrambled to right my top and then glanced around for my bikini bottoms.

"It's a damn good sight to see though." He smiled and tucked himself back into his suit pants. He wasn't bad to look at either. I saw how my arousal still glistened on his cock, how his abs flexed as he looked down to buckle his belt.

I tried a different angle. "You know, I bet she's with a couple of guys too. You be happy to let them have a look at me?"

There was that look of jealousy I shouldn't have loved so much.

"Fuck me," he growled and hurried to button up his shirt before he walked around the bushes. I heard him greet the group of what sounded like all women.

Of course that was my luck, but I was able to get my halter top back on and my bikini bottoms back in place. And that's when I heard it. The softest whisper of angry voices through the trees toward Lucille's house.

Immediately, I thought of Earl. I heard a deep low growl of frustration. I jumped over a pile of leaves and tried my best to tiptoe in my heels.

When I got near enough to Lucille's side of the property and leaned in though, I heard Jameson's voice. It was rougher, meaner, and not at all like the Jameson I knew. He was always so mellow, bouncing Franny on his leg, joking with me about our high school memories, but now his voice sounded menacing.

Maybe I shouldn't have eavesdropped, but this was what a small community was all about. Plus, Lucille was nowhere to be found and his voice was coming from her yard.

"That's not going to hold up."

"Well, I don't really care at this point. I'm tired of hiding him anyway."

I knew something was off about Earl. She must have been keeping him indoors for some reason.

"Lucille, knock it off. It's going to be fine. This was my idea in the first place. Let me follow through with it before you get jumpy."

"It was your idea. But I'm quite proud of my implementation, so I'll go down for it if we can't get a person here by next week."

I froze mid step and tried to lean into the shadows now. What was next week?

"My guys will be here next week," Jameson confirmed, and I saw how he pinched the bridge of his straight nose. "Don't worry about it."

"Melly is watching my every move. If I keep him in the basement much longer ..."

My mind raced with what they could be discussing. Was she holding Earl hostage? Was he going against the secret society? I should have immediately gone to call the cops. Yet, I wasn't exactly sure that's what was happening. I didn't want to jump to conclusions and the sheriff knew Lucille. Everyone did.

Instead, I needed to make sure, do some research, read more about this society. Could I ask Dimitri for help?

That's when I knew I'd drank too much. He couldn't know about this society. He'd destroy it. And I didn't want that for our town. The realization shocked me, and I hiccupped at the thought. Freaking hiccupped like a child.

And then I heard a tiny voice by my legs. "Excuse you. Also, who are we spying on?" Franny, the little sweetheart that was just as curious as I was and shouldn't have been following me, said.

Both Lucille and Jameson's heads snapped toward us.

"Franny," Jameson said, and then his voice got lower.

"Olive Bee. What are you doing?"

"Well, Grandpa and Grandma said we go to the party too." She threw one tiny hand over her shoulder to point as she talked fast like she knew she'd done something wrong. "They talking to Melly sooo long. I saw Olive and wanted to spy with her! I like playing spy!"

"And what good spies you were." Lucille smiled at both of us, but her eyes were on me, and they held something darker than I wanted to be a part of. "Why don't you all come into my house? We'll get you some yummy treats and discuss everything you learned."

"Oh, that's okay." I tried to back up a step, but Jameson was faster. He hurried forward and grabbed my elbow.

"We insist, Olive," he said loudly for his daughter to hear. "We'd love to have you try Lucille's secret cookie recipe."

And with that, he dragged me forward into Lucille's home. I wiggled my arm the whole way. "Hey, what are you doing?" I finally managed to free myself once he practically pushed me through the doorway and shoved me into a seat at her dining room table.

"What were you listening to us talk about?" Jameson sat down across from Lucille's wooden table to glare at me.

"Nothing," I blurted out fast.

Franny immediately sat down in front of the TV and turned it on to watch cartoons. Lucille hummed about in her giant kitchen, moving around a few jars to pull out a cookie for Franny. Then, she turned toward me, her hand a little shaky as she asked, "Want a cookie, Olive?"

"No thank you." I cleared my throat and glanced around, trying to not make eye contact with either of them.

Lucille's house was immaculate with pretty little statues

everywhere, not a speck of dust on any of them. She had antique furnishings that seemed to fit her personality perfectly. It was clear she'd been collecting beautiful pieces for years. Gold-framed art adorned every wall and matched some of her painted wood furniture.

I'd never really taken a moment to see everything she had here, though, because she kept her and Earl's life pretty private, which I now questioned more as I saw how her embroidered drapes were drawn shut.

"You had to have heard something if you were listening, Olive."

"Jameson, you know how I am." I chuckled nervously. "I just heard something and wanted to see what it was. I'd got to the corner of Melly's hedges and, well, you know."

He was searching my face for the lie, and I remembered Esme's words. I suddenly knew I couldn't just sit there and let him interrogate me. I'd crack.

Lucille came over to pat my shoulder. "She's fine, Jameson." It was her mother hen tone, the one she used on most of us in the community and we all sort of fell in line when she did. "If she heard anything, she would have told us. Honestly, it was just me and Jameson discussing a bad stock trade that he and Earl made. A bit embarrassing, but nothing to get worked up about, right?"

Jameson squinted at her.

"She grew up with you, Jameson. She's not going to think any less of you, right, Olive?" Now Lucille looked at me with a wobbly smile. "With that curiosity you have, though, I should have you helping me write the Paradise Grove News every single quarter. Not just the next. Would you like to? We could get together maybe on Monday and talk out your next article along with other things?"

"Well, I have my thesis to work on, and I'm starting to do hair at the salon—" I stumbled over my words just as the doorbell rang.

"What do you think, Jameson?" Lucille asked as she walked to the door.

"I think that's a very good idea." He crossed his arms and stared at me like I was suddenly a criminal rather than his friend.

"Oh, Dimitri, hi," Lucille announced, and Dimitri peered in. His muscles tensed when he saw Jameson and me at the table.

"There you are," he said slowly as his eyes ping-ponged between us.

"Yes, Jameson and Olive were just catching up. Franny wanted to come over for a cookie."

Franny held it up at the TV and didn't even look our way.

"Olive, I have an early flight in the morning."

"Right, and I'm starting to get a migraine. We should get going," I said as I rubbed at my temples. Truly, I was starting to see spots as my alcohol wore off and my mind raced. I shoved the chair back fast. "I have to stop back over at Melly's to grab my cover-up and—"

He held up my things. "Got them, Honeybee. Said bye to your family too. Time to go home to *our* bed."

Jameson scoffed but he got up and gave me a hug as he whispered, "I'll be texting you about meeting for lunch very soon."

"You really getting a migraine?" I asked her, immediately concerned that the birth control change hadn't worked.

"No." She shook her head fast. "It was just a way to get out of there."

"So, you didn't want to catch up with—" I stopped my question as we walked across the street to our house, and instead we both stared at the large box in front of our door.

"I think that's our mattress."

I sucked on my teeth before nodding, not wanting to think about having her sleep on it upstairs tonight or any other night.

"I'll bring it in tomorrow morning."

She shook her head. "I can help you after I change."

"No. I'm fine bringing it in myself, Olive."

"Whatever." She waved off my offer. "I can carry one side and you the other. It'll be easier with two people, and I should open it so it can air out. The foam ones normally smell a bit weird for a few days."

I knew my jaw was clenching up and down. "Go change, Olive. I'll get this up there myself."

"But—" I lifted the box and her jaw dropped at how easy it was for me. "Okay show-off. I guess it's easy for you to carry it all by your freaking self," she grumbled as she threw the door open and held it for me.

I stomped up every one of those stairs, pissed that there would be no reason to keep her in the primary suite with me now.

"Go shower, Olive," I told her again as I heard her creeping up the stairs. "I'll set this up."

She sighed and stared at the box like she didn't exactly enjoy the idea of it, but then she nodded and disappeared down the hall. It didn't take her long to rinse off or me to pull apart the cardboard box and rip open the plastic to find the mattress practically unfolded itself as it absorbed air.

I came down the stairs with the garbage and said, "You're right. It's going to take a few days to air out. No one will sleep up there tonight."

She narrowed her eyes. "Dimitri, if this is—"

"By the way, what the hell were you and Jameson discussing at Lucille's?"

"Oh, um, nothing." As always, she jumped right in with her answer when she lied.

So, it was obvious their conversation was intimate. "You expect me to leave that alone after you got jealous of Melly?"

"It wasn't jealousy. It was ..." She drifted off with her explanation and looked away from me.

"What?"

"I don't know. Insecurity? A feeling of no self-worth, probably?" Then she winced as she let her feelings show. "Okay, maybe a little jealousy."

"So you don't want to tell me what you and Jameson discussed?"

She shook her head no and stretched her arms above her head. Then, she rubbed her own shoulders. "Maybe later. I'm pretty tired."

I stepped in and rubbed them for her. "It's okay if you don't want to tell me." It absolutely wasn't. I was honestly considering firing up all the security I'd installed throughout this community but hadn't turned on because of the HOA's holdup on the approval. I could have seen why she went into Lucille's and how close she and Jameson had been standing.

My investment in Paradise Grove was going to shit already, but I wasn't about to lose the one thing I wanted most in it. And after her meeting with Jameson, suddenly, she was a closed book when I wanted her fucking open. I couldn't figure it out. She had been completely willing in the woods, like she wanted something more with me and now I was going to pry information from her.

"There's nothing between us, Dimitri. He doesn't want me the way Melly wants you."

"I don't believe that for a second. There'd be something between you two if he could have it that way, Honeybee."

She looked up at me with those beautiful eyes and smiled softly. "I don't think so. If it makes you feel better, I thought I heard him talking about something, so I was eavesdropping. He just wanted to know what I'd heard."

"You were spying on them?"

"Well ..." She shrugged and hummed as I kneaded her shoulders a bit more before I pushed my fingertips into her curls so I could massage her scalp too. "It wasn't really spying. Just listening closely." She had no boundaries. "Plus, what if I heard something about the board? It would have helped us."

I shook my head at her. "Don't go snooping around while I'm gone," I frowned, thinking back to Jameson's stare tonight. "Jameson didn't look happy about you listening."

She chuckled but I saw how she glanced away.

She wasn't telling me something and that thought infuriated me. Sometimes I could swear she was more reckless with that curiosity than I was with the risks I took in my business.

I tried to give her space as I made calls that night and did things I shouldn't have done. I wasn't going to leave Olive unprotected. I showered in the upstairs bathroom and toweled off before going to the primary suite with the towel wrapped around my waist. She'd already gotten into bed and had the light on her nightstand turned off.

She texted away on her phone though. For some reason, after what we'd done in the woods, I wanted all her attention. "Who are you texting?"

She looked over her shoulder at me as I laid down with my head right beside hers. She didn't say anything for a second as I scooted close. "You're lying up here again?" she whispered, her breath shaky.

I love that I affected her in the same way she affected me. "I won't have you in my bed for a while. You think I'm going to pass on sleeping up against your ass on my last night?"

"How romantic." She chuckled as I yanked her close to me.

She turned her phone off right away. "Who's got your attention over me?"

She hesitated for a second before she said, "No one."

"Mr. Perfect?" I lifted a brow. "You texting men on that dating app while you're dating me for real now?"

"Um, we sure that's happening? What you said in the woods doesn't have to be serious. We can go back to—"

"I was serious. Better tell that guy so. Or you plan on meeting him while we date?"

"I don't know." I felt her shrug and then she admitted, "I've never casually dated before. Rufford and I got serious fast. I don't know if someone is going to be okay with me sharing a bed with another man."

"Another man who happens to be your boyfriend." I slid my hand into her shorts. "And happens to know how to play with your pussy just right."

"Dimitri—" She sighed but her legs opened immediately for me to touch her clit before sliding into her pussy.

"Damn, you're already wet for me. You can go ahead and tell Mr. Perfect our relationship is exclusive."

"I shouldn't. We should just see where this goes, Dimitri. It's too new," she clarified. "If you go out with someone and it works better with them, we can stop. It'll be much less complicated anyway. If I go on a date with him, I'll stop too."

"Would you?" I whispered as I nudged my cock into her ass. "It seems this is working out pretty good for you."

She moaned as I pinched her clit and then she rolled her ass harder into my cock. "It is. It's so good," she murmured.

"What is? That I fuck you better than any man you've been with?"

"Yes." She rode my hand in her shorts faster, but I wanted her to realize I would give her more than she ever could get from someone else. I slid my other hand down her ass cheek and let my thumb graze over her other hole.

Her whole body quivered as she gasped, "What are you doing, Dimitri?"

Her voice was unsure, but I knew right then, no man had ever fucked her there. I knew right at that moment, too, that no other man ever would but me.

"I'm giving you an orgasm before I leave," I said against her neck.

"But I've never ... No one's ever done anything to me there."

Hearing her admit it had me pulling my cock out from my shorts and nudging it against her right there. I wanted to feel it pucker on my tip, so tight and soft at the same time.

"Well, if you're going to start fucking around with other men, you'd better know what you like beforehand, right?" I'd never let another man touch her. "I'm your boyfriend. I'm the one who takes care of every part of you now. And I'm going to show you, Honeybee, just what you like." She'd like only me. My cock inside her. Where I belonged.

"I want you again, Dimitri. Get a condom this time."

I listened to her right then, but I wasn't sure I always would.

CHAPTER 30: OLIVE

That night, he gave me orgasm after orgasm, and I fell asleep with him still massaging my pussy like he wanted to give me more.

I dreamt of him, moaned for him, whimpered and begged for him. It felt so good having him sliding in out of me, calling me his.

"My cock belongs in you, Honeybee. You feel how you take me? How you stretch for me?" he told me in my ear. His dick was so huge and rock hard that I had to bend myself over further in the bed as I laid on my side to take all of him.

"You feel so fucking good bare, baby," he murmured. It sounded so real, felt so real and raw. There was no way it was a dream.

I opened my eyes in a flash. "Dimitri—"

He pumped into me harder, holding my hair. "Take it, Olive. Don't act like you don't want it."

My pussy wanted it. It was practically clenching around him as my ass rocked back to meet his thrust. "You have to stop right at the end."

"Shut up, baby. Just shut up and take my cock like the good girl who wants me to fuck her like I am."

How could I stop him? His arm was around my waist, his other hand in my hair, and then he flipped me onto my stomach and thrust into me harder. "I think you want my baby."

"Dimitri, I don't," I told him. But then I moaned so loud.

"Want me to stop?" His voice was controlled he thrust in again.

"You have to. We're going to be done with each other sooner or later."

"Not if you're having my baby, Olive. Not if you're carrying what's mine. When you are mine."

"I can't. I won't be good at it." I felt myself starting to hit my high though, felt myself losing control and toppling off the edge. "Harder, Dimitri. Harder," I told him because I wasn't good at denying myself this pleasure. I couldn't.

"Tell me to stop," he growled.

And now I was pushing my hips back to meet his just as fast. "Don't you dare stop. Don't you freaking dare."

He came in me hard and then took his time pulling his cock from me afterward. He didn't let me turn away when he did either.

He took his finger and dragged the come dripping from my pussy back up into me. "I hope you're fucking pregnant, Honeybee. And I hope you know I'm not letting you go. Not after this investment bullshit is over. And not ever."

He got out of bed like nothing had changed.

And I really tried to act like nothing had.

Yet, the next day, I woke to him quietly packing up his suitcase, all dressed in his suit and tie while I still laid there wrapped in the plush comforter of our bed. And my heart rebelled at him being gone. Fear snaked through my veins while thoughts of him leaving for good invaded every corner of my mind. Doubt will sneak up on a person and choke out their joy.

He kissed my forehead, brushing those rough hands over my cheek before he murmured, "Should I fold you up in this blanket and take you with me?"

I tried to hold onto the haze of our lovemaking bubble without sounding panicked. "It'd hardly be a work trip then."

His head tipped slightly like he was considering that. "Even still, sure you don't want to come?"

The fact that I wanted to follow him around on business trips and make sure he was only with me, that he wouldn't abandon me, and that I would be the only thing on his mind was enough for me to say, "I can't. Thesis." I tucked the blanket under my arms and held up fingers to tick off. "Article. Board meeting prep. Desk delivery."

"I can take care of all that remotely." He placed both hands on my pillow and caged me in. "You could come, and we could make a stop to see Kee to tell her—"

With that, I let go of the haze of our lovemaking bubble. It literally popped, and the gravity of the situation spread in the air, making it hard for me to take a deep breath. "No." I squeezed my eyes shut. "It's ... this is the time to take it slow, right? And you'll be working most of the time, Dimitri. You have to work, don't you?" He groaned like a child not wanting to do homework. "Plus, seeing Kee might not be such a good idea." I looked away, not sure how to broach the subject.

"Still don't want to tell her a single thing about us?" His forehead fell onto mine.

"Let's just take it slow." Or back away from the idea entirely, I thought when I considered the outcome. If I was this fearful of losing him now, I'd end up devastated when this was inevitably over. "No one needs to know right now. We should see how things go before announcing it to our close friends."

"Because you think it won't work out?" He shook his head against my skin, and I felt the scruff on his jaw, making me shiver.

"I'm just trying to be cautious."

"I think you're trying to protect that pretty heart of yours by not committing." He finally pulled away and studied how I reacted.

What could I say? I'd been burned before. "Let's keep it casual right now. Give me time to see, please?"

"Casual?"

"Yeah. See if you want someone else when you're flying around. See if we miss each other. See how we do." The words almost tasted like acid coming out of my mouth, but it was for the best.

"I could answer all those questions now," he said. He combed a hand through his hair and relented. "I'll try, Honeybee. For you."

CHAPTER 31: OLIVE

I threw myself into every task I needed to accomplish while Dimitri was gone. I called my doctor to request a different birth control. I walked every day and bothered my brother. He'd turned over a new leaf after the grill out, it seemed, and would play H-O-R-S-E with me every morning now. Then, I would go home and rewrite the article and then my thesis, day and night. I went to the spa to talk with Madi about doing hair and I knew the drill by the end of that day. I worked myself to the bone so much so that I didn't even have time to miss him at all.

I didn't miss him lying next to me in the bed, didn't miss his snuggling, didn't miss his scent, didn't miss his outrageous mouth. Didn't miss one thing about him.

And every time he called, I made that clear by not picking up. Every time he texted, I responded with one-word answers.

Instead, I practiced my calligraphy and didn't even jump when the phone rang. I'd stare at my mother's journals and look at her own calligraphy pen that she'd handed down to me. I didn't know why there was so much she didn't share with me, but I knew I wanted to learn. I knew I wanted to focus on that instead of anything else. I slid the necklace on and went out about my day, touching it every now and then like the weight of my mother was with me now.

Dimitri had been right, I was trying to protect my heart from more trauma. I didn't want to fall in love with him and lose him. I'd endured it once and didn't know if I could again.

Maybe my plan of avoidance would have worked had I not gotten a call from Zen. She informed me that on her days off from the library, she also worked at the spa, and that I already had a client. She needed me to come fill in halfway through the week because Madi wasn't able to make it.

I pulled my curls back and threw on a black maxi dress that I could move easily in. Then, I speed walked to the salon, trying to avoid seeing anyone from the grill out a few days ago.

I didn't need to run into Lucille or Jameson just yet, not when they were concerned about what I'd heard. But of course, when I walked in, not another customer was in the spa other than Lucille.

The quiet symphony music played in the background and Zen waved me in, while Lucille lifted the tiny sky-blue teacup in her manicured nails as a welcome. "Come in, darling. We have a few things to discuss."

I hadn't stepped over the threshold onto the marble tile quite yet, but Zen yanked me forward and slammed the door behind me, locking it.

The clinking of the china on the paper-thin saucer as Lucille set it down was distinct with no other chatter in the salon. "So happy to hear you're available today, Olive Bee. I need a trim."

I glanced at Zen and placed a hand on my hip. "Really?"

Zen winced and wrinkled her nose before starting to straighten some of the plants on the white granite countertop. "Esme might have disclosed to Lucille that you know a little something about the library stacks."

"Might have?"

"Come on now, dear." Lucille fluffed her blonde curls, not one gray hair to be seen even though I knew she was well past seventy. The woman was particular about some things, especially when those things were in Paradise Grove, threatening her harmony.

I played with the gold fountain pen on the necklace as I stood there, not sure how to proceed. "I don't know that much, Lucille," I admitted.

Lucille's gaze zeroed in on the necklace, and she gasped, Then, she pointed to it before curling the finger toward her, beckoning for me to come closer. "Is that your mother's? Are you ... You're finally wearing her fountain pen."

Her voice shook in disbelief, and then her blue eyes shimmered with tears. One of them tracked down her face slowly. When her hand clutched her heart, I didn't hesitate.

I approached her fast, bending at the knee to meet her gaze and grab her frail fingers into mine. "Lucille? Are you okay? What's wrong?" It didn't matter if we were keeping secrets from one another, it didn't matter what I'd heard the other night or what would happen in the future, I cared for the older woman beyond all that.

"It's nothing." She waved her other hand in front of her face. Then she pulled at the small chain of the necklace at my collarbone and held it up as if I should understand. "Your mother just ... she wanted this, you know?"

"I don't understand," I whispered and looked at Zen with concern. "Can you get her some water?"

"I'm fine." Lucille took a deep breath before she squeezed my hand in hers and let it go so she could grab part of the fountain pen. "Did you open it?"

I frowned and looked down. "What are you talking about?"

She sighed before she carefully unscrewed a part of it and in there was a small rolled-up scroll. I frowned as Lucille pulled it out and handed me the tiny paper. "Your mother was always creative. She loved her calligraphy, you know. She wanted you to have this letter when it was time."

"Time for what?" I stared down at the letter Lucille held out to me but didn't take it from her. My hands shook as I stood and stepped back, away from the weight of what that note might hold.

"She said once you came home, Olive Bee, came back to her, it would be time for you to read it."

"I don't ... Maybe I'm not home for good," I blurted out.

Lucille frowned. "You're starting a family, no?"

"I don't ... I don't know." I gasped at the words I let fall from my lips, because they were the truth. I might have been playing pretend with Dimitri, but I didn't know anymore. "I ... I truly don't know if I'm ready for any of it."

"Oh, sweet girl." Lucille stood and pulled me into her arms. For some reason, the fears and the pain and the trauma of what I'd been through flowed out of me. I let Lucille hug me and share the weight. I let my old friend shoulder some of the pain my heart had held on to, and sharing it felt like I could breathe for just a second.

"Let it out, Olive Bee. No one's supposed to bottle any of this up." Lucille hurried me over to the waiting area. We sat down together as she said, "She wanted you to go where your soul desired until you were ready to be back here. You're ready for all of it now."

She pulled my hand into her lap and opened my closed fist softly before placing the rolled-up paper in my hand. "Read it."

A mother takes care of her family, Olive Bee.

You needed to see the world and I hope you did. I hope you flew through it and saw every corner.

I didn't tell you about the Diamonds because as a child I wasn't afforded the opportunity to live without the responsibility of being a part of the Diamonds. I wanted different for you and Knox.

The Diamond Syndicate and your father agreed. I hope they've upheld their end of the bargain. Your responsibility should have only been to love life and live it how you wanted. You'd come back when you were ready for the responsibility of more. It seems you have.

I trust you to make the Diamond Syndicate what you believe it should be for the next generation. Now, you're home.

"What does this mean?" Her words flowed through my veins, filling in gaps of pain and questions of the secrets she'd kept but they left stains of more questions, droplets of fear of the responsibility that I knew shouldn't be mine.

Picking at the tweed of the white skirt she was wearing, Lucille sighed. "Being a part of this influential society means making hard decisions. She didn't want that pressure placed on you before you'd seen the world, found out who you were—"

"I still don't know who I am." I cut her off with what I shouldn't have admitted. I shook the note in my hand. "I truly have no idea. And I make terrible decisions, Lucille. I was sleeping with my professor, and he cheated on me. Did you know that?" I don't know why my mouth decided to blurt that out, but the rambling couldn't be contained as panic set in. "I mean, did you hear Melly the other night? I'm chaos and don't know up from down, Lucille. I can't even keep the plants alive in front of our house. I'm noncommittal to a fault. I can't decide if I want to be a journalist or hair stylist, if I want to be here or not, if I want to be with Dimitri or not, and if I'm capable of having a b—" I stopped. Lucille and Zen were both leaning in like they were watching the good part of a movie and taking notes.

"Oh, honey." Lucille cleared her throat, frowning like she was disappointed. "That isn't being noncommittal at all. That's just figuring out what you're willing to commit to. Thank God it's not a professor who doesn't treat you well. Who cares if you can't keep a plant alive? Just means you have the wrong plants in your yard. Which reminds me, we'll get some cacti for you. Start there. Much easier in this type of climate, I promise. Plus, you'll need to learn to be a bit pricklier now."

"What for?" I shook my head in confusion.

"The hard decisions are made with the weight of the responsibility that comes with them. You'll have to embrace that. You should have, quite frankly, when Melly was being a little witch the other night."

I looked toward the ceiling and recalled what I read in that book. They were making huge monetary decisions that impacted millions socially and personally. I tried not to be rude as I told her, "This isn't for me, Lucille. I can't be a part of this. My mother was wrong if she thought—"

"Your mother was not wrong. If you weren't nervous, I'd be worried," Lucille said. "You're ready for anything life throws at you now, Olive Bee. I know you are because I heard about how you handled Melly at that grill out.

"What did you hear? Because all that happened was I went to cry in the woods!" I threw up my hands.

"Yes." She patted my hand. "Good. You still feel all the

things you should. Let yourself feel them. Your mom was concerned about that."

"Concerned about what?"

"Well, that you would bottle it all up. It's my thought you should let the anger out a bit more though. It's what you did in the woods after. I heard you made it known who you're with. It was quite clear, my dear. So, sometimes it pays to be prickly, like the cacti I'm going to help you grow." She smiled to herself like she'd just given me the best advice. "Anyway, you'll learn to be as you make hard decisions with us as time goes on. We've made partnerships with extremely large companies. Your grandparents and their grandparents are—"

"Are intertwined. I saw in the book and did the research to piece together what's happening."

"So you know," Lucille reached out for the water Zen brought in a clear pitcher and poured some in two glasses she set down. "We can influence state ordinances, make sure some people have more power and—"

"Others don't." I finished for her. Generation after generation kept business dealings quieter and quieter. We all knew our families came from money, but I recalled the times I asked my mother.

"Your grandparents were wealthy, Olive Bee. We're all very fortunate here. It's been a morality issue in the past, that's for sure. We've struggled to maintain power over other groups like mob families and there has been concern, as you can see, about Dimitri. His sisters are married to Armanellis." She cleared her throat and straightened. "I have found them all to be quite pleasant, but, well, some others don't agree. That's why, at some point, you'll take your family's seat within the Diamond Syndicate here in Paradise Grove. Your father won't serve that role anymore. You can make decisions instead."

And then I heard the rev of a motorcycle, one I'd heard only a few times before, but I knew the sound. Jameson didn't ride it every day. Mostly, he kept it in the garage, unless Franny wasn't with him. He pulled up right in front of the salon and cut the engine. In a black tee, black helmet, and with the tattoos on his arms on full display, there was definitely a formidable quality about him.

Zen rushed to unlock the door, and he walked in, pulling his helmet off, his blue eyes focused only on me. "Good. They got you here."

"Guess you couldn't wait for lunch," I grumbled, not sure if I should feel like I was in some type of danger. My high school friend was a lot bigger than he used to be, and I knew he probably held sway too. Yet, I wouldn't shrink away.

He set his helmet on the counter and leaned on it as he looked at us. "So, Lucille fill you in on what you need to know?"

"I just started, Jameson. It's ..." Lucille paused and looked at the note again. "It's a delicate matter. Her mother wasn't like your parents."

"I'm aware." His hands fisted together before he admitted, "I wished I'd had a mother like that. She shielded you from a lot."

"I'm seeing that." I crossed my arms. "Not sure if it's to my detriment at this point."

"Well, she probably didn't know you'd get involved with a Hardy and that he'd be involved with the mob."

"Barely a mob when they're reformed," Lucille said like she'd been won over by them long ago. "I've told you this, Jameson."

"I heard you. And I'm inclined to believe you. I'm just

wondering if Olive is truly in bed with the enemy or not. It's all very coincidental, her being with Dimitri. It either means she's working against him or with him. And in turn, against us or with us."

"You can't honestly believe she's faking the chemistry she has with him for intel for her father, Jameson." Lucille chuckled. "We just talked about this. She doesn't even know her father is involved with the Irish."

I froze, The drink I had in my hand clattered onto the table, water spilling everywhere. "What?"

"Oh, Olive Bee. Sorry to drop the news." She sighed and grabbed for the napkins Zen was hurrying over. "Only a few of us are confirming this, but I do believe it's true."

At that point, I saw how Jameson's jaw flex. His muscles coiled like they were ready to strike, and then he paced over and sat down in the chair beside me, sharpening that blue stare on me. "Are you giving your father information, Olive Bee? Or trying to sway Dimitri out of town?"

"I don't know what you mean," I said, completely confused. We'd faked a relationship but for the complete opposite. "I want Paradise Grove to prosper, Jameson. It's the reason I'm here, and the reason I think Dimitri's offices with the Armanelli businesses are a good move."

As I said the words, I felt the truth of them settle like cement in me. Jameson wasn't as convinced though, and his hand shot out to the leg of my chair to pull me close. I gasped at our proximity and was reminded of the appeal he'd always had.

Darkness lurked behind those blue eyes, wild and vicious. I knew he must have had deep, cavernous secrets that caused pain, that he hid, that he could tap into. He'd let that darkness out with the right instigating, I could tell. "Olive, I want honesty.

Don't lie to me now. You and Dimitri, that's real?"

There was no lie as I nodded and whispered yes. Even if I was scared as hell of what that meant, I knew I couldn't fool my heart. "If I'm going to have a family here with anyone, Jameson, it's going to be him."

"We'll see," he growled before he sat back and flicked his gaze over to Lucille before saying, "I'm not here to intimidate you."

"Really?" I blurted out. "Sure seems like it with the stare down."

"Thatta girl," Lucille said softly. "Give them prickly for the win."

Jameson cracked his knuckles before a small smile formed on his face. "Leave it to you to make me feel like an ass."

"Well, you did drive in on your motorcycle like you were on some mission and stomp in here all puffed up," Lucille countered for me.

Jameson frowned and peeked over at me with sheepish eyes, probably in hopes I'd help him out. "She's right. The motorcycle especially was over the top."

"The motorcycle wasn't even a damn part of talking to you. Franny's with her grandma for two weeks in Italy, and so I'm getting a few rides in before—"

"She must be afraid of how loud and intimidating that motorcycle can be too." Zen winked at Lucille and shot a saccharine smile his way. "Quite frankly, I don't know why you drive one at all. They're extremely dangerous."

"You might end up needing someone to save your life one day with that bike." He'd had one since high school. His father seemed oddly okay with it, but I was pretty sure they were all in some club with a motorcycle factory being a couple hours away.

"Olive Bee, you know as well as I do, I'm careful as ever on this thing."

Zen beat me to schooling him as she softly retorted, "Can't be careful if someone else isn't driving carefully by you."

He scoffed in irritation before he got up and swiped his helmet off the counter. He was close to Zen, but her arms were crossed as the tension between them crackled. "Want a ride? I can show you how careful I am right now."

It was like they were the only two people in the room for a moment before her eyes widened and she almost jolted away from him. He blinked once, shaking his head before he turned to me and tried to dispel the moment. "Or I'll give you a ride on the motorcycle, Olive. You know I'm careful."

"Yeah, Dimitri would love his girlfriend hopping on the back of another man's bike," I said sarcastically.

"If that's actually true, I'm happy to rectify you being his girlfriend if you want." He cleared his throat and rubbed his gloved hands together like he'd enjoy it. I didn't have a thing for bikers, but Jameson still pulled it off well as he combed his hand through his dark hair. I think Zen saw that, too, as she bit her lip and walked away.

"It's true, Jameson." I held his gaze this time, trying to get that point across.

"Good. Because I want what's best for this community. Your hometown and mine." He slid his helmet on. "And for your brother. And my fucking daughter. She deserves the world. She's all I got. I wouldn't risk any of this if it wasn't for her. She deserves a damn good childhood, and I'm not going to give her any less than that."

"I wouldn't want you to. I mean that. I'm not sure what the goal is here but—"

"I'm not sure what you heard at the grill out." I opened my mouth, willing to tell him at this point. "But I'm trusting that you know Lucille and I have it under control. Keep what you know about the Diamond Syndicate to yourself."

"But—"

"Just for now." He took a deep breath. "The less you know the better. And the less everyone knows is better. I've got two weeks to iron this out. Lucille and I will do just that."

He turned toward the front of the spa, unlocked the door, and left just like that.

"He's such a drama queen," Zen grumbled.

Lucille rolled her eyes and hummed in agreement. "He's right though. Don't talk to anyone about it, okay? Just give us two weeks."

"That's up until the board meeting." I tilted my head. "What about the article I'm writing?"

"Ah, by then, everything will be fine." She waved away any concern. Then she turned and looked out the window. "Oh, look. Knox is being driven home. I know that SUV. You should go see if he'll play some basketball with you, Olive. Make sure he's doing okay."

I studied the older woman and her tactics. "Don't you need a hair trim?"

"Oh, that can wait till next week." She chuckled, already making her way toward the door. "I have to work on my garden anyway." She held the door open for me.

"Well, this was fun," I mumbled without any joy in my tone.

"It'll be fun to catch up with Knox. He needs you now more than ever," she said, cryptically. "Remember, no secret spilling."

Easy for her to say. She didn't have an obsessed Dimitri

Hardy texting her.

When I walked out of that door, another message came in from him.

> **Dimitri: You're being short with me when I want long texts. Paragraphs. Novels from you.**

> **Me: I've just been busy. And stressed.**

> **Dimitri: Headaches?**

> **Me: No but that doesn't mean it's because of the birth control.**

> **Dimitri: I beg to differ, Honeybee. If you're stressed, take a day of rest.**

> **Me: I'll be fine. Don't worry about me. Go work.**

I took a deep breath, thinking of all that Lucille said. So many commitments and choosing what I wanted to commit to. I encouraged Dimitri to leave me alone, pushed him away because there was fear in getting attached to something that could potentially destroy you. I sacrificed the butterflies and giddiness I felt in getting responses from his texts for the safety net of loneliness.

I walked home and tried to focus on my responsibilities by calling Knox. My attention needed to be on him anyway. We'd been playing H-O-R-S-E every day now, and he looked like himself more each time. Would he tell me if he knew something? Were we getting that close again?

I wasn't sure I cared one way or the other. The weight of the information was a lot, and I think, more than anything, I just wanted the comfort of his presence. We'd played that game as kids. It was a safe place for both of us even if my mind was a mess and he was struggling through whatever pulled him toward taking drugs.

Maybe we were broken. But families had a way of either completing breaking you or holding you together and piecing you back up. I'd wanted us to be the latter for each other, thought we were moving toward that.

Yet, he didn't answer my call. Nor did he answer the next morning. He wasn't there for basketball when I walked by at the normal time either. And his phone went right to voicemail.

I waited all day with the phone in my hand.

I waited until I got the call. It wasn't from him, though, but my father.

CHAPTER 32: OLIVE

The gruff voice of my father was irritable rather than loving when I picked up the phone call. "Knox wanted me to let you know he won't be playing ball for the rest of this week."

"Okay." I dragged out the word in question. It was late in the day, but I pulled out my calligraphy supplies to work at the table in the dining room, holding the phone in the crook of my neck. "And why exactly couldn't he just text me that?"

He scoffed at me like he was disgusted that I even asked. "Because he talked to his father instead. We have a lot of stuff going on, Olive. You can't expect people to drop things just because you're back home. It's quite selfish if you ask me."

"I'm being selfish?" The question bubbled up fast. I unscrewed the ink and slammed it down harder on the table than I would have liked.

"Why are you back here stirring all these things up? Doesn't your friend Kee need you?" It was almost as if he was pushing me to leave.

"I'm here for Knox and—"

"You know, he's trying to level out his medications, and your stepmother says you just keep calling him in the early morning hours to play basketball? He's been helping me with business and needs rest. I can't keep dealing with—"

"Wow," I cut him off, hurt that Knox had told him that because it was true. I had called him but only because I thought we were on the same page. I laid out the different nibs and sat down at the table, trying to stay calm during the call. "I thought that—"

"I don't care what you thought. We don't want to be bothered with you. You shouldn't be here." His tone stabbed at my heart. Had I really let him down so much that he didn't want me there ever? "My family needs stability right now."

"Your family?" I inquired softly as I tested a new nib on the pen I'd ordered. The stroke I made was heavy and rough. I set down the pen and folded my fingers together, trying my best to cull the emotions rolling around inside me. You had to be delicate, precise, and handle calligraphy with care if you wanted the writing to come out perfectly, the flick of my wrist and the pressure on the paper changed every part.

"Yes. Georgette and Knox. So, leave him alone." He said it with finality. No inclusion of his own daughter. And suddenly Lucille's words started to make a bit of sense. Instead of feeling hurt and ignoring the anger, I embraced them both.

I narrowed my eyes on that heavy stroke of ink I'd made, feeling the anger of it. "What business are you two working on anyway?"

"It's not your concern."

The rage and prickle came out in my voice then. "It's always my concern when it has to deal with my brother, Father. I won't call him if he doesn't want, but I'll be here, ready to answer, when he calls me. I'm not going anywhere. You can bet on it."

"You're impossible," my father retorted before he hung up on me.

And I think my heart broke in another way that night. My father had said I wasn't a part of his family, and I accepted that as I stared out the window that night, but I felt the pain of the bond truly severing.

When I got another text from Dimitri, I ignored it.

Another day, another time to ignore.

The next day, he texted again.

Dimitri: You must still be stressed.

I got an alert then from an unknown number that the whole spa was booked for me next week and the message said, "Congrats on booking your spa day."

I knew the culprit and tried not to smile at his over-the-top effort. I took a screenshot and sent it back to him.

Me: What is this?

Dimitri: A spa day for you to relax.

Me: Dimitri, I don't want that. Cancel it.

Dimitri: It's not refundable.

Me: You own the spa!

Dimitri: Yup, and as the owner, I know when to shut down the spa to outside guests so my future wife can pamper herself in it and relax.

> **Me: No. As your casual girlfriend, I don't need extreme gifts. Give them to someone else. You're flying around the world. Enjoy it and all the women you can have fun with.**

> **Me: Which is fine, by the way. Of course. I'm enjoying all the men here too.**

I winced at my stupidity. My own fun? Not really.

My stomach twisted and dipped and rolled at texting him to do that. I missed him. I knew I was getting feelings I shouldn't. It's how I knew I'd be hurt when he texted me back that he'd probably hooked up with every girl in every country he'd been in since he left last week.

It showed me I needed to start denying what I felt better and faster. I needed to be realistic that this charade would come to an end, that his desire for me would come to an end, that I wouldn't be able to keep him.

I sighed and closed iMessages and put my notifications on Do Not Disturb. Too much was happening in Paradise Grove for me to be falling in love with Dimitri Hardy. So, I opened up the dating app instead and tried to go down the path of less complications.

> **Me: How are you? We haven't talked in a while.**

> **Mr. Perfect: Been busy but doesn't mean we shouldn't be talking. What are you up to tonight?**

Me: About to go to sleep actually.

**Mr. Perfect: Would it be bad if I said
I wanted to see that, Flower Girl?**

I smiled at his nickname for me. I appreciated that Mr. Perfect had kept things between us quite PG so far. This was the first time he'd pushed the boundary a bit. It was an open invitation to pick a path. To make a hard decision, especially considering Lucille had said I would have to make more in the future.

I knew I was going to stay in Paradise Grove, and Dimitri wouldn't want that forever. He'd forget me while he flew around the world. Rightfully so.

I threw a bare leg over the white sheets and took a picture of it to send to Mr. Perfect.

**Me: That's just a little. Maybe if we
actually meet, you'll see more. I'll
be near Rooster Rock tomorrow
evening. We could have a drink at 9?**

When my phone rang and Dimitri's name popped up, I dropped it like it was a hot potato, feeling like I'd somehow done something completely wrong. I wasn't cheating on Dimitri. We were just casual. So, I don't know why I stared at the phone with a feeling of guilt swelling through me.

Cautiously, I picked it up and stared at it. He had no idea what I was doing just like I had no idea who he was doing over there.

"Hello?"

"What the hell are you doing?" he growled out.

"Um, hi to you too." I frowned at the phone. He sounded livid.

He took two deep breaths before he said, "You didn't answer my text."

I pulled up his texts quick to see what he'd said.

> **Dimitri: Who the fuck are you having fun with?**

> **Dimitri: Don't make me drop everything to fly home early.**

> **Dimitri: I will fly home early if you don't answer, Honeybee.**

"Are you threatening me with your presence?" I asked coyly, already feeling my messy emotions for him bubbling over into the conversation.

"Why aren't you answering my texts?" His tone was sharp.

"I put them on silent," I admitted.

"Why?"

"Because ..." I didn't really know how to divulge that I was jealous of what he might be doing in another country. "I was about to go to sleep."

"You know ... I'd believe that lie had I not known the truth."

"Which is what?" I narrowed my eyes because there was no way he knew I was messaging another guy.

"I think you are having fun with someone else. You just wrote that in a damn text."

"If that was the case, I wouldn't have answered the phone." I rolled my eyes as I rolled over in the bed and touched the empty spot where he'd lain next to me just weeks ago.

He hummed like he was thinking about all of it. "I'll be home late tomorrow. Wait up for me."

"I can't." I paused before I breathed out the next sentence. "I'm going on a date." There was the line. I was drawing it so we both had a clear view of what it meant for our casual relationship.

"A date?" he murmured. "With who?"

"Mr. Perfect." I hesitated. "I think. He hasn't answered back yet. But I figure I should try, right?"

There was a beat of silence before he said, "If that's really what you want, Olive. I'm warning you though, I don't play nice with competition."

"It isn't a competition. It's taking things slow and being sure."

"I am sure. Sure as the sky is blue, that you're not supposed to be with anyone but me. Wait up for me after your date then?"

"If I don't stay out with him all night." I chuckled.

He didn't laugh with me. I think I heard a snarl instead. "Not happening, Honeybee. I'll see you tomorrow night."

With that, he hung up, and I was wound so tight from our interaction that I didn't even bother texting Mr. Perfect back after he wrote ...

Mr. Perfect: I'll be there. Look for the tall guy who makes it clear I'm there for you.

I threw the phone down on the carpeted floor and went to sleep.

CHAPTER 33: DIMITRI

"What are you looking at over there?" my brother Dom asked as we sat in his office. I'd flown out to see him as my last stop.

"None of your business." I squinted at the camera footage. What the hell was that woman doing over there?

When Dom leaned over to see what was on my phone, though, I clicked it off. "Don't tell me you're doing dumb shit like Dex was."

"Was or is?" I threw back. We all knew his ass still watched his wife's every move. I didn't actually knock him for it now.

"I saw a damn surveillance video on your phone." Dom combed a hand through his dark hair and then crossed his arms. "Your security system is up and running in Paradise Grove and we all know it."

"Are you guys watching what I'm doing with my own investments?" I tried to sound offended, but it was really no use.

"Of course we are. Kee's your best friend, and Dex watches her mental health like a hawk on steroids. You're causing her stress."

"Why? I'm just checking on Olive," I tried to reason.

"You sure about that?" He lifted an eyebrow. "The investment in a dating app last week an indicator of you just checking on her?"

"I'm not discussing that with you," I growled out. "What I do with my money is—"

"Your business. It's only my business when it affects the family."

I leaned on the desk to look him in the eye. "Stay out of my shit."

"Stop watching her on the cameras and—"

"I'm not going to stop." I slammed my hand down on the desk and tried to take a deep breath so my heart would stop beating wildly against my chest. It was a futile attempt. It was never going to stop beating just for her now. "She's my girl and—"

"Ah." Dominic smiled then. My eldest brother was always pushing us. "That's all I needed to know. I think you need to take this call I have with Bane Black then."

Bane was a partner in our newest resort endeavor. We'd begrudgingly given into a deal with him after we found it was the only way to get the resort and casino up and running. His rap sheet was questionable, his ties to different groups loose and murky, and his demeanor sinister most days. I didn't need the guy dabbling in more of my investments.

"For what?"

Dominic sighed, "That Paradise of yours seems to have bigger connections that we'd originally thought, and they span the United States in a way we need to be careful about."

Normally, I would have been excited about this news. Throw a curveball my way and let me swing at it. But I felt the fear rush through me, and all the blood drained from my face, from my heart, and sped through my veins. "What exactly are you talking about?"

Dominic pulled up a video chat with Bane. He sat there looking at another screen, his angular face barely in view as he greeted us. Then, Dominic announced, "My brother doesn't know about your Diamond Syndicate, Bane. Not sure Olive does either."

Bane turned toward the screen and I sat back as his piercing blue gaze bored into me. His look was always formidable with how the tattoos snaked up his neck, how he didn't look away once he caught your eye, and how he always felt coiled, ready to strike. "Diamond Syndicate is a very secret society. One I've been a part of since I was born. It has afforded me opportunities I otherwise wouldn't have. But we don't flaunt our status like you Hardys or the men your sisters married. Those Armanellis have made quite a name for themselves." He chuckled.

"What's your point?" I murmured.

He explained how Paradise Grove was just like the exclusive community he'd grown up in, a Diamond Syndicate pod. All of these communities worked together to quietly influence the world, and to make sure certain groups weren't allowed to overrun the United States.

"So, you're practically your own mob, keeping down the actual mob?" I threw back after listening to what essentially was an elevator pitch.

He chuckled. "Say what you will about us, Dimitri. I'm not here to win you over. I'm here to let you know you invested in Paradise Grove and their players have misstepped. They've aligned with partners we don't approve of. We're handling it discreetly." He cracked his knuckles in irritation on the screen and then started typing away on his other laptop. "I'm dropping files to you that you can go through."

My phone pinged with notifications from him. I pulled up the first file and saw the history of the Diamond Syndicate right away.

"I've got to give your sister Izzy credit. She's been digging into this information with her husband, that Armanelli of hers, for a little while. She seems to think this can be smoothed over."

There were ties to the Irish mob, to selling drugs, to trafficking within the last year. "Smoothed over? The Armanellis have reorganized to not have any of this within their family. I'm not going to have it in mine," I whispered in disbelief. There was absolutely no way. I stood abruptly. "I need to leave."

My brother grabbed my shoulder and yanked me down. "Calm down." When I tried to pull my elbow away, he held on. "Man, I said chill. I agree with you. You know we all do. Everyone is safe right now. Olive's fine. But we'd like her to stay that way. We're still confirming who's working outside of the syndicate and partnering with the Irish."

I pushed away from the desk and paced up and down the room. "Please don't tell me you think it's her—"

"No. But her dad? We are working on confirming who's involved."

"Well, fucking make sure and call me," I growled before I stood up. "And, Bane, funny that you're investing with us when you're part of a damn secret society that essentially wants to bring down our family."

"The Diamond Syndicate's always had a moral compass. I may have been born into it"—he smiled, but it was sinister— "but that doesn't mean I was born with the same compass."

"If I wasn't partnering with you, I'd beat your ass."

"Yeah, yeah. Your Armanelli brothers said the same a few days ago. And honestly, the Diamond Syndicate approved of the reform they've brought within their Italian family. We aren't working on bringing the Italians down."

"You wouldn't be able to." I crossed my arms.

His laugh was low before he rubbed at his jaw. "Don't be so

sure. Look how fast we can make a community prosper, Dimitri. There's a reason you invested. Anyway, our battle isn't with you. You're not a problem at all. It is with whomever is betraying us." He sighed. "Just keep an eye on Olive and be cautious for the next few weeks."

"Cautious of what exactly?"

"Well, there's a reason you've gotten so much pushback on your condos and offices. If the Irish Mob is influencing a few to push all the others to vote against you ... they want you gone, and if they look at Olive wrong because she's with you—"

"I'll kill them," I responded without a second thought.

Bane laughed and Dom leaned back and held his hands up like he'd finally proven his point. "Well then ... Just like Dex."

"First of all, we're in agreement what Dex did was warranted." My brother had gotten rid of someone who had hurt his wife.

"Of course." Dom didn't even hesitate.

"If these fuckers threaten any part of my family, they deserve just as bad as what Dex has done or worse. They're not going to look twice at my girl without me coming for them."

Dom said quietly, "Not just a little business transaction between you two anymore?"

"Look"—I felt my jaw popping up and down—"don't tell Kee and Dex. Not yet."

"Jesus, I'm not your secret keeper, Dimitri. We aren't twelve. Just tell them quick."

"I will." I nodded. "I already would have had it not been for Olive asking me to keep it to ourselves. Right now, I have to get back. Things are happening in Paradise Grove that I shouldn't be missing. Tell Clara I said hi."

Dom nodded. "Don't fuck it up."

I stared at her text the whole flight home.

There was no reason to respond to it.

She'd understand soon enough how serious I was.

CHAPTER 34: OLIVE

I'd taken an Uber thirty minutes out of town to meet up with Mr. Perfect.

I'd put on my best red dress, my best shoes, and my best makeup while FaceTiming Kee and Pink for help. Pink stared at the phone for a second before saying, "More red lipstick and the red flower in your hair."

"Are you sure?" I switched out my normal pink plumeria to a red one. "What do you think?"

"Fucking hot." Pink nodded at me and Kee smiled.

"I'm so excited for you." Kee looked like she might even tear up.

"I'm nervous he won't show or won't look like I want him to."

"You've barely talked with the guy, right?" Pink shrugged. "So, if he's terrible, who cares?"

"He's the only one I've talked to in a couple weeks. And I haven't been matching with anyone else in this area." I wasn't going to admit I really hadn't been trying because of Dimitri.

"This is good. Get out there. Try out some new men." Pink was rattling off things now. "Forget your ex ever existed. Jump back in the saddle, ride a cowboy and—"

"Enough." I heard a deep voice in the background.

"What, Bane?" Pink handed the phone to Kee who started to walk away from them. "It's the truth. We all need to forget about the past."

I heard his growl and then, "You're never forgetting about anything with me."

Kee laughed as she walked into another room and gave me a look. "So, Bane just arrived on a private jet to see Pink. She's not happy about him showing up, obviously."

"How's that going?"

"About as well as you'd expect." Bane and Pink had a complicated history that none of us completely knew the specifics of, but we were aware of their love and extreme hate for one another. "Anyway, call me after your date. It's going to be great."

"I will. We'll catch up then. It feels like forever since I've seen you."

"You and Dimitri. You two are stealing each other from me." She turned the corner, and Dex was there to put his arm around her neck.

"Looks like you're doing just fine without us. Love you, and I better go because my Uber is here."

I ran out in my wedges and hopped into the car. After ten minutes or so, Dimitri texted me.

Dimitri: Tell me you reconsidered your date.

Me: Can't do that. In an Uber.

Dimitri: Send me the driver details and your location.

Me: Get real.

Dimitri: Don't make me act unhinged and find a way to hack your phone.

Me: This is ridiculous. I'm on my way there already.

Dimitri: What place are you going to?

Me: A little bar I'm sure you haven't heard of.

Dimitri: What's the name?

Me: Rooster Rock. Dive bar outside of town where no one will see me.

Dimitri: That's thirty minutes from our house if I'm speeding. Send me your damn location so I can track the driver.

Me: Fine. Sent. Happy?

Dimitri: No. You're going on a date when you're my girlfriend. Why the hell would I be happy?

Me: We're CASUALLY dating.

Dimitri: Did it feel casual when my cock was so far inside you that I could practically feel your heart beating?

Me: What we say and feel during sex is sorta moot outside of it, don't you think?

Dimitri: Is it really? Because I hope I knocked you up.

Me: Dimitri, that's nearly impossible.

Dimitri: But still possible. And then I get you forever.

Me: People raise kids separately all the time.

Dimitri: So you'd keep our kid?

Me: I don't even know why I'm having this conversation. I'm not pregnant!

Dimitri: We'll see, Honeybee.

Me: Don't be ridiculous. You've got engagements and people all around the world that you need to commit your time to.

Dimitri: What if the only one I care about committing to is in an Uber on their way to see another guy?

I looked around the bar for a tall man who would make it clear he was here to see me. I didn't see him at first, so I sat down in a booth and ordered a drink.

One minute passed.

Then another.

I stared at my phone until a text came through. Not from Mr. Perfect though.

> **Jameson: Lunch sometime next week at Paradise Grove Golf Club? Preferably before the board meeting and before you turn your article in.**

> **Me: Just let me know the day and time.**

It was only five more minutes into me sitting there sipping on a drink that I saw him. Tall, probably six six with green eyes, perfect navy suit, and a devilish smile on his face. When he got to my table he leaned in and whispered, "Hey, Flower Girl."

Dimitri Hardy. Not Mr. Perfect.

My breath caught on the way he said the nickname, how he smelled, how my body ached immediately to touch him and pull him in for a kiss. I bit my lip to try to restrain myself from all of it. I'd missed him but he didn't get to know that. "What did you just call me?"

"You heard me." He pulled at one of my curls and then he sat down across from me.

"Dimitri, what the hell are you doing here?"

"Meeting my girlfriend for a date." He tilted his head and then looked me up and down. "Or ruining the date she thought she'd be on. One or the other."

"No." I shook my head. "That's not possible. Where's Mr. Perfect?"

"Mr. Perfect was a douche." He sucked on his perfect teeth as he looked toward the ceiling for a second before he said, "I'm having a hard time seeing you in that stunning dress. Red, Honeybee? For a guy other than me?"

I glanced down at my dress and smoothed the fabric on my hips. "I wanted to look good for someone."

"You always look good. In a sweater. In your glasses. Without them. With red lipstick. Without it, even though your lips look hot as hell now that I'm imagining them wrapped around me, which means some other guy would have been imagining it too. With red flowers in your hair. And a gold necklace around your neck." He reached out to play with the chain and studied it. "This new?"

He recognized it so quickly, something that was different in my appearance that it made my center hot with need. I took a deep breath before I answered, "It was my mom's. It meant a lot to her. She used to wear it before ..."

"It looks stunning on you." Then his eyes swept up and down my body. I chewed the side of my cheek, trying to wait for the heat in my body to cool off but it just spread further through me. "Fuck, I missed seeing you."

I felt the blush heat my cheeks and hated that my thighs clenched at his assessment. "Should I ask again? Where is Mr. Perfect?" I whispered.

"Mr. Perfect wasn't perfect. Not for you." He looked a tad remorseful, and I grabbed my drink to take a big gulp of it. I figured I was going to need it, and I was right when he admitted, "I bought the dating app you were on, Olive. I needed to make sure you wouldn't date anyone but me."

I choked on the drink. It literally spewed out of my mouth before I grabbed a napkin to wipe it away. "You what?"

"In my defense, you said it was a great dating app."

"It's a terrible dating app. It just started!" I slammed down my drink and it sloshed over.

"True. The start-up only launched about a year ago, and I'm pretty sure they were happy with my offer of a couple million, which means they weren't making much."

"You dropped millions on a start-up app? For what? Because I said it was good?! That's the most idiotic thing I've ever heard."

"I dropped a couple mil on an app because you were on it trying to find a match when you're my *only* match." He said it so casually as he leaned back in his seat and stretched his arms across the booth.

And that's when the anger bubbled inside me. "I'm ... not ... yours," I stuttered out, trying to piece together everything that had just happened. "Did you—? What happened to Mr. Perfect? How did you get his information?"

"I got access to all the profiles, obviously." He shrugged. "And when I looked him up to learn more about him, I found you weren't a good match."

"You helped match me with him! How could you possibly know that?"

"He wasn't me, Honeybee. I'm the only match for you."

"We'll see. Let me meet Mr. Perfect, and I'll tell you."

"Not possible. I took over his profile for a fair price."

"You paid him off?"

"I'll pay off every guy who matches with you from here on out."

"I haven't matched with anyone in ... You aren't giving me matches, are you?"

"Again, they aren't me."

"You're out of your mind."

"Or you're in denial about the fact that you're my exclusive girlfriend at this point."

"We've barely spoken this past week."

"You barely answered me, sure. I've been texting and calling your ass nonstop."

"You know, I thought your brother was crazy over Kee."

"I'm crazier than him."

"It's not something to be proud of." I stared out at the people in the bar. "I don't need a boyfriend. I had one, and he was—"

"Absolutely an asshole to you. I won't be."

"I don't even know what to say." I shook my head at him but then a laugh bubbled up from inside me, and I hiccupped. "When did you buy the app?"

"The day after you matched with him."

"So, it's been you the whole time?" I narrowed my eyes. "You got the picture of my legs."

"That's why I called you immediately." His hand crinkled a napkin on our table. "You were sending pics to some other guy."

"You were flying around the world meeting up with women," I blurted out.

He frowned. "What?"

"I—" My mouth snapped shut. "I might have talked myself into thinking that you were. Because Ruff—"

"I'm not him." Dimitri cut me off. "I'll never be someone like him."

Then, I rubbed at my temples. "I think we need to get through this business with Paradise Grove first."

"Agree to see only me and we will."

"Jealousy doesn't suit you." It totally did. "So, no more dating apps?" I tried to sound dejected, but I hadn't been putting in any effort towards them anyway.

"You think I'm not going to be enough or you? You need another man to fulfill your every need?"

It was at that moment that my phone lit up, still face up on the table, and a text came through.

> **Jameson: Franny's still gone next week, so I can do 1 p.m. on Tuesday for lunch to talk more?**

When my eyes shot up to meet Dimitri's, his were burning with that jealous green ember that my body reacted to.

And all he said was, "No."

CHAPTER 35: DIMITRI

Her honey-colored eyes twinkled at me as she smirked. "See. Jealous. You're not telling me who I can and cannot go to lunch with, Dimitri." Then she grabbed for her drink, but I swiped it away from her before waving the waitress over to hand her my card. "Bring her a water and close our tab."

I wanted Olive at home in bed with me safe. I wasn't about to divulge the information I'd learned from my brother and Bane earlier, but I knew now that I was going to be keeping a much closer eye on her. I didn't regret placing security throughout the town or turning it on before it was approved. I'd break the law for the woman I loved. I wouldn't regret it either.

"Water?" Olive lifted a brow.

"Might be pregnant, Honeybee." I dropped each word with weight, trying to make her see how serious I was. "Means we should be avoiding alcohol and talking about a wedding, not a lunch date you're not attending."

She closed her eyes like she was trying to tamp down her frustration with me. And even as she sat there angry, I admired how the pink hue of her cheeks matched the red flower and red dress she had on. Fuck. I wanted to ravage her here in the bar.

She took a deep breath before she folded the napkin in front of her. "You know, as much as I didn't want to think about having a kid, Dimitri, I *did*. I thought about it because you brought it up, and it actually made me contemplate the out-of-this-world commitment that would bring. Have you looked at my life?"

"Yes?" I answered, confused.

"But really considered it? Because, honestly, I've been avoiding things I care about for a long time. I left this place after my mom died, you know? Probably because I was so rooted here, and I didn't want anything else to happen that would hurt me more. Then, I just sort of drifted until I found Rufford. I committed to him, right? And then ... well, that didn't work either. I don't think I need more commitments. If I have them, I'll just worry."

"Worry about what?" I frowned.

"About you." She looked away. "I always worry now. If I care this much now, what will it be later? What will I worry about then?"

"I'll ask again ... about what?"

"That you'll find someone better than me," she whisper-yelled. "That this won't be enough. That I won't be enough, and my heart will break so much it won't be repairable."

I reached for her hand to reassure her that that could never be the case, but she snatched her hand back. "No. Don't console me about it. I hate that I can't have the confidence or take the risk, but it's gone."

The waitress came over right then to hand me the check. She'd put little hearts and her number on it too. I saw how Olive's eyes widened, and she blushed in jealousy and embarrassment that another woman was so blatantly hitting on me.

"Excuse me." I stopped the woman and handed the tab back to the waitress. "Get me another bill. One without your number on it." Then I shook my head, got my card out and murmured, "Matter of fact, just run the bill."

The waitress stuttered out a sorry and hurried away.

She sighed. "See? I am perfectly justified to worry about things like this."

"And see how I cull your worry right away? You better do the same with any man who approaches you," I told her as she reached into her purse to try and hand me some cash. I shook my head. "You're not paying. It's our first date."

"It should be our last date." She frowned as she pushed her curls from her face. "You have to accept that I'm not ready."

"I'll wait for you to be ready. In the meantime, I'll be ready enough for the both of us."

She scrunched up the napkin and met my gaze. "Dimitri, you know you'll hate that. Especially when I still intend to Uber places, take cabs home, go on dates, go to lunches."

The air swirled with the tension between us as I held her gaze. She was going to go head-to-head with me, I could tell. She didn't know what she was up against.

"Try to take a cab home tonight. See how it works out for you."

She stood right then. "I hope she brings your card soon." Her smile was saccharine as she walked out, her hips swaying in that scarlet dress like a red flag in front of a bull. I was the bull.

And I wasn't letting her leave without hitting my target.

I threw a hundred on the table and grabbed my card on the way out just as I saw her waving down a taxi.

I mumbled to the valet to get my car and walked up to her fast before she got in. There was no arguing with her at this point.

She wasn't going to listen. She'd made up her mind, but I'd made up mine. So I bent and tucked my shoulder into her waist before scooping her up and over my shoulder. She screamed as

I did it, but I said, "Don't make a scene or you'll be talking to the cops tonight."

"You're using freaking force to get your way?"

"And I always will when it comes to your safety, Honeybee," I countered as I walked toward where the valet had pulled my car up to. He then opened the passenger door for me to throw her in.

"You're the most ridiculous, stubborn—"

I slammed the door in her face and tipped the valet generously. He smiled and said to have a great night.

I rounded the front of the car and got in. She was still screaming. "And quite frankly, I bet Mr. Perfect would have been better in bed."

I shifted the car into first and gunned it as I looked at her. "You and I both know that's a lie. I fuck your pussy better than anyone because it's mine. You were made for me. Don't deny it."

"Oh my God. Your ego is so stupidly big for no reason." When we came to a stop sign, she yanked on the door handle. "Let me out."

I didn't even look at her. "You know I'm not going to."

"If you don't let me out of here, I'm going to roll down the window and scream," she warned me. "It won't be good for you around here and you know it."

Didn't she get that I didn't care one bit about my reputation in Paradise Grove anymore?

CHAPTER 36: OLIVE

Dimitri got off on a thrill, loved the risk, would do something completely stupid just to see how it ended up. He loved when someone pushed him or defied him. He got that burst of fire in his green eyes before one side of his mouth lifted. "Go on then, Honeybee." No fear at all that it could ruin his reputation. If anything, he was like a trained military dog that had just been hit, wagging his tail ready to lunge into chaos. "Scream loud."

Then he accelerated—rapidly—in that insanely expensive car.

"Holy crap." I gripped the handle above the door and gasped as the speed climbed so fast. "You're breaking the speed limit."

"I'll risk the ticket." He shrugged and kept going.

"Well, how about not risking my life while you're at it!"

He glanced at me then and slowed the car abruptly enough that my body leaned forward but his arm was fast enough to shoot out and catch me. "No one's on the road. I'm trained to handle this car."

"You're trained? Really?" I rolled my eyes.

"Took lessons with the best," he told me, and I believed him because there was no reason to brag at this point. "I shouldn't speed though. Not with you in the car. It's a risk I won't take."

"Oh good. So you do understand the idea of risks." I tried to reason with him another way. "You realize us trying to be in a real relationship is a huge risk to each of our friendships with

Kee. And what about us? We're fri—"

"Don't you dare say we're friends, or I'll pull this car over and fuck you on top of it."

"Do you hear yourself?" I threw up my hands. "We're in the middle of you trying to make a good impression on the people around here and you're talking about fucking me in public."

"Your point?"

I swear he wanted to get a rise out of me, and I didn't care anymore. I gave him one. Like Lucille said, people deserved prickly sometimes. I threw my hand so hard on his dashboard, I wanted to dent it. Instead, though, I immediately snatched it back and rubbed it as pain shot through it. "Crap." He glanced over at me with concern and slid his hand in mine fast to take over rubbing it. "What are you doing?" I murmured as I looked down at it.

"Taking care of you."

Those five words. Him worrying over me. Him taking care of me and rubbing my hand for just a moment. It shifted something in me. I blinked back the tears that had started to fill my eyes. "You don't understand, Dimitri. Everything around here is a mess. And so am I. I'm the biggest mess of all. You can't want me."

"But I do. And I'm going to show you. Deny me all you want. I'll be waiting till you don't."

After he pulled into the garage and turned off the car, silence descended on us.

"I'm scared I'm not enough. I'm scared to commit and then find out I wasn't enough." I swiped at the first tear that fell before I shoved through the door to the backyard instead of inside. I stared out at the clear stars over our backyard. I didn't spend much time out here. I'd told myself the lawn service would handle it, but I saw how the lights twinkled over the fences, how our overhead lights provided just the right dim glow.

"Just because you don't see yourself as absolutely one in a hundred billion doesn't mean I don't."

"A hundred billion, huh? That's pretty exact."

"There's about a hundred billion stars in this galaxy, Olive. I know because I was on a plane discussing another business investment I'm considering. And you know what I kept thinking of? You. You shine brighter than the hundred billion stars for me."

I stared out at them. And then I looked out at how we could see other backyards connected to ours in the moonlight, how the hills rolled into the stars on the right and the city lights to the left.

This whole community was so intertwined, and I'd missed how we all fit together. How I could fit in. How I should. Yet, pieces were falling into place, and I wondered if Dimitri would fall into place with me.

I sighed and glanced at the hot tub. I shoved off the lid and felt the steam swirl out into the night air.

"Going in?" Dimitri murmured behind me.

"I shouldn't." I shook my head. "I should go work on my thesis and finish figuring out exactly what our proposal should be for the board meeting. You should want me to do that."

"And yet I want you in the hot tub instead." His voice vibrated against the soft skin of my neck in just the right way, making me shiver.

I turned to look up at him in the moonlight. He stood right against me, and I fit there with him. Then he pulled me even closer by my waist so I could feel how hard he was. "If I say yes, it doesn't mean yes to everything."

He gripped my hips and moved me forward toward the stone hot tub steps. When I hesitated for a second, he gripped me tight and lifted me right over the edge of the hot tub and set me in it. "I'm not asking for a yes to everything right now, Olive." His hand brushed against my neck and then to the red straps of my dress. He pulled on one and then the other until it fell fluidly into the water.

"My dress is going to be ruined," I murmured as I stood there in the red bra and panties I'd picked out for tonight.

"Good. I'll buy you a new one that goes all the way up to your chin and down to your toes."

"For all the dates I'll be going on later?" I said as I shoved the dress down into the water and stepped around it.

He was shaking his head at me as he undid his shirt buttons and pulled it off. "You know I took my jet back and had them speed half the way."

"Why? You were Mr. Perfect at that point. You knew no one else was going to show," I reminded him as he unbuckled his belt. He pulled it through his belt loops and walked up the stairs to the hot tub, unbuttoning his slacks and getting rid of them.

"Some other man was bound to see you sitting there alone and hit on you. I couldn't have that."

He stepped in, right up to me, and I practically moaned as his wet skin touched mine. Then he reached over and turned the bubbles on. Every sensation was heightened now that he was in there with me and the hot water moving around us. I felt his cool breath, the touch of his soft lips against my cheek, the way his hand dragged the hot water across my stomach. "I can't have another man look at all this. I've missed it too much for anyone else to admire."

"Don't be ridiculous," I murmured but I was already wrapping my arm around the one he had against my body and pressing my ass into him because I'd missed him too. So much.

He stepped us back enough to pull me down as he sat, and then I was in his lap, leaning my head back as he kissed my neck and ran his hands over my bra, behind my back to unhook it, and then I pushed the straps off.

His hands immediately covered my breasts, and I reached behind me to shove at his boxers. He moved away though, not ready to let me have him yet. "I want you. I want you right now, Dimitri."

"I know, Honeybee. It was too long," he murmured in my ear. "I love seeing how much you really want me though. Give me another minute, huh? Let me make you feel good first."

"It'll feel good when your cock is in me," I whimpered.

I felt the scruff on his jaw as he shook his head against my neck. "I spent too much time away from you. I won't again. I need to apologize to this pussy of yours first, baby. Spread your legs."

"No. Please." But Dimitri was done with my requests. He yanked the thong from my legs and it ripped under the water, the red fabric floating up away from my sex, leaving me bare with the bubbles moving right against me and my arousal. His hand cupped me, and I jolted into him.

"How can you beg for my cock when this pussy wants it all?"

He slid a finger in, and I spread my legs immediately. I felt his cock against my ass then, too, and he shifted it so the tip pressed right against my other hole, making me whimper and moan. He chuckled and flexed his hips just a little, making my ass tense against the tip of him.

"Dimitri, please." I didn't even know what I was asking for at this point. I placed my hands on his knees for leverage and pushed back on his cock. He swore as my ass stretched just a little and his fingers thrust in me fast as this thumb rolled over my clit.

All the sensations, the hot water rising and falling on my breasts, him biting into my neck, my body missing the feel of his. Every part of me coiled up and burst apart as I cried out into the night.

My body shook with the orgasm that rolled through me so fast that the water splashed around me as I arched back into him. He was quick to keep his cock from moving further into my ass, but he thrust his fingers up and down to milk my aftershocks as he murmured, "That's it, Honeybee. Take all you want. Fuck my hand with that pretty little pussy of yours and show me just how good of a girlfriend you are. See how you take it. How you want it. How you're mine."

I was shaking my head back and forth against his shoulder now as he moved his thumb over my clit again, like he was testing how sensitive I was. "It's too good, Dimitri. I can't have another."

He hummed. "I think you can. This pussy is mine. I know how much it can take. Now ..." He bit my ear. "How wet are you in here? Put that pussy on me. Let me feel it."

"Last time you go bare before my new birth control kicks in." I rocked my hips up against the tip of his cock now. I was spreading my legs, moaning and whimpering at the feel of it.

"Olive, you okay over there?" I suddenly heard. And I froze.

It was the middle of the freaking night, but we were still outside, still in public. And it was right then that I saw Jameson's silhouette walking over from his side of the yard and knew in a second he'd see us in the hot tub.

"Better say something or your old crush is going to see how much of a boyfriend I really am to you." Dimitri's voice was low in warning, restrained, almost unhinged and off kilter.

He squeezed my hip hard, and I loved how it felt, the rush of it all. He'd unhinged something in me too, something I didn't want to bottle back up. It was bold and wrong and taboo and completely something I never would have done before, something I'd wondered about, though, something I would be doing just for me.

I also knew Dimitri wouldn't be doing this for himself at all. I saw the conflict in his eyes, and for some reason, I felt the pull, the need to indulge in this. Rufford had hid me from everyone. I wasn't publicly desired—or even privately.

"I've never done this with anyone," I whispered to Dimitri. "But I might want to."

Dimitri's jaw clenched up and down. "Jesus, and you're the only woman I absolutely don't want to do this with." But then he leaned in close. "Only for you, Honeybee."

I relaxed into Dimitri and said loudly, "I'm more than fine, Jameson." I purred out his name and his face appeared from the shadows as he squinted over at us.

I bore down on Dimitri's cock and gasped as I took him all the way up in me, my breasts floating in the water as I sank down onto him. Dimitri pinched and rolled my clit hard as if to punish me for my decision, but the pain mixed with pleasure as I stared at Jameson's eyes raking over us.

"You two are asking for trouble out here," he murmured, but he didn't step back to go inside. Instead, he walked forward slowly.

"You're asking for trouble taking my girl to lunch without

me," Dimitri told him in a serious, quiet voice, and I imagined they were staring at one another because Jameson's gaze was trained right past me.

"You sure she's yours? Sure it's real between you two?" Jameson was goading us for his own agenda, I knew that. Yet, Dimitri thought he was taunting us about our relationship.

The rumble in Dimitri's chest was enough of a response before he sucked on my neck. "Tell me you want to go in, Honeybee. I'll fuck you just the way you want inside."

His restraint was about to snap. And I knew right then, I wanted it to. I needed it for me. I wanted him to take this risk with me just as I was taking a risk with him. "You want to go inside instead of showing Jameson how much you want me?"

It was a challenge. He knew it and so did I.

His jaw clenched once, then twice before his hand wrapped around my breast. Then, he thrust into me hard. I felt the power of it, the stretch in my pussy, the way there was possession along with passion.

And then he lifted me to bend me over the edge of the hot tub, my knees on the seat, my tits on display for Jameson out of the water. "Watch how I fuck her, Jameson. Know that she's mine."

He didn't hesitate then, nor did I. He brought my ass back and thrust his hips forward, over and over again. The hot water splashed around us, matching our rhythm and showing our passion. I lost myself in how good he felt, how his cock stretched my walls, how he slid in and out, how his hands gripped me with bruising precision and didn't let go of me, not even for a second. The stars shined down on us, the moonlight illuminating how Jameson watched as I unraveled in the ecstasy of knowing Dimitri was willing to lose control for me, to show another person how important I was to him in that moment.

There was a sort of rush and appeal for a man doing something for me even when he didn't want to. I'd felt his hesitation, felt how possessive he was in that moment, because right after he got off with me, he wrapped his arms around my body and pulled me back into the water. Then he commanded Jameson, "Go inside."

Jameson nodded to us both. "I think you two might be the real deal. See you at lunch, Olive Bee. Don't be late."

I turned to look at Dimitri after Jameson disappeared and saw how his jaw was clenched, his neck completely tensed. "That lunch will be over my dead body."

I chuckled and got off his lap, hopping out of the hot tub fast and running toward the door. "Stop stewing and get inside before someone calls the cops on us."

I ran inside and glanced at the primary suite's hall. I should have been showering upstairs and sleeping there now. That had been the deal. The bed was all set up. So, I went up there and took a shower immediately.

Dimitri wasn't done with me though. I heard the door open and felt him step in behind me before he said, "Why the hell are you up here showering?"

"That was the original plan, Dimitri."

He pushed me up against the stone wall and stared down at me with fire in his eyes. "Are you trying to drive me insane?"

"What?" I felt his cock rising along with his temper as we stared at each other.

He lifted my leg and crouched a bit to slide his cock into me slowly, inch by delicious inch. "Does this feel like we're sticking to the plan of me being your fake boyfriend?"

"Dimitri—"

My nails dug into him as he lifted my other leg too. Then he reared back and thrust into me hard. Again and again and again. "You're. Mine." Another thrust. "Mine in my bed." Another thrust. "Mine in the hot tub." Another thrust. "Mine everywhere."

"I don't think—"

His hand went to my throat. "Careful what you say now, Honeybee."

I couldn't say a single thing. The heat in the shower when he'd clamped down on my throat increased a hundred degrees, and my body convulsed around him. And I felt how he released himself in me, too, his body flexing and uncoiling the tension he held. He didn't hold back as he pumped into me.

And when I'd settled against him, he didn't let me go even as I tried to pull away. Instead, he grabbed his soap and started to wash every part of me—quietly, softly, meticulously.

We showered in silence, but the connection was too loud to ignore. It was getting harder and harder to deny this relationship was real.

I tried not to focus on it and let him carry me to the bedroom downstairs, where he firmly planted me on my side of his bed. "Don't even think about sleeping in the spare bedroom," he grumbled.

"Seems like that's a talk for another day," I murmured.

"Or never," he retorted as he turned out the light and circled the bed to get in, completely naked. "You sleep next to me in our house every day."

"Won't be our house when you sell it," I reminded him.

"Not sure I can sell the house when I have memories of fucking you in the hot tub."

I groaned. "Don't remind me. I can't believe we did that in

front of Jameson."

He nuzzled up against me. "I'll never do that again. Not even for you."

"Do what?"

"Fuck my girl in front of another man just because she likes it, or just to prove a point."

"I didn't— Well, I was curious how it would be, and it was ..."

"It was what?" He bit my ear.

"Well, I know why people are into voyeurism now."

He almost snarled. "I'm not. Never again, Olive. These tits, this pussy." He slid his hand over me, and I moaned. "These sounds are only for me." He sucked on my neck, and I whimpered as he nipped at my skin. "Do you understand?"

"Dimitri—"

He slid his finger into me again, and I spread my legs, my body ready for anything he was willing to give.

"Say you understand, Honeybee. That you belong to me."

I knew I did. The truth settles deep in my bones. I said it over and over. But I wondered if he'd feel the same once the news of the Diamond Syndicate came out.

CHAPTER 37: OLIVE

The next morning, I rolled over, ready to tell Dimitri we had to talk about the society.

Except the man who could sleep in for an hour after me was gone. And I felt the stress of it all weigh down on me as I stared at his empty space. I'd been doing so well with working at the salon and then coming home to practice calligraphy and look at my thesis notes.

But Lucille and Jameson had jumbled up my thoughts on my thesis now.

My relationship with Dimitri was all jumbled too.

I stared at the dresser which hid the leatherbound book. How would I tell him about the syndicate? I got up to stare at the people outside my window. How would I explain that I didn't think Lucille was a danger and that Jameson only wanted what was best for his daughter?

Did I even believe that?

I squinted when I saw a truck with a trailer packed with a lawn mower and gardening tools parked out front. It must have been the lawn service Dimitri hired. I didn't know why my stomach turned at the thought of them here now. Like I couldn't take care of my home myself. *Mine.* In my community. The one I should be learning about and taking care of and helping to flourish.

I touched the necklace and thought of my mother's words. They were getting to me. Or maybe Lucille's words were ... and maybe Dimitri was too. The idea that I needed to do this, to take care of the lawn myself, suddenly burned in my gut before I stomped over to the closet and threw on some shorts and a sports bra. It was going to be a hot day, but I was going to do this myself either way.

I hurried down the stairs and whipped open the doors. "You all can stop working on the lawn."

Two men looked up and the other didn't even hesitate to walk the mower back over to his truck. "Do as the lady says," he told his colleagues.

"I'll make sure to reimburse you for—"

"We've been paid through the year."

"Oh, right. Well, how about you come once a month to clean up anything I have missed?"

"Okay?" He dragged out the word and rubbed at a bit of dirt on his chin. "You own this home?"

"Yes, with my boyfriend, Dimitri Hardy. He'll confirm. Anyway, would you like some lemonade before you head out?"

"Sure." He smiled big.

But his friend nudged him and grumbled, "Dude, Dimitri ain't going for this."

"I got plans with my girl tonight. I'm leaving if she lets us," he responded back.

Of course I was listening to the whole conversation as they followed me inside. "You should pick her some flowers before you see her," I offered.

"Good idea." He smiled and it lit up the room as I gave them some sparkling lemonade that we'd stocked from our last grocery visit.

"I appreciate you all coming by," I told them before they left with no argument. I pushed the flower behind my ear in a bit further and smiled to myself, excited to get a workout, smell a fresh-cut lawn, and quiet the thoughts in my mind with the loud mower.

Except we didn't have a lawn mower when I looked in the garage because ... why would we? We were going to move.

I shoved that thought down and waved to Lucille across the street as she sat out on her porch. "You have a mower I can borrow?"

She smirked. "You even know how to turn one on?" she quipped before opening her garage. She then yelled to Jameson. "Olive's going to mow the lawn."

He was out on his porch as well, looking at a newspaper in a rocking chair. Making eye contact with him was a bit difficult after what I'd done last night, but when he frowned at me, my embarrassment turned to determination. "What? You don't think I can, Jameson?"

He rolled his eyes and rocked away. "I'm going to enjoy watching this."

"Jameson!" I frowned at him, not sure if he was making a comment about last night.

"I'm being honest." He shrugged, sipping his morning coffee.

"Don't you ever work?"

"On sabbatical." He smiled like he might never go back to work just to irritate me. "Had to fire Franny's last nanny so I figured some time with her would be great. Plus, I had to figure out some things here anyway."

My eyes narrowed. "How's that figuring out coming?"

"Why don't you just mow the lawn?"

"You're really going to watch me mow the lawn?"

"You betcha." He waved us on, and Lucille waved back.

"I just have to get it out of the garage." She disappeared for a minute and then came back. I looked at the mower and she chuckled. "Here's how to get it started." She explained how to fire it up and stop it. "Good luck." She winked at me, and I scoffed. I couldn't believe none of them thought I could do this.

I had mowed a lawn before. It was probably only once or twice when Kee and I were traveling and we'd stayed at a friend's. I'm pretty sure it was more of a dare sort of thing. I wasn't that much of a princess though. I could handle this.

I smiled big when I found the primer that Lucille told me about. It didn't seem to be doing anything, but I grabbed the handlebar and yanked the string thing with my other hand and it revved to life.

I glanced up at Lucille who was clapping and then at Jameson who was giving me a thumbs-up. I was so proud that I got right to work by engaging the other handle that supposedly helped to propel the mower forward.

A small chore like this brought me such joy that I didn't even notice I'd conquered half the lawn until I heard, "Olive. Cut the mower! Why are you mowing the fucking lawn?"

Hearing his voice over the mower meant Dimitri was yelling. The man never truly yelled at anyone. I heard him on the phone talking sternly, but he had such an even keel nature, that was as harsh as he got—except when he was talking dirty to me.

I tried not to consider what it would be like if he was really angry and talking dirty as I turned to see him standing in his three-piece suit. The scowl on his face made him look powerful and dangerous. I wanted him even more now.

Truly, my body was starting to be completely disconnected from any logical way of thinking. I knew he wasn't good for me, yet he was all I craved every single part of every single day.

I turned off the mower and took a deep breath. Then I swiped away some of the sweat on my brow before turning around to face him. "You concerned about your girlfriend when you're at work?"

I glanced around just so he was aware there may be an audience. "Work?" He frowned and then shook his head like he didn't seem concerned about that. "I hired a lawn service, Honeybee."

"I know. I invited them in for lemonade and then told them they could go home." I didn't think Dimitri would mind that I canceled the lawn service. What did he care as long as it was done?

Yet, his stare was vicious as he said, "And they just left?"

"Well, what did you expect them to do? Stay?"

He growled, "Get inside now."

"Dimitri, the lawn is only half done and—"

"You won't be finishing the lawn. I hired those men to do a job. I expected them to do it, not let my girlfriend do it instead."

"Guess the show's over," Jameson announced as he stood from his chair on the porch. "See you on Tuesday, Olive."

"If you see her, you'll also be seeing me," Dimitri made it known. "Happy to have lunch with you too, Jameson."

Jameson cracked his knuckles but didn't say another word as he walked inside.

"You're being absolutely ridiculous right now. I can mow a lawn and go to lunch by myself." I spun back to the lawn mower and turned it on.

He stomped over, balanced the two cups he was holding in one hand, and turned the mower off. "I was getting you a coffee. And you're not mowing the damn lawn."

"Okay ... well, you weren't even home," I pointed out and crossed my arms. "Is this some weird male thing?"

He walked up and kissed my cheek before handing me the coffees. "Please go set these inside, Honeybee," he grumbled while unbuttoning his suit jacket. Knowing my lack of control with him, I should have looked away, especially when he undid the top button of his freaking collared shirt.

"What are you doing?" I squeaked, my eyes widening.

"I'm not mowing the lawn in a long sleeve." He handed me his jacket and collared shirt and then proceeded to take off his undershirt too.

And there he stood in slacks and no shirt on, a billion abs on display for the whole neighborhood to see. He yanked the pull cord of the mower and was off. He buzzed up and down the lawn and not one woman looked away. Not Lucille. Not me. Not Melly. Even Zen stopped to watch as she walked by.

Thankfully, he was much faster than me and was done within twenty minutes. I wasn't proud to admit that I hadn't moved the whole time. I leaned against one of our porch posts and tried to keep the hunger in me at bay as the sweat glistened across his chest.

Dimitri Hardy was a perfect specimen with ten million abs, biceps and forearms of steel, and tanned skin that almost shimmered in the sun. There was no way I was leaving him outside by himself while he did this. I understood the need to mark territory now, understood why he maybe didn't want men watching me while I did manual labor, because watching him was freaking intimate. My body heated and my thighs clenched while I stood there, consciously rigid, trying to not walk up to him and stop the mower.

Finally, he pushed through the last line of grass and the

sound of the engine ceased. Right away, Lucille and Melly started walking over. Melly basically had her claws and teeth out, ready to pounce on him. I saw how she sauntered, wearing the shortest shorts ever. I frowned at him. "Great job drawing half the town's attention by mowing the lawn half naked," I whisper-yelled at him.

He had no shame as he stuck a finger in the waist of my yoga pants and yanked me close to him. Then he dragged that finger up my stomach as I sucked in a breath. "I could say the same about you. How long did Jameson sit on his porch watching?"

"Dimitri, that's not the point—"

"It is. I'll make sure Melly gets the same amount of time because I like that look of jealousy on your face." One of his dimples showed as he shot me a lopsided smile.

I was about to tell him he was a dick and drag him in by his damn ear, but Lucille called to us, "Yoo-hoo, Dimitri, seems you weren't at work too long today." She glanced up meaningfully at our house and winked at him. "What made you come back so soon?"

I looked over and frowned. There, by the corner of our garage—and quite frankly on every corner of the house—I now saw small black security cameras.

"What the hell are those?" I pointed to them and the smile that spread across his face held not one ounce of remorse.

"Cameras. For security, of course."

"That's such a good idea," Melly said in her bubbly fake tone as she bounced over. She would have said anything Dimitri did was a good idea. "I especially like the idea of you adding these on street corners too. It really would add such a feeling of safety for me."

"You're talking about installing them throughout the neighborhood?" I narrowed my eyes at him.

"Yes, Honeybee. Just testing them for now."

That's when Jameson decided to add from his porch. "Seems to be something you need approval for."

"Interesting," Lucille said softly.

"Awesome. That the only reason you want them on the street corners and around our home?" I lifted a brow and then scowled at him.

He rubbed a hand over his five-o'clock shadow before he responded. "Oh, around our house? Those are to make sure I know what my future wife is doing all the time, Olive. I like watching you. You know this."

CHAPTER 38: DIMITRI

"Stop with the future wife!" She slammed the door of the house after I'd followed her inside.

"Never gonna happen. Until we're married. Then, it'll just be wife," I said as I laid my shirt on the chair and smiled over at her. Steam was practically coming out of her ears as her eyes widened at my nonchalance of the term.

"You make all this sound so normal! And I know it's not, Dimitri. Like you've considered marrying all the women you've ever been in a relationship with?" Her eyes narrowed. "It's ridiculous."

"Absolutely. Because the *only* serious relationship I've ever had is with you.

"Well, I'm not happy with our serious relationship right now because you're being a misogynistic asshole who won't let his girlfriend mow a damn lawn. No one would ever want that."

"So, you're saying it's serious?" I stepped closer to her. "Melly seemed quite happy about it, and—"

"Don't you dare talk to me about that little—" She poked me in the chest and then stopped when I grabbed her wrist and held her hand there.

"Go on. I'd love to hear what you think of her." I wrapped a hand around her waist and pulled her closer.

"No. I don't even care about her. I'm freaking mad at you, Dimitri." She tried to cover up her jealousy, but I wanted it. I wanted to see it. I wanted her as unhinged as I was. If I was going to lose my mind, she was going down the path of insanity with me. When I saw her smiling at Jameson before she mowed our damn lawn, I'd practically run out of the coffeehouse. The cameras I'd set up alerted me to motion outside, and now I was inclined to look all the damn time when it came to her.

"Because I wouldn't let you mow the lawn?"

"Let's not gloss over the fact you're watching me on those cameras *without my knowledge.*"

"I'll be installing them throughout the house too." I crossed my arms, not willing to bend there. "I'm admitting it now. So that way, when I watch you shower, you're completely aware."

"Stop it." She bit her lip and blushed. But then she poked me again. "You can't be all manly and not let me do things I want to do. That's absurd. I can take care of myself." She sighed. "And I enjoy doing it. I don't like hiring every last person to come in and do every single thing for us. If we have everyone do everything for us, how is it our own anymore, you know? And I feel like I want to know all these things—"

"Because you're curious about everything?" I finished for her.

She chewed her cheek and the blush that spread across her face made me want to pull her close to tell her not to be embarrassed about who she was. "I know I have a nosy streak."

"That I'm not sure if I find that cute or completely detrimental to your safety. It's likely the latter most of the time."

She nodded, then she sighed. "This place is ... well, people care about it. They put in hard work and time and effort, and they want to protect it. I figure we should put in some hard work too."

"Honeybee, I'm only putting in hard work for you and protecting you at this point," I emphasized so she'd understand.

She folded her arms across her chest as she scowled at me, but I saw the blush on her cheeks. Olive couldn't hide that she wanted my attention, that we were meant for one another at this point. "You need to take a minute to cool off and think about what you're saying. I am going to go shower. *Upstairs.* You better not freaking watch."

"Upstairs?" I growled out the word. No one belonged up there unless they were a guest. And her ass knew she wasn't that. I strode across the room, and her name rumbled out from my chest in warning. "You shower in our bathroom."

"Or what?" The challenge rolled off her lips as she threw a smirk over her shoulder.

That was all the invite I needed to grab her by those curls on the stairs. "I'll show you where you belong right here right now."

"Maybe you shouldn't have been staring at me through secret cameras either." She turned fully to face me, one step above me on those stairs, her lips now aligned with mine. She licked them, letting them shimmer like they wanted to be bit.

"You know I'm going to stare at you all I want for the rest of my life, Olive. It'll be my right."

"Is that so?" She planted her hands on her hips and glared those amber eyes at me. "Even if you're my future husband, Dimitri Hardy, you don't get to look unless I want you to."

"There's no question about it anymore. You will be mine. And I'm already yours." I looked down at my length, rock hard for her under my slacks. "Can't you tell?"

Her eyes dragged down my body now and her hand slid over my chest, then my abs, and then into my pants. "I wish every woman outside could tell too. Some of them seem to forget." She gripped my cock then, biting her lip.

"You can tell them, Olive. Or I'll keep telling them for you. I'm yours." She pumped her tiny fist up and down my cock as I groaned. "I'm always going to be yours."

"Why do I feel like I might lose you at any moment then?" Her voice was breathy now as she held my gaze. "I watched you mowing our lawn, Dimitri. Watched how other women looked at you—"

"Just remember I'm only watching you. I'm here for you. I'm doing it all for you."

She whimpered, then said, "I want you."

"Good because I'm taking you on these stairs. I should take you on our front lawn too. I want to take you everywhere in this house so you remember every second of every day while you're here that this is how much I want you always."

"How much?" she breathed.

I leaned in and told her, "Turn around, walk a step up."

She did and then asked, "Now what?"

I ripped her thin yoga pants down. "I'm going to burn every pair of these so no man can stare at the curve of your ass anymore."

"I'll just get more." She giggled.

I smacked her ass then. "Get on our knees, Olive Monroe. I'm going to fuck that pussy to remind you who's in charge."

She did as she was told and I shucked my slacks down, ready to have her right then and there. Yet, she threw her curls over her shoulder to glance back at me. "Maybe *I'm* in charge. You make me feel that way, Dimitri. You have a hunger in your eyes for me sometimes where I swear maybe I am the only woman for you."

"You are." I pumped myself once as our eyes locked. "You're the one I want forever."

"I'm starting to believe it," she whispered before she glanced down and murmured, "Maybe I want you to show me now. Show me you want only me. Show me how much, Dimitri Hardy. I want you to fuck me hard. So hard I feel that cock through my whole damn body."

With that comment, she put her elbows on the step and arched her back so her beautiful ass was on display for me. I grabbed the railing to steady myself at the gorgeous sight. Her pussy was perfect, dripping for me already, her skin was so smooth and delicate that it felt made for me too as I took her hips in my hands. "Olive, if I take you here—"

"You better. And you better make it rough."

No more hesitation, I did what she told me. She was in charge. I thrust my cock deep into the center of her, wanting to feel every single inch of her then. I roared her name as I did it, and she screamed mine.

Our skin slapped together in the silence of the room, her pussy soaked my cock exactly the way I liked, and her honey-apple scent swirled around me as I took what was mine.

"You're it for me, Olive Monroe. You're the only one I'll have forever. The only one for me."

Her mewls of pleasure filled the air. "I want that. I do. It might be wrong, but I do."

"Can't be wrong when it feels this right." I groaned as I slid my cock slow this time out of her so she could feel how I stretched her, and how empty she would feel without me in her.

She gasped as I did, and when I stopped for just a moment, with only my tip touching her entrance, she whined, "Please. I need you in me again. Now."

"Do you?" I leaned forward and raised her sports bra above her tits so I could roll them into my hands.

She gasped. "Oh my God. It feels too good. Dimitri, they ... I need you to fuck me when you do that."

"Honeybee, these tits feel so good in my hands right now. Maybe I'll take some time to just play with them."

She whimpered as I rolled the nipples in between my fingers. "I'm going to orgasm. I can't take it. Please, screw me now."

I didn't give her my cock, but I did slide one hand down to brush over her clit. Her pussy was dripping so much arousal onto it that my fingers slid fast against it as I rolled one nipple and her clit at the same rhythm.

"I'm so sensitive. I don't know why." She sounded almost in pain, but I knew it was because she was holding back feeling that pleasure.

"Take your orgasm, Olive. I want to see you unravel. Let go on *your* stairs, in *your* house, with *your* future husband. Let go for me, Honeybee."

She did. She threw her head back, and I saw the woman I loved give in for me. She gave in to the vulnerability she didn't want to embrace, and she gave in to us even when she was scared. I hoped she'd do it again even when it was outside of the sex we were having.

I shifted my hips so I could rub our arousal over her clit now as she came down from her high. She shivered with the sensation. "I'm good, Dimitri. Just take what you want now."

"No," I told her. "You're not done. You'll be even better in a second, Honeybee."

"I don't think I can—"

"You'll take another orgasm. You know why?"

She was shaking, her skin shimmering, her breath coming fast, but her back arched into me again as she said, "Tell me why."

"You do need me. Just like I need you. Don't forget that, Olive. We need each other. We always will."

Then I reared back only to thrust into her again. Hard. I reached around to pinch her clit too, to give her every sensation she needed right then. She met me thrust for thrust, and then we both climbed toward another high, her pussy squeezing my dick like she never wanted me to leave the inside of her.

I didn't want to leave either. This woman was my home, and I intended to make her see that as I roared that she was mine again, rocking into her with all I had this time and emptying my seed into her. Her pussy was still pulsing, like it was milking the last of my come into her, and I held myself inside her, hoping every drop of it stayed in.

I took my time sliding from her, careful with how sensitive we both were. I then scooped her up, wanting to make sure we went downstairs instead of up. "I should screw you again in our bed just so we're clear that all I want is you, day in and day out."

I set her on the bed, and she smiled lazily at me before she spread her legs. "Do it then, Dimitri Hardy. Make me believe it."

I wasn't about to disappoint her. Like I said, she was the one in charge, not me.

CHAPTER 39: OLIVE

Dimitri went to finish the lawn in the backyard in a black T-shirt and gym shorts, completely satisfied with how he'd had his way with me. I couldn't really complain. Other than the fact I made sure he had a shirt over that chest of his before he went out back.

I only had our soft bedsheet wrapped around me when I heard a knock at the door and saw Jameson standing on the porch from out the window.

I padded down the hall and glanced back at Dimitri still mowing, before I hurried to the door. "What's going on?"

"I was going to discuss this at lunch with you, but it seems it can't wait after the text I got. And you're going to have to decide what you want Dimitri to know too." His eyes glanced behind me.

"Well, if it's serious, I probably should. Dimitri's reasonable."

"He's not. Not when it comes to you." He shook his head and his eyes seemed to glaze over with darkness. "I wouldn't be either with the girl I loved."

I wanted to argue there was no way he loved me. Not yet. It was all too soon, but I felt the weight of my feelings for him in every one of my blood cells. I knew my heart was being won over by him. He'd made me feel like he'd never look away from me.

It's what I wanted. What I needed in that moment, and

he'd given it to me. No one could be immune to that.

"You look like you're not sure, Olive. He tells you right?" He lifted a brow before he continued. "He'd better be telling you, because it's obvious he does. Anyway, the text."

"What?" I asked as I stepped out onto the porch with him now while he held his phone up for me to see. A text from an unknown number read...

Unknown: Suspicions confirmed. He's got the kid working with him.

"Who's the kid, Jameson?" I said but my blood ran cold because it couldn't be. I told myself over and over there was no way, but my gut was already turning with the answer.

"Knox is in on that deal with the Irish, Olive Bee. He has to be."

That's when the mower cut in the backyard. Other than the birds chirping, it was silent now. As silent as it seemed my world was, it screeched to a halt with Jameson's statement. "No." I shook my head. "No. No. No."

Dimitri's footsteps were loud and hurried before the front door swung open from behind me. "What the hell is going on?"

I wanted to tell Dimitri all about the Diamond Syndicate, but I needed him to have the correct picture, not one of my brother involved in drugs and trafficking. I stuttered over my words, "Jameson just stopped by to talk over the board meeting and ... um ... the office space, Dimitri."

Dimitri wasn't dumb. He must have heard the tremor of emotion in my voice, because he came to stand beside me and look me in the eye before he stepped in front of me. "Whatever the hell is happening, it's done now. We're done here." He stood with his arms crossed and his feet wide, like a wall there to protect me. "Don't look at her, don't talk to her, don't breathe the same air as her."

"Are we done though?" Jameson met his stance head-on. "Because you know as well as I do there is shit going on in this community." Jameson's tone was hard, but his words were damning for Dimitri.

"Wait." I peered around my barrier of a man. "What does he know?"

"Dimitri should be getting a text from Bane or Dom about the Diamond Syndicate soon. He knows about them. And he's about to know that your father, my father, and Earl have all been involved in deals with drug trafficking with the Irish." He took a breath while all the air seemed to leave my lungs. I couldn't breathe, not with what he was telling me. "But it's harder now because of Knox—"

"Stop." Dimitri's voice boomed out through the town. "Don't say another damn word."

Jameson looked at me with fear finally in his eyes. "We have to talk, Olive. There are things you'll need to make decisions about. Dimitri, you know—"

Dimitri cut him off. "Don't involve her by saying more. What the hell are you thinking?" And then he looked back at me, fire in his green eyes. "Honeybee, you knew? You should have told me." I felt the way his body shook, the way his muscles were coiled and ready to carry me the hell out of there.

"Shouldn't you have told her too?" Jameson countered.

My glance ping-ponged between them, and suddenly I felt a fear whoosh through me at those words. If he knew, could he be in danger? Why hadn't he told me? The fury of that question came next. "And *you* knew?" My tone was accusatory.

He shook his head. "Damn it. I've been trying to protect you," he said, and I didn't know whether to lean into the anger or the fear of what this meant or the pitter-patter of my heart that he cared enough to try to protect me.

"You can't protect her from her birthright," Jameson continued. "I need to talk with her."

"I'd rather drop dead than allow that. She's not safe with you."

"Like you can't watch her every move around here anyway." Jameson tsked, and Dimitri glared at him.

"You're right. I can and I will," Dimitri responded immediately, no remorse in his growl.

"Those security cameras aren't approved on the streets yet," Jameson pointed out. "It's illegal to have them on."

"You think I give a fuck?" Dimitri was admitting to committing a crime, and I didn't know whether to be flattered it was for me or concerned. "Let me be clear, I don't live by morals, Jameson. I don't live for my life anymore, quite frankly. I'm living to protect hers. I couldn't care less about a damn law. Take me to jail. I'll live there happily as long as I know she is good. The only life I'm trying to save here is the love of mine. Don't get it twisted."

I gasped at his declaration and whispered out his name. He glanced back at me for just a second and his brows knitted together as he murmured softly, "Honeybee." It was just a nickname, but I felt the love in it, the unwavering support.

Then, he looked back at Jameson and snarled, "I'll break every law and every bone in your body if I think for a second she's unsafe."

"She's safe with me," Jameson declared, and his voice was loud now too. But when his blue eyes met mine, I saw the genuine look there that I'd seen when he'd come to my mother's funeral, the look of a friend and of someone I could trust.

I took a deep breath, knowing I was about to piss off the one man I didn't want to, and touched Dimitri's back. "Dimitri, just a minute."

His whole body tensed, every single huge muscle, before he cranked his neck to look over at me. He was already shaking his head. "Don't ask me to do this, Honeybee."

"I have to," I whispered out. "You need to let me have a moment more with Jameson."

"I'm not going to hurt her, Dimitri."

"I don't trust a damn thing that comes out of your mouth." He pinched the bridge of his nose and let out about ten swears before he pulled me close. "I swear I do things for you I would never do for another soul. You talk to your friend, and you let him know he's not a friend after this." Then he wrapped his hand around the nape of my neck and kissed me, dragging his lips over mine slowly and deliberately. "Don't agree to anything either." Jameson sighed as he watched Dimitri glare at him. "You got two minutes, Jameson." And then he went inside, slamming the door.

Jameson chuckled. "Completely irrational and completely in love when it comes to you."

I waved off his assessment, more focused on the text he'd received now. "If what you're saying about my father and Earl and everyone is true, how do I get Knox out? How do we make this right?"

"You are going to do nothing for now. Act normal, stay safe"—he sighed and pointed toward the door—"with your bodyguard. As for Earl, we're taking care of it. But you're going to stop poking around. You're causing concerns. We don't need to tip your father off to anything more. You're going to tell Dimitri to get in or get out, too. If we push through approval for his office, that comes with us aligning with the companies he has partnerships with. That means the HEAT empire is tied to the Italian Mob and the Armanellis. The Irish will not be happy, especially after your father and Earl promised them an alliance."

"I want my brother out of this." I felt the roots I'd avoided planting digging themselves deep into Paradise Grove. "I'll do whatever it takes. You can't possibly want this type of home for Franny either. We have to make it better." I touched my necklace and stared out at our street, at my community, at my home. "Sometimes you have to take the chance ... and enjoy the dance."

He sighed. And then he touched my cheek. "If you weren't with that man in there, Olive, I'd probably kiss you for that. I had my doubts about you both at first. Wasn't sure what either of you knew or what you were trying to do."

I felt the blush on my cheeks as I chewed on my bottom lip. "It's real," I whispered.

"We'll get through this. In the meantime, think about what you want with your dad. Once we figure out our plan with Knox, we'll have to make a decision about him."

"Don't do anything about Knox without me. There's got to be a way to get him out of this. He can't possibly be thinking right if—"

"I know, Olive. I know." He leaned forward still and kissed my cheek softly. There was a moment that passed between us as I looked into his blue eyes. They were full of ice-cold determination. Knox was a part of his family too. He wasn't going to let anything happen.

He shifted his weight a little and a floorboard under him creaked, making me jerk back and look down.

He tsked at it. "This piece is going bad. You should replace it." He murmured, "I'll come over with some tools and work on it for you after this is all over. You'll be here, yeah?"

"I will." I said those two words with the most confidence I'd felt since I'd been home.

CHAPTER 40: DIMITRI

I was only allowing the interaction between Jameson and Olive because I knew I could watch every damn second of them out there on that porch. I pulled up my security system, but that's when the first text from my family came in.

> **Izzy: So we should probably have a chat about this little mob issue going on with the Diamond Syndicate. Saw your girl just met with Jameson, Dimitri.**

My sister was used to being involved in all this. I'd become accustomed to the fact that she'd married Cade, the brother of the head of the Italian Mob, and a man that essentially could hack into any system in the world. He'd promised he was reformed along with this brother, and so far, their investments with us had been clean.

He'd also helped clean up Dex's mess. And smiled at every ounce of violence he witnessed. He was deranged and we all knew it. Still, he was family.

> **Me: Are you hacking security cameras again, Izzy?**

Cade: Yup. My wife seems to think watching all of you is a great use of her time.

Izzy: So what if I am? Dimitri, you turned on these cameras before they were legal, so I am just being a good sister and seeing what's so important over in that little Paradise.

Kee: Dimitri, you owe me a phone call about turning on those cameras. Are you watching Olive?

Lilah: Should we all stick to the matter at hand? The hubs says we've already partnered with Bane and Black Diamond Casino. It's essentially the same thing as backing the Diamond Syndicate, so we should consider doing it. I also vote yes.

Izzy: Yeah. Probably best-case scenario doing that. You good with it, Dimitri?

Dex: Dimitri? How about if I'm good with it? No fucking way.

Kee: Don't be overprotective for no reason, Dex. It's ridiculous.

Dex: It's not ridiculous to think the Diamond Syndicate could be catastrophically dangerous to this family in that some of them are partnering with the Irish Mob.

Izzy: Only like three people. Out of thousands across the United States. Bill Monroe, Earl and a few others have ties with the Irish Mob, but we're working on pinpointing the ringleader, and if we make our own partnership soon, we can stop that alliance in their tracks.

Declan: It's messy.

Evie: It's logical.

Izzy: So smart.

Me: At the potential detriment of what? The family's safety? Olive's? No fucking way is right. I'm with Dex.

Kee: Pink swears that it's the best move.

Me: The fact that you're talking to Pink about a secret society alliance with the HEAT empire is a problem, Kee.

Dex: What Dimitri said. I'm done with this conversation.

Declan: If Dimitri and Dex aren't on board, neither am I.

Dom: Guess the boys have spoken.

Clara: Dom, just because the guys have spoken doesn't mean the decision has been made.

She was right in most cases, but in this instance, it was for the good of the family—for my nieces and nephews and everyone's safety.

I watched Olive and Jameson on the camera that I shouldn't have had operational. I saw how he offered to fix our porch, how he kissed her cheek, how she let him. I swung open the door just as I heard her say, "When will it blow over exactly? And what will that choice be?"

Jameson crossed his arms over his chest, and I swear his ass was trying to puff his chest up as he glared at me. "You know I'm only telling her to lay low."

"Your two minutes are up."

"Man, I'm warning you about that too. She's my friend. And we're always going to be friends. You understand that, right?"

Like I gave a damn. He was circling too close to my girl and he knew it. "And we're always going to be together."

The guy had the audacity to goad me by looking Olive up and down in the bed sheet before he smirked. "Sure?"

Motherfucker. "Sure as the sun rising in the east and setting in the west. She's mine, and I'm never leaving her."

"What if she leaves you?"

I smirked. "Then I'll follow her through whatever heaven and hell she dreams up for me on my damn knees, pleading with her until she takes me back."

CHAPTER 41: OLIVE

I tried to listen. I tried to lay low and keep my mouth shut for the first night. Dimitri and I didn't indulge in anything other than him holding me close and me snuggling against him as my thoughts turned and turned.

He was quiet next to me, like he knew now wasn't the time to argue about what we'd kept from each other or talk about the large diamond elephant in the room.

He held me, like the unwavering rock of support that he was. Like the man I needed. Like my person. Like the love of my life.

I still woke the next morning feeling as if I hadn't slept at all. My stomach was a mess with nerves, my body jittery from wanting to do something to help. I was trying to listen. I really was. Yet, this involved my family. My brother. I felt absolutely sick to my stomach that morning, so much so that I reached for my phone and texted him.

> **Me: I know what Dad said. But we need to talk, Knox.**
>
> **Me: Please call me back.**
>
> **Me: Please.**

There were dots that showed up on the screen, but then

they stopped. Our relationship had just started to mend, so I didn't know how much more I should push. I also didn't know how deep into it he was, if he would listen to reason.

Without him answering, there was nothing I could do, so I tried to focus on other things. I wrote out my thesis and stared at what I'd done. Suddenly, my degree didn't feel so important. Suddenly, I knew I was going to be here in Paradise Grove where I belonged anyway.

Sometimes, even when life feels like a complete mess, the path you've been searching for makes itself known through the storm of chaos. I sent my thesis in, pulling everything I'd previously written about the syndicate, and chose a deliberate path. It was one where I protected my home and my family.

Lucille had booked a blow out for that morning and it was the perfect thing for me to do while I waited to hear from Jameson or Knox.

"I'm walking to the salon," I announced on my way out after putting on my black maxi dress.

"I'll walk you there." Dimitri immediately closed his laptop like he was ready to keep me wrapped in his bubble for all of time.

"No. I'm fine. You're going to have to let me take care of myself, Dimitri." I shook my head at him.

"Or I could just walk you," he suggested again. "If I don't, I'll be pulling you up on the damn cameras."

"That's a complete waste of time." I rolled my eyes at him but felt butterflies in my stomach at the way he wanted to watch over me. He got up from the couch and packed up his laptop in a briefcase. "It's just a walk for me, Honeybee."

He wouldn't take no for an answer and even held my hand the whole way. This was supposed to be normal, something we'd been doing for a while, but somehow it felt more intimate, more real, and more magical all at the same time.

He kissed me in front of the spa when we got there and murmured, "I'm going to stop at the drugstore next door, then I'll be sitting at the park across the street. Call me when you're ready to go."

Minutes later, I was set up to give Lucille a blowout. She sat down and asked, "How's Dimitri? See he's out there keeping watch."

"He's been a bit overly protective, but fine." I didn't divulge anything else to her, but I saw how she narrowed her eyes.

"I'd think you'd be thankful a man was doting on you so much," I heard from about ten feet away. I hadn't noticed Melly sitting in Madi's chair, and she was glaring at me now.

"What?" I knew today wasn't the day I should listen to her. My brother hadn't called, a migraine was growing by the minute, which meant stress must have been the culprit, and I was worried about the syndicate. I didn't need my high school bully adding to all that.

And it probably wasn't good that Lucille grumbled under her breath, "Be prickly. The girl needs a lesson."

I understood I was different than her, that I didn't have my life as together as she did, didn't make all the right moves right away, and that she thought she was better than me because of it. But she had no right to talk down to me.

"I said you should be happy Dimitri treats you that way. I mean, at least someone is interested in you." She stared at me, her beautiful blue eyes lined perfectly in makeup, the lashes feathering out as if she'd spent hours coating them.

I felt my eyes well with tears, which was silly. She meant nothing to me. Why was I so emotional about it all of a sudden?

Lucille patted my hand quickly and shook her head slightly at me as if she was telling me not to give in. And Zen walked by and nudged my back as if to push me to keep going. I blurted out the next question. "Are you insinuating that he shouldn't be?"

She sighed and looked at her nails. "Olive, when are you going to learn you've never belonged here really. This is an upscale community, and Dimitri is taking it to the next level. You're not exactly on par. You and I both know that. Everyone does. That's why you left. Why you should leave again."

I think maybe Lucille had talked me up about cacti too much. Or maybe I really hadn't had enough sleep. And then she tilted her head toward the hair dye.

"I'm sorry you feel that way. But just because I left doesn't mean I wasn't a part of Paradise Grove, Melly. And now I'm back with the man I'll marry, and we'll likely settle here." I said the words fast, but I didn't stutter or trip over them. They felt good, right, and they settled in my soul even as I tried to keep a lid on my emotions. The fury in me raged now. She'd crossed lines before, but this, at my job, in front of friends, was too much.

"Zen, what color are you doing in Melly's hair today?" Lucille asked and when Zen looked over, Lucille winked at her. Zen looked at me and lifted her eyebrows.

I shouldn't have nodded. I was basically giving permission. Yet, these people encouraged me to be over-the-top for once, and I was taking the opportunity.

"Same as always," Zen said as she combed through her precious chestnut brown hair and went about dying her roots.

I told her how wonderful she'd look when she was done. She rolled her eyes at me like she couldn't be bothered to talk to me anymore. Lucille and I watched as Zen put the black temporary dye in her hair and spun Melly away from the mirror so that she wouldn't be able to see as she typed away on her phone. She made sure to get every strand too.

"You're all set," I whispered to Lucille just as Zen murmured to Melly that they could go wash out the dye.

"Not set until I get to see that little brat's face."

As Zen walked Melly back to her seat, she said, "You know, Melly, not all of us were sure we'd fit in here. I'm sure Olive felt the same."

"Yes, well, that's all I mean by it. She gets it." Melly laughed and rolled her eyes, still looking at her phone.

Didn't she realize no one here fit in perfectly? We were all shapes jamming ourselves into the wrong indentations. The problem was she was so judgmental that we kept trying to do it. "You're of course right. This community is so lucky to have you."

And then Madi turned to me and asked, "Can you just blow dry her quick? I need to make a call."

Melly smirked at the idea of me having to work on her hair, but I did so with joy. I wanted to be the one to spin her in the chair and see the look on her face up close.

It was wrong of me to smile now. To even start giggling under the sound of the blow dryer. She wasn't paying attention to me though. I was just the help pretty much. She didn't care if I was staying at Dimitri's house either. In her mind, she'd steal him away sooner or later. She'd wear down my confidence enough that I'd leave.

Except being in this town had built me back up in a way I hadn't realized I needed.

I turned the chair and smiled at her. "Voila, Melly. I hope

you enjoy the color. It suits your soul."

Her scream was brutal, like she was dying. I didn't expect her to do much more than that. Yet, I'm pretty sure when Dimitri and the rest of the town got to the salon after hearing the screaming, we were on the floor, fighting.

Lucille was cheering me on with the delicate gold-rimmed china teacup we'd given her to sip out of. And then when Dimitri rushed forward to grab me, she said, "Melly deserved it."

Melly scrambled to her feet and brushed off her outfit as I tried to right my sweater even though Dimitri had me in his arms. "You're a classless wannabe, Olive," she spit out.

"Watch it," Dimitri said in a low voice.

"Dimitri!" Melly whined and immediately tears sprouted in her eyes. "She did this to me. My hair! You don't want to be with someone like that."

Dimitri started backing out of the salon as I wiggled in his arms. "Oh, I'm already with her. I intend to have children with her, fight with her, experience her explosions with her. I'm all in ... with her. Don't forget it."

With that, he carried me out of the salon while I whacked at his back. "Let me go. I don't need anyone to fight my battles. And I'm not letting her push me into pools anymore." The rage flowing through me was doing the perfect job of it instead.

"Do I even want to know?" he asked as he hiked me higher up on to his shoulder.

"Can you please put me down?"

"Not happening, Honeybee. You've got some explaining to do. What happened to just going to work? Want to talk about that?"

"Well, I try to keep my emotions at bay, but we all have a temper," I admitted through clenched teeth. I knew this was a bit outrageous, even I could confess to that. "I'm stressed. I might be getting a migraine. There's way too much going on."

"You don't say?" He sighed. I couldn't see whether or not he was mad, but I felt his muscles tighten under my waist. Trying to wiggle out of his grip hadn't helped, but maybe if I rolled just the right way, I could fall into the grass and save some of my dignity.

Yet, when I shoved up on his back and cranked my body that way, his arm tightened around my legs and his other hand landed loudly and firmly on my ass.

I gasped at him spanking me. "Are you kidding right now?"

"Stop trying to outmaneuver me. It won't happen."

"Just let me down. Everyone is looking at us."

"Everyone's already heard about you at the salon. There's no getting around that. So, me walking you back to our place is the least of our problems."

And it really, truly was. When we got there, he still didn't put me down. He walked me all the way to our bedroom and then said, "Take a shower. Cool off."

And he left me in there like I was a child being scolded by her parents and told to think about her actions.

After showering, I pulled on a sweater and was about to sit down to practice a bit of calligraphy when I heard a loud bang. Immediately, I jumped out of bed and ran to the window to see what was wrong.

The whole house shook with the pounding, and when I couldn't figure out where it was coming from, I ran down the stairs and whipped open the front door.

"What on earth are you doing?" I stared at him with a freaking tool belt on. Dimitri Hardy. The most eligible bachelor I'd ever seen, swinging away at the floorboards of the porch like he couldn't afford a construction crew.

"You complained about a floorboard creaking on here."

"No. Jameson mentioned ... Dimitri, he said he would come by and fix that board. Did you—" It occurred to me then that Dimitri shouldn't have known any of that because it was from our conversation on the porch. "Were you listening to us?"

"Yeah. I'm aware of what he offered." He wedged a crowbar-looking thing under the floorboard and cranked on it hard. Much harder than necessary. The wood crunched and cracked.

Now, I was concerned about his mental state, not mine. "Dimitri, are you okay?" I asked softly. I knew I'd acted out but now he was acting more than a little angry. His face was red, and there was a sheen of sweat across his forehead.

"I'm trying my best not to be pissed at this community right now. I really am. Melly's a little ..."

"Yep. I agree." He wrenched the crowbar into the floorboard again.

"Dimitri, I think, maybe, you're doing it wrong." I tried to approach this lightly. "That's going to ruin the wood."

"That's the point. I'm pulling it all up."

I sighed. "What for?" I started toward him now. I loved this porch.

"To let off some steam. Plus, you were with Jameson out here. I tried to let it go. But I'd rather not."

"Let what go?" I stared at him, beads of sweat rolling down his temples now, saw how his muscles flexed as he stood up to face me and really look me over as I asked the question slowly one more time.

"He kissed your cheek on this porch, Honeybee."

"Dimitri." I said his name softly, not knowing if I should even be entertaining the idea of consoling him. "It was a kiss on the cheek as a frien—"

"Yep," he blurted out. Then he threw the crowbar down. "I saw your soft skin being touched by his fucking—"

"Okay." My love for him and the way he loved me settled deep in me with the look of frustration he had on his face. For me. All for me. "So you were definitely watching the cameras again?"

"Of course I was! And through the doorbell." He pointed behind him. "I watched. You're damn right I did."

"I feel like you should apologize for spying on me."

"I feel like you should apologize for being with someone other than your future husband."

My mouth opened. Then I closed it. He took that moment to grab the crowbar and crank the tool into the wood again. It snapped in half, splintering into a bunch of jagged pieces.

"Maybe we should take a step back." We needed to hash out our feelings, get through the next few weeks, and try to understand where all this was going. "We need to be mature about all this. We can stop sleeping together and discuss—"

"We're sleeping together right after I finish redoing this porch." He grunted like it was an absolute sure thing. So sure of us that I actually smiled, because there was no question in how he felt about me or how I felt about him now.

Even still, I squeaked out, "The whole porch? I'm pretty sure you're not finishing that today." Did the man know anything about manual labor? "It would take a whole team of very hot men sweating all around this house of yours to redo the porch, which, by the way, I'm not at all against, but we should plan for that before ruining the perfectly good porch that we have here."

He made a ha sound, and I thought he liked my joke at first. But then, his laugh became somewhat sinister as he cranked on another board and then another before he stood again and wiped his brow. There was something in his eye that I couldn't quite place as he nodded to the screen door behind me.

"No other men will be helping you around this house. Ever. You and me, we can do it all ourselves. Together."

Then he got up and marched into the house. I followed him, not sure if our conversation was over.

He grabbed a bag from the bathroom cabinet and threw it on the bed where I was standing. "We need to build a safe home with safe people around, Olive, and you want to know why?"

I stared at the bag for a moment and my heart started to thump. "Why?"

"For our kid." He pointed to my belly. "Go take the test in that bag."

"What?" I frowned at the bag and then opened it to peer in. I stumbled back. He couldn't be serious. "That's not possible, Dimitri."

"It is." He combed a hand through his hair and glanced out at the porch one last time. "Think about how sensitive your body has been. Think about how you were today at the salon—"

"I was just giving her what she deserved. The dye is temporary!" I bit out, feeling the anger swell inside me immediately. I gripped the back of the dining room chair though as I started to think harder about it. I shook my head back and forth. "No. This can't be happening, I just started taking the pill again."

"We had two weeks of you not taking it though, right? And pregnancy tests can be accurate as early as ten days after conception, Honeybee. And—"

My stomach rolled. "I'm going to be sick, I think."

"Exactly. Probably because I put a baby in you." The man

actually smiled wide, and I wanted to smack him.

"This isn't a joke, Dimitri!"

"Okay, I know. But just—" He cleared the space between us as he strode over and took my hands in his. "Think about it, Olive Monroe. Take the test. If it's nothing, fine. If it's everything, the way a baby with you would be for me, then consider it. You make the decision on what you want, of course, but just consider it. Consider the life you want and if I'm in it. If a kid you had with me is in it."

"The life I want?" I breathed out, a storm of emotions now creating a hurricane within me.

"And me too. Because I want all of my life with you. I want one where I wake up next to you every morning. Where it might be raining outside, but it's always sunny inside our home with kids running around calling you Mom and me being thankful every day that I get to still call you Honeybee. The one where I'm right about the fact that you're mine and about the fact that we get to take the chance and enjoy the dance. It's going to be a good dance, I promise. Because I love you. I'm going to take care of you. Always. Even if you don't end up wanting kids, I'm going to be here. For you."

He didn't hesitate or look away from me while he said the words. The emotions that swirled around inside me stopped, my world stopped, everything stopped. Everything but my heart beating for him.

"Dimitri," I whispered, "I don't know if I can do this." I said it honestly, but he pulled me close to kiss the top of my forehead.

"Take the test, Honeybee. Then we figure it out together."

"It's just not possible.

"It is. It lines up. Have you gotten your period?"

"Well no. But ... it's not even time yet, and with you messing with my birth control ..."

"Take the test."

"It wouldn't even show up," I whispered.

"Then it will say negative."

I grabbed the test like I was in a daze as I mumbled, "I can't have a kid."

"Why not?"

I spun on him and threw up a hand. "Because I'm not ready! We're not ready. We just started dating. Some secret society might be causing danger to my family. There are a million reasons."

"*I'm* ready. I'll be ready for both of us if you want me to. And I'm going to keep you safe. I promise you that. Take the test, Honeybee. We'll figure out whatever you want after, okay?"

I walked slowly into the bathroom, carrying the box like it was a bomb, and then I closed the door behind me so I could take a breath, so I could center myself while I looked in the mirror. My curls jumped out in every direction, the flower askew in my hair, and my sweater was wrinkled about ten different ways.

I'd been all over the place this summer and couldn't really even comprehend how I'd gotten here, in a bathroom, about to take a pregnancy test.

Yet, I wasn't alone. Dimitri stood outside that door patiently waiting. Never did he waver in his support for me. Dimitri was my rock, the man I knew I could see myself with forever, that I'd want my kids to call dad.

That last thought had me wondering if I would be a good enough mother. I'd stood up for myself today, backed by women who supported me. I'd finished the article for Lucille and my thesis was submitted. I was home, and it had somehow brought out the best in me.

I'd deal with whatever it came with.

I took a breath and smiled at myself. A sense of calm washed over me. I opened the box, read the directions, and peed on that stick.

With or without Dimitri, with or without a baby, I would be okay.

My path in life might not have been exactly perfect, but it was mine. I was choosing the right way for me, taking a chance and enjoying the dance.

I waited and waited for the lines to show up on the stick.

My heart pounded while I stared at the white little window on the stick. It must have been fear. It had to be. But there was a fear of not being pregnant and then being pregnant, like suddenly I wanted a child.

Then I sat in that bathroom, staring at the lines before I finally looked up at him with tears in my eyes.

"You're pregnant." He smiled. "And we're going to be the best parents."

He said it with conviction and I bit my lip before admitting back, "I think you're right, Dimitri. I think you might really be right."

He pulled me close to hug and kiss my forehead over and over. I cried in his arms, realizing I was ready to put down roots here in Paradise Grove, just like my mother had said.

It should have been the most surreal day but it was just minutes later my phone went off in our room.

My father's name was on the screen. When I picked up, he said softly, "I'm so sorry, Olive. Knox OD'd."

CHAPTER 42: OLIVE

How do you save someone when you don't even know how to save yourself? How do you rip someone away from an addiction when it's preying on their brain, the very thing that gives them the logic to stop? How do you stop a teenager from seeking out a drug that makes the pain go away, especially when that drug is morphing their brain, lacing it with chemicals so that as it develops, the paths for addiction are fully formed, embedded, permanent?

My nerves were fried. My worries after the initial shock of the test were back with a bit of a vengeance as I thought about Jameson's request, about what we'd talked about. I couldn't comprehend everything that had just happened, how I'd made such a misstep, and how I'd sat on that bathroom floor with Dimitri looking down at me, not feeling anything but joy.

It could have been hormones. It could have been the shock. But everything seemed to fall into place. I understood now why my mother protected me, why she hadn't told me a thing about this society. I understood that I'd do anything for the baby growing inside me and for my brother. It was what a family did, what a community did, what I knew I could do even if I hadn't felt strong enough to do so before.

I now knew I had to get to the bottom of exactly what was happening in the Diamond Syndicate.

"I want to see him!" I screamed at my father as soon as I got to the waiting room.

Dimitri whispered to me, "Do you want me to handle this?"

I stopped and looked at the man I was pretty sure I was in love with, the man who didn't scold me for acting out at a salon but who stood by me and took care of me when I needed it. "No. This is for me. I want every single second of this conversation with him. Father. To. Daughter."

Dimitri was protective. Over-the-top protective. Possessive too. Yet he stepped back and murmured, "Yeah, I'm not stopping you from this. No one should. Be strong, Honeybee. I'll be right behind you but he's all yours."

And then I turned to speed walk toward my father and shouted, "Tell me his room number now."

"Calm down. Your stepmother is talking to the nurses now, and she'll—"

"She won't do a damn thing. She's done being the middleman between him and his doctor."

"Olive." His voice was so consoling, like he'd been around the whole time. So soothing like he cared. "She's been helping him from the beginning of this. She knows what to do."

"She's almost killed him. Or you did," I threw out, and it wasn't nice and it wasn't caring. It was dramatic like they'd all accused me of being. "Where the hell were you?"

"Well, sweetheart, now I've had business. It's probably best if you let us handle this. Why don't you go back to work with Kee and—"

"Dad. Do not play dumb with me." I cut him off. "You tell me what the business is. Was Knox with you?"

He frowned, and although people said he was one of the best, most charming men around, I knew all of his tells. He would fiddle with his hands more, go to grab a drink as if he was parched when really he was thinking up what to say. He tried to play dumb at first, "What are you talking about, Olive?"

"I know about the Diamond Syndicate."

This time, he didn't try to play with me at all. His face contorted in anger, and his eyes burned with an evil in them I'd only seen a few times, one being when he hit me the night I left home. "You think you can come here and take it from me?"

"I don't want a damn thing from you," I threw back, not exactly sure what he was talking about. "I want my brother safe, though, that's for sure. He isn't with you."

"Olive Bee. Just like a bee." He massaged his gray temples. "You're buzzing in things you shouldn't be."

"Too much curiosity." I smiled menacingly at him now. "Funny, though, because Mom loved it. She loved you too. God, she stupidly loved you through the cheating, the lying, even bringing you into the society like you deserved to be there. She must have been so scared, knowing she was leaving us with you."

"Watch it, Olive."

"No." I felt the tears then, felt them spring to my eyes, but I wouldn't let them run over. "I held her hand. I read her books, I sang her songs, Dad. Where were you?"

"I was–"

"You were with Georgette!" I shook with rage. "Were you two planning your freaking wedding while your kids cried over their dying mother in the next room? Were you planning this deal all along?"

"Hey, now. I lost a wife too," he said like he was remorseful for a second.

"You did." I sniffed and stood up straighter. "You lost her the moment you ruined her trust in you. You left her for

Georgette because you weren't strong enough to stand by her side."

"I tried," he growled before he paced away from me before turning back. "I didn't want to see her waste away, Olive. It was difficult and—"

"I know it was difficult. I witnessed it. I saw how she lost so much weight that her high cheek bones hollowed out. I saw how her curls fell from her skull. How every breath she took became ragged. I went there every day after school, sat there doing schoolwork remotely when it got too bad and I didn't want to risk going to school. I witnessed the fear in her eyes every day when she told me to go live my life after she was gone, like she knew being here with you would be too much. I saw though her love for you drain from her eyes and that might have been the most difficult."

"Well ..." My father didn't even really argue his piece anymore. What could he even say? "I tried to provide for you. Now, I have a new family to provide for, and Knox and Georgette need me and the Diamond Syndicate. So, you need to leave."

"You think I'm just going to leave?"

"Look, you're blurring Knox's focus. He needed a reminder, okay?"

"A reminder of what?" I whispered but suddenly I knew. I didn't even need to ask.

My father had done something I'd never forgive him for. He sighed and his gaze darted behind me like he was considering his words as Dimitri stood there. Then he scratched his jaw. "The doctors say he's doing fine. He'll be okay, and we're going to make sure no batch from the Irish is laced with anything anymore. I didn't think he'd have this reaction, but we can't back out of our deal with them, Olive. You understand right?

The HEAT empire cannot—"

"Wait a second." I stopped him, holding up a hand. "Please tell me you weren't a part of your own son ODing, Dad."

There was too much silence before he started to spew words that didn't matter. "Look, it's not what you think. Knox was just providing information for neighboring less-fortunate communities, and we wanted to know what the atmosphere was like at *those* schools. The boy needed purpose. And we needed him to experiment a little with the drugs. I ... It was Earl's idea. He thought—"

"You're a monster," I whispered, feeling a rage in me so ferocious I wasn't sure if I'd be able to stand there with him for a second longer. I knew I had to though, knew I had to know everything. "You broke the whole code of the Diamond Syndicate. To keep our community clean. To protect it. To protect your family. You didn't."

"This *is* protecting it. There's no way around the mob anymore. They have their hands in everything. We pick and choose our battles as a society, and we evolve to be better."

I pushed past him, not willing to hear the excuses. There were none. Instead, I went to the nurse and asked for my brother's room number. "Are you family?"

"His sister."

"Right now we are asking that only—"

"This is a HEAT hospital correct?" Dimitri murmured behind me.

I jumped at his voice. I'd almost forgotten he stood back and told me I was strong enough to say what I had to my father. He didn't interfere. He believed in me enough to know I could handle it on my own.

I leaned into his touch as he said, "I'm Dimitri Hardy.

Check your security detail and let me scan my watch. I have access where needed within this building, as does my wife."

The nurse moved the scanner out to him and Dimitri held his wrist over the device. It beeped green. She then glanced at my wrist.

Dimitri rolled his eyes. "Had a feeling they might ask." He slid a small watch that looked almost like a Rolex but with a digital screen as the face of it onto my wrist. "Scan."

I narrowed my eyes. How could he have known? But the device beeped green.

As we walked away, I murmured, "Your wife?"

He murmured back, "You might have been faking this relationship a while back, but I wasn't. And you're going to marry me one day soon, Honeybee. Might as well start using the wife pronoun now."

"But you got me a watch when?"

He shrugged. "Got it synced up with my access when we moved in together."

"Dimitri—"

He scoffed. "You weren't ever really fake. I might have denied it for a while and only acted on my desire, but I think I knew you were mine the second I saw you cry at my best friend's wedding, Olive."

Georgette stood over my brother as I walked in. She was wringing her hands with worry and when she looked up and saw us, the worry turned to anger. She glanced behind us and said, "Why are they in here?" to my father who had trailed behind us.

"That's his sister, Georgette," my father said.

"This is a liability. All of it. I can't protect you and myself if we get taken to court when this all comes back to us," she seethed.

She wasn't concerned for my brother at all, and that's when I looked at Dimitri. He knew the look immediately, knew I was done with them, that I would forever be done with them. "You can all get out."

"What?" She narrowed her eyes.

My future husband didn't hesitate. "This hospital belongs to my family, you realize that?"

"So?" my stepmother threw out. "That's my son—"

"Stepson," I corrected her. "And you're not here for him."

My father thought he still had some control. "Now, Olive, that's no way to talk to—"

"How can you be even the least bit concerned with how I'm speaking to her when Knox is on a ventilator, Dad? He could be brain-dead and—"

"That would be a blessing," Georgette murmured.

My jaw dropped before I lunged for her. Dimitri caught me just in time. "Don't give her the satisfaction right now, Honeybee."

I took a deep breath. "Go. Please. Because once I'm done taking care of Knox, I will leave this hospital and I will do everything in my power to never be a part of the partnership you're creating. Matter of fact, I'll make sure I'm more of a liability than you will ever be able to silence."

My father's face curdled. "Fine. Be dramatic and stubborn. But it's not something I'll ever respect. It doesn't suit you, Olive. You've always been a brat of a—"

"Watch your mouth," I heard from behind me, and all I

had to do was lean back to feel Dimitri's chest as solid as a rock behind me.

"What did you say to me, boy?"

"I said, watch your mouth when you're speaking to my girl, or I'll break it apart so you don't have to," he said to my dad, his voice low.

"She's my daughter. I'm her father."

"She might be your daughter, but she's the woman I'm going to marry. The mother of my future children. I wouldn't ever talk to her that way, so I'll be damned if another man—father or not—does." He took a deep breath. "Matter of fact, I'm going to need you to apologize."

"What?" my father whispered.

He cracked his knuckles and kept his eyes on my dad. "Apologize to your daughter before I make you apologize, Mr. Monroe. And try to mean it because after this, your lives as you know them are over. I hope you both realize that, but if you don't apologize and leave right now, not even your daughter will be able to convince me that you shouldn't endure excruciating amounts of discomfort in the future. I will make Dante's inferno look like heaven. Do you understand?"

My father's stare was full of anger, but he murmured an apology, and then Dimitri growled, "Now, get the fuck out of my hospital."

He pressed a button on his watch, and security rushed to the room as my father and his wife were exiting. After they left, I held Knox's hand. It felt stronger than my mother's had at the end, but the pain of being there with him in that bed was the same.

I wanted to cry, to break down, to curse whatever higher being was out there that let this happen. But instead, I recited my mother's favorite lines of a book to him. I told him he would be okay, and I fell asleep there for hours and hours.

Dimitri never left my side. He talked with the doctors, and we found that there were lethal doses of fentanyl in him that nearly killed him. He would be kept on a ventilator for longer than I liked, but his brain waves seemed stable, good.

Promising even, the doctor said.

What a word to use when you felt like your world was a storm crashing down on you.

CHAPTER 43: DIMITRI

Olive had stayed overnight but finally let me talk her into going home the next day. She was exceptionally quiet on the way, so quiet that I was the one who ended up waving to Lucille as we pulled up the driveway.

I didn't give the woman the opportunity to walk over, but instead closed the garage behind us. She'd ask about Knox and try to pry, and right now, we couldn't take that. My concern was nothing but for the woman who had the pink flower from her hair now in her hands, twisting it round and round.

I turned the car off and we both sat there quietly. I couldn't console her because I knew no words would help.

"I know he's going to be okay," she whispered. "I can feel it. And you heard the doctor. He's stable, his brain activity is great. He's going to be fine. I know that." But then she looked at me with tears in her eyes and said, "I'm just not sure he will be next time ... if there is a next time. And then I'm not sure if I'll be either."

"We won't ever know."

"Right." She nodded fast over and over. "Right. You take risks every day knowing there's always a chance of it turning out a disaster."

"Taking a risk with my business isn't the same as enduring one with family," I corrected her. "Give yourself grace, Honeybee. You can take time to—"

"I've taken my time. I ran away from what I thought was

hell with my father. My mom told me to go live my life before she died. Do you know that? And I listened. I up and left him."

"You grew up. Your responsibility as a sibling isn't to be the parent to your brother."

She sniffled. "Right. But whose responsibility is it then, because my father didn't take it."

I nodded and knew I had to explain something to her. "My sister is an addict. She's been sober a long time now, but Izzy used and lost someone close to her during that time." Olive listened with her big honey eyes, as if I could promise her Knox would turn out the same way. "I don't know if Knox will get through it. I think Izzy considers if she's getting through it still sometimes. It's a journey, but we'll be there for him."

"This isn't your responsibility."

"Honeybee, it will be our responsibility. Just like the baby you have in you now. Ours. Together. We're in all this together now."

She chewed on her cheek like she was thinking things over, and then she murmured, "I should go shower." Taking a deep breath, she walked inside with that flower not in her hair but still in her hand. It was symbolic of something, the brightness in her, the burst of energy and emotion that she hid from the world sometimes was shown through that flower. I wouldn't let it die out. I'd make sure she put it back in her curls by the very next day.

I growled and went to find my laptop. I was trying to give her the space she needed now, but it proved to be one of the most difficult things I would have to learn to do when all I wanted was to be beside her. Forever and ever.

I tried to work on my investments, tried to make calls, but I didn't listen to any of my clients, and then I found myself wondering if we'd have enough room in the house for a little one.

My girl was pregnant and if I had to give her space, I'd at least start focusing on making sure we had everything we needed for her pregnancy. I started researching rocking chairs and high chairs and bibs and formula, and I even googled what pump would be best. I'd ordered over $10,000 worth of items before I slammed my laptop shut.

I'd spent an hour doing that after I stopped working, which meant she'd been in there for at least ninety minutes. My brain wouldn't shut off, and I figured 5400 seconds must have been enough time for her, right? Quite frankly, at that point, I regretted having a tankless water heater because it didn't force her to come out.

Finally, the water stopped, and I was acutely aware of every single sound that came from the bathroom. I could only blame myself for deciding to work in the primary suite where I could listen. Yet, I couldn't bring myself to move. I heard a cupboard opening and then closing. A drawer sliding out and then back. Did I hear a sniffle? Was I going insane? Yes, I think I was because I ran over to the door to knock on it.

"Honeybee, you okay in there?"

She definitely sniffled before responding. "I'm fine. Just finishing up."

"Open the door. You sound like you're crying."

"I'm not." She whispered now. Yet, she didn't open the door.

I leaned my forehead on the door and reasoned with her. "Babe, let's not make me break down this door to get to you. Open up."

I heard a deep sigh. "If you break down the door, it'll take you longer to sell this house, Dimitri."

"You think I care? I'm not selling this house anyway."

"Why?" I heard her say softly.

"Because this house is ours. I'm fucking you in every room of it, remember?"

Through the door, she continued to talk, "You should sell. Paradise Grove homes are probably a couple million."

"And I'd risk triple that to make sure you're okay. Scratch that. My whole bank account, Honeybee."

I heard a chuckle and then a sniffle before she said, "You know, if we're going to really do this whole together thing, we might need to talk about your frivolous mentality on finances."

"True. I spent five figures on baby gear just now."

"What?!" she screeched before I finally heard the lock click. I took a step back, and she opened the door with a towel wrapped around her hair and body. "Why are you buying all that? We haven't even been to the doctor."

"Honeybee." I took her face in my hands and brushed my thumb over her nose that was tinted cherry red, her eyes puffier than usual. "Because I wanted to."

"You're planning way too far ahead," she said, but her hands were around my wrists now. "We have months and months to get things, Dimitri."

"There's a lot. We need a crib, stroller, rocking chair. Something called a MamaRoo. Some bassinet that detects the baby's needs, but I'll be up—"

"Dimitri." She stopped me with a hand on my chest. "You know you're so over-the-top that most people wouldn't be able to handle you right?"

"Are you saying you can't?" I frowned at her, my heart dropping at the thought.

She shook her head slowly. "I'm in here crying about how I'm going to handle it all, but you know what you continue to make me realize? I don't have to handle it alone now. You're here. You want to be. And I want you to be here too. With me. For as long as you want."

"Which is going to be forever, Honeybee."

"Good. Because today was freaking hard." She took a deep breath and pulled me close. "I'm scared about what's to come, but I'm not scared about you anymore."

"I'm here, Olive. I'm not leaving. We're going to get through it. Together." She frowned but nodded at me, tears threatening to spill over her pretty eyes.

"I believe you, Dimitri. I freaking believe you. I'm just scared of everything else in the future. So make me forget today, make me forget my fear, if only for a little."

I pulled her to our bed and unwrapped the towel from her to see her skin glistening almost a golden hue, still dewy from the moisture in the air. That night, I didn't fuck or screw her. I loved her softly. Cherished every part of her.

The secret society had their own code, and I think I made one of my own that night. I vowed to protect her, to love her, to do anything for *her*. Even if it meant ruining every single thing I'd worked for.

CHAPTER 44: OLIVE

It was another week of me visiting my brother in the hospital and of Dimitri and I laying low around town. He stayed close to me and reassured me everything would be okay. We talked about telling our families about the baby once we went to the doctor and knew he or she was healthy.

I wanted to keep the news to ourselves for now and Dimitri agreed, saying that when I was ready to share with more people, I'd know. I realized that he wanted me comfortable at all costs and I had been. I'd feared having a family because I'd lost so much of mine at one point.

That didn't mean I couldn't rebuild it or that I couldn't create a new one. I saw the strength in myself now, saw the support I had around me, and knew I deserved a family if that's what I wanted now.

My brother was a part of that family I wanted. I wanted him out of the hospital and getting well. I hurried to get ready the day before the board meeting and was ready to drive to the hospital when I glanced out the windo and saw my brother sitting in front of the porch on our steps.

I ran out there. "Knox, you're out of the hospital? They didn't call!" I leapt over the broken floorboards to hug him. "How are you? When did you get out? Are you okay?"

"One question at a time, Olive Bee." He chuckled. "I was released this morning. Told them not to call anyone. I needed a minute to think. It was early. I'm eighteen, so technically an adult and they didn't mention my release to Dad. Don't worry. I went home. No one's there."

"He contact you?"

"No." Knox took a deep breath. "He won't Olive. It wasn't good before ..."

He didn't finish his sentence, and I didn't know how to ask him the rest. I put my hand on his arm and murmured, "You can tell me when you're ready."

"I should be ready now." His jaw flexed while he combed a hand through his curly hair. "I'm not proud of what happened. I'm not even sure— I'm sorry we put you through this, Olive." His voice broke off, and his face crumpled as I sat down next to him on that porch. He cried on my shoulder, and I wrapped my arm around him.

It was just a moment. A single moment in time that I knew I would never take for granted. My brother was home, and he was breaking in front of me, but he was here, where we could figure things out together.

Once he had enough composure, I told him what I knew, told him how I'd confronted our father, and he winced.

"I shouldn't have taken a hit from him. I shouldn't have tested anything for them, but I knew the product and ... It was dumb. I'd been doing better." Knox admitted that the Irish had told them their drugs were clean, and my dad literally had Knox try them on their way back from the city.

"I'm going to get out of town," Knox murmured. "For a few days. Jameson stopped by the hospital right as I was about to be released. Sounds like he's about to have it out with the Irish. I got security on me till then."

"He thinks it's that dangerous?" I glanced down the road.

"I think it's mostly dangerous for Dad since the board is

going to vote to approve whatever companies Dimitri would like in his office building tomorrow."

"That's good, right?" I said slowly, not sure where he stood right at that moment.

"Yeah." He nodded. "It's going to be all good."

I wasn't sure he thought so, but I didn't want to overwhelm him, so I focused on something small. "Should we go inside? Leave my mess of a porch?"

"Dimitri do this?" he asked, pointing to the broken wood.

"Unfortunately, he's not much of a handyman." I chuckled.

"Doesn't look like handiwork. Looks like demolition work."

"What do you mean by that?"

"I'm pretty sure he's in love with you." My brother took a sip of the water he had in his bottle. "I'm pretty sure I'm in love with Esme, and I fucked up my whole life because of it. We cause destruction when we think our hearts are in jeopardy of being broken."

I froze at his confession and looked up at him. "Wait. Did you say you love Esme?" He nodded and smiled a little. He looked so young and innocent when he did. "She's such a beautiful and nice girl, Knox." I hoped this was his step in the right direction.

"She's dating again. Not me. Went to get coffee with a guy recently." His jaw worked up and down. "I'm not going to freak out anymore, though. I'm sorry I did and made the wrong-ass decision with Dad."

"That's not your fault."

"It is. I was mad about her, and then, damn, I don't know. Just didn't care in the moment." He sighed. "I should have answered when you called too. Didn't know what to say, and I didn't want you worrying."

I chose honesty rather than white lies. "I'm always going to worry about you."

"Yeah, I know. I worry about me a lot too." He flexed his hand over and over on his water jug, a sign I was getting used to understanding as his nervous movement. "You think Esme will talk to me again if I go to rehab and therapy?"

"Is that the only reason you'd go?" I asked softly.

He grunted. "No. I'm gonna go either way."

"That's good. That's really good, Knox." The words I'd wanted to hear so badly hit me hard. "Can I ask one thing of you?"

"You name it."

"Don't ever go back to those men again, and if Dad or Georgette calls—"

"I won't be answering. I don't think they're worried about us, honestly. They're worried about the Irish. It looked like he cleared out a lot from our house."

To think that man had left his family, his son and daughter, to flee like the coward he was.

"Right ... So," I cleared my throat and sat up a bit straighter. "I'm going to go to therapy with you if that's okay. I'm so mad at our father, I don't think I'll get over it otherwise." I grabbed his hand to stop his nervous movement. "Please say yes."

"If I said no, what would you do?"

"Still go."

"Right." He rolled his eyes. "Guess that's what siblings are for."

I nodded. "I think everyone needs a bit of therapy in their lives, and what better way to get through the hard stuff than with someone who loves you? I've got some stuff I'm going to need your help with too." I took a deep breath and closed my eyes before I told him, "I'm pregnant and kind of freaking out about it."

"Pregnant?" My little brother whispered like he couldn't believe it and his eyes dropped to my belly. "Freaking out why?"

I frowned, not sure I should be overwhelming him right then. "We don't need to talk about this right now."

"Of course we do. You're here for me, and I'm here for you." He nudged his shoulder into mine. "Tell me what's freaking you out."

I chewed my cheek and looked out at the neighborhood. "At first, I was scared to have a family. Now, I'm scared I might do something wrong and lose him or her. I've known now for a week and I don't know if I'm doing everything right. Like what if I'm not eating right? And then what if I don't get enough therapy and mess him or her up in some way later on?"

It was his turn to squeeze my hand and soothe my nerves. "You're going to do everything right. And when you don't, Dimitri and I will be there to help."

"You mean that? Because I'm going to stay here in Paradise Grove, Knox," I told him. "I'm going to stay, and maybe you will too?"

He nodded. "You probably got to figure out what the hell you're doing with Dimitri first."

"He can either stay with us or he can go."

Knox laughed. "His ass isn't going anywhere, Olive Bee. He'd burn in hell with you if that's where you were."

"Well, we might have to go through it first to get this over with."

He pulled me in for a hug and then said, "Let me know when you're starting the fire, and I'll help."

I nodded and hugged him back. "You need to help yourself first. You can't stay with Dad and Georgette. They're too—"

"I know. I'm going to look into some other places, and I talked with D."

"About what?" I frowned. "When?"

Dimitri appeared in the doorway and opened the screen door. "You two are going to kill yourselves out here with the jagged edges of this porch. Get inside."

"What did you talk to my brother about?"

"About how he's going to rehab and then staying here. With us."

"But wait?" I shook my head. "When?"

"He left the hospital and they updated me. So I called him and let him know."

"But we didn't discuss—"

"Nothing to discuss when it comes to family, Honeybee." He was so damn sure of himself that I almost melted at the way he spoke about my brother, because technically that wasn't his family, yet.

"Anyway, I'm going to stay for a while, and we've found a rehab place." Knox nodded at Dimitri like they'd become friends.

"You did this for me?" I whispered to him.

"No." Dimitri shook his head. "This one I did for your brother, who I'm pretty damn certain is going to be my brother."

"Dimitri," I sighed. "Don't start. Do you want more water or something to eat?"

"Erm ... You two are planning to get married already?" Knox looked surprised, and I practically stumbled as I walked toward the kitchen.

"No," I said as Dimitri said, "Yes."

He chuckled. "That's going to be interesting."

"He gets ahead of himself," I told Knox.

"She's in denial a lot," he responded immediately.

Knox laughed at us both, then we all laughed together, like we didn't have a million other problems to solve that day. When we sobered enough, Knox murmured. "I'm probably going to fuck up a lot, guys."

"Great. You and your sister can both sit in this house and think about your fuckups at the same time since her ass was down the street fighting with her childhood bully out in public for all to see."

"Am I missing something?"

"Please shut up." I shook my head and pinched the bridge of my nose. "Now is not the time, Dimitri."

He started to laugh and then turned to my brother and put his arm around his shoulder. "Come on. I'll tell you all about it." And he proceeded to walk Knox into the living room, telling him all about my temper tantrum at the salon.

Knox's laugh boomed throughout my house so loudly I couldn't help but snicker. Then he looked over at me and said, "Mom would have been proud of you, Olive Bee. Sticking up for yourself and being dramatic. It's what she loved most about you."

I turned away fast before they both saw me tearing up and rushed around the kitchen to whip up some dinner.

That night, we talked about where Knox would stay, how he could pick out his own furniture for his room, and how we'd look into therapy and rehab together. Later, when Knox went upstairs, I turned to Dimitri and said what I should have a long time ago. "I've been in denial about falling in love with you, but I've fallen all the way down the tunnel now. I'm not sure I'll be able to climb out of this one."

"Thank fuck."

"What?" My mouth dropped.

"You heard me, I'm happy."

"You're happy? And thankful? That's it?"

"Well, *I've* been in love with you practically this whole time, so I'm happy to hear you think you're almost all the way down that rabbit hole with me."

My stomach got butterflies as I giggled at his confession. I dropped my head onto his shoulder as we sat there. "You're taking in my brother," I whispered.

"Who's also going to be my brother." He kissed me then and I cried in his arms. I didn't hold back. I let it all out. Knox was right. My mother would have been proud.

Everything had been going so well, so perfect. I shouldn't have jumped out of the bed when I heard a car door slam outside. I shouldn't have snuck down the stairs to get a closer look at the dark shadows moving over on Lucille's driveway.

And I definitely shouldn't have gone out the front door into the night when I saw Jameson and Lucille putting something very large into a man's car.

CHAPTER 45: OLIVE

I pushed Lucille's lawn mower over as an excuse. I mean, it was midnight. I didn't really need one. They knew I was being nosy, but I waved at them both and shoved the mower hard toward her garage just as Jameson tried to step into my way.

"What the fuck are you doing outside?"

"I could ask you the same," I whisper-yelled as I peered around at Lucille who was shaking her head at me with wide eyes.

"You need to go back into your house and act like you never—"

"Is Earl in that car?" I took a deep breath. "Dead?"

"Oh, Jesus," Lucille said as Jameson slammed the car door shut.

Jameson glared at me. "What the hell would make you think that?"

"Earl started all this—"

"He was always disloyal." Lucille harrumphed and crossed her arms. "And violent, Olive. Don't forget." Lucille didn't look remorseful at all.

"We're helping Lucille with a few things. Earl has been *out of town*."

"Knox was in the hospital because of my father, because of them. You get that right?"

Jameson pinched the bridge of his nose. "Let's talk in the morning, okay?" he whispered.

I knew he was asking me to trust him and the syndicate right then. So I took a deep breath, thinking of Knox, thinking of what could be with Dimitri. I stepped back but not before I said, "You need to make sure you're righting the wrongs, Jameson. Otherwise, there's no hope for Paradise Grove."

I spun on a heel and went back inside where I was met with Dimitri rushing down the stairs. "What the hell are you doing?"

"I ... felt like a walk."

He frowned and glanced outside, his jaw going up and down, up and down. "Since I just saw the headlights of the car, why don't you try again?"

I sighed and closed my eyes. "All I know is that maybe Earl hasn't been out of town, Dimitri. I happen to think he's gone."

"Gone how?"

I chewed on my cheek. "They put something very large in that car," I whispered.

"You're kidding me?" His eyes widened. "And they saw you watching?"

"I ... Well, Jameson said we would talk in the morning."

That's when Dimitri really started moving. "Wake your brother up and tell him to watch the house. We're leaving."

"Leaving for where?" I shrieked. "I am not leaving."

"Oh. You are," he grumbled as he stomped up the stairs. "Pack a suitcase or you'll be on vacation with nothing but the clothes on your back."

"This is silly, Dimitri."

He whipped around. "I'm trying to protect you, Olive."

"I don't want protection," I told him. "We need to know what was going on."

"You need to stop putting yourself in harm's way."

"That's what you wanted. That's how all this started," I screamed. "You wanted information on Paradise Grove."

He punched his fist into the wall. "Not at the expense of you," he bellowed. And then he looked at me with true fear in his eyes. "Never at the expense of you."

Agreeing to a vacation for a few days after Knox sided with Dimitri was really all I could do to smooth the waters.

Dimitri had called Jameson and they'd all agreed it was best. "My brothers and I are pulling out of the investment here. Olive and I are going to stick around for a while and see how everything goes, but we can't endanger ourselves with the Irish."

"The Diamond Syndicate is still going to vote for the offices. We're going to establish a line in the sand that we won't work with the Irish."

"We're establishing our line too. We're not working with any of you. I'm going to pull my investment. My family doesn't like it."

"You'll take a huge hit monetarily, but I understand. Still best for you to get out of harm's way with Knox and Olive. Their father wronged the Irish. They'll be looking to make an example."

Dimitri gave me a look, and I finally sighed and nodded toward his phone. He'd put Jameson on speaker so I could hear.

I agreed to leave for a week.

We were all packed and walking through the airport when I got a text.

> **Unknown: Go to the bathroom. Make it believable if you want everyone to be safe.**

I glanced up, heart thumping as I looked around fast. I told Dimitri I was running to the bathroom before our flight. I had a few minutes to spare and wanted to take a few deep breaths to settle my nerves about leaving.

In the bathroom, I took a deep breath as I stared at myself in the mirror, then threw some water on my face.

"We got this." I rubbed my belly just as a woman I never expected to see there walked in.

Lucille with her pretty pink lipstick and her proper woven pant suit. She leaned over the sink and grabbed a lip gloss from her black bag. "Who's we? Are you ..." She glanced down at my belly. "Are you pregnant?"

"What are you doing here?" I whispered.

"Well, the pregnancy complicates things a bit," she murmured to herself. "Although, Olive, I'm so happy for you! You're going to be so happy."

"What's going on, Lucille?"

"Well, I'm quite positive your mother would want you to reconsider what you're about to do. Going on vacation when you could make history by merging the Diamond Syndicate with the HEAT empire?"

"What?" I whispered as my heart dropped. She stood between me and the door, but I felt the sudden rush to run, the blood pumping fast in my veins with the adrenaline screaming at me to move.

"Don't run. I don't want to have to bring someone in to fight you. I have men on the other side of that employee door though. Jameson and I believe you want this. Right? I was scared at first, too, of doing something so drastic."

"What did you do exactly, Lucille?" I whispered as I glanced to my right and left. To my dismay, there was nothing to use as a weapon should I need to defend myself if she brought in those men. Hand towels. That's all I had going for me.

"Look, we've got men surrounding Dimitri, and he's big, but I think he'd only be able to bring down three of them, maybe four. I made sure to have five on him though. Plus, then the cops will get involved, and it just gets messy. We're all going to have a nice chat, but we can't afford to have you flying out of state. We want this to ultimately be your decision today anyway." She glanced at her HEAT watch and read a text that must have come through. "There's a back door for employees we can take so we can talk with the women before the guys arrive. We're the only logical ones at this point. Come with me?"

"You didn't answer me, Lucille. What did you do?"

"Well, I did kill my husband, if that's what you're asking." My gut twisted with her confession even though I'd already known it to be true. "He deserved it." She said it almost exactly in the same tone she used when I'd fought Melly.

"Lucille," I murmured softly.

"Oh, don't act surprised. You knew it when you came out to return my lawnmower in the middle of the damn night while Jameson helped me dispose of the body."

"I couldn't be sure—" I felt the vomit coming, the shock of her confession making me weak and queasy on my feet.

"Well, anyway, Jameson is such a gentleman. He told me he was going to do it after he'd found out what Earl and your fathers had been doing with the kids. Knox was the last straw. They had him drive around neighborhoods noting the optimal students to target, the ideal schools to sell drugs into. Knox wanted to please your stepmom and dad so much, and Earl encouraged it. Had I known ..." She shook her head in disgust. Then she looked at me. "Your momma told me to take care of you two once she was gone. I got overwhelmed with Earl being so controlling most days. That was until Jameson told me. Once I found out, I was done with him."

"So you killed him?"

"He hit me one night quite hard, Olive Bee. It was self-defense." She fluttered her eyelashes. "Anyway, the disposal took much longer than we anticipated, and I've had to navigate those Irish men coming to my house asking for Earl and reminding me that blocking Dimitri's office requests was best. I didn't realize they didn't want the Armanellis around nor did they want more security in our town to tip off residents. Earl thought he was so smart."

I shook my head, not believing all of it.

"It's why they supplied Knox with more drugs, got him more addicted. They wanted to be able to pay off more people in town before the next board meeting. They knew I was working on turning the tide, and then you came back and, well, they're going to make moves if we don't make them first."

That's when the vomit came. I bent forward over the trash can and let it out while Lucille patted my back the whole time.

"I want you to know, Olive Bee, I've always been an ally of your mother's. Of the Diamond Syndicate. Of most everyone you know and have ties with, except your father. You're like a granddaughter to me, I hope you know that."

And I did know that. I knew she wouldn't lie to me either. "What do you need me to do?" I asked softly.

"I need you to make that clear to Dimitri and his HEAT empire. I'd rather Paradise be safe under them than the Irish Mob." I took a step back. "Unfortunately, I won't be able to protect your father. He and your stepmom will most likely be going to jail after we're through with them. They are being brought in though. That will be your decision. I hope you know that. But you need to convince Dimitri to trust us. We want to align with HEAT, and their wives agree. It's a good partnership but he won't if he thinks you're in some type of danger."

"But—"

"We'll discuss on the way." She held up her hand and motioned toward the employee exit. "Please?"

With that, I took one step toward the back door. And then another. And another.

Not because of curiosity. But because I had a mother who had trusted her, a brother who needed me, and a baby I planned to raise in Paradise Grove.

I wouldn't let them down. Not again.

CHAPTER 46: DIMITRI

I'd waited three minutes outside that bathroom door before I called her and when she didn't answer, my gut rolled in fear.

It wasn't a new sensation with her, but one I knew I would have always now. My greatest risk and my greatest reward. I'd fear for her and care for her in a way I'd never done with anyone else.

Now, I knew something was wrong with the mother of my child. Before I could barrel in there though, Jameson stepped in front of the door. "Your brothers are on their way, and Olive and Knox are safe. If you want it to stay that way, you'll follow me out of the airport." There was no hesitation. My hand went to this throat as I shoved him into the brick wall. He wheezed, "You kill me here, you'll be arrested and not find your girl, Dimitri."

So, I'd gone. I drove my car, following him back to Paradise Grove and up to the Seymour Hall where we waited to have a garage open up. As it opened, I saw the floor underneath it open, too, and our cars, along with motorcycles, swerved to follow Jameson down into a secret tunnel with brick roads that led to parking and then opened up to sliding glass doors.

If I hadn't been worried about Olive, I would have been impressed. Instead, I called Dom first who'd told me, "Yeah, I'm on my way. Dex said he's already there. Don't do something dumb. Bastian, Cade, Dante, Declan, and I will be there within an hour. Everyone's safe, Dimitri."

"She's not safe if she's not with me," I threw back.

"Clara left early this morning too," he growled about his wife. "She woke up and was texting and texting and then she said she needed to meet with the girls. Cade let me know Izzy is gone, so are Kee, Evie, Pink, and Lilah. They're together with Olive."

"Whose idea was this?"

"I mean—"

"Know what? Never mind." I hung up on him as I got out of my car and followed Jameson through glass doors and down two brick hallways before it opened up to a huge conference room of ornate furniture and men dressed in black suits. Some had helmets resting on the large oak table. Others were walking around fixing their cuff links while they stared at the expensive art on the walls.

I saw my brother Dex immediately get up to move to my side. "You made it."

Jameson turned and smiled at us. "He did. He was actually quite nice once—"

That's when I punched him in the face.

The first blow felt good. Cathartic almost. My knuckles hit his cheekbone hard enough that I felt the sting up my elbow. The man had had it coming since the day I met him. He'd been eyeing up my girl like she wasn't mine for a long time, and now he'd orchestrated her disappearance.

"Fuck, man." He spit blood onto the floor. "I know you're mad, but you realize none of this is my fault. Olive went willingly. So, you get that one hit."

"That so?" I cracked my knuckles and stared at him. "And who do you think is going to stop me from hitting you again?"

He glanced at Dex who looked at me and nodded slightly

like he was giving me the go ahead and chanting silently, "Swing, swing, swing."

So, before he answered, I swung again, and he barely even tried to dodge.

"God damn it. Okay, I deserved those two." He wiggled his jaw. This time a few men at the table stood, and I saw Bane Black out of the corner of my eye, moving forward. I didn't give a fuck. I'd punch and kill whoever I needed to get Olive back.

"Where the fuck is the mother of my child?" I stepped up to him and bellowed.

This time, he cracked his neck and smiled in my face slowly. "You know what?" He sucked on his teeth and wiped the blood from his chin. "Go on. Hit me again."

"Yeah." Dex saw how Jameson smiled, and I think we were all ready to come to blows. My brother crossed his arms over his chest and said, "Hit him again. Harder this time because you're losing it, bro. Didn't even knock him out after he kidnapped your girl."

"I'm going kill you," I growled. But just as I swung, Bane shoved me back and Dex sighed as he did the same.

"Go sit down and cool off," Bane told me, his tone not leaving room for argument.

"I'm not sitting down anywhere." I turned my fury on him. "How long have you been a part of this?"

"I told you, since I was fucking born," he said without any remorse in his haunting pale-blue eyes as he stared at me. The only thing I saw was a darkness in them about what he may have experienced. "And it wasn't as nice as the Paradise Grove community over on this side of the country. So, watch what you say in here," Bane grumbled to me like he was trying to help me out.

The men in the room were already mumbling. "What? You all offended?" I yelled out. "You think I give a fuck, Bane?"

He'd done a deal with Dex and me on the Vegas resort and casino. He knew he should have disclosed his dealings with societies then.

Just as Dante, Dom, and Declan walked in along with Cade and Bastian Armanelli, they all came to stand by me. I said, "If Olive Monroe isn't brought to me within another minute, I will personally find a way to ruin every one of you motherfucker's lives. I don't care how offended any of you are."

Bane groaned and Cade pinched the bridge of his nose.

"That so?" Jameson murmured as he leaned his hip on the conference table, glancing at a few of the biker guys sitting there and then at Bane.

The truth was, none of them mattered to me because Bastian looked at Cade and Dante, who looked at Dom and Declan, who in turn looked at Dex and me. Then, they all nodded. We all agreed right then. More men fanned in behind us. Bastian, Cade, and Dante pulled weapons.

"This not a cordial meeting now?" Jameson asked but I saw a wild look in his eye before he nodded over at a few other men. They pulled weapons too.

"It won't be if I don't see Olive very soon," I replied.

"The girls planned this, you know. They wanted Olive's approval, but it was their doing. We're all here because of them," Jameson ground out. He stared at me like he wanted me to understand before he sighed and nodded to one of his guys and the man went out the doors only to hold them open for Lucille to walk in, a small little black bag hanging from her arm in one of her wool suits, dressed to the nines.

Then, one by one, my sisters came in to stand by Dante

and Cade, my sisters-in-law went to stand by my brothers, and then my Olive walked in. She walked up to me and kissed my cheek.

"Sorry, Darling D."

"Honeybee ..." I murmured as I held her face in my hands. I tilted her head to one side, then the other. I smoothed my hands over the clothes she'd been wearing just an hour ago. "Are you hurt?"

"No. I went willingly."

I took a deep breath. "How can I protect you if—"

"No one is protecting me from something I'm a part of, Dimitri. I've always been a part of it ... was born into it, even if I didn't want to be." She stepped back and looked around the room. "And that means making the tough decisions."

"We're having nothing to do with this." I shook my head at her.

"I know you want nothing to do with them, Dimitri. It's why I had to hear out the other side."

"What the fuck could they possibly say to you? This partnership is—"

"What I want." She stood there, looking at me with those honey-brown eyes, and murmured, "It's the only thing that feels right when I know I'm going to stay here. I'm going to live here in Paradise Grove with Knox, and I'm going to make this place my home all over again. With or—"

"Always with, never without, Olive Monroe," I growled. She wasn't leaving me out of her life. I wouldn't even have her voice it as an option.

"Then you need to listen and figure out a way to make this work."

"Fuck me," I grumbled, and then I looked over at most of

my family standing there waiting to hear what I had to say. I took a deep breath before motioning toward the door to them and the twenty other men milling about in there. "I want a moment alone with my girlfriend."

"Just your girlfriend?" Kee was the first one to speak up, and she tilted her head like she needed more clarification.

That was fine. "My future wife. The mother of my children. My Honeybee. The one I'll kill for and die for. Not *just* my girlfriend. My life." I stared at Olive as I said it, then looked over at my best friend. "You want me to clarify further?"

"Nope." She smiled big. "Just making sure." And then she turned to her husband and wide-eyed him like he was an idiot. "Let's go. He needs a minute."

"Yeah, why the hell are you guys still standing here like you can't understand English? Get the fuck out." Pink shoved at Bane. He glared at her before bending to throw her over his shoulder and stomping out.

Every man and woman filtered out of the room, and then I stared at Olive. Her hands were folded in front of her as she waited for my response. "You really want this? Do you know how dangerous it could be?"

"I know that according to Lucille, she killed Earl because he made a drug distribution deal with the Irish Mob."

"Jesus Christ." I looked toward the ceiling. I'd read some of the information Izzy had sent me. I knew this was going to be a dirty and dangerous partnership, but this went deep fast.

"She explained to me on the way to the meeting with all the women that Jameson told her he was going to do it. I still think he might off his father, honestly. Or mine." She sighed but there wasn't any sorrow in her voice. "They all deserve it."

"This isn't our battle."

"But it is. Because it's what is best for this town and for the state and for your businesses, quite frankly."

"My business is as much yours as it is mine."

She puffed out a breath. "Okay, well, you say that now."

"I'll sign on the dotted line tonight if you want."

"Okay." She waved away my declaration. "Either way, this is the right thing to do. The Armanellis are working with the United States government—and with you and other big companies—to make sure money is legitimate and not coming from sex trafficking or drugs or smuggling—"

"Yes. You're right. But we can't stop them."

"You can stop the Irish Mob from infiltrating a huge secret society that has pull, Dimitri. If Jameson and Lucille, along with all of the Diamond Syndicate, have your support, they have the Armanellis'—which is the biggest Italian Mob family on the globe. They will think twice about hurting anyone or spreading their business in the way they already have. This was a desperate grab for them anyway."

I nodded. I'd done the research after I'd gotten the information from Bane. I just didn't want anything to do with it. "My job isn't to protect the world, Olive."

"What is it then? The HEAT empire practically prides itself on that with the Armanellis—"

"My job and sole purpose is to protect you now. And our baby. And this is fucking dangerous."

"More dangerous than letting them continue to do what they're doing?" She lifted her chin, so much confidence in her all of a sudden. Olive was home, finally comfortable in the place she knew she belonged. "I know where I stand, Dimitri. I'm going to stand here in Paradise Grove with them. I won't leave." She whispered out the words like she was sure about it, but then her next ones wavered. "The question is where do *you* want to stand?"

Didn't she know already? Didn't she understand that this was forever between us? "I'm always going to stand with you, Honeybee. Even if we're burning in hell together," I responded, because it wasn't a question for me at all.

"You think that's what will happen?" I finally saw a flicker of vulnerability in her eyes and knew she understood the gravity of the situation.

I chuckled as I shook my head at the whole situation. "The funny thing about all this, Olive, is I would have signed on to fuck around with an alliance that would have pissed people off so fast before we came here. Now, I want nothing to do with it. I don't want to risk it with you." I thought about the moments she was out of my reach, the seconds she'd disappeared at the airport, about losing her again, and tried one last-ditch effort. "You could say no, Honeybee. We could go to Hawaii for a while. A lifetime if you wanted."

She sighed. "I hated the memories here but loved them all the same. The pain in this place was rooted in my love for it too. I think a hometown always has all that, no?"

"It's a great risk partnering with this syndicate. You realize that?"

"Take a chance and enjoy the dance, right? Someone told me that once." Her eyes twinkled as she said it to me.

"So, if I do this ... you're going to marry me, yeah?"

"Are you negotiating this partnership now, Dimitri?"

"Yes."

"If I say no to that?"

"I'll renegotiate until you say yes, but why deny what you want, Olive?"

"I'm not, Dimitri Hardy. There's no reason to deny how much I love you at this point anyway. I want to marry you and live in this twisted little place I call home for as long as possible."

THE END

EPILOGUE: OLIVE

Life always seems to make you lemonade even when you think the only ingredient you have is lemons. Or maybe Dimitri showed me how to take a few more chances and enjoy the dances, because my life had completely changed.

Dimitri proposed the morning of the graduation. I'd come down the hall, grumbling about not being able to find my necklace but then I saw the gold gleaming on the dining table where Knox and Dimitri sat.

I glared at them both and went to grab it before I froze. It was laying on top of the *Paradise Grove News,* a special edition. On the cover was a picture of Knox, Dimitri, and me that we'd taken earlier that month and the headline article that was featured on the front read "Marry me, Olive Monroe."

I was crying even before I saw that my mom's gold fountain pen had a diamond ring threaded around it. Knox cheered for us as Dimitri rounded the table with intentions to kneel, but I lunged for him and jumped into his arms, screaming yes and bawling.

So now I was on my way to graduation with a family, a baby, and a fiancé along for the ride. Even though I'd told Dimitri and Knox a million times that I didn't need to go to the ceremony since I'd been in an online program, for God's sakes, they'd absolutely insisted.

It made sense now.

And then, after the ceremony, they both proceeded to

whisper "Told you so" in my ear when I cried and hugged them, diploma in hand.

It wasn't just having that diploma, it was seeing what had come of my last semester. I stood there looking down at the family I knew would be there for me always. I had Knox and Kee and Pink. I had Dimitri's sisters and brothers. I had Lucille and Jameson and Franny. Other Paradise Groveians and even Bane Black stood in the crowd.

When the speeches were done, we'd invited everyone to our place later that night. I walked hand in hand with Dimitri to our car, and when we were only a few steps from it, Rufford, barely recognizable from the weight he'd lost and the facial hair he'd allowed to grow in, came barreling toward us.

Dimitri stepped in front of me immediately.

"Oh, don't act like I'm going to hurt her," Rufford sneered while he stood up tall, toe-to-toe with Dimitri, and patted his wrinkled brown suit. "I'm just coming over to congratulate her."

"It's fine," I murmured to Dimitri, but he didn't move out of Rufford's path.

"Congratulations, Olive, on ruining my life. For blocking me and not giving me a chance. All so you could be with him. You think you'll be happy settling for this—"

I stepped out from behind Dimitri to confront him. "I don't think I'm happy"—I leaned against Dimitri, who immediately put his arm around me—"I am. I've achieved—"

"Nothing. You got a degree, and now you'll go ... what? Make a bunch of babies and settle for some suburban life?"

He said the words like they were an insult. "I'd be lucky to do that, Rufford. And I'll be lucky to live my life in any way I want, whether it's doing research or doing hair or taking care of my kids. You know why? Because it's my life to live. Not yours.

I'm not seeking your approval anymore. If you're looking to give it to someone, you should look elsewhere."

"You changed." He wrinkled his nose at me. "You used to have so much potential—"

"Alright. Enough." Dimitri kissed my cheek and told me, "Please tell me you're done here? I can't deal with this man causing you or our baby more stress."

"Baby?" Rufford gasped and then he glanced at my belly. My black dress was a flowy one. Plus I wasn't really showing yet.

"Yeah, I'm done with him. Have been since the night I found out he cheated on me and hooked up with you instead."

"You better be lying—" Rufford started.

"Or what?" Dimitri laughed and opened the car door for me. I got in and he closed it but I heard his deep voice through the window. "You threatening my future wife, Rufford? Please tell me now so I can make sure that not only do I ruin your career but I break every bone in your body too."

"Dimitri," I tried to calm him with saying his name softly.

"She blocked you, didn't answer your calls, and never contacted you again. Take a fucking hint, or I'll use my fist to make it clear. Fuck off. Forever."

Rufford proceeded to listen that time, and I had a feeling I'd never ever hear from him again. It didn't stop Dimitri from complaining and cursing him the whole way home.

When we pulled up to our driveway, though, I cursed my husband as I got out. "Dimitri Hardy!" I groaned as I opened the door to seeing another package being dropped off in front of our house. "Stop ordering stuff for the baby."

Kee and Pink got out of their black SUV behind us and snickered while I thanked the delivery guy for dropping two large boxes off that I was sure were more strollers. They were too bulky to be anything else.

"He's not going to stop." Kee sighed and rubbed her belly too. I don't know if it was the hormones or the fact that my best friend and I were venturing on the journey of motherhood at the same time, but we cried together that day.

Dex draped an arm around her shoulders and pulled her close. "Why don't you think he'll stop?"

"Because you just ordered five different high chairs to test out. So ridiculous."

"Yeah?" Dimitri now looked curious. "Which one was best?"

"You two are ludicrous, Kee's right," I grumbled, walking inside and waving everyone in. "We need to focus on getting this place ready for tonight, not thinking about babies that are coming next year."

"Give them a break. They're just being good daddies." Pink chuckled and plopped down on my couch, throwing her combat boots on the new coffee table I'd bought from a boutique furniture store in New Haven City. "Plus, we don't really have to do anything for that party right? I feel like Lucille's got a whole damn crew in your backyard setting up."

"I have no idea what's she's doing." I groaned. "It's like she's the grandmother of the century."

"Well, can't complain, considering she's doing what your mom always wanted, I'm sure. And ... well, can't speak for your dumbass father—"

I groaned and sat down next to her. "Don't remind me." It had just been a few months now that I'd made the decision to negotiate my father's future with the Irish mob. The Diamond Syndicate actually orchestrated delivering him to the Irish Mob. It was a bargaining chip of sorts. They wanted him to suffer, we wanted him to pay for the wrongs he'd committed. They'd agreed to let him live as long as he went to jail. His sentence was for much longer than it should have been, and he'd taken the fall for more than a dozen of their crimes along with a few other Groveians who'd been working with him. Paradise Grove now didn't owe the Irish anything, especially because Jameson and Lucille had done the dirty work of taking care of Earl.

It was a begrudging agreement, one Dimitri and the Armanellis weren't sure would hold. For now, though, everything was paradise in Paradise Grove.

Dimitri walked over, loosening his tie, to come and kiss my forehead over the back of the couch. "Yeah, don't remind me about her father. Damn bastard."

I sighed and moved my hand so Dimitri could rub my belly now. He'd been obsessed with trying to feel the baby kicking. "At least we're through the woods, Darling D."

"You shouldn't have ever been a part of that, Honeybee," he grumbled, his tone clipped. Dimitri still hated that I was a part of the Diamond Syndicate and that there was a risk to making decisions for the future of the communities. Yet, he'd accepted that it was part of who I was and wanted to be.

Paradise Grove was my home and where I felt the roots of my mother still most days.

"Don't start complaining about it again. I can't take it." Kee sat on the beige love seat and threw her feet up on the coffee table too. "When do you think we need to start getting ready for this party? I want relax and eat food instead."

"Preferably ice cream," I agreed.

"I have cookie dough in the fridge from the last time you asked and—"

"I want a fruity flavor. Like maybe grapefruit," Kee

hummed and closed her eyes.

I swear the baby kicked like she wanted it too and Dimitri smiled down at his hand over my stomach, "Feels like she must be hungry for that flavor, too."

Pink peered over and then groaned loudly. "Are we talking *for* the baby now, Dimitri?"

"Yeah, I'm talking for my kid. She's hungry." He stood and swiped the keys off the counter. "I guess I'm going to find grapefruit flavored ice cream for you two."

"And maybe some turtle sundae," Pink blurted out.

Dimitri frowned. "Are you pregnant too?"

He opened the door and Bane was standing there. Bane leaned forward and glanced around the room before he made his assessment. "Pink, you better not be fucking pregnant."

"So what if I am?" She pulled at a thread on her ripped jeans, not looking at him at all.

He growled and his eyes never left her as he walked in and leaned over to whisper something in her ear.

"Yeah, so what if she is. We're delightful when pregnant, right, Darling D?" I gave him my best doe-eyed look.

He chuckled and grumbled, "Fuck it." He glanced at Bane, "Go get the ladies some ice cream. I'm taking my wife to bed."

"Hey!" I slapped his shoulder as he scooped me up. "I'm not married to you yet."

"Tell Lucille that again, please. She'll have our wedding planned in the backyard next month."

I laughed as he took me down the hall. "You're right, and I won't complain either, Dimitri Hardy. I can't wait to marry you. I won't deny it."

"Good. Because you're going to be a fine-ass Olive Hardy soon, Honeybee. Very, very soon."

For additional content, including bonus scenes, sign up for Shain Rose's newsletter: shainrose.com/newsletter

And are you ready for the start of the Diamond Syndicate Series?! Jameson is coming. So are Bane Black and Pink!! Please join Shain Rose's Lovers of Love Group for updates here:

https://www.facebook.com/groups/shainroseslovers/

ALSO BY SHAIN ROSE

Hardy Billionaires
Between Commitment and Betrayal
Between Love and Loathing
Between Never and Forever
Between Desire and Denial

* * *

Tarnished Empire
Shattered Vows
Fractured Freedom
Corrupted Chaos

* * *

Stonewood Billionaire Brothers
INEVITABLE
REVERIE
THRIVE

* * *

New Reign Mafia
Heart of a Monster
Love of a Queen

ABOUT SHAIN ROSE

Shain Rose writes romance with an edge. Her books are filled with angst, steam, and emotional rollercoasters that lead to happily ever afters.

She lives where the weather is always changing with a family that she hopes will never change. When she isn't writing, she's reading and loving life.